Uncommon Prayer

A Father Flenn Adventure

By Scott Arnold

Uncommon Prayer

Uncommon Prayer

Copyright © 2019 Scott Arnold

All rights reserved.

Published by Farne Press

ISBN 978-1-7337524-0-4

Arnold, Scott.

Uncommon Prayer : A Father Flenn Adventure — 1st edition

 1. Fiction-Thrillers-Espionage. 2. Fiction-Crime

United States of America

No parts of this publication may be reproduced, stored in a retrieval system, or transmitted in any form or by any means, electronic, mechanical, photocopying, recording, or otherwise, without the prior written permission of the copyright owner.

This book is sold subject to the condition that it shall not, by way of trade or otherwise, be lent, resold, hired out, or otherwise circulated without the publisher's prior consent in any form of binding or cover other than that in which it is published and without a similar condition including this condition being imposed on the subsequent purchaser. Under no circumstances may any part of this book be photocopied for resale.

This is a work of fiction. Any similarity between the characters and situations within its pages and places or persons, living or dead, is unintentional and co-incidental.

Cover Photography: Peter O'Connor, Bespoke Book Covers

Interior Design: Jim Brown

Editor: Margaret Shaw

Dedicated to:

My Dad.
Always in my heart.

CHAPTER ONE

Father Scott Flenn bolted upright as his hand dove underneath the pillow for a pistol that hadn't been there in years.

Cold sweat trickled down his forehead as the priest peered into the darkness from his four-poster, mahogany bed. Everything was still, other than a breeze from the furnace fanning the tapestry on the wall behind him. Father Flenn could just make out the silhouette of the antique dresser on the other side of the room.

The priest sighed. *It was only a dream*—the same one he'd had for the past three nights. In it, two men had been dragging him down a long corridor toward a third, a repulsive figure; someone he'd recognized in the dream, but not now that he was awake.

At least tonight he'd been able to make out the face of one of the men pulling him down that corridor. It was a face from the past, from Flenn's days with the CIA—*the face of Zack Matteson!*

Father Flenn closed his eyes, trying to shake off the nightmare. He reminded himself that Zack Matteson had always been one of the good guys. Zack, in fact, had once been his best friend. But things change; at last they had for Flenn.

The priest told himself that Zack still had a *number* of redeemable qualities. *After all,* Flenn thought…*'One' is a number.* And Zack Matteson's one redeemable quality is, was, and always had been, his unabashed loyalty to the United States of America.

Flenn checked the clock. Five a.m. No use trying to go back to sleep now. He climbed out of bed to make a pot of coffee and get ready for his morning run. Thankfully, it had just been a dream; Flenn hadn't heard from Zack in nearly two years.

Two very peaceful years.

****

Damn! The package was nearly empty. The spy was certain he'd had plenty when he left London. *What to do now?*

Cursing, Zack Matteson stuffed the bag's contents, a few remaining jellybeans, into his pants pocket as he stepped onto the tarmac at Ankara Esenboga International Airport. A faint scent of Snowdrop and Windflower hung in the late November breeze—a musky smell from flowers long used by assassins for their deadly poison.

His passport read *Matthew Stevens, 41, from Detroit.* In truth, he was six years older than that, but his boyish good looks, and the fact that there wasn't even a speck of gray in his thick, jet-black hair made Zack look much younger. His trim, muscular build was evident in his blue jeans and tight-fitting tee, but what stood out most were

Zack's ocean-blue eyes, especially today in a sea of brown-eyed travelers.

The customs agent robotically plodded through all the usual questions, and Zack answered as any travel-weary, automobile company representative would have:

Yes, he was here on business.

Yes, he was meeting someone – Mr. Erdem Firat, from the Askam automobile manufacturing company.

No, this was not his first visit to Turkey.

He'd be staying at the Four Seasons.

Finally, the woman waved him through. Outside, Zack met his contact, Erdem Firat. Erdem really did work for the Askam manufacturer, a subsidiary of Chrysler, but he'd also been on the payroll for the Central Intelligence Agency for the past 15 years. The man was short, slight, and rather mousy-looking. He wore a simple white button-down and a pair of threadbare khakis. The ring on his right hand was the only evidence of the prosperity that Zack knew Erdem privately enjoyed. Zack followed Erdem outside to an orange Askam pickup truck—a vehicle that would have stuck out like a sore thumb back home in D.C.; but here in Ankara, it blended in with the other work trucks parked around the airport.

"Mr. Zack, it is very much agreeableness to look upon your face again," Erdem Firat said as he climbed into the driver's seat.

"Good to see you, too, Erd," Zack replied. "I see those

English classes are really making a difference." Erdem either didn't notice the sarcasm, or didn't care. He reached under his seat and handed Zack a small paper bag. Inside, Zack found a mobile phone, a pistol, and two magazines of ammunition.

"I was surprised, but delighting, when you telephoned me this morning to arrange to meeting you," the Turk said. "However, my boss was not so delightful when I called in sickly." The little man grinned. "Of course, it helps that my boss is also my cousin."

Zack handed Erdem a $50 bill. "As I recall, this is what usually makes your cousin happy."

"Yes, indeedly," agreed Erdem, stuffing the bill into his shirt pocket. "So, what marvelous journey will we be going upon this time?"

"Nothing exciting," Zack said. "Just take me to the Four Seasons." Zack gazed past the parking lot, toward the city. Not much had changed in the three years since he'd last been here.

"Will you be needling my services later today?"

"Yes," said Zack, "and maybe the rest of the week as well."

Erdem frowned. "My cousin will be very much unhappy to hear this."

Zack sighed as he reached into his wallet and pulled out three more fifties. Erdem looked at the bills and smiled. "Erd, I'm going to need you to tail someone for me, and I'm going to need you to be discreet."

Erdem pretended to look hurt. "Mr. Zack, am I not always discreet?"

"Yeah, right," Zack chuckled. "What about last time? You never told me that woman had a husband!"

"I was very discreet, Mr. Zack. It was *you* who was, how do you say it… undiscreetish."

"Indiscreet," corrected Zack, rubbing his chin. "As I recall, he wasn't a very happy husband, either."

"Nor would I have been! She was a beautifullish woman, no?" said the Turk. "I trust you got away with all your parts?"

Zack tucked the pistol in his waistband. "Parts? Yes. Clothes, no."

Erdem shook his head. "She was lucky to be Turk. The Saudis would have stoned her to death—or worse." Zack wondered what could possibly be worse.

Erdem turned down a single lane road full of early morning foot traffic, swerving to avoid a boy carrying two chickens in cages stacked one atop the other. "So, who am I to be discreetable with this week?" Erdem asked.

Zack fished in his backpack for a photograph. He handed the image to Erdem, who studied it for a moment.

"This man looks like me, no?" Erdem said with a grin.

"Don't kid yourself, Erd. You're not that handsome."

Erdem had to admit that the man in the photo was striking. Stocky build, dark hair, olive skin, high cheekbones and brown eyes.

"He is Turk?"

"A Guatemalan, actually. At least his parents were."

Zack fished in his pocket for a jellybean. "He was born in America. Name's Daniel Romero. He's staying at the Four Seasons, which is why I'm going there." Zack had texted someone he knew at MI-6 from the plane. The British agent texted him back in minutes: Romero had used his own name to book a suite at the Four Seasons. Using the plane's wi-fi, Zack had called and made a reservation.

Erdem rounded a corner way too fast, just missing an old man on a bicycle. "Anything else I need to be knowing, Mr. Zack?"

Zack thought for a moment. *Was there anything else he needed to tell Erdem? Probably not.* It wasn't that Zack didn't trust the man. Erdem wasn't one to work both sides of the fence; but Zack was here solely on a hunch, and it would be best to keep that hunch to himself for the time being. Zack smiled as he remembered how his former partner, Scott Flenn, used to scold him: "Hunches are for horseraces," Flenn would always say. "Stick to the facts!" Flenn had been the logical one back then. Zack usually just followed his gut. *Maybe that's what had made their partnership work so well.* Zack fished in his pocket for another jellybean and wondered what Flenn would have said about this little adventure.

Three days ago, Zack had happened to catch sight of Daniel Romero in London. There was nothing extraordinary about a billionaire traveling abroad, except this particular billionaire was traveling alone. Zack thought it odd that the heir to the largest telecommunications company in Central America was in

London by himself: no wife or girlfriend, no bodyguard... no one. He'd thought it even odder that Romero was having tea with the man Zack had been assigned to keep an eye on—Carmel Fahook, a known intermediary for Iranian interests.

Zack had followed Romero to Heathrow this morning, where the tycoon had booked a flight to Turkey. Zack had made a snap decision to buy a ticket and follow. There'd been no time to clear it with anyone, but then, there really wasn't anyone to notify. Zack was what the CIA called a "cowboy," an agent who worked alone, always looking for the next big rodeo. It had been that way for years now, ever since Scott Flenn, his longtime partner, had left the agency. There had been something unique about the way the two of them had gotten along back then. Zack had never been able to replicate that sort of relationship with anyone else. It took the CIA some time to accept the fact that Zack did better on his own. Since Zack's hunches paid off more often than not, his superiors were usually willing to give him a long leash.

Luckily, there had been no problems getting through Turkish customs; no one had asked why he had no luggage. All he'd had time to do before the flight was to grab his backpack from the car he'd left parked at Heathrow. If he ended up staying in Turkey longer than a day or two, he'd have someone to pick up his things in London. For now, he'd simply purchase whatever he needed—starting with a fresh bag of jellybeans.

Erdem pulled up at the hotel. Zack climbed out of the

car, surveyed his surroundings, then leaned back inside. "Stick around, Erd, I may need you later." As Zack walked inside, he glanced around the spacious lobby. There was no sign of Romero, so he made his way over to the bar where he ordered a double bourbon, neat. He fiddled with a video game on his personal phone—not the disposable one Erdem had given him. He was beginning to have second thoughts, wondering whether he'd made the right decision to follow Romero all the way to Turkey. Once again, he had acted on impulse, something Flenn used to berate him about back in the day. *Flenn would probably have called his trip to Turkey nothing more than a wild goose chase,* he thought as he switched off the game and checked his phone for return flights to London.

The preacher was tired of the girl's complaints. Tonight was supposed to be a celebration! Sure, she had been exciting enough, but he had expected her to be more... compliant; especially with what he was paying her. She could at least pretend to enjoy it!

The young blonde glared at him. "You didn't have to be so rough, mister!" He liked how she called him "mister." He looked into her pale blue eyes and saw... what was it? Anger? No, that wasn't it. Fear? No, that wasn't it either. Despair? Maybe. In the end, what did it matter? At least this one had been prettier than the other girls the pimp had provided him in the past. The essence of youth, she had a tiny frame, watery blue eyes, and long golden hair which had been pulled back into a ponytail. He hadn't noticed the butterscotch freckles on her nose and cheeks... at least not at first.

The preacher's wife hadn't attracted him in years. His secretary was still eager, but he'd grown bored with her as well, which was why he had suggested to his friend that they get a hooker tonight and meet at his family's old cabin. This way, they could each do what they wanted. He certainly had.

The blonde pointed toward the bedroom door. "I don't care how much you are paying me, I'm not doing this again—not with that other guy, not if he's anything like you!"

"Oh, he's not at all like me," the preacher said, leering at her as he slowly opened the door to leave. "He's much worse."

CHAPTER TWO

Zack Matteson was on his second bourbon when Daniel Romero sauntered into the bar. The spy pretended not to watch as the tycoon ordered a drink and pulled out a cell phone to make a call. From his vantage point, Zack was unable to hear the conversation.

Romero finished the call and quickly downed the cocktail. He checked his watch, then signaled the bartender for another drink. A teenager entered the bar from across the lobby and walked straight up to Romero. She was wearing too-tight-for-her-age blue jeans, a flimsy pink blouse, and heavy makeup belying her age. If she'd dressed like this in any other Muslim country, she would have been arrested. Even in Turkey, a girl could be beaten up in certain neighborhoods for wearing such an outfit. The tycoon looked her up and down as if appraising a new car. The way Romero smiled at the girl made Zack's skin crawl; she couldn't have been much older than Zack's eldest daughter back in Virginia.

Romero reached into his pocket. Whispering into the girl's ear, he pressed what appeared to be a room key in her hand and then patted her bottom. She flashed him a practiced smile, then slowly turned and walked away. Romero's eyes followed the girl as she made her way

across the lobby and out the door. He checked his watch
again, then gazed up at a soccer match on one of the bar's
flat-screens. At the top of the hour, Romero finished his
third drink and headed for the front door. Zack watched
as a limousine pulled up to the lobby entrance. He sent a
quick text to Erdem. As the limo pulled away from the
hotel, a bright orange pickup truck headed off in the
same direction. Confident Erdem would keep him
informed of Romero's movements, Zack checked into his
room, showered, and slept for a couple of hours.

Erdem's call woke him.

Daniel Romero had traveled east to a non-descript
diner a couple of miles outside the city. According to
Erdem, no other patrons were in the restaurant this
evening. Erdem was watching from a small market just
down the road. "Mr. Zack, I'm not sure I should stay
here much longerish. My truck might be conspicual."

Zack thought for a moment. *This was probably nothing,
just another horse-race-hunch.* "Come on back, Erd. Find a
different car for tomorrow in case I need you. Call me in
the morning—early, okay?"

Zack could almost see Erdem smiling at the thought
of more $50 bills coming his way. "Right, Mr. Zack. I will
borrowing my cousin's Toyota. Now, that is one fine
ride!" He paused before adding, "My cousin will want to
charge me for it. Maybe two hundred dollars."

Zack rolled his eyes. "Your 'cousins' are expensive,"
he complained. Zack knew Erdem was pocketing as

much as half of what he was extorting from him. It
wasn't that the CIA was underpaying the Turk, but little
extras here and there were always expected. It was how
the Middle East operated. Zack sighed. *Who was he
kidding? It was how the whole world operated!*

Zack's cynicism had been well earned over the years.
In his line of work, he'd found people rarely meant what
they said or said what they meant. The biggest exception
to that, of course, had been his former partner, Scott
Flenn. Or, just *Flenn* as he always insisted upon being
called. Flenn was the real deal, always had been. Flenn
had been a straight shooter during their time together…
which was why Zack had questioned Flenn's sanity on
their last assignment in Edinburgh over a decade ago,
right after Zack had married Donna. Flenn still swore it
had all occurred just the way he said it did back then, but
it was about the craziest tale Zack had ever heard! If it
had been anyone else but Flenn, Zack would have called
the person nuts. *One thing was certain,* Zack reminded
himself, *Flenn believed it. Flenn had even given up being an
agnostic to become a priest, of all things!*

Since Edinburgh, Zack had tried to keep in touch
with his former partner, but Flenn's break with the CIA
had been absolute and there'd been little room left for
Zack Matteson in Flenn's new world.

Zack had developed few friendships since those days.
Ever since he and Donna busted up, he'd come to prefer
a life of bourbon, one-night stands, and chasing after bad
guys. People like Erdem were the closest thing he had to
friends these days—contacts and informants hired to do

a job, nothing more. Zack had known the Turk for years, but knew next to nothing about the man... other than that he was expensive. Zack assumed Erdem was putting it all away until he could retire one day... *far away from his cousins, no doubt!*

Zack dusted pocket lint off his last jellybean—a cheaper alternative to the cigarettes he had given up years ago. *Nicotine and sugar, both deadly, but jellybeans didn't make his breath smell bad.* He pulled out his phone and used Google Earth to look up the restaurant where Romero was dining tonight. It certainly didn't look like a place a billionaire would choose to spend the evening. Judging from the location, and Erdem's description, Romero must have gone there to slip away from prying eyes, maybe to meet someone... but whom? *Since Romero had been meeting with the Iranians, the most obvious answer was that Romero was searching for a way his corporation could skirt around the sanctions in place against Iran.*

Erdem had said there were only two cars outside the restaurant tonight, which meant the place had most likely been reserved for the evening. Zack closed his eyes and asked himself if this was this simply a fool's errand. *Probably; but then, why had Romero been meeting with Carmel Fahook in London?* Zack shook his head, *No, if Fahook was involved, then someone in Iran's inner circle was interested in something Romero had to offer, which meant that there would likely be more meetings after tonight.* He'd need to keep Erdem on the payroll a while longer.

Despite what Flenn used to say, in his twenty-plus years in the CIA, Zack had learned to rely on his gut, and his gut was telling him that there was something to all of this. *Even Flenn would have questioned Romero's meeting with Carmel Fahook,* Zack told himself. He needed to contact the agency in Istanbul to get a camera and a listening device with decent enough range. Such things were expensive, and delicate, but the agency here should have at least one or two on hand. Zack made the call and was told to expect a delivery by noon the next day. With nothing else to do, he called it a night.

The next morning, the eavesdropping apparatus and the camera arrived shortly after room service delivered breakfast. Zack finished off his orange juice while familiarizing himself with the listening device. As for the camera, he managed to hide it inside a flower arrangement on a table down the hall from Romero's room. Through an app on his phone he was able to keep an eye on Daniel Romero's door. After Erdem called to check in, Zack went down to the lobby and picked up a local newspaper which he used to try and blend in as he sipped coffee and passed time checking the camera feed from outside Romero's room.

It was mid-morning when he saw two men in dark suits and sunglasses enter Romero's suite. A moment later they came back into the hallway, propping up someone between them. Zack recognized the young girl from the bar the night before. She was limping badly. The men were having to carry her as they made their way swiftly to the stairwell. Zack dropped the newspaper and hurried outside to the parking lot where he stood next to a blue Lexus and pretended to talk on his phone. A dark Mercedes pulled up just as the two men exited the building with the girl. They quickly shoved the girl inside, climbed in beside her, and sped away—but not before Zack got a picture of the license plate. Less than 10 minutes later, Zack was nursing a fresh cup of coffee in the hotel lobby and reading a text from a CIA contact in Istanbul. The car was registered to the Iranian embassy.

First, Carmel Fahook, and now this! What on earth did Iran want with Daniel Romero? Zack asked himself. *And, what of that poor girl?*

Zack wanted answers, but so far all he had were questions. Questions—and a disposable phone, an eavesdropping device, a hidden camera, a pistol with two magazines of ammunition, and an assistant who spoke only pidgin English. He shook his head. *Where in the hell was Scott Flenn when you needed him?*

The preacher put on his shirt, walked outside, and lit a joint. It was the middle of May, but the night was hot and humid. He took a drag as he walked the familiar path from his childhood.

No doubt his friend would take his time. Now, he was beginning to wish that he had. It just simply hadn't lasted long enough. Part of the problem with getting older. He had to admit, this girl had been a cut above the other two that lowlife pimp had supplied... she was even cuter than the Mallory twins. His secretary, Jessica Mallory, was okay, but her daughters even better.

This kid tonight, though, had potential. Experienced and eager to please—at least she had been at first. Maybe he had taken things a bit too far; but if his friend was acting the way he used to when they shared a dorm room years ago, then the girl was probably wishing for him right about now.

The preacher knew he would have to make it up to her if he ever wanted to use her services again. He decided to give a generous tip and to explain that his friend was in town for only the one night. She didn't need to know why; that they were planning something huge— bigger than anything even the preacher's celebrated father had ever dared imagine!

He ambled down the path toward the dock where he and his brother used to fish when they were kids. The preacher smiled, remembering how he had treated Junior back then. The kid had always seemed to invite it. He was a weakling, a mama's boy—a fat, whiny kid with lots of smarts but no ambition. The preacher still recalled the day his parents brought the little brat home from the hospital. Everyone had been there—aunts, uncles, neighbors—all making a fuss over the stupid baby! It still bothered him. Maybe that's why he and his wife never had kids. He couldn't stand them.

Of course, teenagers were a different story. He and his friend had found that out in college nearly 25 years ago. It had been Daniel's idea to attend high school football games and pretend to be scouting cheerleaders for a university eager to give free rides to those deemed worthy. It had always worked best with the freshmen and sophomores anxious to help their parents with future college costs. The preacher laughed. They had gotten a free ride all right!

He and Danny had remained in touch over the years, even serving as best men at one another's weddings. Their wives, however, had never become close. No matter, thought the preacher as he walked up to the dock overlooking the river; he and Danny never talked about family anyway. Just as well; the preacher had hated his ever since he could remember.

He killed time by tossing rocks into the water. The inlet where his family had built their cabin had been a great place for fishing when he was a kid. He remembered how he used to like watching the fish flop around on the dock, gasping for breath.

At times he and his father had sat out here, just the two of them. The old man had been gone so much when he was a kid that he'd relished those moments together when he was little. Then later, as an adolescent, he grew to hate his father—as well as the memory of those earlier times. His mother, he had learned how to manipulate, but never his father. The old man seemed to be able to see right through him. Many were the times he had fantasized that his father would be killed in a plane crash or by a fanatic's bullet, but no such luck. Instead, he'd had to wait until time took its course. Thank God, it looked like that could be any day now!

The preacher looked at his phone. No messages. Good. He didn't want any distractions, not tonight. He and Danny had a lot to celebrate. He checked the time; his friend should be done by now. He thought he might even be up for another round. He had learned that those little blue pills really did work, sometimes more than once, as the Mallory twins could attest. True, their silence had cost him the promise of a new car when they turned 16, but it was worth it. His clueless secretary would simply assume he was giving her daughters the cars for her having been nice to him.

He began to laugh. Life is good, the preacher thought as he looked into the heavens, daring the fates to prove otherwise.

CHAPTER THREE

"Blessed be God, Father, Son and Holy Spirit."

Father Scott Flenn read the opening words of the communion service for the first Sunday in Advent to a congregation of just under two dozen. A solitary blue candle burned brightly on the Advent wreath near the center aisle.

With chiseled cheek bones, tall and trim, Father Flenn looked handsome in his white robe and blue stole. But it wasn't his green eyes or wavy, sandy-brown hair that had first impressed the congregation of Saint Ann's Episcopal Church, it was the fact that he had come free of charge.

The dwindling congregation could no longer afford a priest on their own, so they had jumped at the chance six years ago to have Father Flenn become their vicar. Flenn's only stipulation had been that the congregation allow him the use of the vicarage as his home, along with the freedom to set his own hours during the week. Granted, Flenn had done some peculiar things since he'd arrived, such as taking part in several protests in Birmingham, as well as leading a variety of social justice committees for the Diocese of Alabama. He had shocked some of his members the year he'd put together a winter ministry to the Fourth Avenue prostitutes, taking blankets and hot chocolate to the working girls downtown.

He had caused an even bigger stir when he'd insisted that every household of the tiny parish turn in a pledge card each year. While everyone knew Father Scott Flenn came from a wealthy New Hampshire family, Flenn had been very clear: he would not pay the parish's bills for them. It was the congregation's responsibility to learn how to make their own way and to build up enough savings so that they could one day hire another priest, should he be called elsewhere. They had originally balked at being forced into making a financial commitment to their parish, but in the end, they had all acquiesced.

Sitting across from Flenn during the service this morning was a gum-chewing acolyte, a lector who had fallen asleep during the sermon, and a substitute organist; the regular organist's arthritis having flared up again. The organist, a student from Birmingham Southern, played brilliantly but had no understanding whatsoever of Episcopal liturgy. This morning, four weeks before Christmas, he'd ignored the Advent hymns Flenn had selected and begun the service with his own jazzy composition of "Silent Night."

Father Flenn was going to have a talk with the dean next week and ask that they teach their organ students some basics about how to serve a liturgical church. Granted, there weren't all that many in the deep South, as the so-called *non-denominational* congregations were increasing in appeal to younger crowds. They were even beginning to draw members away from the deeply-entrenched Southern Baptist congregations, a feat thought impossible only a decade ago. Drop down screens, rock bands and pews with cup holders were not things Father Scott Flenn would ever allow, no matter how long he lived.

After the service, Flenn greeted his flock at the door and exchanged pleasantries as people scurried off for lunch or an afternoon nap. He was amused when the lector told him how much he'd enjoyed the sermon.

Flenn found the young organist chatting with Elaine Wells in the sacristy as she cleaned up after the service. Elaine was one of two women who comprised Saint Ann's altar guild, the other being the volunteer parish secretary, Iriana Racks. Flenn removed his chasuble and stole and hung them up neatly. "Mike, can we talk?"

The organist looked at his watch. "Oh, I'd love to, Father Flenn, but I'm supposed to be at Hill Street Church of God for a rehearsal of tonight's Christmas pageant."

Flenn raised an eyebrow. "A pageant, already? Christmas is still four weeks away!"

"Oh, I've been busy for a couple of weeks now," the young man replied. "The Nazarenes had their Christmas cantata last week."

"Before Thanksgiving?" Flenn would have asked more but the kid was out the door before he could say another word.

Elaine chuckled.

"What's so funny?"

"Why, you are, Father! You've been here all this time

and still get shocked at the way other churches do things down here."

Flenn shook his head. "It's just wrong. This is Advent, not Christmas!"

The sacristan filled the sink with warm, soapy water. "Father, you're fighting an uphill battle." The woman began washing the chalice and paten. "I know you New Englanders are all old-school Anglicans, and think the rest of the world should be too; but fundamentalists run things down here. They don't understand our liturgy, or reading prayers from a book, or using wine instead of grape juice at communion, or..."

"Or," Flenn groused, "that playing Christmas carols during Advent is just plain wrong! The rest of the Christian world understands the ancient traditions of the Church. Why can't people down here?"

The woman peered over her shoulder at him. "Really, Father? The rest of the Christian world?" She shook her head. "Maybe *we* are the ones who should try and be more understanding."

Flenn sighed, a bit embarrassed by his tirade. "You've got me, Elaine. You're absolutely right. Just chalk it up to my arrogance; another one of my many sins."

The woman put down the paten and turned to face him, hands on her hips. "Come now, Father Flenn. You, of all people, are not arrogant! I am surprised at you though, not knowing how fundamentalists think; you're being so tight with the folks over at the Rye Foundation and all. I mean you can't possibly get any more evangelical than Willy Rye."

Flenn reached for his black suitcoat. "I'm not 'tight' with them. My father was close to Willy and his wife, Elizabeth, that's all. Dad wasn't much of a churchgoer but his father was, and gramps was a big supporter of Willy Rye way back when Willy was still preaching tent revivals. Gramps went on to serve on the Rye Foundation board for years. He could be very generous when he saw someone doing something he thought was worthwhile."

"Sounds like someone else I know." She smiled and turned back to finish her work. "What about your mother, was she a friend of Willy and Elizabeth Rye as well?"

Flenn shrugged. "Not so much. It was mostly gramps, and later dad. When the Ryes were building their gigantic headquarters here in Birmingham, dad and gramps gave enough money to pay for half of those enormous windows." He finished taking off his robes. "Personally, even as a boy, I thought that place looked atrocious."

Elaine rolled her eyes. "I won't argue with you about that!"

"After dad died, Willy tried to get me to serve on the board."

"Did you?"

Flenn shook his head. "I was too busy—plus, I hadn't quite, as they say, 'come to Jesus' yet. And, I was," he paused, "taking care of family business interests overseas."

"Do you miss it?"

"What? My old job?" Flenn thought about his time in the CIA, something neither Elaine nor his congregation knew anything about. "No. I don't miss it at all." As far as any member of his parish was concerned, Flenn had simply been a representative for Flenn Industries after he'd left the Air Force.

She caught him before he headed out the door. "But wasn't it exciting, traveling the world and all?"

Flenn turned and winked, "Nah, not nearly as exciting as singing Christmas hymns during Advent!"

Flenn made his way down a long corridor to his office. The small parish hall was empty now except for the priest. He had just sat down with a fresh cup of coffee, his fourth for the day, when his computer chimed with a new email. It was from Minerva Wilson. Minerva's family had been the first African-American members in Saint Ann's history. With a sharp mind and a love for all things Anglican, Minerva had become an instant friend. He had mentored her as she was discerning a call to the priesthood. Flenn had been impressed—to the point that he'd personally paid her way to the University of the South, an expensive Episcopal seminary in Tennessee. Minerva had done well in school. Afterwards, their bishop, Tom Morrison, convinced the rector of Saint Latimer's in Mountain Brook, one of the wealthiest parishes in Birmingham, to add her to his already bulging staff.

Flenn opened Minerva's email. Instead of her usual warm greeting, it read: *"Flenn, I need your help; I'm at a crossroads. I can't eat or sleep. I've lost fifteen pounds in the past month alone…"* Flenn raised an eyebrow. Minerva was slender to begin with, maybe 120-pounds tops. She couldn't afford to lose that much weight. "...*I need to talk to you. I thought about going to the bishop, but I already know what he will say. He'll just give me the standard line of the Church—which, believe me, I've been trying to toe—but I don't know how much longer I can keep it up. I will be at the quarterly clergy meeting at the cathedral on Tuesday. Please set aside some time where we can be alone. I desperately need to talk to you!*"

Flenn read the email a second time. Minerva Wilson was as stable a priest as anyone he knew. *Could her husband, Wayne, or one of the kids be ill? No, the bishop would have been supportive if that were the case. Just what was she going through? An affair? A lapse of faith?*

Flenn knew Tom Morrison as both bishop and friend. He couldn't imagine why Minerva thought Tom wouldn't be willing to help her. Tom had certainly been supportive of Flenn over the years, even after Flenn had chased a couple of families away from Saint Ann's. It had happened shortly after his arrival, when the two wealthiest families in the parish had threatened to take their money and leave if the vestry didn't "put a lid" on this new priest's "activist agenda." Flenn had driven his red, Saab convertible over to their homes and handed them each a personal check covering what they had donated to the church for the past three years. He'd also given them notice that while he had no grounds to officially excommunicate them, he did not expect to ever see them again at Saint Ann's. Something in the priest's eyes had told them he meant business. *If they had known anything at all about his past, they'd have understood just how right they were.*

Father Flenn rarely thought back on his old life, even though he'd been an operative for nearly 12 years. When he'd announced his departure, no one at the agency had understood, especially his former partner, Zack Matteson. For an agency that prided itself on assimilating information, the CIA never seemed to have figured out what made Scott Flenn tick. He had often wondered how his personnel file at Langley read. He assumed there would be detailed dossiers on his accomplishments in Bosnia, Korea, Saudi Arabia. No doubt, London's MI-6 would have shared their perception of what had occurred on his last assignment—the one in Edinburgh. He sat back in his chair and couldn't help but wonder about that particular report. *Of course,* he thought, *the Brits would have gotten it all wrong.*

Flenn doubted there'd been much written about some of his other missions, such as the incident in Afghanistan, or the time he and Zack Matteson had dropped completely off the grid in Moscow. Nevertheless, Flenn had served his country well in both the military and the CIA.

Except for Bishop Morrison, all anyone in the diocese knew about Flenn's past was that he had served a stint in the Air Force and then left the military to help manage Flenn Industries' interests overseas. It had been a believable cover. Solar power, heavy-duty earthmoving equipment, water purification, and a half-dozen other interests had made Flenn Industries one of the most successful privately-owned conglomerates in the nation. His grandfather had insisted the company was never to be be traded publicly on Wall Street, which had left Scott and his brother, David Jr., both billionaires after their father died.

Scott's father, David Sr., had been painfully aware of his son's clandestine career, but he had carried the secret to the grave, not even informing Flenn's sainted mother. She'd died thinking her son some sort of gadabout playboy, traveling the world, seldom calling home, and never settling down with a wife and family. Years later, when Flenn had explained to his father the strange things he'd experienced in Edinburgh, and that he was leaving the CIA as a result of them, his father had absorbed it all without comment, except to urge him to move back to New Hampshire.

The experience in Scotland had affected more than just Scott Flenn's career; it had led him back to the church of his late mother. Oddly enough, it had been his dad who had been the first one to suggest that he speak with New Hampshire's bishop about pursuing holy orders. Aside from his father, Bishop Arnholt was, at the time, the only other person outside the CIA who knew of Flenn's former life as a spy. Much of it Flenn had told the bishop inside the protection of confession. Episcopalians are as strict as Roman Catholics about the sanctity of confession, and nothing could ever be repeated—no matter what. The penalty was huge and often included the loss of one's orders.

"Scott," Bishop Arnholt had said that day, "God has called you from a broken world to a whole new life. I have never been more certain of anyone!"

Bishop Arnholt had been one of the few to call him by his first name. It had been the same way with his dad. Most people had always referred to his father as Flenn, and so it was only natural that Scott Flenn wanted to be called the same. It had stuck. Scott had been "Flenn" at school, "Flenn" in the Air Force, "Flenn" in the CIA, and now, after following Bishop Arnholt's advice, it was "Father Flenn."

During his last year in seminary, Flenn realized that he wanted to serve a unique congregation, one that truly *needed* him—which was how he'd found Saint Ann's, a dying parish about to be closed by the Diocese of Alabama. Six years later, the parish remained small, but what it lacked in numbers it now made up for in enthusiasm, even producing a priest from one of their own—Minerva Wilson.

Flenn read Minerva's email again, picked up the phone to call her, but thought better of it. Her Sundays were busier than his. Saint Latimer's had three morning services, plus Evensong. No, he wouldn't call today, and since tomorrow was going to be a full day for him, visiting nursing homes and taking communion to homebound parishioners, he'd just have to wait until the clergy meeting on Tuesday. He sent an email saying that he would meet her at the cathedral and that they could have lunch together.

What on earth was going on? he wondered. *Whatever it was, it would just have to wait until Tuesday.*

CHAPTER FOUR

It was mid-afternoon, and Daniel Romero had only opened his door once since the girl had been taken away, and that was to allow room service to bring in a large tray. Apparently, Romero had worked up quite an appetite the night before.

Zack Matteson had spent the day in his hotel room dividing his time between checking the video feed outside Romero's suite and searching the web for any connection between Iran and the budding telecom giant. Daniel Romero was a U.S. citizen, born in Texas into an immensely wealthy Guatemalan family with telecommunication interests throughout Texas, New Mexico, Guatemala and Honduras.

Why had a man of Romero's stature been travelling alone in London? Zack wondered. *And, what was he doing with the Iranian that day? Any business with Iran would be illegal. Decades of sanctions prevented companies, such as Romero's company AlphaNet, from doing business in Iran. No doubt, AlphaNet would love to get a foothold in Iran before his competitors did once the sanctions were eased. Was that why Romero was traveling alone? Was he trying to avoid detection from the competition? Surely there were easier ways.*

Zack searched the internet for loopholes in foreign

trade laws which might allow Romero to skirt around the sanctions. He discovered that AlphaNet, was making inroads in Oklahoma and Arizona, but that the company had absolutely no overseas connections. Were the Iranians offering AlphaNet a path into the Middle East, and if so, why? Zack rubbed his temples, trying to sort it all out.

The girl from last night had apparently been a gift from the Iranian embassy. The fact that Romero had roughed her up had made Zack see stars. He hated it when the strong bullied the weak. So much so, that he'd almost turned in his resignation after the last election. Almost everyone in the CIA now knew that the results of the primaries, and later the election itself, would have been different had it not been for foreign intervention—something which still sent shivers down Zack's spine. In the end, Zack had decided to stick it out. As it turned out, President Ripley had become only the second person ever to resign the presidency. Vice President Margaret Shouse also left office shortly afterwards, which resulted in Speaker of the House Jillian Claxton having become president. However, Claxton was fighting pancreatic cancer and had announced that she would not be running for the post in the next election.

Zack was thankful he'd trusted his gut and remained in the CIA, trusting that the recent turmoil in the Oval Office would never be repeated.

****

Some 1,200 miles away in Tehran, photographs were being passed across a massive olive-wood desk to Sadar Abbas, director of Iran's foreign and domestic intelligence.

Abbas had been appointed a year ago, after the previous director had died suddenly from a heart attack. *That was the official story.* Abbas knew the truth; his predecessor had failed one too many times in the tasks assigned him by those who truly ruled the country. On paper, the spy chief served President Rousaan Hajjani, but Abbas actually answered to the Supreme National Security Council, and they were not known for having a forgiving nature.

"Excellency." a short, squat man with closely-cropped black hair, moustache, and a graying beard stood at attention before him. "After my men did a routine check of the passenger manifest of Mr. Romero's flight yesterday from London, we did turn up… *something.*" Colonel Haamad Amir passed his boss a picture of a muscular, Caucasian man with jet-black hair boarding a flight to Turkey.

Abbas studied the photograph. "Just who is this?"

"His name is Zachary Matteson, but he's traveling under the name Matthew Stevens." Amir shifted his weight slightly. Years ago, Col. Amir had an encounter with Matteson and another agent. Amir still had the scars. "He is known to us, Excellency. Mr. Matteson is CIA."

Director Abbas put down the picture and stared at Amir without so much as blinking. When Abbas finally spoke, it was in a hushed, deceptively casual tone—one which the colonel knew to be most dangerous.

"So, tell me Haamad, what is Mr. Zack Matteson, CIA, doing on the same flight as our Daniel Romero?"

Colonel Amir swallowed. "We do not know, sir." People had died for uttering similar words to the colonel, and now he was having to say them to his boss. "Matteson's last known location was in London. We have yet to discover why he was on that flight." His eyes narrowed. "But, we will, Excellency, we will!"

Sadar Abbas reached for a cup of scalding hot tea and studied the man standing in front of him. Colonel Amir was a loyalist, one who had proven himself many times in the past, but he was also a holdover from several previous directors. True, the colonel followed orders blindly. Abbas simply assumed that was because the man had not entertained an original thought in years. *Fortunately, Col. Amir was afraid of him,* Abbas told himself. *Fear was not always the best motivator, but it generally kept subordinates in line.* "I trust you understand that we cannot afford any interest in our new friend at this juncture?" Abbas said.

"Yes sir. Our people did not know about Matteson until we reviewed these photographs. If he were in Tehran, we would, of course, be able to find him immediately. As it is, our agents are well known to the Turks; they do not allow us to move about as freely as we would like. In fact, Turkish agents followed our car only this morning to the hotel. I am told that they are parked outside our embassy at this very moment."

Sadar Abbas frowned. "That could make it difficult to dispose of the girl's body. I assume *that* particular task has been taken care of?"

"Moments ago, Excellency."

Abbas took a sip from the delicate china cup. "Good. Have your people find this Zack Matteson. Look under every camel dropping in that God-forsaken country if need be. I want to know if the CIA has wind of our plans. If they do, it will ruin everything." Abbas' eyes narrowed. "That would not be good for me, Colonel; but I assure you, it would be even worse for you."

Outside came the late afternoon call for prayer. Abbas stood and smiled—the smile of a man who was accustomed to holding all the cards. "Colonel, will you join me for prayer?"

It wasn't a question.

"Of course, Excellency." The two men walked down the hall to the entrance of a large room, where they slipped off their shoes. Amir's prayers would be in earnest this day... all for his own safety.

The preacher could see the cabin lights as he walked toward the driveway. He hoped Danny hadn't been too rough, although the generous tip he was planning to give the girl should smooth things over. He was nearly to his car when the screen door flew open and the girl ran naked across the porch, jumped down the step, and fled up the long driveway into the night.

Danny appeared at the door, doubled over in pain, but trying to put on his sneakers. "That little witch kicked me! Go after her!"

The preacher looked from Danny to the girl, who was now halfway up the drive. She had a head start and was young, but she was also barefoot and didn't know the terrain the way the preacher did. Once she'd made it to the top of the drive, there was nothing but a dirt road that went on for a couple of miles before emptying onto a long stretch of divided highway. There was a shortcut the preacher and his brother used to take up to the mailbox. The deer had kept the path passable; it would be easy enough to cut the girl off at the top of the hill.

The girl's feet were bruised from the gravel drive. She had acted on impulse; more angry than scared. She'd agreed to a night with one man, not two! No matter what she was being paid, it didn't include being repeatedly called degrading names or being hurt. The second man had just laughed at her protests. Finally, she had kicked him hard in the groin and taken off for the door.

She didn't see the preacher waiting for her at the top of the driveway. She fell, bruising her face on the ground as he tackled her.

"Let me go! Damn it, let me go!"

Danny was limping up the drive. "Tell me that you've got her!" he yelled. The preacher stood up and shook his head as he looked down at the girl. This was going to cost him a lot more than a hundred-dollar tip.

"What the hell happened back there?"

Danny pushed him away and positioned himself over the now frightened girl. This was not what the preacher had planned for tonight; his friend was out of control. "Come on, stop it, she's had enough! Let's just clean her up and play nice." Danny ignored him. "Come on man, not here!"

Daniel Romero caught his breath, his rage unmistakable even by moonlight. "All right; have it your way! Take her back to the cabin!"

The girl was crying as the two of them jerked her onto her feet and led her back down the hill—back into hell.

CHAPTER FIVE

Detective Guy Rainsford was waiting for a pimp.

He had purposefully held off an impatient coroner who'd been called in early this Sunday morning. There had been a nasty multiple vehicle accident on I-65 last night, plus two gang related killings. The woman had not been particularly happy when Guy had called downstairs.

November almost always saw a rise in the number of murders in Birmingham, though no one had ever been able to come up with a reason why. Birmingham's per capita murder rate surpassed that even of Chicago's at times, a fact which kept Guy snowed under most of the year. Gang activity was on the rise, dope was plentiful, and sex trafficking was worse than ever before. Over the years, Guy had watched as city officials spent tax revenues on sport stadiums and parking garages—hardly ever on law enforcement. He tugged on his too-short, plaid tie as if it were a noose. Guy despised wearing the things, although not as much as he despised the current city government. Between bankrupting the city and crucifying one another in front of the media, the council seldom paid attention to the city's soaring crime rate.

Birmingham had been built as a railroad town after the Civil War when rich deposits of iron ore had made the city the steel capitol of the South. The coal mines had brought German, Polish, and Irish workers across the Atlantic in search of the American dream. What they found instead was backbreaking labor and black-lung disease. All of this, while coal industrialists amassed huge fortunes. A mixed labor force of European immigrants had worked for decades alongside the grandchildren of black slaves. Bloody rivalries had run rampant throughout the city's history. Over the decades, both the industrialists and organized labor capitalized on ethnic tensions. Poor whites were purposefully pitted against poorer blacks as the mine owners and steel magnates profited beyond their wildest imaginations. Unions, for their part, promised more than they could deliver, profiting off of the same atmosphere of fear and distrust. As a result, Birmingham was a city that had been built on greed and injustice.

As far as Detective Guy Rainsford was concerned, not much had changed. The mines were closed and the mills long gone, but the massive poverty left behind drove most of Birmingham's drug deals, burglaries, and prostitution. Guy had seen the victims and arrested the perpetrators for more than 20 years and was long past burnout.

Ironically, just outside the city were communities that were ranked amongst the safest places to live in the state. So, it was odd that the girl's body had turned up in Shades Creek, not far from Helena. It was nothing short of a miracle that the body had been found at all. If the girl's killer had used chains to weigh the body down instead of rope, she might never have washed ashore. Something had eaten through the ropes, or maybe the fiber had simply dissolved. Either way, it was obvious that the girl's body had spent weeks, if not months, under water.

Guy hadn't been particularly busy Friday, so he'd ended up being the lucky one assigned to investigate. Some kids had been making out down on the creekbank when they'd seen a hand sticking out from the murky water. They had rushed into the creek thinking to save a drowning victim, only to find instead a girl's naked, decaying body, her face smashed beyond recognition. The press had jumped all over the story, reporting that the corpse might be that of a missing debutante—the teenaged daughter of Councilman Mac and Juanita O'Reilly. Fifteen-year-old Rochelle O'Reilly had disappeared last May and hadn't been seen since.

"Young, Blonde, and Naked," had been the tasteless headline two days ago in the *Birmingham Post*. Underneath, the tagline read: "Has missing Girl Finally been Found?" Guy tugged again at his tie. He hated reporters about as much as he did the city council. *The press had gotten ahead of themselves. Again!* Guy could remember the days before 24-hour cable news; back when reporters were less willing to risk the facts over their rush to publish a story.

The parents of the O'Reilly girl had come to view the body yesterday. They told the police the child in the morgue wasn't their daughter. The girl's fingerprints weren't on file, although it wouldn't have mattered anyway since most of the skin had either worn off, or been eaten off this poor kid's hands. Dental records wouldn't matter either, since whoever had beaten the girl had destroyed most of her face in the process. There was only one other missing person's report that might fit the description, and it had been turned in months ago by none other than a pimp—the same one Guy was waiting for now.

Guy longed for retirement on days like this. The semi-balding detective stood up from behind the pile of paperwork and crossed over to one of the floor-to-ceiling windows of the Twenty-First Street Station. Guy's job depressed him, but then so did life. It always had. Relationships never seemed to work out, no one was at home waiting for him, no wife or kids—just a couple of dogs. His bank account was always low, as were the number of people he could count on as friends. His caseload was usually assigned from the bottom of the barrel, which meant that only a few ever got solved. Guy had found that drinking helped, but he hadn't become particularly successful at that either. About the only thing he did for amusement was to go to Region's Field, eat a hotdog and watch the Barons play baseball. The minor leaguers, unlike Guy, had hopes for better days. Guy simply accepted there were no better days ahead. It was easier that way.

His depressed demeanor and dress had long ago earned him the nickname "Eeyore" around the station. He knew; just didn't care.

Guy peered down through the accumulation of dust

and grime on the window to the city streets below. It was beginning to rain. The weather girl from the radio had said it might even snow. He looked up at the sky. *Nah. It wouldn't snow.* Even if it did, it wouldn't stick—just as it would be hard to make any charges stick against this pimp. *After all, the coroner wasn't likely to find a lot of evidence from a body that had been under water as long as this one had.*

He rubbed his eyes. He hadn't slept much this weekend, trying to figure out if the body in the morgue was that of a teen prostitute named Lindsay. Ironically, it had been her pimp who'd filed the original report. Guy knew the weasel—Valentino Ramirez; he catered to some of the wealthier clients in town. Ramirez had wanted to find this girl badly enough to come to the police station and fill out a missing person's report. *That, in and of itself, was unusual. Damned unusual.* Guy recalled how careful Ramirez had been when filling out the paperwork. He'd simply noted that the girl was a *friend*, and that her name was Lindsay. No last name—just Lindsay.

Valentino Ramirez wasn't cut of the same cloth as most pimps Guy had arrested. From what Guy had been able to determine, Ramirez simply made the arrangements; the girls could agree or not. There was never a consequence for refusing work; although the word on the street was that Ramirez's girls seldom refused, probably because he let them keep up to half of whatever they made. Girls could come and go as they pleased, and work whenever they chose. As far as the detective could tell, Ramirez didn't abuse his girls, or fine them for pulling fewer tricks the way most other pimps did. *If there was such a thing as a lazy pimp, Valentino Ramirez was it.*

The detective had spoken with a couple of the working girls he knew—both professionally and in the Biblical sense—who'd told him that Ramirez was known for offering specialty services. Judging from the age of the child lying on the slab downstairs, *specialty* translated *young.*

His captain, Maurice Toone—*Toone the Loon,* Guy had nicknamed him—had never liked him, which was probably the reason Guy had been assigned to Lindsay's murder in the first place. Guy got a lot of unsolvable cases, which meant he was constantly being passed over for promotion. It had started years ago when he'd made a crack about the captain's wife at the annual Christmas party. *Of course, if the woman hadn't been sleeping with every other officer in the department, he wouldn't have said anything in the first place!* As a result, Guy took great delight whenever he did solve any of the captain's crappy assignments. A month ago, he'd come close to throwing a file on Toone's desk and performing a touchdown celebration after solving a seemingly impossible case. *Maybe he would really do that if he managed to figure this one out!*

He sighed.

Okay, maybe not.

Guy had sent two patrolmen to bring Ramirez in and see if the pimp could identify the body downstairs. Ramirez must have gotten word, because he had called an hour ago and agreed to come to the station. Guy fiddled with his tie again, finally taking the blasted thing off and tossing it on the desk behind him.

"Detective Rainsford?"

Guy hadn't heard the patrolman come up behind him. "Dispatch sent me upstairs to find you. They got someone downstairs; says you've been lookin' for him."

Guy nodded. "Bring him up."

He looked out the window again, still trying to put the pieces of the puzzle together. Two girls, close to the same age, both vanish around the same time. *One a Birmingham councilman's daughter; the other...* he shook his head. *Prostitution? Pornography?* Probably both if she had been involved with this scumbag on his way upstairs. Guy's former partner, Teri McCaleb, worked for the Alabama Internet Crime Division. He wondered if he should talk to Teri about this girl.

"I hear you're looking for me," said a short, dumpy man with closely cropped hair and bushy eyebrows. Guy stared at Valentino Ramirez and sneered. The pimp had on a camouflage jacket, torn jeans, and $600 shoes.

"Nice shoes."

"Yeah, man," Ramirez shot back. "I'd say the same thing about yours, but I don't like to lie."

Pleasantries over.

Guy pulled out a chair. "Sit down." Ramirez was a lot of things, but defiant wasn't one of them. He sat in the folding chair across from the detective's cluttered, gray-metal desk.

"My condolences," Guy said.

"For what?"

"Judging from that jacket, business must be bad."

Ramirez flashed a smart-ass grin, displaying a mouth full of gold crowns. "Man, business is just fine; but thanks for askin'."

"I don't know, looks like things aren't going so well. I've never seen you dressed like this. You certainly don't look like a pimp... well maybe those shoes."

Ramirez bristled. "How many times I got to tell you people? I ain't no pimp."

Guy raised an eyebrow. "Oh yeah, that's right, you called it... wait a minute, it will come to me..."

The pimp straightened. "Man, I'm simply a business manager."

"Yeah, that's right... a *manager*." Guy's smile vanished. "Well, Mister Business Manager, I need you to look at something for me."

"What's that?"

"Let's just call it part of your portfolio. Come with me." The detective led the pimp down four flights of stairs and then to the other end of a deserted, dimly lit, yellow and gray hallway.

"Man, don't you people have an elevator?" Ramirez complained.

Guy walked in front toward a steel door at the end of the hall, placed a key in the lock, and opened it. "Never use it. I need the exercise. Besides, we reserve the elevator for our more distinguished guests." He stood back to let Ramirez walk through first.

"Distinguished? Man, ain't nobody more

distinguished than me! Besides, you don't get much of a workout walking *down* steps."

Guy smiled. "We will when we walk back up."

Ramirez stopped. "Come on man, I ain't walking up no four flights of ..." He wrinkled up his nose. "Oh, God, what the hell is that?"

"What?"

Ramirez closed his eyes. "Smells like somebody's dead down here!"

"As a matter of fact, they all are." Guy closed the door behind him. "Welcome to the morgue."

The Birmingham morgue looked a lot like the ones Ramirez had seen on television. It was a large room with cement walls, lined with what looked like huge, metal filing cabinets. The only difference was that on TV no one ever commented about the smell. Truthfully, Guy had never gotten used to it either, but he wasn't about to let on in front of this lowlife.

They walked over to a woman wearing a green jumpsuit and surgical mask, looking as if she had just come from surgery. And she had—of a sort. Detective Rainsford had pulled her out of the latest autopsy—a 58-year-old taxi driver involved in the wreck last night—to let this clown view the body of the girl they had fished out of the water.

The woman opened a drawer, dragged the body-trolley in front of them, and pulled back a white cloth.

"Oh, hell!" Ramirez turned away.

"Come on Valentino, man up!"

"I don't want to look at... at that!"

"I don't have all day." Guy reached over and turned the pimp around and forced him to look at the demolished face of the blonde teenager lying on the examiner's table. "So, is that her?"

"Man, I can't even tell that it *is* a her!"

The detective nodded to the woman in green. She drew the sheet further back, revealing the girl's entire body. Her legs and torso had several long welts, cuts and tears running at all angles. Small bits of flesh hung loose from various parts of the body.

Ramirez turned and vomited on the floor. The woman in green rolled her eyes.

"Before we get you a mop," Guy quipped, "I want you to take a good look at her. Is this the girl you reported missing last summer?"

Ramirez glanced at the face and body of the dead girl. "No man, I don't know this bi…" he caught himself… "this young lady."

"You sure? Look closer."

Ramirez forced himself to look again. "God, she's all cut up!"

The doctor explained, "The cuts were most likely from objects the body encountered in the river bed. The wounds to the head were not. We'll know more after the autopsy."

"Will you be able to tell if she had sex before she died?" Guy was asking the examiner but looking straight at Ramirez.

The woman shook her head. "She's been under the water a long time, Detective."

"Man, get me out of here!" Ramirez turned away, his face turning green.

Guy blocked his way. "Not until you tell me if this is her! Is this Lindsay?"

The pimp grimaced as he turned to look at the girl's face again. One eye was missing; the other half open. Her mouth was nearly gone, and if she had ever had a nose, there was no way to know what it had looked like now. "Look, man, how am I supposed to know if this is... Oh, my God!"

"What?"

Ramirez was staring at the girl's feet.

"No! Oh God... Sweet Jesus. . . her left foot!"

Both the examiner and detective followed Ramirez gaze. "What about her foot?"

The pimp began shaking. "No! Oh, hell no." He looked up at Guy. "It's her! It's Lindsay!"

"The girl you reported missing last May?"

Ramirez nodded.

"You're sure?"

"Man, I know everything about my girls'... I mean... my friends'... bodies. Look at her middle toe. It's stubbed, shorter than it ought to be. She told me she was born with it."

Guy looked at the girl's foot; sure enough, the middle toe was about half the size it should have been.

"You're positive this is Lindsay?"

Ramirez grimaced, but made himself look at the girl. "Whoever did this is one sick mother. I ain't saying nuttin', but if I ever had a girl work for me, I'd do a better job of screening clients than allow someone to do..." he pointed to the girl's face, "...to do this."

Ramirez couldn't help it; he turned and vomited again. Guy glanced over at the examiner. "Get him a mop!" he said as he stormed out the double doors and into the hallway to wait.

The pimp came out a few minutes later, the color drained from his face. He leaned against the wall. "Man, what happened to her? Nobody should go through nuttin' like that!"

Guy sneered. "That sounds funny, coming from you."

"Man, I ain't never hurt *nobody*! I protect my friends."

Guy's face hardened. "I wouldn't call what you do *protection*."

The pimp wiped his eyes with the back of his hand. "They come to me. I'm not like the others. I don't recruit. Girls come to me. They want me to fix them up, that's all."

"For a fee," Guy quipped.

"*You* said that. I didn't. But even if I did take a piece, it ain't no different than any other escort agency."

"Except that escort agencies are illegal in the state of Alabama."

"Look, I ain't saying crap, man. We done here?"

Guy's eyes flashed fire. "We're done when I say we're done! That kid was beaten to death! I'm guessing she was underage. It wouldn't be hard to prove she worked for you. And right now, I'd say that makes you the prime suspect!"

Whatever color had managed to return to Ramirez's face completely vanished. His legs buckled and he collapsed to the floor. "I ain't never killed nobody," he cried. "You cops know me, man, I ain't built that way! I never hurt nobody... nobody!" Ramirez was trembling. "Girl wants to go to work for me, fine, but she can come and go as she pleases." He shook his head. "I ain't never hurt none of 'em!"

Guy knew plenty of pimps; most were hard as nails. This one was a cream puff.

"I treat them with respect, man. Nobody forces them to do nuttin'." Ramirez was incriminating himself, but Guy was starting to realize he needed an ally, not an enemy, if he was going to solve this case. Sure, he could arrest Ramirez, but he'd be free by the end of the day. Plus, Guy's gut told him Ramirez didn't kill the girl, although he might have an idea who did. *Better to play him now than lose him later,* Guy thought. As much as he couldn't stand pimps, the detective softened his tone. "Valentino, somebody beat that kid really bad."

"It wasn't me, man. I swear it."

"Then I need you to work with me. I need to know everything about Lindsay. Was she moody? What were her likes, her dislikes, what kind of music did she listen to—everything." Guy also wanted a list of Lindsay's clients, but he knew Ramirez wasn't about to hand that over.

"I don't know man, she mostly kept to herself." Ramirez wiped his eyes. "Found me online. She only worked on weekends... sometimes two or three clients a night."

"So... she was popular?" Guy asked, secretly wishing

there was someplace he could drag this creep for about an hour.

Ramirez wiped his eyes. "The young ones always are. I mean…"

"I'm not charging you." *Not yet, at least!* "I just want to find Lindsay's killer."

"Fourteen or fifteen-year-olds… I mean is that so different from sixteen?" Ramirez said. "Alabama lets you do whatever you want with a 16-year-old girl."

Not for pay! thought the detective, barely managing to keep his hands from Ramirez's throat.

"I mean they all tell me they're eighteen, but look at her, man. She was fifteen, tops. Who would do that to a kid?"

A kid you sold for sex! Guy was doing his best to conceal his rage. He took a deep breath. "She certainly didn't deserve what she got."

Nor had Ramirez. Guy thought. *Not yet, at least!*

Guy despised men like Ramirez, but right now he had to try and use him to find out who had killed the girl. He wondered if the pimp's tears were from grief or if the man was just scared. *Did Ramirez know who did it? If so, was he afraid that he might be next?*

"Look, Valentino, I know you take care of your… um, *friends.* I know you're not like those other guys. Maybe you're right, you're more like a…" it wasn't easy to get the words out of his mouth, "…a *manager.*

Guy knew how to lie, it just went with the territory, but some lies were harder than others. It didn't hurt that Guy had one of those faces that people just seemed to trust. He didn't look like a cop. Dark hair—what was left of it—a thick moustache, round face. Dressed like a used car salesman down on his luck, Guy looked like the kind of fellow you might hang out with after work and knock down a few. But it was the detective's eyes which drew you in: warm and inviting, able to make you feel as if he had nothing but your best interest at heart. He'd managed to coax more than one suspect into a confession with those soft, bluish-grey eyes. Plus, when he wanted to, Guy was a master at making people feel as if he cared—which he hardly ever did anymore.

"Listen, Valentino, I know you never wanted Lindsay to get hurt. Did she ever say anything about someone... I don't know... somebody who liked it rough?" Guy knew it was risky asking the pimp about his clientele, but the man's defenses were down.

"Not to me, she didn't."

"Well, somebody hurt her." He handed Ramirez his handkerchief. The pimp blew his nose and tried to hand it back. "That's okay, you keep it." Ramirez put it in his inside jacket pocket, where Guy caught a glimpse of his cell phone. *That phone was a treasure trove of information!* Guy's mind began to race. *It might take a bit of convincing to get a judge to subpoena the phone records. Maybe there was another way... perhaps Teri McCaleb would help him out—for old time's sake.*

"What else can you tell me about Lindsay?"

"Not a damn thing. I ain't lyin' to you, man. It's just like I said when she went missing last spring. Lindsay never told me where she lived, or who she lived with, or what she did during the rest of the week. Never talked about no school, no parents, not a damn thing. Just called me on Friday afternoons to see if..." his voice trailed away.

"To see if you had a client for her?"

Ramirez didn't respond.

"How'd she get to her, uh... appointments?"

Ramirez hesitated. "I guess she took Uber. Everybody's doing that these days." *The pimp wasn't stupid. He knew that if he admitted to driving a girl to meet a client that the case for sex trafficking would be that much easier to make.*

"An underage kid turning tricks, with enough smarts to get herself to and from a client's house every weekend? Doesn't sound to me like she needed a manager."

"Man, I've said too much already."

Guy shifted gears. "So, how can I reach you later if I need to get hold of you?"

"Same way you did this time. Just put word out on the street, I'll find you."

"No good. Give me your address." The pimp knew he wouldn't be able to leave otherwise, so he took the pen and paper offered and wrote down the address of his complex, although he listed the wrong apartment number.

"Look, Valentino, let's just keep all this between you and me for the time being." *Lying to a pimp wasn't really lying.* "I just need you to sign a piece of paper saying that you know the girl, that it's Lindsay."

"Man, I ain't signing nothing."

"You can't get in trouble for identifying a body. Besides, you clearly didn't kill her. For Chrissake, we have you on record as reporting her missing. Why would you do that if you had anything to do with her death?" Guy kept Ramirez's gaze and talked fast. "Good thing you did, or nobody would know who that poor thing is lying on that slab in there." Guy couldn't afford to lose whatever morsel of trust he'd just gained. Unfortunately, the truth was that he still knew next to nothing about this girl. Right now, all he had was Lindsay's pimp, so he'd have to keep playing him until he could gather something more substantial.

"Tell you what... let me give you my private number. You can call me anytime."

The pimp wiped his cheeks. "Yeah, all right, what is it?"

"How about you give me your number and I'll call it right now, then you'll have my number on your phone."

Ramirez wasn't about to give the police his private cell phone number. "Don't you have a business card?"

"Nope, fresh out."

Another lie.

"Okay," Guy offered, "how about I give you my phone and *you* can call your own; that way you can..." (he almost said, "add it to your address list," but then Ramirez might have figured out what Guy was really doing) "...have my number anytime you need it." Once he had access to the pimp's phone, he could ask Teri to run the contacts. *She still owed him a favor... or did he owe her?*

Ramirez reached for the detective's phone, then turned his back so the detective couldn't see what number he was calling.

Guy heard a phone ringing from inside the pimp's coat pocket.

What an idiot!

CHAPTER SIX

Last year, the first day of December had been freezing, but this morning, exactly a year later, it was already in the mid-seventies and still climbing as Father Flenn made his way through Homewood toward a shelter for women in downtown Birmingham. Just yesterday, the weather forecast had been for snow!

He put the top down on his aging Saab as he pulled into a burger joint drive-thru for coffee. As soon as he did, the priest was nearly blinded by the reflection of early-morning sunlight off the enormous glass structure that housed the Rye Foundation. The building sat atop a small hill in Homewood, one of the oldest suburbs of Birmingham. At certain angles, the gigantic, mirrored edifice reflected the bare buttocks of the city's prized statue of Vulcan, the god of fire. Locals often referred to the semi-clad figure as: "Moon Over Homewood." Fortunately, Flenn was spared that particular this morning as he waited for his coffee.

Flenn had known Willy Rye for what seemed like forever, but in a sense, so had most of America. Rye's evangelical crusades had been televised across the nation for decades, having once been a staple of Sunday night television. Flenn knew that Willy Rye was as authentic a preacher as fundamentalist Christianity had ever produced. Before televangelists had soiled evangelism's reputation, Willy had been filling stadiums with Bible-toting believers for nearly 50 years.

The evangelist's popularity was rooted in his authenticity. Willy Rye said what he believed and believed what he said. His message was simple: "Confess your sins, ask Jesus into your heart, and believe that the Bible is the literal word of God." Willy had preached that same formula to millions. As his popularity skyrocketed, he'd been invited to pray with the heads of state of more than 30 nations, and had personally prayed with every American president since Eisenhower.

Over the decades, Willy's prayers had taken several turns. He had prayed for the American school system, that it would again sanction prayer in its classrooms... that abortion would not be made legal... that the leaders of communism would repent (or perish)... that teenagers would be saved from the temptations of the hippies... that morality would win out during the era of Vietnam and civil rights... and that America would once again become a Christian nation with everyone attending church on Sunday morning. Every four years Willy prayed that the nation would vote, "properly and in accordance with God's will, and that the nation would take a stand against the wiles of the devil"—which were, of course, plentiful.

Willy and Elizabeth had raised their two boys, Benjamin and Willy Junior, with warnings about what they considered worldly evils: premarital sex, drugs, gambling, homosexuality and alcohol. Both boys had gone to fundamentalist schools, and neither had been allowed to have friends without parental approval. Junior had followed the rules with blind obedience, seldom questioning his mother, and never his father. He'd made good grades in school, dated only one girl throughout college and married shortly after graduation—to the utter delight of his parents since Junior hadn't inherited his parents' good looks. Junior had suffered from severe acne as a child, leaving his face permanently pock-marked. His lifeless, thin, black hair always looked greasy, no matter how often he washed it; and his weight had forever been a problem. At only 5'6", Junior had resembled a Sumo wrestler as early as sixth grade. His wife, Mary Lou, was nearly as big, and their three daughters were well on their way to becoming lifetime candidates for liposuction.

Yet Junior was a genius with numbers, so it was no surprise when he announced that he wanted to become an accountant. Nor was it a surprise when he had difficulty establishing himself on his own, his appearance being the biggest drawback. As a result, Elizabeth had insisted her husband hire Junior to work in the accounting department at the ministry's home office.

Junior's older brother, Benjamin, was on the opposite end of the spectrum. Handsome and self-confident, Benji, as his mother nicknamed him, had enough self-esteem for a dozen kids. Tall and slender, with thick locks of dark, wavy hair, Benji had chiseled cheekbones and a pronounced chin that made him appear studious, though he had been anything but. Benjamin's green eyes sparkled with... *something*, although no one could ever determine just what. His mother had labeled it early on as mischief; his father thought it something more diabolical. Elizabeth eventually came to feel that way herself, especially after Junior's cat was found hanging inside the tree house. She had sent Benjamin for counseling after that; and, while her son never repeated the act with any of the family pets, Elizabeth couldn't help wondering every time a neighbor's cat or puppy went missing.

Willy lived by the proverb, "spare the rod, spoil the child," but Elizabeth insisted that her husband let her handle Benji her own way, with counseling and tenderness. Despite her best efforts, problems continued, as did complaints from teachers and neighbors. Elizabeth initially believed her son's protests of innocence, but the evidence always seemed to prove otherwise: broken windows after he'd gotten his first BB gun, beer cans in his room in junior high, marijuana and pills she found in his dresser during high school... not to mention the claims of several distraught young girls over the years. All this Elizabeth handled quietly and alone while her famous husband was away leading people to the Lord.

She had told Willy about a few of the incidents at first, but the agony on her husband's face had been too great for her to bear. So, instead of going to Willy, she paid restitutions, saw that damages were repaired, hired more counselors and made sure that absolutely nothing made its way into a courtroom—or worse, the newspapers.

Most pastors' families are accustomed to feeling as if they live in a fishbowl, but the Ryes weren't like most pastors' families. Whatever was true for the typical preacher's household was multiplied a hundred-fold for this first family of Christendom. Elizabeth worked diligently behind the scenes to make sure that the family of the man who counseled presidents, preached to kings and queens, and brought thousands to Jesus always looked their best. Willy suspected that there were things his wife wasn't telling him about their eldest son, but his calling as God's champion meant that he had to trust that Elizabeth would be able to handle the boy.

Willy had been greatly relieved the year that Benjamin was accepted to Princeton, but he had been astonished when his son had actually managed to graduate. Scott Flenn had felt pretty much the same way since he had expected Benji Rye to be in prison long before he turned 21. Flenn had known Benji, along with the rest of the Rye family, ever since he was a kid. Flenn's grandfather had admired Willy in the early days and had donated millions to the Rye Foundation, and so, in turn, had Flenn's dad. As a result, the Flenn family had been invited down from New Hampshire to Birmingham to spend summers at the Ryes' home by the river. Flenn always hated those summers. The brutal Alabama heat was bad enough; putting up with Benji Rye had proved next to impossible.

Flenn was still dubious about Benji's sudden conversion to Christianity a couple of years ago. It had been a bit *too* convenient. It put Benji, as the eldest son, in the driver's seat of a lucrative evangelical empire once Willy passed; which, from all indication, would be relatively soon.

Driving away with a large coffee in hand, Father Flenn looked into his rearview mirror at the towering glass structure fading into the distance. Not for the first time, he felt a sense of unease about Willy Rye's impending death. He shook his head. *If Benjamin Rye was soon to be at the helm of his father's empire, God help us all!*

The girl glowered at them from the bed where Daniel Romero had thrown her. Benjamin Rye was gathering her clothes to take her back into town, upset that he'd have to find a different girl next time... if there was a next time. Danny was not likely to risk further exposure.

Danny had been way too rough on the girl. The preacher kept telling the kid that he'd make it worth her while, but she wasn't listening. "It'll be okay," he said for what seemed like the thousandth time.

"Benji, shut up!" Romero ordered as he paced around the room, lost in thought. Rye winced. Danny had just used his nickname! That was probably okay since he hadn't called him by his full name. Rye had a little over $900 in his wallet, which he had decided to hand her when they dropped her off downtown. That should keep her mouth shut.

The girl somehow managed to finally put her pain and rage into words. "What is wrong with you?" She was staring straight at Danny. "You didn't have to do that. I was doing what you wanted, you didn't have to be so damn mean!"

"And you! she said, glaring at Rye. "Why didn't you stop him? I mean, you being a famous preacher and everything!"

Romero stopped pacing.

CHAPTER SEVEN

Father Scott Flenn bounded up the steps of the former tenement building two at a time. What had once been a dilapidated eyesore was swiftly becoming an attractive home for battered women and children—thanks mostly to Flenn's own private donations.

Work continued outside, evidenced by the scaffolding surrounding the north end of the building and by workers busily sandblasting years of grime and graffiti off the brick walls. A security fence and full-time guards prevented unauthorized entry but no one challenged the tall priest this morning; instead, the guards waved good naturedly.

"Father, good to see you on this beautiful Monday morning!" The director of New Beginnings greeted Flenn warmly as he walked into the spacious lobby. A heavyset workman was coming down a rickety ladder. Flenn grabbed hold of the ladder to steady it; the man nodded his thanks and went about his work.

"Always good to see you too, Ashleigh," he said with a warm smile. Ashleigh Nieves was a slender brunette of Peruvian descent who looked years younger than her age, which Flenn happened to know was 36. He'd been the one to steer her to the board of directors just last year.

She was a member of his parish and a licensed social worker. Impressed with Ashleigh's credentials, the board had been eager to hire her.

"Nice save there," she said, pointing to the ladder.

"Well," Flenn offered good-naturedly, "we can't afford to lose any workers right now, can we? There's too much to do around here!"

Indeed, much had already been done—new floors, brightly painted walls, updated fixtures, warm lighting. It had been a three-million-dollar upgrade, two-thirds of which had been donated by Scott Flenn. "Please tell me the electrical contractors arrived this morning?" Flenn asked. "They promised me they'd have that wiring upstairs finished before Christmas."

"Just got here," Ashleigh reported cheerily. "You can go up there if you want. I sure hope they'll be done by then; I'd like to open that third-floor dormitory after the first of the year. Lord knows, we need the extra space."

"Yes, the Lord does know," Flenn smiled. "But as usual, he's left the work up to us."

Ashleigh reached over and put her arm around the priest. "Well, he certainly knew what he was doing when he sent you to us!" she said, hugging him tightly. *Maybe a bit too tightly.* Flenn shrugged. He'd gotten used to it over the years. *Occupational hazard,* he often told himself. As an unattached, friendly, good-looking pastor, Flenn had caught the eye of several people around town—still he hoped Ashleigh's flirtations were nothing serious. His heart belonged elsewhere, and always would.

He gently slipped his arm out of hers and headed

toward the stairs. "Thanks Ashleigh, I think I'll go grab a cup of coffee and check on those contractors now. See you Sunday?"

Ashleigh played with her hair as she smiled warmly. "You betcha!"

CHAPTER EIGHT

Zack Matteson walked out of the hotel's gift shop, delighted to have found a bag of jellybeans, even if nearly half of them were licorice. *Maybe he'd give those to Erdem.*

He checked his watch and thought about what Erdem had told him over the phone. Romero had gone to the same restaurant again last night. Erdem had followed, this time in a different car, and had parked outside the marketplace again. Just like the previous night, there were no patrons except for Romero and whomever he was meeting.

Zack leaned against a large tile column in the middle of the lobby and opened the bag of candy. *Romero hadn't come all this way for the cuisine, especially since Erdem described the place as a Turkish version of a greasy spoon.* Zack pulled out his phone to make reservations for tomorrow night. Since the diner had been booked the previous two nights, if they had a table open then Romero wasn't likely going to be returning for a third.

"I am sorry," the man on the other end of the telephone said in perfect English. "We're completely booked tomorrow evening. Perhaps you can come another time?" English is commonly heard in Turkey, but this guy's was a little *too* good. *Obviously educated beyond the level of someone who would be working in an out-of-the-way bean wagon.* As a precaution, Zack turned his telephone off and removed the battery to avoid being traced.

Well Flenn, old buddy, Zack thought, *looks like some hunches do pay off after all!*

****

"Who was on the phone?" asked Ambassador Javaad Lajani.

"I do not know, sir," replied a man in a dark suit and black tie. "Someone wishing to make reservations for tomorrow night. He sounded like an American."

Ambassador Lajani had been advised of Zack Matteson's presence in Istanbul. A photograph and detailed description had been sent to the embassy with orders to notify Col. Amir immediately if Matteson turned up. "Let me know if he calls again," Lajani ordered. He silently cursed that he had no way of tracing a call to this dive. The ambassador had promised to pay the owner handsomely for the exclusive use of his diner. Lajani's attaché was answering all calls while he met with Daniel Romero—*a good thing, too,* Lajani thought, *since the simpleton who owned this vomit-hole couldn't speak a word of English! Still, there were many Americans in Turkey; there was no reason to believe a spy of Zack Matteson's caliber would be so brazen as to simply call and ask for a reservation.* Lajani tried to swallow a bite of what passed as a salad.

Daniel Romero, for his part, appeared to have a healthy appetite and seemed to be enjoying this slop.

"So, bottom line," Romero said between bites of manti (dumplings with meat), "is that as long as I agree to this one thing, then I will have your full support?"

The ambassador was not accustomed to such frankness. He forced a smile. "Absolutely, Mr. Romero. The terms, of course, will be finalized tomorrow night, but if you agree to what we are asking then we can almost assure you that your ambitions will be fully realized."

Romero cocked his head. "Almost?"

The ambassador continued his practiced smile. "Of course, you will have to do your part in securing the working class... along with your religious right. Our research shows that they will be crucial in this next election. Even with our technical help, you will still need them solidly behind you."

Now it was Romero's turn to smile. "That won't be a problem." Romero wiped his chin. "In fact, I have already set that into motion."

"That's good to hear," said the ambassador. "When Colonel Amir flies in tomorrow, he will be anxious to know more about this. Once he is assured that everything is in place, you will be able to announce your intentions publicly."

Ambassador Lajani took a bite of tomato and followed it with a few olives, pretending to enjoy the food just as he was pretending to enjoy the company. In truth, he despised this man from Texas, just as he'd despise anyone who would betray his own country.

"When will your people act?"

The ambassador wiped his mouth gingerly with a paper napkin. "You mean, free ourselves from the threat of an ancient enemy?" He tossed the napkin on top of his mostly uneaten food. "Not until your second year in office. That way you and your administration will have a tight rein on everything. There will be reaction, of course. Your Jews will be particularly difficult."

Romero stiffened. "They are not *my* Jews!" He took a sip of hot tea, wishing for something stronger. Muslims did not drink alcohol. *Neither did Southern Baptists,* he reminded himself, *at least, not when anyone was looking.* His friend, Benjamin Rye, had introduced him to that bit of hypocrisy years ago over several martinis.

"Still, you will need to be prepared," Lajani said.

"I have someone who will soften any reaction to the Jewish response. By the time he's done, no one will give a damn about what the Jews think."

"How is this possible?"

"Social media, my friend. Twitter, Facebook, Instagram—they're the new opiate of the people. When coupled with a man who knows how to work the fundamentalist base into a fever pitch; then, truth will be whatever we say it is." Romero picked up a forkful of rice and stuffed it in his mouth. "Do you remember how that last guy in office was able to take decent, hard-working Americans and make them believe the absurd? My guy can do it even better; he has God on his side!"

Javaad Lajani looked dubious. "You are certain of this?"

"You ever hear of Willy Rye?" The ambassador shook his head. Romero took a bite of the overcooked lamb. "He is an icon in our country. Sort of like your Ayatollah Khomeini." The ambassador shifted in his chair, trying not to react. "Willy Rye has been a religious leader for decades, someone everybody trusts. He's still around," Romero shook his head, "just barely." He leaned in toward the ambassador, "His son is taking over. Benjamin is his name. He's a friend of mine; we're very close. We were roommates at Princeton. We both have similar interests, if you know what I mean." Ambassador Javaad Lajani didn't. Romero shot him a wicked smile. "I'm referring to last night."

Lajani picked at his dessert—*completely tasteless!* "Oh, you mean the girl?"

Romero smiled. "He and I like to revisit our youth from time to time. He likes the teenagers as much as I do."

The ambassador wondered if this Benjamin Rye person would also beat a girl within an inch of her life. Lajani had been appalled when the order had come to kill the child. She was only 16, the daughter of poor Turkish parents who had been well paid for her services on other occasions. *Now the parents would have to be killed, as well. There could be no trace, no connection to the embassy.*

Romero looked up from his meal. "By the way, I assume another girl has been found for tonight?"

"She will be waiting for you at your hotel." *One more family will have to pay the price for this man's perverse appetite! Yet,* Lajani reasoned, *if Romero made good on his promise, Iran would finally be able to claim the ultimate prize in a few short years. His country's greatest enemy would be destroyed, and America would do nothing to stop it!*

Their business was nearly complete and the stage set. Colonel Amir would fly in tomorrow and meet with Romero over dinner here in this God-forsaken place. The ambassador knew Amir would be spotted by Turkish intelligence if he came to the embassy. *It had been difficult enough for Lajani's men to sneak him out of the compound tonight; it would be next to impossible to go unnoticed once Col. Amir arrived!* The plan was for the colonel to come here and meet with Romero as soon as the plane landed. By the time the agents at the airport reported that Amir was on Turkish soil, the colonel would be well on his way back to Tehran.

Lajani looked around the room at the cracked plaster walls and the dying plants used for decoration. He wondered what Col. Amir would think of this dung heap. *Probably wouldn't even notice,* Lajani thought. *The man is from peasant stock, completely lacking in the finer graces.*

"Coffee here is not as good as in Guatemala," Romero said as he drained the small cup. "But, it's stronger. Which is good, since I'll be up all night!" The way he emphasized the word *up* made Lajani's skin crawl.

The ambassador stood, anxious for the evening to come to an end. "My driver is ready, Mr. Romero. You are welcome to stay and complete your meal. I regret that I will not be with you tomorrow, but Colonel Amir will be your dining companion. I know you will have much to discuss!"

Romero shrugged. "Sounds like it's all settled to me. Just so long as we both keep our ends of the bargain. Looks like I'll have to get busy as soon as I get back to Texas."

The ambassador offered his hand. *Thanks be to Allah; this man was now Amir's responsibility!* Lajani forced one last smile

"Good night Mr. Ambassador," Romero said, turning back to finish his meal.

"Good night, Mr. Romero. Or should I say, Mr. President."

CHAPTER NINE

The Episcopal Church of the Advent had served as the cathedral for the Diocese of Alabama since 1982; over a century after Advent had first been built as a large wooden church in the heart of the new city of Birmingham. The church's current structure had been erected a dozen or so years later of local stone. At one time it had been the tallest, and arguably the grandest, structure in the city.

Ninety-three priests and deacons gathered together under the roof of Clingman Commons to hear Bishop Tom Morrison address a variety of diocesan events, from further expansion of Camp McDowell, to upcoming changes in marriage rituals. Tempers flared among a handful of priests when Bishop Morrison explained that the soon-to-be-published new *Book of Common Prayer* would eliminate the phrase "man and woman" from the marriage rite. Flenn knew that Episcopalians habitually resisted change; however, his denomination had long ago authorized same-sex weddings. It was just that now, with a new prayer book on its way, everyone would see those changes in black and white.

Flenn knew that clergy were the ones who had to handle the complaints and cancellation of pledges when their members were upset with changing policy. The new prayer book would cause yet another uproar in a church which had seen more than half its membership depart since the 1960's. Many congregations had been divided back then over civil rights. Thousands left over the ordination of women in the early 1970's, and even more over the changes in the old *Book of Common Prayer.* These days, congregations had been divided over the issue of sexuality, many even refusing to speak with one another. It never ceased to amaze Flenn how people who routinely spoke of unconditional love and understanding were often reluctant to give either.

Bishop Morrison concluded his remarks just after 11:30 as the group of priests and deacons rose to enter the nave for Holy Communion. Afterwards, boxed lunches awaited as everyone went off to sit with friends and colleagues and catch up with one another over turkey and cheese on white bread. Minerva Wilson sat next to Flenn during the communion service. She looked awful, Flenn thought, a shadow of her usual self. During the passing of the peace, when he'd hugged her, he noticed that she felt like a skeleton. As they stood to sing a hymn, he pretended not to notice the tears falling down her soft, brown cheeks. Afterwards, they picked up their lunch boxes and made their way upstairs to a Sunday School classroom above the parish hall. Minerva didn't bother to open hers. Flenn nibbled his sandwich and waited patiently as she sat quietly, eyes closed in silent prayer. She was shaking when at last she opened her eyes.

"I was praying that God would forgive me for what I am about to do," she said. "I'm just not sure where to start."

"Sometimes," Flenn said kindly, "it is best just to jump in with both feet." She wiped away the tears, took a breath, and this time looked straight at him.

"I may have killed a girl."

CHAPTER TEN

The pizza had no flavor. Guy blamed it on his head cold, which was getting worse by the minute. He sat alone at Tony's Pizzeria, where he had stopped for a bite before going home to Buster and Rolly, two retrievers who shared the otherwise empty house which Guy had called home for the past 20 years. Why the waitress had insisted on seating him at a booth big enough for six when hardly anyone else was in the place was beyond him. Just one more annoyance to an otherwise lousy day. The only other patrons were a young family sitting at the opposite end of the restaurant celebrating a birthday.

Guy stared down at the mostly uneaten sausage and onion pie before finally pushing it away and picking up his beer. He glanced over at the family—two parents, along with twin infant boys, an elderly couple and a four or five-year-old blonde, who was reigning over the ceremony as queen for the day. The little girl looked at him and stuck out her tongue. Guy made sure the adults weren't watching when he returned the gesture.

Birthdays had never been a big deal in Guy's family. His dad had tried, but his mom had never seemed to want to put in the effort. He remembered his dad attempting to bake a cake for his ninth birthday. It was a total disaster. At least his dad had made the effort; his mom seldom had. If there was a Christmas tree in the house or a basket of candy on the kitchen table at Easter for Guy and his sisters, it had been their dad who had provided it.

Guy gazed down at the empty bottle. He hadn't been able to taste the beer any more than he had the pizza, but that didn't keep him from ordering a second. The little girl looked at him again, this time smiling at him before blowing out her candles. It wasn't that Guy disliked children; in fact, he had once envisioned himself having two or three, but that hadn't been in the cards. Now, approaching 50, he'd had to settle for long nights with Buster and Rolly as his only companions.

He took a swig from the second bottle and watched the little blonde open her presents. Gradually, his thoughts turned to the teenager on the slab at the morgue. The autopsy had been delayed and wouldn't be until late tomorrow afternoon. *Doubtful he'd be any closer to figuring anything out even after the examiner's report.* He nursed his beer as the girl received the customary applause for blowing out the candles on what was obviously a homemade birthday cake. A decade from now, he realized, this little girl would be the same age as the kid at the morgue. *Once upon a time, Lindsay had been a little girl. Had anyone ever given her a birthday party?* he wondered, as the image of Lindsay's battered body flashed through his mind.

Who in God's name could have done that to a kid?

That thought had been swirling through his brain

ever since he had first seen her mangled body on the creekbank. It was unusual for a case to get under Guy's skin the way this one was starting to do—he was long past being shocked by anything that sprang from Birmingham's underbelly. *There was something about this kid.* He couldn't put his finger on it, but he wanted; no, he *needed* answers.

He looked down at the cold pizza and began drumming his fingers slowly on the table. He went over the few facts he had managed to put together so far. *Whoever had killed Lindsay had to have been beyond rage to have beaten her so viciously.* Even with all that Guy had seen as a cop, thinking about this case kept making him shiver. *Or was it just his cold?* Guy felt a knot forming in his stomach and hoped he wasn't getting the flu.

He signaled the waitress for a carryout box. At least Buster and Rolly could enjoy the pizza. As he stood and turned to leave, he felt a tug on his trousers. He looked down to see the little girl holding up a green paper plate with a slice of yellow cake and too much frosting smeared over the top. "Mister, you look grumpy," the little girl said. "Here, take this; maybe it will make you feel better." She smiled up at him. "It's my birthday!"

Guy stared at the cake, thinking twice before accepting it. "Thank you," he said, forcing a smile.

The girl looked behind her to make sure no one could hear, then lowered her voice. "Don't tell my mom, but it's disgusting."

CHAPTER ELEVEN

Zack Matteson adjusted his earbuds and offered Erdem a handful of jellybeans (all licorice) as they sat in a car down from the diner where Daniel Romero was meeting with Col. Haamad Amir of Iranian intelligence. Zack had recognized the man as soon as he'd stepped out of the limo. Amir was not someone easily forgotten. He and Flenn had nearly been killed by the Colonel and his men in a standoff in Afghanistan.

Zack set his hand-held surveillance device at an angle so it wouldn't be noticed from outside Erdem's tiny car, or more specifically, his "cousin's" car. All Zack had heard so far was idle chatter. Amir had said very little. Romero was doing most of the talking.

"Colonel, if Iranian food is as good as Turkish food, then I must visit you in your country one day!"

"Anything may be possible in the future," Amir said, smiling. Silently, he agreed with Ambassador Lajani's review of this place; however, Lajani had, at least, found an out of the way location. The food was lousy, but they weren't at risk of being overheard. A customary sweep of the restaurant had found no eavesdropping devices; plus,

reports were that Zack Matteson had likely gone on to
Izmir, where several other CIA agents were known to be
gathering ahead of a visit from the new American
secretary of state in a few days. *Most likely it had simply been
a coincidence that Matteson and Romero had been on the same
flight out of London.*

Colonel Amir would have ordered his agents shot had
he discovered the truth—that Matteson was right under
their very noses, even staying at the same hotel as Romero.
Zack had remained inside his room most of the time, and
Amir had not ordered surveillance inside the hotel, but
had simply arranged for a car to sit outside in case Romero
left the Four Seasons on his own. *Why would he?* Amir had
reasoned. *The man had everything he could want right there in
his room!* The colonel had heard that the second girl had
fared little better than the first. At least she had been able
to walk out on her own accord. *Not that it mattered anymore.*

Zack was growing bored listening to Romero go on
and on about drivel. He cringed, however, when the
subject of the two girls had come up. Earlier, he'd
witnessed the second girl leave Romero's room with the
same two men from yesterday. She had appeared even
younger than the first.

Erdem, unable to hear the conversation, simply drank
a soda and nibbled at something he'd brought along.
Whatever it was smelled awful. Zack leaned closer to the
open window.

"So, let's be sure we are, as you Americans like to say,
on the same page," Col. Amir offered. Romero had
finished his soup and was popping small olives into his

mouth. "My government can assure that the voting will go your way in Florida, Washington, Ohio, New York, New Hampshire, Pennsylvania, along with one or two other states. So far, we have been unable to penetrate California or the states that are not planning to switch to the new voting software. However, I am told you will carry every state which has implemented the new program by a comfortable margin."

Romero seemed disinterested. He'd heard all this before, several times in fact. The Iranians had approached him months ago. How they had known he was considering a run at the presidency was beyond him. In the end, it didn't matter. The Iranians could help him get what he wanted, and even sooner than he'd imagined! The details had been spelled out again in London. Rye had traveled to Turkey because he had insisted on a face-to-face meeting with his benefactors. The Iranians had tried to dissuade him. "Too risky," they had said, but it was the only way he would go through with their offer. Now that Romero had met with the ambassador and Col. Amir, he would go home to Houston and begin to assemble the rest of the people he'd need to make his presidential bid a reality. His original plan had been to wait another four years when the political firestorm from the last election had grown cold. If Iran wanted him to run now, then he wanted to be able to look them in the eyes before getting the ball rolling. In truth, that proverbial ball had begun to roll a few years ago when the nation had seen a populist claim the White House. Romero knew if a man such as that could be elected then his own chances would be extraordinary. An independent with policies nuanced to appeal to both sides of the aisle would be considered balm for a nation fed up with so much division. Romero had people even now coming up with those very policies. He didn't care what they were, he could always change them later.

Of course, the far left would be unreachable. Romero had given up any plans to appeal to them, other than paying lip-service to subsidies for higher education. No, he'd first have to appeal to the moderates in both parties. After that, he'd have his friend, Benjamin Rye, rally the evangelical vote. However, nothing in politics was a sure thing, especially for someone from outside the beltway. That was precisely the reason why he was here. If Iran could indeed deliver on their promise, then he would be the next President of the United States!

"Colonel, do your people understand that my government has hired an army of anti-hacking experts after what the Russians did last go-round?"

Amir rolled his eyes. "The Russians are fools! They always leave too many clues behind. So do the North Koreans. China is better; but we have surpassed all of them." The colonel didn't appear to be gloating, just stating what he believed to be the facts. "We have been doing this for a long time, and no one has discovered us, at least not since the early years. Amir smiled. "Plus, your new voting system has been ours to manipulate from the beginning."

Romero raised an eyebrow. "I don't suppose you're going to tell me just how that came about?"

"Many lives and fortunes have been spent to ensure this," Amir said, sipping his tea. "Let us leave the details for another day."

"Still," Romero countered, "all that fuss over the Russians—it wasn't pretty."

"Trust me. We can run circles around those fools. You will win by a margin of four percent. High enough to be acceptable, but low enough to be within your pollsters' margins of error. No one will suspect a thing. Of course, there is still the matter of your Southern states to contend with. So far, other than Florida, none of those states have purchased the new software."

Romero smiled. "Yes, well, that is where I believe I can be of some assistance."

"Ambassador Lajani told me." The colonel looked unimpressed. "We have looked into your friend, Benjamin Rye. I must confess that we know very little about him, other than he is the son of a popular preacher, William Rye, that he had a troubled youth, is married but has frequent affairs with his staff members, and apparently their daughters as well, and that he spends money lavishly."

Romero laughed as he speared an overcooked onion. "Sounds to me like you know a lot!"

Amir tried to manage a polite smile. *What did this fool know about intelligence?* "We also found that your friend had a conversion experience of some kind two years ago. I think you Americans refer to it as being 'born afresh'."

"Born again." Romero corrected, as he shoveled a mouthful of fava beans. "Benji had to fake all that crap or else his brother would inherit daddy's position at the Rye Foundation. I seem to recall he played it up big, too! His past indiscretions were well known and too much of a liability. He had to show lots of remorse to convince the old man. His daddy bought it—hook, line and sinker!"

"But, you did not?" The colonel sipped his tea.

"Of course not! I've known Benji a long time. He's in it for money and power. His lump of a brother might have eventually taken over their father's mantle, so Benji simply took advantage of the old man—just as you are trying to do with me right now." The colonel did not respond.

"Benji and I have had long discussions over the past year about how to win the evangelical vote once I announce; which, by the way, I wasn't planning on doing for another four years. But now that your offer is on the table, or should I say *under* the table, Benji and I are prepared to move things up. Benji's going to maneuver himself away from the Republicans, which right now will be pretty easy to do, and throw all his support into a third-party candidate, namely *me.*"

"How certain are you of this?"

"Just as certain as you are of ensuring I win in all those states with that new voting software." Romero played with his fork. "Colonel, you, of all people, should know that fundamentalists are naive, no matter what their religion. They will vote for whomever they're told by their leadership. Just look at what happened in America last go-round." Romero shook his head. "No, I won't be making the same blunders that guy did once

I'm in the Oval Office. I will build enough bridges to stay beyond just half a term. Trust me, I won't give them any reasons to go after me the way they did him."

Colonel Amir scratched his head. "You want to be president in order to *build bridges*?"

"That's just an expression. It means to bring people together; but no, I want to be president for the same reason every other leader does... power." Amir raised an eyebrow. "Come on, Colonel," Romero said. "We *are* being honest with one another, aren't we?"

"Yes, of course."

"My company doesn't have the clout of the larger telecommunication companies in America. Regulations and restrictions are keeping us from expanding. I plan on fixing that." Romero leaned back in his seat and stared at the Iranian intelligence officer. "Your people want me to agree not to allow America to intervene when you invade Israel in a couple of years. That's a tall order—a very tall order." He shrugged. "Not that I can't do it. I'll just have to select people on my cabinet who will do what I say, not what some whiny, liberal Jew has to say. And by the time Benjamin Rye has all those simpletons eating out of his hand, even *they* will be more than willing to reject their traditional support of Israel.

"I mean, you've seen how the masses can be manipulated in your own country. It's sort of like taking candy from a baby, *if* you have the right man. And trust me, Benjamin Rye is the right man!"

Zack Matteson dropped the bag of jellybeans on the floorboard. He felt sick to his stomach. *It wouldn't be the first time a billionaire had finagled himself into the White House, or that good, honest, voters had the wool pulled over their eyes, but what he was hearing right now was worse than any of that. Romero intended to sell out a crucial American ally! If what Col. Amir was promising turned out to be true, then the Oval Office could well be within Romero's reach!*

Zack had heard it with his own ears. In return for their assistance, Iran wanted Romero's assurance not to get involved when they attacked Israel in a couple of years. Without America to intervene, a conventional war would end in Israel's certain defeat. Syria and Lebanon would ally themselves with Iran, as would several other Islamic countries. Even Russia would likely offer its support. The big unknown would be whether Israel would use its nuclear arsenal. Strategists in Iran had to be planning for that very possibility even now. *If the Iranians could get so deeply into American technology as to swing an election, their cyber efforts might also prevent Israel from firing its nuclear weapons as well!*

Unable to hear the conversation inside the diner, Erdem couldn't help but wonder why Zack kept swearing, but it was not his place to ask. Instead, he contented himself with finishing the dinner he had brought along.

Zack was cursing himself for not thinking to have ordered something to record with when he had asked for the listening device. *So much for Flenn's, "Hunches are for horseraces!"* Had Zack not followed his gut and shadowed Romero... An icy chill raced down his spine. *Outside of Iran's leaders and Daniel Romero, he was the only man alive who knew the danger the world might soon face!*

"Colonel," Zack heard Romero ask, "are all of these men in here yours?"

"The cooks, wait staff, and the owner are Turks. The rest of these men are with me. Why do you ask?"

"Just don't want to be overheard, that's all," came Romero's voice.

"Trust me. We have taken the necessary steps to ensure our privacy this evening."

Zack Matteson cursed himself yet again. *He had been lazy!* He had assumed this was simply a businessman trying to navigate around sanctions. Zack had not taken the usual precautions. *Damn, Damn, Damn!*

As soon as Romero and Col. Amir left, he would have Erdem drive him to a different hotel and then send him back to gather his belongings, along with the hidden camera outside Romero's room. It was no longer safe to stay anywhere near Daniel Romero.

Zack checked the rearview mirror. People were milling in and out of the marketplace. One man was walking a camel up the street. He was beating the poor animal with a stick and swearing loudly. It was difficult to hear anything now over the man's cursing. Zack pushed the earplugs in deeper. *Damn! Why didn't the man hurry up?* When the camel finally did pass Erdem's car, Romero and Col. Amir were saying farewell. Zack and Erdem watched as several men in dark suits exited the restaurant and drove away in separate limousines.

"Let's wait here for a few minutes and give them time to clear out," Zack said to Erdem, "then take me to the Sheraton."

"The Sheraton, Mr. Zack? You wish to changing hotels?"

"Yeah. The Sheraton." No explanation was offered.

"Whatever you say, Mr. Zack, but the Sheraton's not so nicely as… " A blinding light filled the street, followed by a loud explosion. The restaurant, where moments ago Daniel Romero had agreed to the unthinkable, had just become an inferno!

Bystanders dove to the ground, others flailed helplessly as flames engulfed them. Zack and Erdem jumped out of the car to help. Ahead, the camel and driver lay dead across the road. Zack ran toward the diner to assist survivors, but it only took a moment before he realized there would be none.

Zack grabbed Erdem by the arm and yelled over the noise, "We need to leave—now!"

It was only a matter of time before Amir's men learned he was here. The Middle East was not somewhere he needed to be right now. And, from what he had just overheard, nor would anyone else soon—unless he could find a way to stop Romero and Amir!

Daniel Romero screamed at Benjamin Rye. "Take her outside!"

"Why?"

"She knows who you are!"

"Everybody in Birmingham knows who he is," the girl said.

"Just do it!" Romero commanded. Rye refused to move.

The girl grabbed for her clothes, but Romero jerked her off the bed and pushed her toward the door.

"What are you doing?" Rye asked, as he followed close behind.

"Stop!" she said desperate to diffuse the situation. "I'm not going to tell anybody. What do I care if he's a preacher? I'm just in this for the money."

Romero was silent. He led her outside across the porch and onto the lawn by the driveway. The woods were silent with only a hint of an early summer breeze. Romero looked around before letting her go and heading back toward the house.

Rye took the girl by both shoulders to meet her frightened gaze. "Don't worry kid, nobody's going to hurt you."

They heard Romero coming down the porch steps. Rye looked up in horror and quickly released the girl who turned in time to see a log of firewood heading toward her face. The blow was so hard it sent her flying backwards into Rye, knocking them both down. Romero bent over and brought the log back down a second time, *but this time she managed to hold up her hand to deflect the blow. Rye heard her arm snap.*

No longer able to defend herself, Romero hit her a half dozen times before she grew still. Then he hit her a half dozen more.

Rye was horrified, thinking he might be next. He got up and inched his way toward his car where he kept a Glock .42.

Romero stood over the girl, breathing heavily, blood splattered across his torso. He tossed the log aside and wiped the sweat from his forehead as he gazed at the girl's mangled body.

"Danny, what the hell... Are you crazy!" The look on Romero's face seemed to say that he was. "You... you just killed that girl!"

Romero dropped the log. "No, Benji. You did!"

"What?"

Romero wiped his brow. "If you hadn't been so damned recognizable we could have let her off with a warning, like we do in Guatemala! The men in my family drill lots of little nothing girls like her all the time. They don't dare open their mouths. She should have known to keep hers shut!"

Rye was paralyzed. Earlier he hadn't been able to take his eyes off the girl's body; now he couldn't bear to look at it.

Romero turned. "Where's the garden hose?"

"What? Um, over there." Rye pointed to a barrel to the left of the wrap-around porch where his family used to sit and drink lemonade and eat sugar cookies in the

summer. Romero connected the hose to the faucet and washed the blood off his feet and legs. *I'm going inside to take a shower and get dressed. Go get a sheet and wrap her up. Be sure you don't track any blood inside, and toss that log in the river!"*

Rye watched his friend climb the steps back into the cabin, then looked down at the carnage at his feet. "My God," was all he could manage to say, and even that came out as nothing more than a whisper.

CHAPTER TWELVE

"What do you mean, *you may have killed a girl*?" Flenn searched Minerva Wilson's eyes. *There was no way this gentle soul could ever hurt anyone.*

"Just that." She looked down at the floor.

"Minnie," he said as calmly as he could, "look at me. What did you do?"

Tears ran down her face. "I kept quiet."

Flenn raised an eyebrow. "Minnie, what in God's name are you talking about?"

Minerva fidgeted with a small cross on her bracelet. "I should have done something... I just didn't know what."

She drew a deep breath, then explained. "A member of my congregation, a teenager, came to me several months ago and told me that her stepfather was molesting her, and that he had been for years."

It was Flenn's turn to take a breath. "What did you say to her?"

"It's not important what I *said*, it's what I *did*... or, worse, what I didn't do!"

Flenn turned his chair toward her. "Tell me."

Minerva took a deep breath. "At first, she'd been too young to understand, but in the past couple of years she said she was becoming suicidal." Minerva looked up. "She told me that she didn't know where else to turn, so she came to me."

"And now you're saying she's dead?"

"Yes... no... I don't know." Minerva looked away. "She's been missing for nine months. For all I know, her stepfather may have killed her."

"You went to the police, right?" Even as he said it, Flenn knew she had not.

"How could I?"

"Minnie, we have an obligation to protect our flock." He tried not to sound condescending.

She stared at him. "Don't you understand what I'm saying? The girl came to me in *private*. She told me every bit of that under the seal!"

His eyes grew wide. "She told you this during a confession?"

Minerva wiped her eyes. "Yes." Flenn was silent. He understood now why Minnie had been so upset, why this had been eating at her for months and why she hadn't gone to anyone. She looked as if she wanted to melt into the tile floor beneath their feet. "And now, I've broken that seal."

He took her hands in his and looked deeply into her brown eyes. "Minnie, this is important, had you actually started the rite?"

She nodded.

Flenn bit his bottom lip. *By divulging to him what had been said in a confession she had just breached one of a priest's most sacred obligations.*

"There's more, Flenn, a lot more, but I don't want to go there. I've already violated the sanctity of her confession." She looked up at him. "It is just that I didn't know what else to do. It's been absolutely killing me ever since she turned up missing. I don't know if she's run away, or if he has hurt her, or if someone else did... I... I don't know what's happened to her! When that girl's body turned up in Shades Creek, I freaked. I was so afraid it would be Shelly."

Minerva looked lost and alone. "Flenn, what do I do?"

Flenn took a moment to think. "Do you have any reason to believe—other than the fact that her stepfather abused her—that he might have actually gone so far as to have killed her?"

She shrugged her shoulders. "You mean, did he ever hit her as well? I don't think so."

"Did her stepfather know about your meetings with her?"

"That's a good question. I've wondered about that a lot." Minerva looked away for a moment, then back at Flenn. "It's possible. Shelly's mother saw her with me in my office a couple of times after church, but she never said anything to me about it." Tears began to roll down her cheeks. "Did I kill that girl, Flenn? Or, is she going through something awful right now because of me?" Minerva fell into his arms and sobbed.

He let her cry as his mind tried to wrap itself around what she was telling him. After a moment, he cupped his hand gently under her chin. "Minnie, look at me. *You* did not hurt that girl. She trusted you enough to tell you what was going on, and you helped her to the extent that you were able." Flenn sighed. "The Church puts a lot of chains around clergy. Granted, it's usually for the benefit of our parishioners, but this time it has bound you in a dark prison. You were just trying to do the right thing for this girl; don't beat yourself up anymore. Let me help you. You said her name is Shelby?"

"Shelly."

Suddenly it clicked. "Not Rochelle O'Reilly, the councilman's daughter?! The girl who went missing last May?"

Minnie nodded.

Everyone in Birmingham knew about the missing girl! The media had reported the story for weeks. Flenn looked away. He didn't want his friend to see the rage forming in his eyes. He knew Councilman Mac O'Reilly, and had never liked him—now, he utterly despised the man!

"Minnie, I need you to listen to me. You know I have a past." Flenn had never told Minerva about his being a spy, but most people knew that he had served in the military. What wasn't known was that he had left the Air Force to go under cover for the government for 12 years. "Give me some time to look into this." He wondered how he could help find this girl, mainly to relieve Minnie's suffering, but also to expose Mac O'Reilly for the imposter Flenn had always suspected him to be. Flenn disliked arrogance, and Mac O'Reilly's well-publicized bravado at both City Hall and each year at

Diocesan Convention had always made Flenn's blood boil. Now, it turned out the councilman was even worse than the pompous prick he had thought him to be. Flenn wanted to do all in his power to find a way to expose Mac O'Reilly; but first things first—the girl had to be found. Minerva would have no peace until that happened.

"Minnie. I can't say whether you did the right thing by telling me. However, I've learned over the years that while the Church's rules are there to lead us to God, on occasion, they can sometimes get in God's way. For now, this will be just between you and me. I'll do everything I can to help find Shelly. If she's a runaway, then she left clues somewhere. If something has happened to her... well, again, there will be clues." Flenn looked into her eyes and offered a comforting smile. "I'm good at finding clues. In the meantime, you've got to start taking care of yourself. She's going to need you when we find her."

Minerva nodded as she wiped her eyes. "Thank you," was all she could manage to say. Flenn hugged her tightly. He didn't know how just yet, but he was determined to find a way to help his friend—and at the same time, expose Mac O'Reilly for the monster that he was!

The two men dragged the girl's body into the light from the porch. Each held her by one of her legs. Romero looked up. "Wanna' make a wish?"

"You're sick!" Rye couldn't understand how his friend had become even more twisted than he'd been in their college days when they used to take advantage of unsuspecting high school girls or even when they hanged the coach's dog after Princeton lost that game to Yale.

Romero shrugged. "Might as well make a joke out of it," he said as they pulled her body onto the white bed sheet. There was blood everywhere. "Damn. I'm going to have to take another shower, why didn't you take care of this like I told you?"

Rye stammered, "I couldn't... I couldn't touch her."

"You didn't have a problem touching her earlier."

"Shut up!" Rye dropped her leg onto the sheet. "How come you aren't freaked out by this?"

Romero positioned her body where they could roll her up into the sheet. "Let's just say this isn't my first rodeo."

"You've done this before?" The wind began to stir the pine trees above them.

Romero fastened a piece of rope around the body, wrapping it several times around her legs which pulled the sheet loose at the top, exposing what was left of her face. In the yellow porch light, Rye saw that even if she had lived, the best of plastic surgeons couldn't have repaired that mess.

"After college, I went to Guatemala for a year. Some people threatened to expose my family's financial

dealings down there. My father showed me how to deal with them—the same way his father had showed him. It's just how we do business."

Rye watched as his friend made a sort of lasso and wedged a heavy rock into it. He then wrapped the rope around the girl's legs several more times. They picked up her body, took it down to the dock, and placed it inside a small rowboat. Except for the wind, the night was deathly quiet. The usual cacophony of frogs and crickets was eerily absent as Rye retrieved the oars from the shed. They rowed out into the stillness of the Cahaba River, where it was at its deepest. As they prepared to roll her body over the boat, both men froze.

The girl moved!

CHAPTER THIRTEEN

Guy Rainsford tossed a cigarette butt out the window, then raised it to keep out the driving rain. December in Alabama was always a patchwork of weather patterns. Two days ago, it had been threatening snow. Yesterday had been sunny and hot; today, cold and rainy. Guy had never learned how to dress in winter—a light jacket, heavy coat, rain gear? No matter what he walked out the door wearing in the morning, he would end up regretting it by midafternoon.

Guy sneezed. *Of course, it would be raining, today of all days!* He was going to be in and out of the car trying to track down someone—anyone—who might have known a teenaged girl whose body was even now being cut open by the medical examiner.

Why even bother with an autopsy? Guy wondered. *It was obvious the girl had been beaten to death.*

Stuck in traffic on Highway 31 near the Shades Valley YMCA, Guy blew his nose and reached into the folder for a copy of the composite drawing he'd had made from the pimp's description. *Who was this girl?*

He stared at the drawing, as if he would see something different this time, something he had missed before. She'd probably been pretty—long blonde hair, blue eyes, high cheekbones, and a dimple on the right cheek. He tossed the drawing on top of the folder. It could have been the face of so many girls... a cheerleader, algebra whiz, a band geek... this girl had been none of those.

What was it that made some kids scholars and others fiends, like the high-schooler he had hauled in last month for beating his girlfriend. Lack of parenting? Drugs? Poverty? What had caused Lindsay to choose a life of prostitution—or had it been chosen for her?

Traffic still wasn't moving. He wondered if the sketch-artist had made her face a bit too round. The girl he had seen in the morgue was tiny. *Why had the artist given her a hint of a smile? What had Lindsay possibly had to smile about?*

The light changed, but nothing moved. A horn honked behind him. Guy resisted giving the man the finger. He sat through two more lights before traffic finally began to creep forward. Thirty minutes later, he pulled into an open space next to the Lighthouse Shelter for men on Third Avenue. The rain was coming down even harder. *Of course, his umbrella would be in the trunk!*

He got soaked sprinting into the place, only staying long enough to speak with the director and to leave a copy of the composite sketch. *Doubtful Lindsay had wasted her time with men who couldn't pay, but maybe one of them knew something about her.* It was his experience that the homeless often knew more about what was going on in the city than did the police.

The rain continued to pour as he made his way to the

women's shelter. Guy cursed his luck when he couldn't find a parking space in front of New Beginnings and had to walk three blocks to the shelter. At least this time he had retrieved his umbrella from the trunk. He sneezed several times as he hurried down Ninth Street. A gust of wind came out of nowhere and turned the flimsy umbrella inside out. He assumed he looked like an idiot fumbling with the cheap thing. He left the piece of junk underneath the awning at the entranceway to New Beginnings.

Security at the shelter was tight. Guy had to flash his badge more than once before being ushered into the director's office. The guard who escorted him inside was huge and looked as if he could have once played for Auburn or Alabama. Guy was instantly struck by the contrast between the men's shelter and New Beginnings with its chandeliers, wallpaper and guards. He noticed everyone here wore an identification badge; even the construction workers who brushed by him wore badges. Above him, Guy heard a mechanical saw and wondered what they were working on upstairs.

The guard introduced him to the director, then waited just outside the door. *Who posts security to watch over a cop?* Guy wondered, slipping off his overcoat.

"What can I do for you, Detective?" Ashleigh Nieves pointed to one of two bright purple chairs sitting across from her small maple desk. Guy noted the difference between this office and the one at the men's shelter. The men's director had only an old 1950's-style metal desk with a few folding chairs. The entire men's facility was little more than an old gymnasium with cots lined up against the wall. By comparison, New Beginnings seemed like an upscale hotel.

"We weren't expecting a visit from the police today," Ashleigh said, obviously irritated by the interruption. Guy couldn't help notice how attractive she was.

"I'm looking for information about a girl," he said, "She was around fifteen or sixteen years old." He pulled out a handkerchief and blew his nose. "She could have been using the name Lindsay. Small, not quite five feet, with blonde hair. Pretty." He handed her the drawing, which the director studied at length.

Finally, Ashleigh Nieves shook her head. "I'm sorry, Detective. We don't have anyone here who looks like this."

"I'm afraid this girl is deceased. I'm trying to find someone who might have known her. So far, I haven't had much luck."

The director took another long look at the drawing. "I suppose she could have come through here at some point, but not in the last year."

"What makes you so sure?"

"I came to work here in January, and I've made it a point to get to know every woman and child that has come through our doors," she said. "Our mission is to get them off the streets and try to instill hope for a better future. We aren't just a night shelter anymore." She handed the drawing back to him. "I'm sorry detective, but this girl hasn't been a resident during my tenure."

She stood up to indicate the meeting was over.

Guy didn't move. "You're sure?"

"Absolutely."

"Let me ask you something. If I were a homeless girl and needed a place to stay, where would I go if I didn't come here?"

The director leaned against her desk and thought for a moment. "That's a good question, Detective. Now, let me ask you one."

"Shoot."

"Any chance she was working the streets?"

Guy raised an eyebrow. "How'd you know?"

"Number one, you wouldn't be here unless she was connected with a crime or was a prostitute. You'd be talking with the schools instead."

Was that anger that flashed in the director's eyes?

"When that councilman's daughter went missing last spring, the police didn't come here to ask me about her. You guys never do, not for a rich girl." Guy shifted uncomfortably in his seat. "Number two, you have the look of someone who would rather be doing something else. Hookers are the bottom-of-the barrel on the street. I suspect you'd like to be investigating something more glamorous."

She had no idea!

"So," he said, trying to remain civil, "*is* there another place?"

"There aren't any other women's shelters in town, if that's what you mean... but I might be able to help you. We have a list of the names of some of the pimps who prey on these kids."

"I'd like to see that list, but I already know who her pimp was—a scumbag named Ramirez."

"Valentino Ramirez?"

Guy didn't bother to hide his surprise. "You've heard of him?"

Ashleigh Nieves sat back down; the look of disgust on her face made it obvious she had. "Oh, yeah, I've heard of him. Thinks he's one of the good guys because he doesn't beat his girls or have sex with them. Tries to pass himself off as legitimate, providing a service to society, or some sort of crap like that."

"That's the scuzzball all right. Know anything else about him?"

"I know he specializes in teenagers. Most of them are eighteen or nineteen, but not all. Recruits them off the internet, then sells them to people with lots of money." She thought for a moment. "Detective, I may be able to help you, but I'll have to check on something first. Can you come back tonight? Say about seven-thirty?"

Crap. Guy had been hoping to turn in early. "I hadn't planned on working tonight; can't you help me now?"

"I have to check with someone first. It's a girl. Worked for Ramirez awhile back." She stood up and walked across to the door. "But that's all I can say until I talk with her first. I'm sure you understand."

"Look, Ms. Nieves, I don't mean to sound impatient, but if you have any information… "

"Detective… *Rainsford,* is it? We work hard to build trust with these women. Some of them have been through things that would make your hair stand on end.

I'm sure you understand that I'll have to approach this girl first, otherwise she's not going to talk to you. She's just turned eighteen and started her first real job over at the Brookwood Mall. She gets off at six. I'll sit down with her at dinner and see if she'll agree to meet with you. I'll do my best, but I can't guarantee anything."

She opened the door. "Come back at 7:30. Maybe she can help you. Now, if you'll excuse me, I have a group session in five minutes." With that, the interview was over. Guy grabbed his coat as the guard escorted him to the door. Outside, the rain had subsided. He walked right past his useless umbrella. He'd get another one later; one that worked

Damn! He had forgotten to ask for that list of pimps she'd mentioned. He'd have to ask for it tonight, though he probably knew who most of them were.

Guy pulled his coat around him and hurried up the street. Half way to his car, it began to pour.

CHAPTER FOURTEEN

Zack Matteson picked at what passed for lunch on the flight to Heathrow. He still had not figured out what his next move should be. *He had no proof of—well, anything. If he went to his superiors, they would simply tell him to gather more evidence. Or, more likely, with the political mess right now in Washington, it was conceivable that his report could get lost in a shuffle of bureaucratic irresponsibility.*

Zack had spent the last two days going over everything in his head. He'd been careful when using the public wi-fi at the Sheraton, but he'd felt safe enough to do a simple internet search on Benjamin Rye. Undoubtedly, he would discover even more about the man once he had access to the CIA's server; although he'd already managed to find out plenty.

There were two Rye brothers: Benjamin, the eldest, and William Junior. There was very little on the web about the younger son, but plenty about Benjamin. Rye had struggled in high school, yet somehow managed to find himself at Princeton, where he spent six years before graduating. *Not all that unusual these days*, Zack thought, *but back then most students were in and out of college within four years.* After finding the school's yearbook online, Zack was able to dig through Rye's fraternity records without much trouble and found that Rye had shared a room with several students before ending up with Daniel Romero. The two had spent their junior year in Laughlin Hall, before moving into an apartment together. During that time, Rye's grades had been below standard and he had been placed on academic probation, but somehow, he'd still managed to graduate.

Post college, Rye had gone to work for a public relations firm but had been fired within a year. After that, he'd tried his hand as a stock broker for a while. He was in and out of several shady trading firms until a couple of years ago when he began working at the Rye Foundation.

Zack had watched a YouTube video of Benjamin Rye's very public spiritual experience two years ago while attending one of his father's New York City crusades. Rye had come up front that night with a crowd of converts during the altar call. He had been recognized by one of the assisting pastors and brought onto the stage to meet his father. There were huge tears in the old man's eyes. Willy Rye had stopped the baritone soloist who was singing, "The Old Rugged Cross," and signaled for the audience's attention.

"Ladies and gentlemen," the old preacher said with a shaky voice. "I have been praying for this day for many, many years!" As grainy as the video was, Zack had seen the pride pouring from Willy Rye's face. The man was absolutely beaming. "My son has come to Jesus!" A thunderous roar of applause echoed through the stadium as the two men embraced on stage.

Zack recalled what Romero had told the Iranian intelligence officer about Benjamin Rye. *Had this simply been a ruse to get his old man to turn the Rye Foundation over to him?* Zack pushed his food aside and replayed the video, which he had loaded onto his phone pre-flight. If Rye hadn't been sincere, he certainly had played the part well. Tears and hugs and smiles filled the stage, but absolutely no one seemed happier than Willy Rye. Zack had seen lottery winners seem maudlin in comparison.

Zack didn't pretend to understand religious experiences, any more than he'd understood what had happened to Scott Flenn in Edinburgh years ago, before Flenn had left the CIA. That experience in Scotland had cost Zack the one man he knew who'd always have his back. It was then that it hit him… *Flenn's right there in Birmingham near the Rye Foundation. Flenn always had a knack for seeing what others missed. Maybe he could be helpful with some of this mess.*

Flenn and Zack had studied together at Langley and had been paired together for nearly 12 years. *If anybody could help him right now it was Scott Flenn—or rather Father Flenn!*

Only one problem: Flenn hated it when Zack came calling for advice these days. When Zack did show up, Flenn always insisted on secrecy, not wanting to risk anyone finding out about his past. To placate him, they'd developed a peculiar telephone code and had found a place to meet north of Birmingham. Zack had often complained that it was too James Bondish, but Flenn had insisted.

Zack ordered a bourbon from the flight attendant. He knew now just what he would do; he'd spend a couple of days in London, then go to Alabama and run all of this by his former partner. He finally felt himself begin to relax. He didn't know if it was from the alcohol or the idea of soon being reunited with Scott Flenn.

****

"What are you telling me? You lost him?" Intelligence Director Sadar Abbas was furious.

"No, Sadar, that is not what I said." Ambassador Lajani had only been semi-apologetic during the phone call. Unlike most in his government, Lajani was not intimidated by the head of Iranian intelligence. "Matteson is on a flight at this moment into London. Our woman at the airport in Istanbul picked him out of the crowd this morning. We just don't know where he was while he was in Turkey; at least, we're not for certain. As you know, our resources are very limited, and our funds are not... "

Abbas cut him off. "I don't want to hear excuses! I want to know where Matteson was while he was in Turkey!"

"I understand that, Sadar. And we are doing our best. One thing I am sure of is that Matteson was not following Mr. Romero! My men watched Romero like an owl watches a mouse. They took all necessary precautions while Amir and I met separately with Romero."

"All necessary precautions?" Abbas scoffed. "I seriously doubt that. Get your people in line, Mr. Ambassador! Next time you call me, I want to know every bathroom where Matteson took a… " he caught himself, knowing the Turkish secret service might have found a way to listen in on the embassy. He'd already said more than he should. "I assume you understand me, Ambassador!" He slammed the phone down before Lajani could respond.

All necessary precautions, indeed!

After a moment to collect himself, Abbas buzzed down the hall for Col. Amir and relayed the details of what Lajani told him. "I want you to keep a close eye on Matteson from this point on. Put your best man in London on it. I want Matteson followed until I say otherwise. I want to know every move that man makes from now on! Our plans depend on it. If Matteson breaks wind, I want to know."

"Yes, Excellency. It will be done." Amir turned and retreated to his office to discover which of his men in London was currently unassigned. There was only one, a junior agent by the name of Farhad Ahmad. Amir was not pleased. Since there was no time to find anyone else, Ahmad would just have to do. Farhad Ahmad was not a seasoned spy, although his record said that he had been an excellent army officer and commando. He also spoke perfect English, which would be a must whether Matteson remained in England or went home to the United States.

Farhad Ahmad was contacted and instructed to

follow Matteson and to report directly to Amir every 24 hours. Amir was explicit: Zack Matteson was neither to be approached nor engaged in any way without his direct order. Ahmad was to simply shadow Matteson at a distance. Above all else, he was to remain unnoticed. Colonel Amir shook his head. He knew Sadar Abbas had inherited the plan to infiltrate the American electoral process from his predecessor. The colonel had followed through with its implementation, even though Abbas had expressed doubts early on. Colonel Amir had been present when his boss had pointed out to the council that if the Americans got the slightest inkling of what was in the works, everything would fall apart, bringing about more sanctions that the country could ill afford. As usual, they had refused to listen. Not for the first time, Col. Amir wondered if other governments were also in the habit of ignoring their intelligence chiefs.

Silently, Col. Amir prayed that Matteson would stay in London and not fly on to Texas, the home of Daniel Romero. If that were the case, it could be an indication that the CIA knew about Iran's plans for the industrialist and the scheme would be dead on arrival—just as he and Abbas would also be. Amir took little comfort in the knowledge that his boss would fare no better. After all, it wouldn't be the first time the head of Iranian intelligence had been eliminated. Although he could never say it publicly, Col. Amir disagreed with Abbas regarding Matteson. *Were he in charge, Zack Matteson would be dead the moment he stepped onto the tarmac at Heathrow!*

****

The flight from London to Atlanta was uneventful. Zack had eaten a few jellybeans and slept most of the way. As Flenn used to tell him, "A tired agent is an agent who makes mistakes." Of course, Flenn said that even though he had never been able to sleep on an airplane himself. Zack could sleep anywhere... and with just about anyone.

Once through customs, Zack rented a nondescript sedan using one of his several aliases. He was anxious to get to Alabama and set up a meeting with Flenn, so much so that he almost backed over a man who had dropped his wallet. The man gave Zack a dirty look, then took his time bending over to pick it up. Zack never saw him place the homing device under his bumper.

Zack drove west on I-85 toward Montgomery—a city that ironically had been both the capital of the Confederacy and the home of Dr. Martin Luther King. He arrived two hours later in Cullman, just before midnight. He paid the sleepy woman at the front desk of the Holiday Inn with cash and went straight to his room. He couldn't help but be aware of the contrast between this room and the one at the luxurious Mayfair where he had stayed the last two nights.

At Flenn's insistence, Zack had agreed never to be seen together in Birmingham, but to meet instead in Cullman, a small town north of the city. Flenn had said he didn't want his old life to interfere with the new— and, of course, Zack was the biggest part of that old life.

Zack was exhausted, not so much from travel as from trying to figure out how to stop Romero and Rye. He'd managed to get back to the United States unscathed, grateful that Col. Amir had known nothing of his time in Turkey. Every seasoned agent in the Middle East knew Col. Amir, if not personally then certainly from his ruthless reputation. Zack and Flenn had run into Amir once before, and Zack knew firsthand just how dangerous the man could be. *Eventually, all of this would have to be reported to Langley, but not until he had more to go on, and not until he had run it all past Flenn.*

Despite all that was on his mind, Zack was asleep as soon as his head hit the pillow. He was totally unaware that, even now, Col. Amir's spy, Farhad Ahmad, was less than the length of a football field away.

A gust of wind rocked the rowboat as the two men watched the linen-wrapped body sink into the dark, murky water of the Cahaba River.

It was Daniel Romero who broke the silence. "So, do you want to say a few words?"

"Shut up, Danny!" Even by moonlight, Romero could see that his friend was as pale as the sheet that was sinking into the mud some 20 or 30 feet below them.

"What? Don't you want to offer a prayer or something?" Romero's mocking smile was even more ghoulish by moonlight.

"Not funny!" Benjamin Rye picked up an oar and gestured for Romero to do the same. "You know I don't believe any of that crap!"

Neither man said another word as they rowed back to the shore, washed the blood into the ground with the garden hose, and remade the bed with fresh linens—even though no one would be using the cabin anytime soon. Rye refused to look at Romero as he headed off to shower.

As they were making their way toward their separate cars, Romero caught Rye by the shoulder. "Look, Benji, you need to forget what happened tonight. It was unfortunate; but we can't let anything stand in our way. You'll forget about this in a day or two."

"Forget about it?! My God, man! How can you say that?"

"Trust me. It's no big deal."

Benjamin Rye looked away. "Maybe not to you, but..."

Romero glared at him. "I'm telling you that you need to let it go. It's over. There's too much at stake here! You and I have come too far to lose sight of what is really important. Come on, Benji, we have a real shot at this! I'm meeting with the Iranians again soon. They're going to help make our dream a reality!"

Rye nearly became unglued. "Our dream? It's your dream, Danny!"

Romero feigned looking hurt. "Hey, don't talk like that. You've been a part of this from the beginning."

"Damn it, Danny! You said it wouldn't be for another four years yet. I'm not ready!"

"You gotta' get ready, Benji. I'm telling you, the Iranians say that they can make this happen."

"My God, man, does nothing get to you?" Rye yelled. "That girl was still alive!" Rye fished in his pocket for the keys to his Mercedes. "Just get away from me."

Romero pushed himself between Romero and the car. "Benji, I get it, you're upset; but listen to me, that girl doesn't matter. She was just a whore. Come on, man, it's over. You gotta' let it go. I need you! Ride shotgun for me, just like in the old days." Rye gestured toward the river. "You can't let this little thing steal your focus. Don't forget, there's something big in this for you too!" The cabinet position had been the carrot on the stick all along, but Romero could see that his friend was teetering on the edge, so he pulled out an even bigger carrot. "You know, Benji, after my first term I'd be able to make you my vice."

Rye stared into Romero's dark eyes. "Vice President?"

Romero nodded. Rye slowly dragged his hand across his mouth. "You're offering me the number two spot?"

"Second term, Benji, second term. It would raise too many eyebrows at first, what with you out there getting the Bible thumpers' vote and all. But after that... just think! You, my friend, would be in line for the next eight years after me... with our Iranian friends' help, of course."

Rye thought about that as a gust of wind blew leaves across the drive toward the riverbank. He no longer felt sick at his stomach.

Maybe Danny was right; the girl was unimportant. Probably a drug addict who'd be dead in a year or two anyway, he told himself. What did her life matter in comparison with this opportunity? The preacher took a deep breath. If there was a God, then he couldn't possibly be interested in people like that tramp. Danny was right. In a day or two this would be nothing more than a bad memory.

CHAPTER FIFTEEN

"There are more than 40 private and public high schools in Jefferson and Shelby counties, Detective. Are you telling me that you're going to go to every single one of them?" The pencil-thin assistant principal gave a cursory glance at the drawing he'd just been handed. "I mean, really, this girl could be anyone. I've got a hundred just like her, maybe two."

"Any of them go missing since last May?" Guy sneezed. His cold had grown worse throughout the day, and he'd already been to three high schools this morning. Now at Riverton, he'd waited almost an hour for the principal to see him, only to be told that she had suddenly gone into labor. He was barely keeping from losing his temper when this arrogant, pale scarecrow, wearing a short-sleeve shirt with a too-short black tie, introduced himself. Guy didn't catch the man's name; it sounded something like Milton Berle.

Milton Berle escorted Guy into a small, untidy side office. The man was clearly annoyed by the interruption. "Detective, students 'go missing' all the time. Parents move away, kids drop out without explanation—and immigrant families, don't even get me started on them!

We can't possibly keep up with everyone." He tried handing the drawing back to Guy.

"You mind keeping that, maybe showing it around to teachers and staff?"

The assistant principal shrugged and tossed the drawing on a file cabinet next to his desk, where Guy figured it would remain until the janitor threw it out. "You've got a big job ahead of you, Detective. I hope you aren't doing this alone." Guy had wanted help, but Toone the Loon hadn't considered this case worth the effort. There were other missing people—some of whom came from big money, like that O'Reilly girl. All the focus had been on finding *her* these past few months, not on some Jane Doe hooker.

"Actually, I was hoping to get *your* help," Guy said, resisting an urge to reach over and punch the man's pointy nose. "After all, you work with kids every day."

"Don't remind me." Guy watched as Milton Berle took off his glasses and wiped them on his shirt.

Guy sighed. He'd endured enough for one day! "Let me show you something." Guy reached into the file and pulled out the photographs of the girl's body taken from the river. He handed them over, face down, and waited for the man's reaction as he turned the first one over.

"Oh, my God!"

It was safe to assume the assistant principal had never seen the naked body of a kid who had been beaten to death. Guy certainly wished *he* never had.

"Is this the same girl?" Milton pointed to the drawing on the file cabinet.

"Same girl. Now do you see why I'm trying to find out who she was?"

Berle turned the next photograph over. "Somebody actually did *this*... to a child?"

Maybe there was a human being inside that skinny shell after all. "Yes sir, and I'm trying to find out just who that somebody was. That's why I need your help."

A plump, gray-haired woman stuck her head in the room. "Mr. Pearle?" Milton didn't respond. He went to the filing cabinet; his eyes darting back and forth from the gruesome photographs to the drawing of what could have been someone's little princess. "Wilton?" The woman persisted. She was all the way in the room now. "There's a fight in Mrs. Holtzclaw's room... again!"

Wilton Pearle looked at the woman. "Oh, great." He stood and offered his hand. "I'm sorry, Detective. I'll ask around," he said, picking up the drawing and placing it this time on his desk. "I wouldn't get your hopes up, though. The girl in that sketch could be anybody."

Guy sighed. "Tell me something I don't already know."

CHAPTER SIXTEEN

Farhad Ahmad had arrived in Atlanta on the same flight out of London as Zack Matteson. The American spy had flown into Heathrow from Turkey two days ago. That was when Colonel Amir had personally called Ahmad in London to order him to follow Matteson. Ahmad had checked into the Mayfair Hotel where Matteson was staying. He'd followed him to the airport this morning and bought a ticket to Atlanta. "Thank Allah it is not Texas," the colonel had told Ahmad over the phone. *Whatever that meant.*

A car and driver had been waiting at the airport. Another man had been sent to the parking lot to tag Matteson's rental car. The agent had pretended to drop his wallet just as Matteson was backing out. Had Zack not just spent nine hours in the air, or had the man been middle-eastern, Zack would have suspected something; but, as he was an African American in blue jeans, the agent had been able to place the homing device under Zack's front bumper as he bent down to retrieve the wallet.

Ahmad and his driver followed Matteson for hours to a small town in Alabama, almost losing the signal twice in Birmingham. Despite a wrong turn where Interstates 59 and 65 intersect at the north end of the city—what the locals called "Malfunction Junction"—the driver managed to adjust his route before the locator was out of range. Unfortunately, the chip was one of the older models with limited abilities, but it had been all that was available when the call came to pick up Ahmad in Atlanta.

The Iranians arrived in Cullman just as Matteson was checking into a Holiday Inn. They pulled into the parking lot of a hotel directly across the street— the *Y'all Come Inn*. The man at the front desk wore a flannel shirt and sported a beard that rivaled those of the clerics back home. The bearded man looked the two olive-skinned men up and down suspiciously before telling them there were no vacancies. Ahmad glanced out the plate glass window. The parking lot was half-empty. His driver slipped the clerk two $100 bills, whereupon a room suddenly became available, although at twice the price flashing on the neon sign outside. The next morning, a woman came to pick up the driver and leave Ahmad with the car from the airport, along with forged identification, a credit card, a pistol and a map of the Southeastern United States. Ahmad had brought his own satellite phone to make his daily reports to Col. Amir.

****

Zack Matteson knew Cullman well, having met Flenn here a few times in the past. Each time, his former partner had been reluctant to assist him, but Zack had learned to wait Flenn out. After a day or so, and with some pestering, Flenn had always changed his mind—up to a point. Flenn was a true convert after Edinburgh, refusing to carry a weapon or do a lot of other things they had once done together. Still, Flenn had been Zack's closest friend once upon a time, and Zack needed a friend right now.

Unlike Flenn, the son of Willy Rye was a complete fraud. According to the info Zack had gleaned from the CIA's server, which he'd finally managed to log into over coffee in his room this morning, Benjamin Rye's conversion had either been short-lived or a total ruse from the beginning. *Most likely the latter,* Zack thought. Clandestine affairs, dope, off-shore gambling... those were how Benjamin Rye spent his free time.

Zack got dressed and drove across town to a local buffet where he had eaten before. He ordered an enormous breakfast of biscuits, bacon, scrambled eggs, pancakes, hash browns and grits. Judging from the size of many of the diners here this morning, Zack figured he didn't need to visit the deep South any more than he did.

Farhad Ahmad sat in his rental car just outside the restaurant. The smell of bacon and sausage repulsed him, but he'd been ordered not to lose sight of Matteson. Colonel Amir had ordered Ahmad to call every 24 hours. This might prove difficult, since phone reception in Cullman was spotty at best. *He was going to have to find higher ground to make calls, which would mean leaving Matteson briefly each day.*

Ahmad waited outside the restaurant for more than an hour, then followed Zack south on Highway 31 to a strip mall where Matteson entered a department store called Belk. Long ago, Ahmad had known an ugly girl in his neighborhood named Belka. He hadn't thought of her in years, not until now. The girl's parents had sold her to a butcher when she was only 12. The last Ahmad had heard she was mother to several children—*no doubt, all with their mother's face!*

When Matteson finally came out of the store, he was carrying a garment bag. Ahmad followed him back to his hotel, keeping several car lengths between them. Perhaps he could come back to this Belk at some point. Western clothes were all the rage back home—*Col. Amir wouldn't have to know.*

****

It never failed. The phone always rang minutes after Flenn's secretary, Iriana Racks, left for the day. Iriana only worked until noon, but Flenn found it uncanny how the phone would almost always start ringing the moment she walked out the door. It was often nothing more than a sales call from some distributor offering the latest Bible study guaranteed to embolden his members and increase the size of his flock. Flenn grunted. Even the church had to contend with snake-oil salespeople from time to time.

Father Flenn picked up the receiver. "Saint Ann's, may I help you?"

An automated voice came across the line. "Collect call from Thomas Cranmer. Will you accept the charges?"

Flenn froze.

Again, the voice said, "Collect call from Thomas Cranmer. Will you accept?" The message repeated itself twice more before he finally hung up. Flenn sat motionless for what seemed to be an eternity before he reached for his jacket and walked out the door, not bothering to turn out the lights.

CHAPTER SEVENTEEN

Sacred Heart Roman Catholic Church had occupied a generous portion of the downtown landscape in Cullman since 1877. Her twin spires could be seen for miles—infuriating many of the town's protestants.

The church's grandeur was due solely to the sacrifices of the town's 19th century German immigrants. They had come to Alabama to build railroads, hoping to escape economic struggles back home. They'd settled in Cullman, where for generations they raised tomatoes, tobacco, and children—many of whom grew up only to work themselves to an early grave in nearby coal mines. The massive church stood as a monument to their grit.

Flenn parked in front of Sacred Heart and looked in his rearview mirror as he straightened his priest's collar. He wanted to make a statement to Zack Matteson. And that statement was, "I have changed."

That change had still been in process when Flenn and Zack had devised their telephone code years ago. Before the residue of his time with the CIA had worn off, he and Zack had agreed to remain in touch. Later, after Flenn was ordained, he had insisted that they not meet in public, and never close to home. As a result, they had developed the *Thomas Cranmer* code—to be used only in

an emergency. It had been Flenn who had suggested
using the name of the 17th-century Archbishop of
Canterbury under King Henry VIII. Cranmer had served
his country well in difficult times, and Flenn wanted to
believe that he had done the same, once upon a time.

Father Flenn climbed the steps of the church, crossing
himself with the water in the font at the door. He was
careful to use the Roman four-point cross instead of the
five-point Anglican one. Flenn didn't need secrecy, but
he wouldn't risk his friend's safety. It was not
uncommon for Zack to have a tail, from an unfriendly
agency or even from the CIA itself, which never trusted
anyone.

The late afternoon sun reflected through the Von
Gerichter windows against the brown-and-gray stone
walls. No one was inside. *At least no one Flenn could see.*
He walked halfway down the aisle where he entered a
pew on the left side of the nave. He crossed himself again
and closed his eyes to pray as he waited.

Flenn felt him before he heard him.

"Long time, no see!" said Zack.

Flenn didn't respond, nor did he open his eyes.

"Is that how you greet an old friend?" Zack asked.
"What are you doing?"

Flenn took a deep breath and exhaled. "I'm praying."

Zack Matteson stood beside him. "What are you
praying for?"

"For you to go away."

"Very funny."

The priest opened his eyes. "Not to me." Both men

kept their voices down. "What is it this time?" Flenn wasn't happy to be here, even if Zack Matteson had once been his best friend.

"Oh, you know, saving the world, that sort of thing," said Zack. "Aren't you going to ask me about Donna and the kids first, like you usually do?"

Flenn shook his head. "You divorced Donna two years ago, and you haven't seen your kids in over nine months."

"Ouch! I thought we were friends."

"We used to be, Zack. I haven't heard from you in years." Flenn got off his knees and sat down in the pew, reasonably comfortable that no one was watching or listening. *Zack would have made certain of that.*

"Hey, that was your choice, remember? Besides, I've been kinda' busy lately."

Flenn heaved a heavy sigh. "I'll ask again, Zack, what do you want?"

"Come on, you know it's important or I wouldn't have used your special code on the Batphone." Zack sat; kneeling was not something he was accustomed to, unless, of course, there was a gun pointed at his head.

"I have to admit I still don't know why you insist on continuing to use Thomas Cranmer as a code phrase. Didn't he end up trying to save his own skin when Bloody Mary threatened to burn him at the stake?"

"Anyone might have done the same after hearing the screams of other bishops burning to death just outside his cell." Flenn looked at Zack. "Well, almost anyone. I suppose *you* would have held out to the bitter end."

"Damn straight."

Flenn shook his head. "Yep, knowing you, you'd probably have lit the match yourself." Flenn sighed. "Okay, Zack, what is it this time?"

Zack evaded the question. "So, when did you talk to Donna? Never mind; doesn't matter. I know I need to call the girls; I just have a hard time doing it. If you'd ever been divorced then you'd understand. Course, you'd have to have been married first."

Flenn shot him a warning glance. "Zack… "

"Sorry. I didn't mean to open an old wound." Flenn had lost the love of his life 12 years ago in Edinburgh, something that Zack still felt a tinge of guilt about.

"Okay, I'll admit it," Zack said, "The divorce was my fault. Well, mostly my fault. I mean I was away for months at a time... I really can't blame Donna."

"Stop." Flenn knew where Zack was going.

"I don't think she loved him, you know, just needed him."

"I said, stop!"

Zack leaned back in the pew. "It hadn't been going on all that long, but I lost my head. Of all people, you'd have thought I would've known that my wife was having an affair. I mean, for Christ's sake, nothing gets past me. There was a time… remember that Russian ambassador? I knew most of his business before he did!"

He didn't want to, but Flenn asked anyway, "So, how come you let the Syrian kill him?" Zack Matteson was silent. "That one just slip by you?"

Zack fished in his pocket and pulled out a jellybean,

dusting lint off it. He offered it to Flenn, who made a face. "Let's just say he had it coming. You do remember Aleppo, right?"

Flenn looked away. "No one will forget Aleppo, or what the Russians did there."

"Anyway, I never told the girls about their mother. That should count for something, right?" Flenn was silent. "When I confronted her, she cried and cried; and then she got angry. You know how Donna can be—especially when she's drinking. She let me have it that day with both barrels, about how I was never there, how I had missed countless school plays, colds, baseball games..."

"Baseball?"

"You *are* rusty, aren't you? A good spy would have known that my Michelle is a great little shortstop."

"Damn it, Zack, I'm not a spy anymore," Flenn countered. "You know," he said, shaking his head, "I really don't want to hear this. Your kids need you, and you need them. End of story, so just call them." Flenn frowned. "Now, tell me: Why am I here?"

Zack grinned. "Come on, you hear stuff like this all the time. Don't people tell priests their life stories?"

"I already know your life story," Flenn said. "Anyway, it's different with you and Donna. I can have a modicum of professional distance from members of my congregation, but you two are like family." He looked away. "At least you used to be."

Zack scratched the back of his head. "Yeah, I know you're right, but..."

"Just go see them." Flenn said. "It isn't too late. You'll have a lot of explaining to do, but those are your girls. They *need* their father."

Zack glanced toward the altar. "They need someone they can rely on, and you know that's not me."

"It was *you* that I relied on in Damascus. You saved my life."

"And you, mine, in Edinburgh."

The priest nodded. "Okay, so we're even." He looked around the church and couldn't help comparing its grandeur with the simplicity of his own little Gothic parish an hour away. "So," Flenn groused, "you used our emergency code just to get pastoral advice?"

"Of course not." Zack said. "Just making small talk."

"Children missing their father hardly constitutes small talk."

Zack winced.

"Sorry." Flenn knew he had struck a nerve. "No, on second thought, I'm not!"

Zack shrugged. "No need to be. You're right. Tell you what, if you help me with what I'm working on, then I'll make the call. Hopefully, Donna will still let me talk to them."

The priest's patience was wearing thin. "I can't be bought, Zack, you ought to know that. And just what the hell *are* you working on?"

"I told you. Saving the world."

Flenn shrugged. *How many times had he heard that before?*

"Listen. Right now, all I need is your willingness to

help. I'll go ahead and tell you part of the story, then I want you to go home and sleep on it. I know you're going to say no today if I tell you everything, just like you always do. Just know that this is bigger than almost anything we've ever done in the past."

Flenn raised an eyebrow. "You always say something like that."

"Well, this time I mean it."

"You always say something like that, too." *Helping Zack Matteson was like jumping on top of stones thrown into quicksand. It might look safe at first, but a couple of stones in and you realize you're in big trouble.*

Zack told Flenn about Daniel Romero and the meeting he overheard with Col. Amir, about Amir's willingness to help Romero win the presidency, and how they planned to do it.

"What do they want in exchange?" Flenn asked.

Zack shook his head. "Can't tell you."

"Can't?" Flenn asked, "Or, won't?"

Zack winked. "Won't. Not until you agree to help me."

Flenn thought for a moment, and then stood to leave. "Zack," he said, "take care of yourself."

"You're not going to at least think about it?"

"Nope, not this time."

Zack stood. "Suit yourself; but, I'll be here in Cullman for a couple of days. It's as good a place as any right now." He handed Flenn one of the hotel's business cards he'd taken from the lobby. Here's the number to my hotel. I'm in room 134."

Flenn turned and headed for the door, "I can't."

Zack called after him. "Can't? Or, won't?"

Flenn hesitated briefly at the huge church door, then called behind him: "Both."

****

Heading home, Flenn stopped at the Cullman Chew and Chat for chili and cornbread. Outside, it was already pitch black. The diner was filled with a dozen rickety tables and a mismatch of wooden and metal chairs acquired over the decades. Most of the tables were adorned with worn, blue-and-white-checked vinyl tablecloths, paper napkin dispensers, and red-and-yellow plastic catsup and mustard containers. The walls were paneled wood, which long ago had begun to fade to gray.

The only thing separating the handful of customers from the open kitchen was a laminated bar with red, vinyl-covered stools. The bar was for eating, not drinking, since Cullman had only recently gone "wet," voting to allow the sale of alcohol in the city. The owners of the older establishments didn't want to risk being criticized from the Sunday morning pulpits.

The waitress brought Flenn a second helping of chili. She appeared to be in her 60s, slender, with dark hair and withered skin. Her smile, even with only a few teeth remaining, was warm and friendly. "Father Flenn, we haven't seen you in a really long time! What brings you up here to Cullman?"

"Visiting an old friend, Irma," Flenn offered.

"Well, I'm glad you came to see us before you left. You just missed Father Brunt from over at Grace Episcopal. Him and his missus and their two young'uns eat here every week, you know."

"Wow, they sure are brave!"

"Oh, Father, you're such a tease. Careful, or Clyde will hear you!" Clyde was the owner of the Chew and Chat and had flipped burgers here since he'd bought the place 20 years ago.

Flenn was glad he'd missed running into Dominic Brunt; he didn't want to explain his presence in Cullman tonight, and he hated having to lie. He'd spent enough time doing that during his days in the CIA. Over the years, Zack had tried to lure him back into the old ways, and always with a good reason—but, not this time. *No, Zack Matteson would just have to find someone else!*

Flenn took his time eating, left a hefty tip for Irma, complimented Clyde on the chili, and walked outside. It was dark now, except for a streetlight on the other side of the road.

Meow.

He looked down at the sidewalk where an emaciated ginger cat was huddled against the diner's wall. Flenn, always a sucker for strays, went back inside.

"Still hungry, Father?"

"There's a cat outside, and… "

"Yeah, she's got kittens. I keep telling Clyde to feed her, but he doesn't want cats hanging around here."

"Damned nuisance!" Clyde snapped from across the

bar. "Oops. Sorry, Father." Flenn went back outside, down a narrow alley and around the back. Sure enough, there were three tiny, multi-colored balls of fluff hiding behind a trash can. Mama cat followed him. Flenn stroked her back and could feel every one of her ribs. He went back inside and asked Clyde for a hamburger patty.

"Father, I'm not feeding those damn... dang... cats," said Clyde.

"I'm taking them with me," Flenn said. "I'll raise them at the vicarage and when they're old enough I'll find homes for them."

Clyde's grin was nearly as big as the hamburgers he scooped up. "Well, in that case," he said, happily stuffing two patties into a white paper bag. "These are on the house!

CHAPTER EIGHTEEN

The weather in Guatemala City had not been at all what Benjamin Rye had expected back in August when he'd first visited. He had assumed it would have been hotter than hell; but the temperatures had only been in the low 70's back then. It promised not to be much different today as the pilot gave the customary weather report prior to landing.

Not a bad place to live; Rye thought, as he looked out the tiny window at the mountainous scenery spotted here and there with villages full of tiny shacks, *if it just weren't for all these damned poor people!*

Guatemala City wasn't much different from the cities in Central America his parents had dragged him to years ago. While his father had been off preaching to the lost souls of Tegucigalpa, Port-au-Prince, and San Salvador, his mother had taken the boys to neighboring villages where the Rye Foundation was bringing food and medicine to some of the poorest people in the Western Hemisphere. Back then, he and his brother had witnessed children their own age with emaciated bodies. His brother had been moved with pity, but seeing the malnourished and powerless people of the world had always given Benjamin Rye a feeling of superiority, even as a child. His parents constantly told him that they were no better than anyone else; *but he was, and right under his airplane window was the proof! Why in God's name his parents had wanted to help these losers was beyond comprehension.*

As he looked down on the city of more than two million, he knew that as the successor to Willy Rye, and the emerging leader of the Rye Foundation, he would be expected to call attention to the plight of the poor from time to time. He'd have to pretend to show compassion. He was already studying how to casually drop Bible verses about helping the poor and such into his monthly letters to the foundation's supporters.

Too much of that book is about welcoming the stranger, feeding the hungry, and clothing the naked, Rye thought as the plane taxied down the runway.

Speaking of naked... Rye smiled wickedly as he wondered what treat Danny would have lined up for him tomorrow night. As he disembarked with the other passengers in first class, he recognized the man waiting for him as the same one who had met him back in August. Ernesto Veracruz was the director of the Evangelical Association of Guatemala—Rye hadn't bothered to learn the Spanish pronunciation.

Rye had convinced the board of directors that he should be the one to negotiate with Veracruz's organization and establish a media hub for the distribution of Willy Rye crusade videos on Guatemala's national television. His dad had never been to Guatemala, but plenty of evangelicals here knew about

Willy Rye. "By opening the doors now," Benjamin Rye had told the directors, "maybe we could lead a crusade there one day." At least that had been his excuse for coming down here. He was really here to meet with Danny to discuss plans for Romero's upcoming presidential bid. A crusade, like the hundreds his dad had led, was the last thing on Benjamin Rye's mind. He was not about to become a clown for Jesus, or anyone else for that matter. No, he would rule his father's empire from a leather chair, sending out missives as necessary, granting interviews to *Fox News* and the *National Republic,* and sending out mass appeals for financial support for ministries his father had started. But *preach? Never!*

Romero had warned Rye against their being seen together in America after the incident with the girl, so they had coordinated their schedules to meet discreetly in Guatemala, where Romero's family owned numerous properties. Romero had offered to send a girl to his hotel tonight, but Rye hadn't wanted to risk any of Veracruz's people discovering her. He was scheduled to meet with Veracruz again in the morning, where he would later have to pretend to be interested in the museums and art galleries the man was insisting on showing him. He'd be free to meet with Romero tomorrow night. After they concluded their business, Danny would likely present him with several young girls from which to pick, just as he had last time.

The incident last May still bothered Rye—not so much the death of the girl, but whether they'd left any clues behind. "No stone goes unturned during a presidential campaign, and an inquisitive press could be disastrous for them both!" he had told Danny. He'd called Romero right after reading that some kids had found the girl's body last week.

"Don't worry about anything," Danny had insisted. "I'll have my man take care of it." Rye knew which man he meant; he had met the Guatemalan back in August. He was huge, built like a Sherman tank, but the thing Rye remembered most were his eyes—dark and empty. His mother would have called them "soul-less."

The Guatemalan spoke English, but even more important was that he was totally unknown to American law enforcement. According to Danny, the Guatemalan was versed in making things look like an accident. Rye was supposed to meet with the Guatemalan again tomorrow night to give instructions on exactly what needed to be done—and to whom. *Two girls were going to be on that list, along with their pimp and anyone else they might have told.* Rye shrugged off a shiver of guilt, but told himself that none of it mattered. *Just so long as it all gets done before Danny announces!*

Personally, Rye believed Danny was cutting it way too close. *With the Iranians' help, it might be feasible*, he thought, *but not without a lot of work.* Tomorrow night, he and Romero would lay out the game plan, then one last girl before having to play the choir boy in front of the public. *Well, except for the Mallory twins. No need to tell Danny and the Guatemalan everything!*

CHAPTER NINETEEN

Prostitution in Birmingham previously confined itself to certain areas of town, Fourth Avenue chief amongst them. But, like everything else, the face of sex trafficking had been taken over by the internet. No longer a street-corner business, it was now almost completely relegated to the world of cyberspace—computer savvy call-girls were available through cell phone apps, social media, and websites designed to find people willing to exchange sex for money. The pimps had wasted no time finding their way into the digital age, delivering girls to hotels and truck stops—just about anywhere. Detective Guy Rainsford knew firsthand just how rampant sex trafficking had become in Birmingham. Not only had he seen it up close, but his former partner, Teri McCaleb, had explained to him just how cunning the pimps had become.

Guy blew his nose as he drove slowly down Fourth Avenue. The stink of uncollected garbage wafted through the car as he peered down a couple of dark alleyways, confirming what he already knew; not a single working girl was on the street. Just a few drunks and a couple of junkies. Guy assumed it was the same pretty much everywhere these days; but here in

Alabama, the very buckle of the "Bible Belt," the hypocrisy of it all had long ago gotten under his skin. Guy considered preachers to be the best advertisement the sex industry ever had. Railing against the sins of the flesh on Sunday mornings seemed to entice rather than dissuade. It didn't help his cynicism any when he heard stories of how fellow officers ushered some of those same ministers out of hotels just before a sex-sting operation went down.

Those busts almost always happened in October. Girls would be arrested right before a city election, only to be bailed out and run straight back to their pimps the next day. City officials would then take credit for cleaning up the streets. Nothing was ever said about the clientele—sometimes some of the same city officials. After the November elections, everything would go back to the way it had been before.

Guy turned left onto 24th Street. *Nothing ever changed!* he thought. *Sure, a few organizations here and there tried to help; some charities had set up halfway-houses and such, but all-in-all it was just a tiny drop in a sea of misery.* He recalled how an Episcopal priest had taken blankets and hot chocolate to the working girls on Fourth Avenue a few years back. *How on Earth had that helped change anything?* he had wondered. Still, he remembered having been impressed that the pastor hadn't tried to convert any of the women, or even try and convince them to leave their lifestyle. Guy couldn't remember the priest's name; the ministry had disappeared, as had the girls, once prostitution fled to the realm of cyberspace.

He made his way down several blocks, and this time managed to find a parking space directly in front of New Beginnings. The rain earlier had cooled things off, but tomorrow the high was supposed to be back up in the upper 70's again! *Nothing like Birmingham weather in December,* Guy muttered to himself, as he walked up to the gate to get out of the night chill.

An armed night watchman met him. Guy flashed his badge. "Detective Rainsford. I'm supposed to meet with Ashleigh Nieves."

"She told me to expect you." The burly security guard was even bigger than the other guard from this morning. "I need to take a closer look at that badge, along with a photo ID," he said. *This one could drop a charging bull,* Guy thought as he looked at the guard. *Anyone would have second thoughts of trying to get in here at night once he saw this piece of granite!* The guard examined the badge along with the detective's driver's license. Guy didn't bother to point out there was a photo of him on the badge. Once the big man was satisfied, he opened the gate and waved him through. Unlike the man from this morning, this one stayed at his post.

A moment later, Guy was knocking on Ashleigh Nieves's office door. The director was sitting next to a freckled, red-haired girl who was wearing jeans and a yellow tee-shirt. "Roxy, this is the man I told you about, Detective Rainsford."

The cop stuck out his hand and flashed a practiced smile. "Just call me Guy." The girl responded with a silent stare.

"Detective Rainsford, Roxy doesn't really trust men all that much right now, including police officers," Ashleigh said. "She's asked me to stay here with the two of you."

Guy sat down in a purple chair next to the girl. "I understand," he said. He set his file folder—the same one he'd carried all day—on the floor beside his chair. "Roxanne. That's a pretty name." The girl turned her gaze down to the floor. *Damn! Why had he said that? She'd undoubtedly been told crap like that by a lot of men.*

Ashleigh saved him. "Detective, maybe you can tell us what it is that you need?"

Guy looked at the director, thankful for the redirection. "Yes… well, I'm trying to find out about another girl. A little younger than you. I don't know her last name, she called herself Lindsay. I'm not even sure if that's her real name."

"Most people don't use their real name." The girl spoke matter-of-factly but didn't look up.

"Okay… well, this girl was small, not quite five feet. Blonde hair, blue eyes. Sixteen, maybe younger."

Roxanne raised her eyes. "Was?"

"She was murdered."

The girl's pupils narrowed. *No doubt she had known men capable of such a thing.* "Who did it?"

"Don't know. Her pimp, maybe. Valentino Ramirez."

Roxanne shook her head. "No way. Valentino never hurt nobody."

"How do you know that?"

"Miss Ashleigh said she already told you I worked for him, about a year ago."

"Yeah, she told me that." Guy raised an eyebrow. "But, why do you say Valentino never hurt anybody?"

"Cause it's true. That fat jerk wouldn't want to damage the merchandise. Plus, he's too big a wimp to hurt anyone. He just wants the money."

"Does he make a lot?" A stupid question, but Guy needed to keep her talking.

"Yeah. Big time." The girl's eyes flared. "At least he did off of me." She looked over at Ashleigh. "Of course, so did I. He lets his girls keep half of what they make."

Guy leaned back in his chair. "I've heard that. How much might that be?"

Roxanne shrugged. "It varies. The younger they are, the more he charges."

Guy handed over the drawing of Lindsay. "How much for this one, you think?"

Roxanne studied the drawing like a pawnbroker looking over a used wedding ring. "Two, maybe three," she said.

"Three hundred?"

"Thousand. Valentino ain't cheap. His customers have money." She looked at the drawing again. "I've never seen this girl before, but she could easily bring in several grand a night."

Guy was deflated. He'd hoped Roxanne would have known the girl. "You sure you've never seen her?"

"Positive. She looks about the age I was when I started. Valentino won't run a girl under 14, and only then if she approaches him like I did."

Guy was incredulous. "How does a 14-year-old approach a pimp?"

"And *you're* a detective?" Roxanne shook her head. "The old days of hanging around bus stations trying to catch runaways are over. Pimps advertise on the web now. A savvy girl finds out she can make a load of money, so *she* finds *him*. Of course, it don't turn out so good for most of them, but Valentino's different; he protects his girls. He likes to pretend he's running some sort of an escort service for gentlemen."

Guy grimaced. "So, I've heard."

Roxanne returned her gaze to the floor. "My clients were lawyers, doctors, city councilmen—hell, even a preacher... but, if somebody tried to hurt me, well Valentino knows some guys. They'd have worked that fool over. Nobody ever hurts one of Valentino's girls." Her tone made it clear she wasn't defending the pimp, just stating a fact.

Ashleigh leaned toward Roxanne, eyes full of compassion. "Those men *did* hurt you, Roxy, even if they didn't beat you." The girl looked at her mentor; the connection was obvious. Guy realized for the first time that Ashleigh Nieves probably had to be mother, counselor, and confidant to the women living here, especially the younger ones like Roxanne. While he couldn't see any outward scars on this kid, he knew there had to be plenty of emotional ones.

Guy broke the silence. "How old were you when you went to work for Ramirez?"

"Fifteen. There were two of us. Denise was younger.

She told everybody she was older, but I could tell—it was the way she acted when we were together. She could be pretty immature at times. She still works for Valentino, last I heard. Probably doesn't make as much a night as we used to, though."

"How much was that?"

"I'd bring in between eight and ten thousand a night on the weekends. Half of that was mine to keep. Of course, I blew it all—drugs mostly."

"You only worked weekends?"

"Believe it or not, I went to school, sort of. But Denise, she worked all the time, lived with an uncle or something."

Guy wondered how a teenager could emotionally handle going to school during the week and then turn tricks on the weekend. "Did anybody know what you were doing? Friends? Someone in your family?"

Roxanne visibly tensed. This time Ashleigh spoke. "Like a lot of our women, Detective, Roxy had a rough childhood." She took the girl's hand. "I'm sure you can understand that she has difficulty talking about it. She and I spoke before you got here. She said it was okay for me to tell you some of it." Guy noticed Roxanne squeeze Ashleigh's hand. "Her mom was in the adult film industry. She's a heroin addict. As she got older, she found out she could make more money by using Roxanne. Roxy was in her first pornographic film when she was only eight years old."

Guy struggled hard not to react. Child porn cases were something he'd only worked twice in the past, and neither time by choice. *Murder shouldn't be the only capital offense!*

Guy knew that kids who had been abused almost always felt guilty for what had happened to them even though *they* were the real victims.

"Roxy," Guy said, softening his tone. "You're a brave and courageous young woman. I can't imagine what it must have taken for you to leave Valentino."

The girl looked up, holding back angry tears. "That wasn't the hard part. The hard part was getting away from my mother!"

Ashleigh interjected, "We've got a restraining order against Gina Lake. She's not allowed to see Roxy, or come within 100 yards of her."

It would be easy enough to go through the warrants and find out more about this Gina Lake, but, for now, he wanted to know about Ramirez's friends. Guy reached into the file at his feet. "Roxy, you said that Valentino knew some guys—tough guys. Any chance one of them could have done this?" He showed her a picture of Lindsay's body on the riverbank. Surprisingly, she didn't look away; didn't even flinch.

She stared at the picture for a moment before handing it back. "No way. Like I said, Valentino never hurt the merchandise. Look, I don't know about this girl, but the one in that other drawing would have made a lot of money." She rubbed her chin. "But, if she ever wanted to leave, Valentino would have let her go. He would have tried to use her later to recruit other girls for him. He always said some stupid thing about catching more flies with honey than vinegar. I didn't know what he was talking about."

"An old expression." Guy slipped the photograph back in the folder. "Could one of Valentino's friends have simply thought Lindsay too cute to resist and things just got out of hand?" Guy was reaching, but he didn't have much else to go on. "Did his thugs ever take a liking to you? Maybe come on to you?"

For the first time since he'd walked into the room Roxanne smiled, more of a smirk, really. "No. They were just like Valentino."

Guy looked puzzled.

She shook her head. "You sure you're a detective?'

Guy raised an eyebrow. "They were *just like* Valentino," she said again.

Guy scratched his head. "They are pimps?"

"No," she said. "They are gay."

CHAPTER TWENTY

A gay pimp, a dead teenaged hooker, and a damaged young woman trying to start a new life—where was all this leading?

Guy struggled to put it together as he drove the hour and a half to Montgomery. Toone the Loon had needed someone to deliver evidence for a drug case at the state capital, and, of course, had sent him. Guy hadn't argued; he needed the time to think.

When Lindsay's body was found, it was thought she might have been that rich kid, the daughter of the city councilman. He had been down in the morgue when Mac O'Reilly had come to identify the body. Apparently, the mother was too shaken up to view the girl's body, but O'Reilly had said it wasn't his kid. The coroner had said something about trying to run the girl's dental records, but anyone could see her mouth had been busted too badly for that. Since it hadn't been the O'Reilly kid, it ceased being a high-profile case—which meant it was up to him to try and figure it out.

As Guy went over what he had learned so far, he realized just how little he had to go on. *Runaways sometimes come to Birmingham, sure, but not very often. It wasn't like this was a popular spot like Panama City, New York, or even Nashville. In fact, most teens generally wanted to get out of the so-called "Magic City." Birmingham was only magical if your parents had money. Kids who felt trapped, either by poverty or family ties, simply had to settle for dreams of leaving.*

No, Guy reasoned, *a kid might run away to Nashville with hopes of being the next Carrie Underwood, Atlanta to get into hip-hop, or the lights of New Orleans—all cities with high child prostitution rates—but not Birmingham.*

Most of the kids on the streets, at least the ones Guy had known about, were from here, born in poverty, abused and abandoned. Something told him that Lindsay had come from downtown. The ritzier hotels were all within a 30-minute walk from some of the poorest neighborhoods in the city. No doubt she lived in one of those very same neighborhoods. Although, when the cops had gone through the projects back in June, they'd come up empty-handed. None of the residents claimed to have ever seen her.

He sneezed repeatedly as he drove past barren trees and brown fields devoid of any sign of life. *This was turning into a bad one!* He made a mental note to stop and get some cold medicine on his way home. The trip to Montgomery was always boring. Not much to see along the way—an aging Interstate, spotted here and there with road kill. Nobody ever bothered to repair the fences to keep the wildlife out. "All the talk about unemployment in the state," he groused aloud, "but how hard would it be to hire people to repair these fences!"

Guy was in Montgomery longer than he thought he'd be and it was getting late. He decided to stop for some barbecue and sweet tea on the way home. The restaurant was loud and smelled of pork and fried onions. He sat at a table with a red-checkered, vinyl tablecloth surrounded by countless other tables that looked just alike. His waitress was short and plump, with pink and purple highlights in her hair and flaming orange lipstick. On her green tee-shirt was a tag that said, "Darla." All the staff wore the same tee. The shirts bore the name of the restaurant along with the phrase, *Delicious Between Buns!* He tried to chase the words out of his head as he looked up at Darla and ordered a large barbecue pork sandwich, sweet potato fries and a large glass of sweet tea.

Guy glanced across at the next table where three large dour-looking men in polyester suits and cheap ties sat eating banana pudding. Each man had a leather-bound Bible sitting in front of him.

Preachers!

Guy had seen plenty in his day. His mother had been a regular church-goer all her life. She had forced Guy and his two sisters to attend church every Sunday, although without their father. Guy's dad had been divorced twice before meeting his mother, worked at the Good Times Liquor Shoppe down from their house, and was a member of the Elks lodge—none of which would have been tolerated at the Third Street Church of God in Alabaster. His mother made Guy go with her on Sundays until, at 13, he had refused. His father had supported his decision; surprisingly, his mom hadn't put up as big a fuss as Guy had expected. He hadn't been to a church service since, except for a few funerals and a couple of weddings. His dad had been gone some 15 years now, and his mother was in a nursing home in Vestavia, just outside Birmingham. Waiting for Darla to return with his food, he told himself he should pay his mother a visit on his way home this evening.

The preachers at the next table were talking passionately about something, but Guy couldn't hear what they were saying. Not that he wanted to; he had no interest in churches or preachers. He'd spent too many hours sitting next to his mother hearing about the evils of integration, homosexuals, Democrats, Catholics, and worst of all... beer.

After Guy finished his sandwich, he left Darla a generous tip and then nodded, out of courtesy more than respect, to the three preachers, who, in turn, nodded back. He walked outside and opened the door to his aging, blue Crown Victoria.

Preachers, he thought. *Biggest hypocrites of them all!*

What was it Roxanne had said? *"My clients were lawyers, doctors, city councilmen—hell even a preacher."*

He shook his head. "Yes sir, biggest hypocrites of them all," he said, this time out loud, as he turned the key in the ignition.

Well... maybe not all of them.

He reminded himself of the priest who'd brought blankets and hot chocolate to the hookers on Fourth Avenue. The pastor's name hadn't stuck in his head, but Guy remembered where the little church was. He thought he might drive by there tonight and see if anyone was around. *Maybe the congregation still has some sort of ministry with the girls downtown*, he thought. *If so perhaps someone would recognize Lindsay from the drawing. It wasn't much, but what else did he have to go on right now?*

He forgot all about going to see his mother.

****

Flenn drove home in drizzling rain thinking about what Zack had told him—that, and how he'd possibly find homes for a cat and three kittens! The windshield wipers on his old convertible needed replacing. Their high-pitched squeal was getting increasingly annoying, but not nearly as much as had Zack's sudden re-appearance out of nowhere.

It was always the same gut-wrenching dilemma whenever Zack came to call. On the one hand, Flenn felt obligated to help out his old friend. On the other, he was fully engaged in his new life, and except for Zack Matteson's occasional interruptions, he'd managed to put the past behind him.

Flenn's life as a spy had been grim. He'd seen things which few people knew existed in the world. He wasn't about to fall back into the darkness he'd left behind. *Still, if even half of what Zack had told him was true, then there was a great deal at stake.* He had said no, but as Zack had pointed out, he almost always said no, only to reconsider later. He glanced down at the passenger seat as he pulled into Saint Ann's parking lot. Mama Kitty had left her sleeping kittens in the back to come up and sit next to him. "What would *you* do?" he said to the cat, who simply twitched an ear.

Flenn sat in the church parking lot, the engine still

running. "Damn it, Zack!" he said aloud as the cat looked at him with feigned interest. He thought about what Zack had said, how he had discovered a plot between a business tycoon and the Iranian government, and how the Iranians may have already infiltrated a new voting software program slated to be used in next year's election. Of course, Zack had not explained what it was that he wanted from him. *Leaving me hanging again, huh, old boy?*

He shut off the engine and reached down to pet the cat before opening the car door. "I'll be back; just got to check a couple of things in the office before we can go home and discuss your new living arrangements. It's gonna' be temporary, so don't get your hopes up. And, young lady, there will be no clawing of my furniture, or confusing my houseplants with your litter box. Understood?"

The cat blinked.

Flenn was turning the key in the parish hall door when a large, blue Ford pulled into the lot. A stocky, balding man got out of the car and sneezed twice as he walked up to Flenn. He wore a wrinkled gray suit with a short red tie; a shabby, tan overcoat fell past his knees.

"Excuse me for asking, Father, but are you the priest who used to bring blankets and hot chocolate downtown a few years ago?"

The man pulled out a badge. "If so, I need to ask you a few questions."

CHAPTER TWENTY-ONE

Spanish was not a language frequently heard at *Chez Bon-Bon*, which is why Valentino Ramirez was surprised to hear someone using it to address him as he sipped his morning latte on the café's terrace. The pimp was enjoying the warm sunshine under a purple and green awning decorated with drawings of cupcakes and unicorns.

"Nice day," the stranger had said in perfect Spanish. "So much more pleasant than earlier this week. Mind if I join you?"

Ramirez smelled trouble. He crossed his legs under the table so he could reach the .22 strapped to his ankle if he needed it. "Please do, sir," he responded, also in Spanish. The stranger was built like a truck. "Your accent," he said, "Honduran?"

"Guatemalan."

"Never had the pleasure." Ramirez offered a practiced smile. "What may I do for you, sir?" *Spanish was so much politer than English,* the pimp thought as the stranger sat across from him.

"It's what I can do for you, sir. You are Valentino Ramirez, correct?" A young woman in a yellow, polka-dotted dress came out to take the Guatemalan's order. He smiled but waved her away.

Ramirez looked around once more to see if anyone else might be watching. "Why do you ask, sir?"

The man pulled an envelope out of his pocket and placed it on the small, white table. He lifted the flap revealing several one-hundred-dollar bills. "Because I may have a gift for you."

Ramirez stared at the envelope. The Guatemalan winked. "I just need a bit of information."

The pimp stiffened. "Sorry, sir, I don't know anything."

"I haven't yet told you what it is that I wish to know."

"Doesn't matter," said Ramirez, looking away. "I wouldn't know it."

The Guatemalan frowned. "I see." He pulled a thicker envelope from his pocket and set it on the table next to the other one. "Then I suppose you do not wish to receive the other nine thousand?"

Ramirez looked at the envelope, trying not to lick his lips. He reached for the second envelope, but the Guatemalan placed his massive hand on top of it.

"What information is it that you want, sir?"

"Nothing, really. Just an address."

The pimp looked up at the Guatemalan. "Whose address?"

"I wish to find a young lady who used to be in your employ. I believe her name is Roxanne. I do not know her last name."

Damn! Ramirez didn't give out information on his girls, even those who no longer worked for him. He stared at the two envelopes on the table. Ten-grand was a lot of money; he'd sell his sister for less. In fact, he had—twice.

"I don't know where Roxanne is these days. We've... well, you might say we've lost touch." Ramirez watched as the man shove both envelopes back into his blazer.

"That is a shame. I was hoping we could do business."

Ramirez leaned forward, "I may know a way to find her mother. She would know where Roxy is."

The Guatemalan pulled out the smaller envelope and handed it over. "Tell me the mother's address, and if I am able to find the girl I will bring you the rest."

Ramirez wasn't born yesterday. If the Guatemalan found what he wanted, he wouldn't be back. "Both envelopes if you don't mind, then I will be happy to help you."

Anger flashed briefly across the big man's face. "Forgive me, sir, but I do not know if the information you give me will be correct."

The Guatemalan stood, as if to leave. Ramirez gestured for the stranger to return to his seat. "I don't know the mother's address exactly, but if you give me another thousand I will tell you how to find her."

The Guatemalan reached into the larger envelope, pulled out several bills, and placed them in the first envelope, which he then slid across the table. "If your information is useful, I will bring you the rest."

Ramirez doubted he'd ever see the man again but told him what he wanted to know. "I've seen Gina Lake on that corner several times," he said. "She's easy to spot.

She's a toothpick with legs. She's has blackish-gray hair; carries herself like someone who used to be a looker. She has a taste for the hard stuff. Her dealer is a guy called Doc. He's almost always on that corner in the late afternoon. He's a mousey, white guy with a long, orange beard and bald head. He wears a silver ring through his left eyebrow. You can't miss him."

The Guatemalan smiled. "Thank you, sir. I am a man of my word. I will be back. I trust it will be a *happy* reunion." The big man waited for the not-so-veiled threat to hit home. The pimp looked away. *Good*, thought the Guatemalan. *He understands.*

"How will you find me?"

"Mr. Ramirez," the Guatemalan's eyes narrowed. "I can always find the people I am looking for… Always."

The pimp swallowed as he stuffed the envelope in his pocket. He remained in his seat so as not to lose a chance to reach for the pistol, just in case. He watched the Guatemalan disappear around the corner before releasing a long sigh. Valentino Ramirez pushed his latte away. *He wouldn't want to be Roxanne right now, not with that bulldozer looking for her.*

CHAPTER TWENTY-TWO

Gina Lake pleaded with the stranger on the street corner where Doc had always stood. "Look, I'm really hurting, I'll do anything you want, but I need that stuff... now!" The stranger had somehow recognized her; he even seemed to have been waiting for her. Odd, she thought, but right now she didn't care. All she needed was what he was selling, and she had precious little today to give in exchange.

The man was built like a mountain; six-feet tall, 250 pounds—all of it muscle. He wore a navy blazer and gray pants—quality stuff, Gina could tell. Doc always wore dirty jeans and a smelly tee, but Doc wasn't here today. This new guy with brown skin and a funny accent had told her that he would be her supplier from now on. She knew what that meant. Gina felt sorry for Doc, but that was how territorial disputes were usually settled. Frankly, she was amazed the little guy had lasted this long.

Gina did her best to look seductive. "Sometimes Doc would cut me some slack, if you know what I mean. Maybe, if you'll be good to me, I will be good to you? I can make it worth your while."

The stranger looked her up and down. "Maybe ten

years ago, baby, but not now." Gina recoiled from the big man's mocking grin. "Tell you what," he said, "I'm in a generous mood today." He showed her the tiny packet in his hand. "Just tell me where Roxanne is and this one is on me."

Gina stepped back. "Roxy? How do you know her?"

"Doesn't matter. You give me what I want and I'll give you what you want. Deal?"

She didn't hesitate before nodding. A free fix would buy her time to find a new dealer, someone she could strike a better arrangement with in the future. *Why should she care what the big man wanted Roxy for? Damn the ingrate for leaving her in the first place!* Roxanne had always brought in enough money to keep the heroin flowing, but ever since Roxy quit turning tricks, Gina had been forced to go back out on the street to buy enough smack to stay ahead of her aching need. As she stared at the dingy, brown packet, Gina figured she might as well tell the stranger what he wanted to know. *She didn't owe that little whore anything!*

"Last I heard she was working at one of the malls somewhere. I think the one up in Homewood."

The stranger pulled back his huge hand. "Not good enough."

Gina didn't take her eyes off the magic powder. Once inside her veins, the world would go away and she could feel *nothing*… and, *everything*.

"She's staying at that women's shelter downtown, New Beginnings."

"See," he said, smiling, "that wasn't so hard." He

handed over the envelope. "Now, just remember, next time be sure to have the money. I'm not running a charity here." He smiled, knowing there would be no next time, not with the extra ingredient he had laced into the heroin.

"New Beginnings," he repeated. "Gracias."

Gina retreated to the tenement she used to share with Roxanne. "Damn little slut!" she said out loud as her rage rose for the thousandth time since her meal ticket had abandoned her.

Clutching the packet tightly, she tried to push Roxanne out of her mind and turned her thoughts instead to Doc. She had no idea just how soon she would be joining him.

CHAPTER TWENTY-THREE

Guy was running late. He had arranged to meet with Father Flenn this morning at 8:30 but an early morning windstorm had knocked down several trees in his neighborhood, forcing him to take an alternative route.

The detective was looking forward to seeing the priest again, though for the life of him he didn't know why. Guy wasn't accustomed to conversing with members of the clergy; yet, he couldn't help feel that there was something different about Father Flenn. They had spoken for half an hour last night before the priest had said something about having to take care of some stray cats. They had agreed to meet again this morning.

Guy hadn't slept much last night, or the night before for that matter. He seldom let a case get under his skin, but this one was gnawing away at him like a rat on a rope. The medical examiner's report listed Lindsay's death as a drowning, but the M.E. had also told him the girl would have died anyway from the wounds she'd received. Splinters had been found embedded as deeply as her brain. Forensics had said the killer had used a club of some kind; that it had been maple, rounded on one side, possibly firewood.

Someone had beaten the hell out of that girl!

No matter how much Guy tried, he couldn't erase the thought of her lifeless body awaiting someone, anyone, to claim her.

****

Flenn looked at his watch as he went over the Sunday bulletin for the third time while waiting for the detective. If the cop didn't show up soon, he'd have to go ahead and leave; he was due across town for a meeting soon. Religious and civic leaders were gathering to discuss ways to preempt a wave of recent racial unrest that was sweeping through urban areas across the country.

Not everyone at Saint Ann's understood Flenn's preoccupation with social issues, but they knew their priest to be a stable and honorable man with a kind heart. He seldom, if ever, preached politics from the pulpit, as some of his fellow priests in the diocese were prone to do; instead, he talked about Christian responsibility to the outcast. "Jesus' imperative," Flenn had repeatedly told his congregation, "was always toward the welfare of others, and required that self-interest and worldly ambition never be sought at the detriment or impairment of another soul." It was a mouthful, but he'd said it so often that many in the congregation could recite it by heart. Perhaps because it sounded odd coming from the heir to one of the largest privately-owned corporations in America. Yet the people of Saint Ann's knew that their vicar lived simply, indulged in few luxuries, and gave massive amounts of money to charity. They may not have always been comfortable with his choice of projects but they were proud of their priest—even if he did push the envelope at times.

His congregation realized that Flenn's wealth and family's good name could have landed him a church anywhere, but that he had chosen Saint Ann's to exercise his ministry. Flenn had told them that his time in the Air Force had taught him that life was to be lived purposefully. His faith, which he attributed to an experience years ago in Scotland, was most assuredly sincere. Although he never spoke to them of what that experience had entailed, it had obviously changed his life.

Waiting for the detective, Flenn thought about the events of the last few days. *Trouble comes in threes!* he thought. *First Minerva, then Zack, and now Detective Rainsford.* On top of preparations for Advent and Christmas, diocesan commitments, and community action meetings such as the one he was to attend this morning, these latest encounters had Flenn feeling as if he were teetering on the edge of an abyss—an abyss he knew all too well, one from which he had only narrowly escaped.

Detective Rainsford had informed him last night that the girl he was trying to identify had been a prostitute, a *teenaged* prostitute! Flenn put down the bulletin and stared at the ceiling. He'd seen so much sadness over the years. Misery, betrayal, death… these had been his world for nearly 12 years with the CIA. Maybe that was why he wanted so desperately to spend the remainder of his life trying to right a few of the world's wrongs. He had been told by the man in Edinburgh that he was being called to be part of the light. That was right before… *it…* had happened. Fewer than five people knew about that experience, but it had altered Flenn's life forever. He left Scotland and the CIA, never to look back on his old life; that is, until Zack Matteson came hunting for him.

Flenn glanced at his watch again. Still no sign of the detective. He went to the kitchen to pour himself another cup of coffee but all that remained were the dregs from the pot. Iriana would be here soon, but he'd be on his way to the meeting by then. Hopefully, he'd have time to stop for another cup along the way. He leaned against the brown and white tiled counter and thought about the policeman he'd met last night. His first impression of Guy Rainsford was that he was a man with very little joy in his life. Priests and spies are notorious for sizing people up quickly. *Goes with the territory,* he told himself as he drained the mug.

He went back to his office, sank into his chair, and fiddled with some papers on the desk. His office was furnished simply, but, like the renewed spirit of this once dying congregation, it was warm and inviting. Flenn had added a few comfortable chairs to the drab gray, cinder-block room and placed some brightly colored icons on the wall. He frequently burned a scented candle next to his red, leather-bound copy of the *Book of Common Prayer.* The book and candle rested on a small glass table separating the chairs. He had lit the candle this morning out of habit, even though he was planning to be out of the office most of the day.

Waiting for the detective, Flenn began to think about his refusal earlier to help Zack. *Perhaps he should reconsider since the stakes were so high—but then the stakes were always high when it came to Zack Matteson.* Still, Zack might be able to help him bring some peace to Minerva.

Zack's help would undoubtedly come at a high price.

Flenn rubbed his forehead. *Was he going to allow Zack to steal his serenity—again?*

The door to the parish hall opened and Flenn heard someone coming through the vestibule. He stuck his head out of the office and recognized Detective Rainsford.

"Sorry I'm late," Guy said. "Traffic." The detective was wearing a white, short-sleeve shirt with an ancient blue tie. He had his jacket draped over his arm, an indicator that it had warmed up since Flenn had come to the office an hour ago.

"Good to see you again, Detective." The two shook hands. "I'm sorry, but this'll have to be brief. I've got a meeting across town."

Guy cursed silently to himself, but said, "This should be quick."

Flenn invited him to sit and closed the door behind him. He sat across from the priest, the glass coffee table between them. "I'd offer you some coffee, but I just finished the pot," Flenn said.

Guy sneezed, then blew his nose into a handkerchief. "Thanks, but I'm good. I'll get right to it, Father. I'd like to know more about your work with the girls downtown. You still doing it?"

Flenn shook his head. "Like I said last night; when we were taking blankets and hot chocolate we were simply trying to offer a bit of kindness. We didn't ask questions. And no, we aren't still doing it. We would, but the ladies aren't hanging around down there like they used to do."

"The girls actually *took* your blankets?"

Flenn understood the question. "Oh, they'd toss them against the building if a car came down the street, but when no one was around they'd bundle up. You know how cold it can get sometimes."

"Except here it is December and today it feels like spring."

Flenn nodded. "What is it they say about Birmingham? We have four seasons, all on the same day."

"Yeah, damndest thing... oh, sorry, Father."

Flenn grinned. "Don't be. I've said worse."

Guy scratched the back of his head. "Wow, Father; there's something definitely different about you."

Flenn laughed. "Yeah, I've heard that before."

The detective shifted in his seat. "No offense. Just... well, there are a lot of preachers out there saying one thing but doing another. Not too many people would go out of their way to help prostitutes on a cold night. And, I've *certainly* never heard a minister admit to cussing before."

Flenn knew what Guy meant. "That's because we live in a world where people think that faith is about being nice, or about not using bad language, or whether you take a drink every now and then."

"You mean it's not?" Guy said, instantly regretting the sarcasm in his voice.

"Christianity isn't about any of those things. And I'll tell you something else, Detective, Christianity isn't even about morality." Flenn secretly loved to watch people's faces when he said things like that. The cop didn't disappoint.

"Morality changes over the centuries. What's proper today was totally taboo in the nineteenth century. And what was considered moral in the nineteenth century would horrify some people today. Take slavery, for instance. For thousands of years it was considered moral to buy and sell people like livestock. Horrible; but, most people didn't think twice. I mean look at morality in Jesus' day—a woman could be stoned for having sex before marriage, but all a man had to do was to pay a fine to the girl's father. That was considered *moral*. No, it isn't about morality; it's about a relationship… a relationship between us and our creator."

Guy felt he had just been given his own personal sermon, the first one he'd heard since he'd been forced to attend church with his mother. He recalled how his mom had often looked as miserable as he had felt back then, listening to sermons about what would happen if you got out of line with the Almighty.

"Father, my job is to look beyond morality. There are times when I've had to arrest people who were doing something with good intentions but were still breaking the law. Other times, I've had to let truly awful people go free because they technically weren't breaking any laws, even though what they were doing was about as immoral as anything you might imagine."

Flenn understood, having seen the underbelly of humanity up close for years. "Detective, I'm genuinely sorry, but unless there's something else, I really do have to leave. I don't think I have anything else for you."

"Father," Guy felt his stomach tighten. He couldn't believe he was about to say this, but he went on: "Maybe you *can* help me… on a, well… on a more personal level." He shifted in his chair. "Maybe you can help me figure out why I'm becoming so obsessed with this case. I have other investigations, but I seem to be consumed more and more with this kid's murder. I'm even starting to lose sleep over it."

Guy hadn't planned on telling the priest any of that, but the emotions he'd been bottling up since seeing the girl's mangled body on the riverbank began to flow out of him. "It's just that she was a kid; a kid nobody cared about, except for her pimp. I mean, to watch a scum-bag like that guy be the only one to shed a tear over this girl is just… well, it's just, I don't know… it's just rotten!"

Guy didn't look at the priest. Instead, he watched the flame of the candle flickering on the table between them.

"I mean, no one has been looking for this girl, nobody. She's just lying there on a cold slab in the morgue with no one to claim her. It's as if she never mattered."

He sneezed. At last, he looked up at the priest. "All

the attention has gone to that rich kid, the one who disappeared last spring. Nobody gives a damn about this poor girl!"

Flenn sat quietly, no longer in a rush to leave. His eyes locked onto Guy, compelling the detective to continue.

"What could have been so bad at home that this girl had to sell herself to men who did God knows what to her? And then one of them—I guess it was one of them—beats her half to death, ties her up and throws her still-breathing body into the river!" The detective's voice faltered, his gaze transfixed again upon the candle's flickering flame... "and nobody... *nobody* cares." The detective wiped his eyes with the back of his hand.

After a moment, Flenn broke the silence.

"And *that*, Detective, is exactly why you are so obsessed with this case."

Guy looked at the priest.

"*You* care."

Flenn went on: "You are absolutely right, this girl deserved to have someone care about her. Since there isn't anyone, *you* have assumed that responsibility. *You* have become her family. For what it's worth, I think that what you're doing is important. You obviously feel you need to do this, not just for the girl's sake, but for *yours*. Trust me, I know there are some things that can latch onto you that just won't let go until you've seen them all the way through. Sounds to me like this is one of those things for you."

The detective nodded slightly, mulling the words

over in his head. He felt embarrassed. He'd only met this priest yesterday, yet here he was baring his soul to him. It was the closest he'd come in years to talking to anyone about his feelings. Guy shook his head. "I'm sorry, Father. I didn't mean to unload all of that on you."

"Yes, you did." Flenn offered a kind smile. "At some level, you did. You needed to tell someone about this girl, about how she's affecting you." Flenn leaned forward. "Detective, you are going around asking a lot of questions and trying to find answers to solve a case, but in the midst of it all you also need to know *who* she was. She wasn't just a hooker. She was a person, a human being. You're searching for more than an identity; you're trying to find her humanity."

Flenn blew out the candle and stood up to leave. "I'll pray you find what you're looking for. I warn you though, once they become human your cases get a lot more difficult."

This time the detective stood as well. "Thank you," Guy said, shaking the priest's hand. "I appreciate your time. I'll be in touch." He made it to the office door before turning around. "Um, could we just keep all this between ourselves?"

Flenn smiled. "Mum's the word."

As Guy pulled out of the parking lot he thought about what the priest had said. *This child deserved to have someone who cared.*

The words resonated within him. *Father Flenn was right. This kid did need somebody to care. She needed family. That rich girl who'd gone missing had lots of people to care. At one point, half the city's police force had been out looking for her. This child had no one... until now!*

Still a bit embarrassed by the encounter with the priest, Detective Guy Rainsford drove away thinking about cursing preachers and caring detectives.

Guy wasn't the only one lost in thought. As he drove across town, Flenn was amazed at how his life had been upended in just four days. *The cop needed him... so did Minerva... and so did Zack!*

"Lord," he said aloud, "I don't know what you're up to, but I guess I owe it to Minerva to let Zack tell me the rest of his story. Unless, of course, you've got a better way for me to help her?" He glanced heavenward. A dark cloud was forming off in the distance. "Oh, please don't let that be a sign," Flenn said.

CHAPTER TWENTY-FOUR

Patience was not one of Col. Amir's virtues, as evidenced by the way he was glaring at the men standing guard in front of the gallows below. The colonel stood behind the guardrail in the oversized, cinder-block room and checked his watch for the third time. If they didn't hurry this up, he'd be late for his meeting with Sadar Abbas.

Twenty state captives would soon be marched out, led to their individual nooses, and unceremoniously hanged five at a time. Although Col. Amir couldn't know it, the reason for the delay was that an order had just gone out to remove the prisoners' blindfolds. A lieutenant had seen Amir watching from the observation platform. He knew that the colonel preferred to watch the faces of the condemned as they drew their last breath.

Amir wasn't required to be here this morning; the law only mandated that two officers be present at state executions. The colonel looked around the room; there were four here this morning. No, Amir was here solely for his wife; after all, he had promised her a full report.

At last, the prisoners were brought into the room, hands tied behind their backs. Most were trying to face their deaths bravely; only a couple were continuing to beg for their lives. One woman was weeping. She was the one Amir had come to see. The woman had been a soldier assigned temporary duty to his wife after her regular bodyguard had taken ill last week. She had been caught with a New Testament in her possession. While Christianity isn't illegal in Iran, trying to convert a Muslim is—which was the official charge against her. In truth, the woman hadn't been trying to convert anyone, but had been overheard calling Col. Amir's wife fat. *It didn't matter that his wife was enormous; it was that the soldier had been heard joking about it publicly.* Colonel Amir glared down at the woman. *The rank and file had to be reminded of what happens to those who disrespect their leaders.*

The first five were finally executed, and their bodies removed. Colonel Amir whispered something to a nearby guard, who went down and adjusted the middle noose, turning it so that the knot would be directly behind the woman's head. This would prevent the neck from breaking, allowing Col. Amir to watch her strangle to death. *He had, after all, promised his wife.*

The show turned out to be disappointing; the woman died in less than a minute. Colonel Amir stomped off, but not before ordering the woman's body be displayed in front of her platoon's barracks. He checked his watch again as he stepped onto the elevator. *At least he wasn't going to be late for his meeting with Abbas.*

Amir dusted the medals on his chest with the back of his hand and thought how he should be the one sitting in Abbas' chair. He had been passed over twice now. This last time he'd been sure he would have been named head of intelligence, but instead the bureaucrats had given the post to one of their own. Sadar Abbas had a cold heart, the colonel gave him credit for that much, but the man had no experience in the field, not like he had. Amir had earned every one of these medals, having served his country loyally over the course of three decades.

It wasn't simply that he disliked Abbas. Whether he liked his boss or not was unimportant. What mattered was that each task got taken care of in an expeditious manner and not left to fester, as had been this matter with Zack Matteson. *Why not simply have Matteson killed?* Coincidence or not, the fact the American had been on the same plane as Daniel Romero should have been reason enough to kill the man. *What was Abbas waiting for?*

As much as Col. Amir wanted the plot against Israel to succeed, he also wanted the American eliminated. Matteson and some other agent—he'd never known the identity of the second man—had once wounded Amir in a shootout with Afghani opium smugglers. The drug lords had been going through Amir to launder money in Iran during the dangerous days after 9-11. The colonel had simply been in the wrong place at the wrong time, but it had taken nearly nine months for him to recover from the wounds he'd received. *Not something easily forgotten!*

He stepped off the elevator and into Abbas' outer office. The secretary pushed a button to announce his arrival. After several minutes, Col. Amir was escorted inside. Sadar Abbas was sitting behind his large desk, studying a file in front of him. The colonel waited, remaining at attention the entire time. *Not once in all his visits to this office had he ever been invited to sit down!* Abbas may not have been military, but he clearly wanted it understood that he was the one in charge.

Finally, Abbas looked up. "I need you to watch someone for me," he said abruptly. "You are to do it personally, and for heaven's sake try and be discreet."

Arrogant bish'our! (idiot), thought Amir.

Abbas continued. "I've just learned that the new ambassador from Syria is coming here for a few days. I need you to keep an eye on him."

Abbas leaned back in his chair and gazed out the window for a moment. "There was a time when Syria was our closest ally, but the way things are progressing... well. . . let's just say our president doesn't trust this new man. The ambassador is thought to have some political leanings toward the West." Abbas glanced back at his subordinate. "You will receive the itinerary as soon as I have it," he said, returning his attention to the papers on his desk. "That is all."

Dismissed, Col. Amir turned for the door. *Ugh! Playing nursemaid to an ambassador. What had he done to turn the face of Allah against him?*

"Amir?" Sadar Abbas, didn't bother looking up as the colonel turned to face him. "Has anything else surfaced concerning Zachary Matteson?"

Amir smiled confidently. "I have him under close observation, Excellency. We know his every move." *Was he about to receive permission to take care of Matteson at last?*

Abbas simply nodded. "Let me know if anything changes." Abbas waved toward the door. "You may go."

Colonel Amir turned quickly before his superior could see the rage in his eyes. *Fool!*

CHAPTER TWENTY-FIVE

Farhad Ahmad stood at attention in the middle of a cow pasture, even though no one else was around. The person on the other end of the satellite phone would have expected nothing less.

"What have you learned, Ahmad?"

"We are still in Alabama, Colonel. Matteson hasn't done much of anything, other than to go shopping."

"Has he met with anyone?" Amir sounded irritated.

"He did go to a Catholic church. I saw no one else come in or go out, other than a priest."

"A priest?" Amir asked. "Did they speak to one another?"

"I do not know, sir." Ahmad had dreaded this moment. *Others had paid dearly for uttering similar words to Amir.* "I could not go inside; I would have been exposed had I entered." There was a long pause. Ahmad felt the sweat begin to bead on his brow.

"Do you know anything about this priest?"

"No, sir, but I am working on it." Ahmad had gone online and found that the church had two priests, although, from the photographs, neither had been the man he'd seen walk into Sacred Heart. Of course, the parish probably had other clergy, as large as it was, but the only way to find out was to walk into the office and pretend to be a convert. Ahmad doubted he could be that convincing.

"The priest may not be important," said Amir, "but if you see him again, make certain you find out who he is. Do not, however, lose sight of your objective!"

"No sir; I mean, yes sir." Ahmad wiped his forehead.

"Do not fail me, Ahmad!" The line went dead.

Farhad Ahmad looked around at the gentle hills of fading-green grass, thankful he was 7,000 miles away from his boss right now. He'd come to the pasture yesterday and today after searching for higher ground to make a solid satellite connection. It meant leaving Matteson for about half an hour, but the tracking device under Matteson's car was still functioning. Besides, the man hadn't done much of anything since arriving in Cullman two nights ago.

Ahmad made his way down the hill, slowing for a moment to gaze at the rich farmland below him. It reminded him of England, especially around Yorkshire, where he had traveled only a few weeks ago. The valleys here were nearly as breathtaking.

He missed seeing the cow pie.

The gooey muck oozed into his expensive loafers and through his socks. As he pulled his feet out of the sticky mess, a rusty pickup truck crested the hill and headed down the dirt road where he'd parked his rental car. Ahmad hastily made his way down the hill; it wouldn't do to have someone asking him questions. Climbing over the barbed wire fence, he tore the inseam of his trousers.

He'd almost made it when the truck stopped in the middle of the dirt road in front of him. Two men got out—one skinny, the other with an enormous belly which bounced as he walked. Both men sported thick, dark beards; the fat one was wearing a dirty-green baseball cap and carrying a lead pipe.

"Habla Ingles?" the skinny man shouted. His yellowish-brown tee shirt was ripped and stained, looking as if it had been rescued from a trash bin. Ahmad kept an eye on the other man, the one holding the pipe.

"Come on, boy! I said, do you speak English?"

The Iranian nodded.

"What were you doing in our daddy's field just now?" the skinny man said.

"Simply making a phone call." Ahmad's English was a mixture of British and Iranian accents, but to these two, any accent from a brown-skinned man meant only one thing… *Mexican.*

"Making a phone call?" said the fat man with the pipe. "Who the hell are you calling from the middle of a cow pasture?"

The skinny one's eyes narrowed. "Probably his boss to tell him he's late for his shift at Taco Bell."

Ahmad was wishing now he had brought his pistol. "I am sorry, gentlemen," he said, certain that it was the first time either of these two had ever heard that term applied to them. "My phone's reception is not very good in town. I will leave now. I apologize to have caused you alarm."

The skinny man moved toward him.

"Leave? No sir, not till you pay us for that!" He pointed down at Ahmad's shoes.

Ahmad looked down at his shoes. "Pay you… for cowshit?"

"That there is our cowshit, ain't it, Roland?"

"Prime, Grade 'A' cowshit, Dirk." The fat man began to twist the pipe slowly in his hands.

"How much you say, that prime, Grade 'A' cowshit is worth?" Dirk said. "Maybe fifty dollars?"

Roland shot him a nearly toothless grin. "I'd say more like a hundred."

"I do not have that much money, gentlemen. Perhaps we should just all go our separate ways. I apologize for disturbing your day." Ahmad backed up slowly toward the passenger side door. The man with the pipe rounded the car behind him.

"On second thought," Ahmad offered, "my wallet is in the glove box. Perhaps you will allow me to retrieve it?"

The skinny man looked toward the car. "Hold on Roland, let me just check what's in that-there glove box." Dirk reached through the open window on the passenger side. "Well, looky here!" He pulled out a Glock G27 and pointed the tiny weapon directly at Farhad Ahmad. His brother, Roland, was now directly behind the stranger. "You wasn't about to reach for this itty-bitty thing, was ya'?"

The Iranian held his hands up and shook his head. "No sir, if you will look again you will also see that my wallet is in there as well." As Dirk turned to check,

Ahmad's right hand came down hard on the man's wrist. The gun fell to the ground as Ahmad's left foot lunged behind him and connected with the fat man's groin. With lightning speed, the Iranian struck Dirk in the throat–so quickly, the skinny man wouldn't have been able to deflect the blow on his best day.

Ahmad kicked the gun out of Dirk's reach, then swiveled as Roland struggled back to his feet. The big man had made it half way when a roundhouse kick to the head knocked him out cold. Ahmad turned. Dirk was writhing in agony, his mouth open in a silent scream.

Ahmad looked around but saw no one else. He picked up his pistol and dusted off the dirt, then he slipped the weapon into his waistband. He reached inside his wallet, which had been in his back pocket all along, and pulled out a $100 bill, which he tossed on top of Dirk.

"You will be okay, my friend, just don't try to talk for a day or two." Farhad Ahmad smiled down at Dirk who was clutching his throat and gasping for air. "Now you must excuse me. I am late for my shift at Taco Bell."

CHAPTER TWENTY-SIX

Zack Matteson paid his admission fee and walked through the gates of the *Ave Marie Grotto* outside Cullman. He was running 20 minutes later than he'd told Flenn. He had spent the time making sure he had not been followed.

While eating breakfast yesterday, Zack had noticed an olive-skinned man sitting in the parking lot. He had seen him outside the restaurant again today. Up until now, Zack had assumed he'd gotten out of Turkey unnoticed. Although he couldn't be certain, it was likely one of Col. Amir's men. He and Flenn had run up against Amir several years ago. Amir now worked under Sadar Abbas, the newest head of Iranian intelligence. Zack had read the dossier on Abbas. The man was as pragmatic as he was brutal.

Zack saw his friend up ahead. Flenn wasn't wearing his clerical collar this morning as he strolled about the exhibits at the Grotto. Instead, he wore jeans, a long-sleeved tee-shirt and a windbreaker.

"So, this is December in Alabama," Zack said. Flenn was standing in front of the Tokyo exhibit. A few tourists passed by them on their way to the other displays which had been created by a Bavarian monk in the early 20th century. Zack read a nearby sign which told how Brother

Joseph Zoettl, a Benedictine, had made the Grotto his life's work. The monk had been maimed in an accident in the 1890s and left severely disabled. With simple, crude tools, he had constructed miniature replicas of famous places around the world out of discarded junk and trash.

Zack looked across the small fence meant to keep tourists a few feet away. "That thing looks Chinese, not Japanese."

"The sculptor wouldn't have known the difference between Japanese and Chinese architecture," Flenn pointed out. "The man never traveled outside the United States after he left Bavaria." Flenn admired the dedication it must have taken for this solitary monk to create more than a hundred recreations of places he had only seen in magazines or on picture post cards.

Zack shook his head. "Still, that doesn't look like Tokyo."

Flenn looked at Zack and sighed. "Imagination is totally lost on you, isn't it?"

Zack folded his sunglasses and placed them in his shirt pocket. "I don't need imagination. Reality is usually more than I can handle."

"What you deal in is *not* reality." Flenn countered.

"You of all people know better than that," Zack said as they made their way down a gravel path toward a bench away from the other exhibits.

"I used to *think* I knew better," Flenn said, "until Edinburgh."

Zack pulled out a handful of jellybeans from his pants pocket, offering Flenn one; he refused.

"I'm sorry, Flenn, but I still have a hard time believing what you say happened in Scotland actually happened. Don't get me wrong. I believe that *you* believe it and all, but… "

The priest cut him off. "That's not why we're here, Zack."

Zack dug in his pocket in search of more jellybeans. "Just why are we here? After all, you're the one who called me last night." Zack scanned the area as a few tourists ambled past, looking for any signs of his tail from this morning. He couldn't know it, but Farhad Ahmad was at that very moment buying new loafers at Belk—praying that the chip planted underneath Zack's car was still working.

Flenn looked down at the sidewalk beneath their feet. "I need your help," he finally said, almost in a whisper.

"Oh, I see." Zack said, pretending to be offended. "*I* need *your* help, and you walk away. Now, you expect me to drop whatever I'm doing and tend to you."

"Don't give me that, Zack. The only reason you're still in Cullman is because you're waiting me out, seeing if I'll change my mind—which, admittedly, I always have."

Zack's eyebrow lifted slightly. "And, have you?"

Flenn watched a squirrel scamper nearby, obviously accustomed to the presence of tourists. "I want you to understand something, Zack; I don't want back in the CIA. I've left that life forever."

"Who said anything about getting back in? I just need a little assistance, that's all."

"I mean it, Zack, you can't tell anyone at Langley that I'm helping you."

Zack fished for another jellybean. "Yeah, yeah. Same song, second verse."

"Stop it! You know I don't like doing this stuff anymore."

"You were the one to call me, remember?"

"Okay, okay." Flenn paused a moment, then began, "There's a girl… "

Zack's eyebrows shot up. "Uh oh."

"Very funny," Flenn said. The squirrel ducked behind the exhibit. "This girl's a teenager. She went missing last spring. She was being abused by her stepfather, a Birmingham city councilman, quite powerful in certain circles."

"Democrat or Republican?"

Flenn stared at him. "Democrat, but why on earth does that matter?"

Zack shrugged. "So, you think her stepfather whacked her?"

Flenn shook his head, as much at his friend's use of the word *whacked* as anything else. "I don't know. Maybe. Or, she may still be alive, but I desperately need to find out. Don't ask me why; I can't tell you." Flenn sighed for a second time. He knew where this would lead. He hadn't wanted to come to Zack for a favor, but he had to find a way to help Minerva, and Zack could make that a lot easier. "I need to know what the police have discovered. I've gone online, checked all the legitimate news feeds and social media sites, but I need to go deeper."

"You want access to the Birmingham police files."

Flenn nodded. "You can do that kind of thing. I can't. All I need is a laptop with the program already installed. I can do the rest."

"Easy," said Zack. "I thought you were going to ask me for something difficult."

Flenn frowned. "Don't make jokes, Zack; this is really important."

"Okay. I guess I shouldn't ask *why* it's so important?"

"No."

The spy looked him. "You know this will cost you, right?"

Here it comes!

Flenn wished just once Zack would go to Langley for help and not to him.

"What is it you want?"

"I need to know who a certain person is going to support in next year's election."

Flenn studied his old friend. "I assume you're talking about Daniel Romero. Who is this 'certain person'?"

"I don't get to ask you, so you don't get to ask me. At least not yet, not until you agree."

There were so many things that Flenn wished he didn't know, so many things that had happened over the years which he wanted to erase from his memory; and yet here he was, with the very same person with whom most of those memories had been created: Zack Matteson.

Taking a deep breath, he said, "Okay. I'm in. Who is it?"

"Benjamin Rye."

Flenn blinked. "Rye is an idiot."

"He's becoming a very influential idiot. What he says goes for a lot of fundamentalist voters. I did some checking. Romero came to Birmingham the last weekend in May. I believe he may have been meeting with Rye."

Flenn shook his head. "You already know he will support the Republican candidate, just like his old man used to do every single election."

"Yeah," Zack smiled wryly, "but Willy Rye could sure make you think he was bipartisan, couldn't he?"

"Not if you listened to what he was saying. Don't get me wrong, I admire the old man. His wife was a close friend of my father's once upon a time, and we spent a bunch of summers at their cabin. But I can't stand their son, Benji. Never could."

Zack winked. "Your old man and Elizabeth Rye, huh?"

Flenn frowned. "Would you get your mind out of the gutter?"

"Sorry, it just sort of stays there," Zack said. "Occupational hazard. I just don't need you siding with the Ryes right now. That could make things... complicated." The squirrel scampered back; Zack tossed it a licorice jellybean. The squirrel sniffed it, then turned away.

"So, all you want from me is to tell you which candidate Benjamin Rye's going to support in the primaries?"

"I don't think the primaries are going to matter this time around. Not if even half of what I told you about

Iran is true. That's why I need you. I need to know who Benjamin Rye is going to back when all is said and done."

"I told you, the Republican."

"Which one? So far, there are seven." From what Zack had overheard in Turkey, he knew none of them stood a chance; neither would any of the candidates from across the aisle.

"If Romero runs as an independent with Iranian support, and your friend Benjamin Rye abandons the Republicans to jump on his bandwagon, then Romero could easily win."

Flenn scratched his head. "You really think that a Southern evangelical, the son of Willy Rye nonetheless, would abandon the Republicans?"

Zack nodded. "A lot of folks have lately. Look, just find out for me, would you? That's all I'm asking."

Flenn envied the squirrel in front of him—*no problems, no enemies, no Zack Matteson!*

"Okay. I'll see what I can do. I'll talk with his mother. We have tea once or twice a year. But, I just can't believe that Romero would have a chance winning the Ryes over or winning an election for that matter. You do know that there's a total of eleven candidates who have announced so far? Do you really think Romero can beat those odds?"

Zack stood up to leave. *There was only going to be one name that would come to the forefront of world history, unless he could find a way to stop it.* "Stranger things have happened," was all he said. Zack took a final look around. "I'll bring you the laptop."

"When and where?"

He grinned. "You'll know when it arrives." Zack didn't say another word, just walked toward the exit of the Grotto.

Flenn looked down at the squirrel. "I don't suppose you'd want to trade places with me right now, would you?" The squirrel scampered off. Flenn shook his head. "Yeah, that's what I figured."

CHAPTER TWENTY-SEVEN

Flenn gently nudged a kitten out of his face and got out of bed, stubbing his toe on a box in the middle of the bathroom floor. He looked at it suspiciously for a moment; the box hadn't been there the night before. There was a time when he would have jumped for cover, but he knew exactly what was in this particular box.

"I've lost my touch," he said to the kitten, now playing with a loose thread on his bathrobe. He reached down; it was exactly what he thought—the computer Zack promised him two days ago. Zack must have brought it sometime in the middle of the night, jimmied the front door lock, and crept by him as he slept. He had probably thought it funny. *At least he hadn't taken a marker and drawn obscene pictures on the walls, the way he had that time with the Libyan diplomat!*

"I've gotta get a dog," Flenn said aloud. "Attack kittens just aren't panning out!"

He decided to skip his morning run and jog after lunch instead. He carried the computer downstairs and made a pot of coffee, nudging yet another ball of fluff aside. *Where in heaven's name was their mother?* She had shown little concern over her brood ever since they'd arrived. The only things she seemed interested in was eating, pooping just outside the litter box, and, despite several lectures, sharpening her claws on Flenn's favorite chair.

Flenn was halfway through his second cup of coffee before he was awake enough to examine the contents of the laptop. He opened it up and pressed the power button. A program titled, "Idiots Guide to Becoming a Priest," popped up on the screen. *Zack had probably thought that was funny, too.* It was indeed the program Flenn had requested, which not only gave him access to all Birmingham police files from the past two years, but also allowed him to drag and drop any items of interest temporarily into an encrypted file for quick reference. Flenn suspected that, in typical Zack Matteson style, both files would delete themselves in a day or two.

He scanned through dozens of records, looking for anything related to Shelly O'Reilly. It didn't take long to find the case file, as well as the lead investigators' notes. Zack had included several weeks' worth of emails from detectives Jay Hollister and Otis Wickes. He'd placed them in a separate file marked, "Merry Christmas."

And a happy Advent to you my friend! Flenn thought as he read through the emails, dragging a few into the encrypted file to go over again later. Thirty-seven emails from Wickes had to do with the case of the missing girl; only nine had any useful information. The rest were personal missives; a few addressed to Detective Wicke's wife–several more to Wicke's girlfriend.

From what Flenn could see, the investigation was at a standstill. According to Wicke's notes, Rochelle–*Shelly*–

O'Reilly had been a loner throughout most of her school years—until last year. Her mother, Juanita O'Reilly, had reported that Shelly had joined a couple of school organizations and clubs last year, and that she had been 'delighted' when her daughter began developing numerous friends. Her mother told the police that Shelly used Uber as a way of getting to and from her friends' homes on the weekends. Wickes noted that her mom had said she'd cautioned Shelly to text her drivers' names to her but that Shelly usually forgot.

Several of Shelly's teachers at the *Birmingham School of Fine Arts* had been interviewed, as had the school principal. *Standard police procedure*, Flenn noted as he pushed a kitten off his computer keyboard for the second time. The acid from three cups of coffee was beginning to eat away at his stomach.

Flenn scrolled through the interviews, all of which said pretty much the same thing: Shelly was an average student, never spoke in class, kept to herself and usually sat alone during lunchtime. Her grades were enough to get by—mostly low C's along with a couple of D's. Flenn questioned why a girl with so many new friends would sit by herself in the lunchroom. *It didn't sound like someone that had suddenly become popular.* Then again, he wondered how a girl who was being abused by her stepfather could function at all. As he continued reading, Flenn found himself unable to reconcile all the slumber parties and sleepovers her mom reported with what appeared to be self-isolation the rest of the time.

Finally, with his eyes needing a break as much as his

stomach did breakfast, Flenn got up from the computer and walked over to the cabinet where he kept the cereal. After he poured the milk, some for himself, a little for the kittens, and a bowl for their mother—who'd suddenly appeared from nowhere—Flenn leaned against the kitchen counter, lost in thought.

Shelly had come from a wealthy home, as had he. He knew firsthand the pressures and expectations placed on privileged kids. He had often felt awkward as a child, especially when so many of his friends came from less fortunate families. Flenn's parents had encouraged him to have friends of every color and socioeconomic background. As a way to ensure that he did, they'd enrolled him in public school. He was thankful for that now, but back then he'd felt embarrassed by his family's wealth. Classmates often taunted him, which had forced him to learn to wield a mean right hook at an early age. Boys respected someone who could take care of himself in a fight, so the name-calling of "Little Rich Kid" didn't last long. Still, he knew that just because the kids weren't saying it didn't mean they weren't thinking it. Shelly, however, had attended a private school with other privileged children. *Private school and a private life.* Flenn figured she must have felt ashamed of what was happening at home and had probably done everything she could to hide it from others—until the day when she'd finally confided in Minerva.

There was no mention of Shelly ever having had a boyfriend. Her mother told police that the girl hadn't expressed an interest in boys or a lot of things kids her age did. Instead, Shelly preferred reading—mostly classics, particularly works by Charles Dickens and Victor Hugo. The file did say that Shelly went to church most Sundays with her mother and stepfather, but that she did not participate in youth group activities or other programs. According to her mother, Shelly spent most of her free time alone in her room.

Reading or hiding? Flenn wondered.

All of that had changed this past year when Shelly began hanging around her new friends. When asked, her mother admitted that she'd only met one of those girls. Juanita O'Reilly couldn't recall the girl's name, only that it began with the letter *D*. When the school was asked for a list of Shelly's girlfriends, they'd been hard-pressed to come up with anyone whose name started with a *D*, or any other letter in the alphabet for that matter.

Flenn scratched his head. *Shelly had several new friends, but nobody seemed to know who they were… she was experienced enough in using Uber to get a ride to wherever she needed to go, but no one had any records of that… her teachers said that she kept to herself regularly and had no love interests or hobbies, other than reading.*

Things just weren't adding up.

Flenn looked at the reports again. Detectives Wickes and Hollister had followed standard operating procedure—but they'd come up empty. *Where does a 15-year-old girl who is being abused by her stepfather go to find solace?* Flenn sat down and pondered the question as he ate his cereal. *A secret love interest was the most obvious answer, but her mother hadn't known of any boyfriends; and the stepfather, from what Flenn knew about abusers, was not likely to have allowed her to date anyone.* Frankly, Flenn was surprised she'd been allowed to have any friends at all.

What was it that Minerva had said? "Shelly had threatened her stepfather with going to the authorities..." *Maybe that had caused Mac to back off.* Flenn had another thought: *Had Shelly ever told her mother what her stepfather was doing to her? Possibly, although abusive parents often bribed or threatened their victims to keep them quiet. Just what had Mac done to that poor girl to buy her silence?* The old Flenn would have known just how to get Mac O'Reilly to tell him everything—but that Flenn had died in Scotland a long time ago. The thought occurred to him: *Should he give Zack a call? Zack never had a problem with the rough stuff.*

Flenn shuddered. "Get behind me, Satan!" he said out loud, startling one of the kittens. Coercive methods in the CIA had been approved, forbidden, then approved again depending upon who was sitting in the Oval Office, but Flenn would have no part of it.

The kitten jumped on the table and stuck her pink nose in the middle of his bowl just as the doorbell rang. Startled, Flenn closed the computer and placed it in an empty drawer. As he walked from the kitchen toward the foyer, he looked out the living room window and saw Delores Dilwicky. *Of all people right now!* he thought. Delores was Saint Anne's leading would-be socialite.

"Yoo-hoo!" Delores waved a gloved hand toward the window.

"Good Lord, deliver me!" he said as he went to the

door. Delores Dilwicky was not someone he wanted to see this morning, or ever, if the truth be told.

"Good morning, Delores," he said opening the door. "What brings you by this morning?"

The chubby brunette with a bulbous bouffant stepped around him and into the foyer. "Why Father, you are still in your bathrobe and haven't even shaved yet." The accusing glint in the short, dumpy woman's eyes made him uncomfortable.

"I haven't made it to the office yet, Delores."

The woman's eyes darted all about.

"They just left," he said with a forced smile.

"Who?"

"The dancing girls—from the wild party last night."

"Oh, Father, you're such a tease," she said, still looking for clues of a scandal.

"Well now that you're here Delores, won't you come in for a cup of coffee?" Flenn led her into the kitchen, glancing at the drawer where he'd stuffed the computer.

"Tea, please."

"Tea it is," he replied, picking up the kitten and what was left of his cereal. "Please, sit down. I was just about to have a bite to eat. Would you like something?"

"Nothing for me, thanks. A girl has to watch her figure, you know."

"Um… yes." He grabbed a bag of cookies and placed the remaining few on a plate, then reached for a box of tea.

"Oh, I hope you have chamomile. I do so love chamomile; don't you, Father?"

"Afraid you will have to settle for Lipton this morning."

"Oh well," she said, pursing her lips, "I'm sure it will be lovely."

They sat sipping their tea and making small talk for a few minutes. Delores kept eyeing the plate of sugar cookies. "Please, have one," Flenn offered.

"Well, maybe just a half," she said breaking a cookie in two and devouring it in a single bite. "Now Father, you are probably wondering why I'm here today."

"The thought had crossed my mind."

She picked up the other half of the cookie. "I'm sure you know that I'm now a member of the Daughters of Birmingham." She waited for an appreciative response, but Flenn simply sipped his tea. "Well, you see," she continued, reaching for another cookie, not bothering to break it in half this time, "our usual venue in Mountain Brook has developed a problem with rodents. Why, one ran right under Mrs. O'Reilly's chair the other day! Father, I tell you, I nearly fainted." She devoured the cookie in three quick bites before reaching for the last two. "It was just awful. Several of the ladies won't hear of going back there again until we're certain that the place has been properly fumigated, or whatever it is people do when they have rodents."

She paused for a moment. "You know these cookies are absolutely delicious, I don't suppose you have any more? No? Oh well. Anyway, I told the ladies that we could meet at Saint Ann's. I do hope that will be okay?"

He looked at the empty plate, his stomach still churning. "That depends on when you want to meet."

"Thursdays at noon."

"Oh, I'm sorry, Delores, but that's when Alcoholics Anonymous meets."

"Couldn't you move them?"

Flenn restrained himself from saying what he was thinking. "No, we couldn't do that."

"Well, the ladies did say we could also come on Tuesdays at eleven."

"Overeaters Anonymous meets then."

Delores looked annoyed. "All these anonymous groups! Who are these people? I will be delighted to call one of them and arrange something."

"I'm afraid you can't do that, Delores. That's what anonymous means."

"Well, I'm told our group once met on Wednesday evenings, I suppose… "

"Bible study."

"Monday afternoons?"

"That's when we pack up items for the emergency food pantry." Flenn didn't even try to look sympathetic. "I'm sorry, I think you'll have to find someplace else to meet." He stood up, signaling their time was ended.

"Oh, Father, whatever should I do? Christmas is a few weeks away and everywhere else is booked. I promised the girls we could meet at my church. I was so happy to offer it before Juanita could offer hers."

Flenn had ushered the woman half-way toward the door when he turned. "Juanita? Is that the Mrs. O'Reilly you referred to earlier?"

"Yes. Poor dear. She hasn't been the same since her

child ran away. You do know about that don't you, Father? You see the girl... "

Flenn cut her off. "Yes, I've heard. Maybe we *can* work something out after all. Go ahead and tell the ladies they can meet Tuesday at noon. The folks from overeaters are usually gone by then."

"Oh, thank you, Father. Thank you so much." She paused at the door. "Are you certain we couldn't meet at 11? It would suit us so much better; you see, I usually have my nails done during lunchtime on Tuesdays, and... "

"Noon, Delores."

"Oh well," she said with a smile. "You can't blame a girl for trying." Delores Dilwicky turned at the door to say her farewells. "I'll call them right away and let them know that we're on for Tuesday. Goodbye, Father! I must make a note to bring you some chamomile next time."

He stood at the vicarage door and watched her leave. *Next time? Good Lord!* Still, having Juanita O'Reilly at his parish on Tuesday might give him an opportunity to speak with her alone. As a priest, Flenn was allowed to be nosy, even expected to be. Juanita wouldn't think anything of his inquiring about her missing daughter. He just needed to figure out the best way to go about it. He felt a moment's shame at his intention to manipulate the situation, but reminded himself that he might come up with a way to help the woman locate her lost daughter.

Flenn made himself a cheese sandwich and retrieved the computer. He read everything over again, this time taking notes, just in case Zack's files suddenly disappeared. He wondered about Shelly's mysterious friends. Who were they, and why didn't the parents know more about them? And just who was this friend whose name began with the letter *D*?

CHAPTER TWENTY-EIGHT

A stocky, yet impeccably dressed guard stood in front of the mansion's gatehouse watching a convertible making its way up the drive. The early morning reflection off the car's red finish made it difficult to see the driver. However, the guard didn't have to see; he had been told to expect Father Flenn this morning.

Flenn turned off the radio—all he could find was Christmas music anyway—and allowed himself to enjoy the early December heatwave. With the top down, he was able to admire the understated charm of the Rye's estate. Sunlight made the dew glisten on the manicured lawn. The guard smiled and waved him on through. "Mrs. Rye is looking forward to your visit, Father Flenn. It's good to see you again. How about this weather, huh?"

"Morning, Nick. Winter in Birmingham, nothing quite like it," Flenn laughed. He pulled up the steep drive and parked between a vintage Cadillac and a six-passenger golf cart. Flenn knew the Ryes used the cart to get around their estate.

Willy Rye's home rivaled some of the New Hampshire mansions where Flenn had spent his childhood. The old preacher was not known for having many extravagances–– other than this 11-million-dollar house along with his wife's passion for antiques. Flenn had seen larger mansions, but few with as much warmth and character as this one, which he attributed all to Elizabeth Rye. Elizabeth was a gracious lady with impeccable taste. Tall and slender with a smile that could melt the coldest of hearts, Elizabeth was one of those people that it was impossible not to like.

An African-American woman ushered Flenn through the foyer into a cozy room finished in walnut trim and cherry-blossom wallpaper. This room had always smelled a bit like Elizabeth, Flenn thought, catching just the slightest hint of jasmine. It was the same room where they'd shared tea several times since Flenn had moved to Birmingham. Elizabeth had called on him as soon as he had arrived… "to reacquaint myself with the son of Davy Flenn," she had told him.

Coffee and warm muffins were arranged on a small table underneath an original oil painting of the famous Puritan, Jonathan Edwards. Across the room hung another painting, a rendering of Queen Elizabeth signing the Act of Uniformity, which had required British subjects to be members of the Church of England. He knew the second painting had been a gift from his own father, and that the irony of it had been totally lost on Willy Rye. Flenn shook his head and chuckled at Willy owning a painting of the event which had established the Anglican Church as the official Church of England and her colonies. His dad had told him about the gift the day Flenn had entered seminary. It had remained their own private joke to the day his father died. His dad had been the one who had insisted Elizabeth hang it in this very room across from the painting of Edwards. On one side of the parlor was order, decorum and reason; on the other, a harsh break from reasoned theology, and with it, the birth of fundamentalism.

The door opened. Elizabeth was her usual stunning self as she greeted him. Even as a kid, Flenn had noticed how she had a certain way about her when she entered a room. "It is so lovely to see you again, dear," she said offering her cheek. "I'm delighted you could come over this morning." Elizabeth made it sound as if the meeting had been her idea. "It has been too long, Scott. Please… " She motioned to a chair at the table that had been set with Aynsley china and Waterford crystal.

Flenn sat, but only after she did. A tall, gray-haired, black man in a three-piece suit entered the room and began to pour their coffee. He remembered Flenn liked his coffee black but offered his employer a tiny white porcelain bowl filled with sugar cubes atop a silver tray.

"Thank you, Edward," Elizabeth said to the man, who left as quietly as he had entered. "I am so sorry that Willy won't be joining us this morning."

Flenn couldn't recall the old man ever having met with them for breakfast, yet Elizabeth always felt she needed to make excuses. She had once told Flenn that her husband took his coffee alone as he read the morning paper in the solarium. The truth was that Flenn and Willy had never connected in the same way that he and Elizabeth had. "Please convey my warmest greetings to your husband."

Elizabeth took the silver tongs and dropped four sugar cubes into her coffee. "I will, but I'm afraid he has been struggling lately with remembering names." She tried to smile. "Although, I must say he is not nearly as bad as poor Ronnie was with dear Nancy at his side." Flenn knew she was referring to the late President Ronald and Nancy Reagan, once close friends of the Ryes.

Edward returned with a large silver tray, which he set atop a table next to Elizabeth. He lifted the top to uncover several smaller trays, from which he dished their breakfast of Eggs Benedict, pork tenderloin, and fruit compote. Edward poured more coffee, took the tray, and then disappeared. They ate their breakfast and spoke, as was their custom, of old times. Elizabeth occasionally referred to her husband's poor health, but would then quickly move on to another topic.

Finished with her few bites of breakfast—Flenn suspected she'd have been much happier with toast and a bit of jam—Elizabeth wiped the corner of her mouth and smiled. "So, dear, to what do I owe the honor of this visit, aside from your concern over my sweet William's health?"

Flenn sipped his coffee and met her gaze with a friendly smile of his own. "Elizabeth, you've got me. I do have a favor to ask."

He set the delicate china cup back on the saucer. "I'm thinking of backing Senator Contreras of New York in the upcoming presidential primaries. I'd be delighted to include you on the roster of guests for a gala I'm thinking of hosting in his honor."

Elizabeth maintained her composure quite well, Flenn thought. He assumed she must be horrified at his asking her to support a Democrat. "Why thank you so much, Scott, for thinking of us. I'm sure it would be grand, but as you know, William and I have always tried to stay out of the political spectrum."

Flenn knew quite the opposite to be true. "Still, I'd like you to think about it. Senator Contreras supports many of the same causes that you and I believe in so strongly."

Elizabeth smiled. "I'm sure that he does dear, however, at our age and in our position, I think it better that we continue to remain neutral in the days ahead, particularly with our nation coming out of that recent unpleasantness."

While Flenn hadn't given it much thought, the previous presidential debacle must have been an absolute affront to Elizabeth's good taste and sensibilities. Her husband had backed the man in so far as he had been the duly elected president, but Willy had been even less enthusiastic about the last president than he had been about any of the Democrats who'd held the office.

"Please don't let the fact that Senator Contreras is not a Republican dissuade you."

Elizabeth smiled warmly. "Of course not, dear. Willy and I have always been bipartisan." Elizabeth took a slow and deliberate sip from her cup. *Probably to keep herself from laughing out loud*, Flenn thought.

"So, you don't have a preference in this next election yet?"

"I simply couldn't say, Scott."

"What about Benji," Flenn said. "I hear that he has a good friend running as an independent." Elizabeth's eyes widened.

"Why, Scott, you never cease to amaze me! How on earth… " she caught herself. "I suppose you are referring to Benji's friend, Daniel Romero. Benjamin has known Danny for years. They met in college, you know. He was best man at Benji's wedding." She stirred her coffee again, and then raised her eyes to meet his. "So sorry you were unable to attend."

Flenn had intentionally missed the wedding, as well as any other event honoring Benjamin Rye over the years.

"You know how I love my sons," Elizabeth said. "At times, however, a mother's love is not enough. I spoiled Benjamin; protected him from Willy's wrath at times, when perhaps I shouldn't have. Benji grew to resent us both over the years, but then I know you're aware of all of that." They had spoken a time or two before of the estranged relationship between mother and son.

"Junior is very affectionate, and a good father—just no ambition." She exhaled slightly. "Benjamin—he's nothing but ambition. That has been his problem all along. He wants, so he takes." Elizabeth stopped herself from saying more. "Please, forgive the ramblings of an old woman."

"No apology necessary," Flenn offered, but continued

to probe. "I've never met Mr. Romero, but if he's running to be the next President of the United States, then I assume he has plenty of ambition himself."

"Among other things." *Clearly, Elizabeth Rye did not like her son's choice in a friend, and with good reason.* "Benjamin told us only recently that Daniel might be running."

"Well, the word is that he will be announcing after the first of the year."

"Honestly, Scott, I don't know how you stay on top of things the way you do." She reached for her tiny glass of orange juice. "Benjamin seems to be quite excited about it all, but his father and I have always cautioned him about not letting friendship cloud one's judgment. The Rye Foundation must not be seen endorsing any particular candidate."

"I understand." And he did. *Benjamin Rye was backing Romero.*

Flenn now had what he'd come for; he would relay the information to Zack and that would be that. *Or would it?* He changed the subject back to remembrances of summers long ago. When it was time to leave, Elizabeth took both his hands in hers and gazed deeply into Flenn's eyes. "Scott, you are the image of your father. Oh, how I do miss him." Elizabeth wiped the corner of one eye. "Davy was a special man." She squeezed his hands, "And, so are you, Scott, so are you."

Flenn gave her frail frame a gentle hug and showed himself to the door. He waved to Nick at the gatehouse. He felt badly about pumping this gracious and gentle lady for information, but a deal was a deal. Hopefully, that would be all Zack Matteson would need from him.

He shook his head.

Fat chance!

CHAPTER TWENTY-NINE

More than two dozen of Birmingham's self-perceived elite began filing into Saint Ann's parish hall just before 11 o'clock. Delores Dilwicky had yet to arrive. Father Flenn apologized profusely as he explained that he had explicitly told Delores that they could have their meeting at noon, not eleven. Since Saint Ann's had only one large meeting space, and it was currently occupied by another group, the women wandered into the Sunday School classrooms and pretended to be interested in the children's artwork on display.

Juanita O'Reilly arrived at the top of the hour, wearing a navy and white dress with a pearl necklace. Flenn knew Juanita, but not well. The two of them had once served together on a welcoming committee for the Archbishop of Canterbury. The councilman's wife was tall, blonde (ish) and looked 10 years younger than her actual age. Flenn recognized the telltale signs here and there of a skilled plastic surgeon.

"Juanita, it's so good to see you."

The woman held out her hand and gave him a practiced smile. "Scott," she said, never having caught on that most people called him Flenn, "thank you for offering us your parish hall for our meeting. I do hope it isn't inconvenient?"

"Not at all," Flenn lied. The folks from Overeaters Anonymous had complained loudly about having to rush their meeting. Flenn had assured them that it was only temporary. He started to explain about the mix-up when he caught a glimpse of Delores Dilwicky coming through the door. Delores was wearing a plaid, knee-length dress and an enormous black hat with tiny red polka dots. "Juanita, may I speak briefly with you after your meeting today?" He looked toward Delores. "In private?" he whispered.

Juanita looked surprised. "Of course, Scott. Is everything alright?"

He nodded. "Yes, I just need to speak with you when you're done. Delores," he called, looking past Juanita. "I thought we were clear that the meeting would be at noon!" Juanita looked at her Rolex and then at the plump woman coming down the hall.

Delores looked embarrassed. "Oh, did we? No, no I'm sure we said eleven."

Flenn managed to contain his anger. "Maybe you forgot that I told you that the other group *always* meets at this time?"

"You mean those fat people?"

It was Juanita who spoke next. "Delores, we could have used any one of a number of rooms at Saint Latimer's."

Delores' expression was that of a child with her hand

caught in the cookie jar. "No, Father, I'm certain you said eleven."

"Well," Juanita said, "obviously there's been a misunderstanding. I can see you don't have room for us here, Father." She glowered at Delores. "I guess we'll just have to cancel today's meeting."

"No, please," Flenn piped up, "I have an idea. Since your members are already here, why don't you use the church? The pews aren't ideal for a meeting, but it should do just for the one day. Then, you're free to use the parish hall in the future—at twelve."

Juanita smoothed the seam of her dress. "Thank you, Scott. The church will be just fine... *today*." She looked directly at Delores. "Next week, we'll meet at Saint Latimer's. Come, Delores, let's go inform the ladies."

Flenn retreated to the safety of his office as two dozen of Birmingham's well-to-do headed noisily to the church's nave. He planned to position himself near the church door at noon to make sure Juanita didn't forget to meet with him; however, a half hour hadn't passed when his door opened and Delores Dilwicky paraded into his office. "Thank you, Father Flenn," she said, with a look of triumph on her face. "We finished early, but we had such a delightful meeting!" Delores showed no sign of distress from the awkward situation earlier. *Probably told them it was all my fault,* Flenn thought. "Just about everyone was here, too! They all absolutely adored Saint Ann's and voted to meet here next week instead of at Saint Latimer's."

Well, thought Flenn, *chalk one up for Delores!*

"Noon, right?" Flenn said, maybe a bit too harshly.

"Yes, right, noon. Although, maybe you could have those other people leave a bit earlier? And, maybe you could make us a fresh pot of coffee, too. Some pastries would be nice. Yes, that would be just perfect. Thank you, Father!"

Flenn felt his face turning red just as Juanita knocked on the open door. Seeing Delores, she said, "I'm sorry, Scott. Maybe we should meet another time?"

Delores didn't take the hint. Flenn stood. "No, please don't go, Delores was just leaving."

Delores still didn't budge. "Oh, Juanita, I was just telling Father Flenn here how the ladies voted to meet at Saint Ann's instead of driving all the way over to Saint Latimer's. I also told him we would need that overeaters group to leave a bit early so we can get settled for our meeting."

"That won't be necessary," Juanita replied. "I'm sure our members won't mind waiting a few minutes. You know, dear," Juanita said, looking Delores up and down, "from what I hear they do wonderful work."

Flenn suppressed a grin. *Round Two goes to Juanita!*

"Um, well, yes, I'm sure they do," stammered Delores. Flenn's bottom lip quivered ever so slightly. "Forgive me, Father, but I must be on my way." Delores straightened her huge hat and walked sideways out the door. Flenn noticed a tiny bit of toilet tissue attached to her left heel. He started to call it to her attention but thought better of it.

"Juanita, please do come in." Flenn shut the door behind them, glad to be rid of the parish busybody. "You all finished early; I thought the meetings were for an hour."

Juanita fiddled with the clasp on her stylish, navy-blue purse. "They usually are, but as you said, pews aren't really suitable for a meeting. We won't trouble you for long; we'll be back in our regular place soon."

"Yes, I heard," he said, inviting her to sit. "Rodents of some sort, wasn't it?"

"Well, you know Birmingham... rats abound."

"They certainly do." Flenn wondered if Juanita knew that she was married to one.

"Juanita," he said sitting down across from her, "I wanted to tell you that your family has been in my prayers. I can't imagine how difficult all this must be on you. I trust your parish has rallied around you? I don't really know your rector that well, but his assistant, Minerva, and I go way back."

"Thank you, Scott," she said, smoothing her dress across her lap. "It has been... trying. To have your child suddenly disappear without a trace is more than any mother should have to endure." *The words seemed rehearsed, but then there was* no *telling how many people she'd had to thank for their concern over the past few months.*

"I can't begin to imagine. Have the police managed to find any clues?" Flenn studied her response... a twitching eye, quivering lip, refusal to make eye contact; all indicators of unease. Instead, she sat stoically, hands folded together in her lap.

"Absolutely nothing, I'm afraid. Shelly goes to school one day, calls to tell me she's going for a hamburger afterwards, and to catch a movie over at the Galleria with some friends... " She took a breath. "I haven't seen her since."

"What about the friends she went out with that night; what did they tell you?"

Juanita picked at a thread on the arm of the chair. "That's just it, apparently Shelly didn't do any of those things. The police went through all the surveillance videos in the theater and from the Galleria. There was no sign of her in any of them." Juanita confirmed what Flenn had already read in the police reports. "There were lots of teenagers at the theater. After all, it was a Friday night in May. But, there was no sign of Shelly."

"So, none of her friends at school know what happened?"

She shook her head. "Do you have children, Scott?"

Flenn's eyes darted to the floor and back. "No, I don't."

Juanita nodded ever so slightly. "Be grateful. Sometimes you want to strangle them, but then something like this happens and you're left..." She didn't finish the sentence.

Flenn felt a twinge of guilt, but still he pressed. "None of her friends had any idea where she went that night?"

She looked down at the loose thread. "No. That's just the thing. Shelly kept telling us that she was going out with all these new friends, but we never knew who they were. I guess Mac and I weren't as attentive as we should have been."

Flenn shifted in his seat.

"We were just so delighted that she was finally living a normal, teenaged life. She had a habit of keeping to herself."

"Juanita," Flenn began the lie he had rehearsed. "As you probably know, my family has lots of connections. One of those is with an excellent detective agency up East. They're very discreet. So discreet, they only hire themselves out to a select few. One phone call from me, however, and they'd be here by the end of the week."

Their eyes met. "My husband said we shouldn't hire detectives, that they would just interfere with the investigation."

I bet he said that! Flenn managed somehow to conceal his anger. "We could just keep it between the two of us. We wouldn't have to tell anyone. Believe me, these people are good at working behind the scenes; as I said, they're very discreet."

"Thank you, Scott. You're very sweet to offer, but… "

Now came the kicker. "If it were my child, I would definitely want these people on my side."

She stiffened. "And yet, as you said, you do not have a child."

He hated himself right now. "But if I did… "

Juanita thought for a moment. "No, but thank you very much."

Was she afraid, or just not used to making decisions without the man?

"Trust me. It'll just be between the two of us."

He searched her eyes for something… anything.

What he saw was neither pain nor frustration. It was something else, something odd, distant.

"If you would like to give them a call, I suppose it would be alright; but just for a consult. I wouldn't want them to interfere with what the police are doing—and not a word to my husband."

Fear! That must be what was behind the cool demeanor. Juanita was afraid of Mac O'Reilly.

Flenn picked up a notepad and pen. "Sure, we can do that. But, I know these guys; they are going to want me to give them as much information as I can, so I'll need to ask you a few questions."

CHAPTER THIRTY

An ice storm was on the way. The temperature had dropped more than 50 degrees overnight. Guy Rainsford couldn't believe it; just yesterday it had been warm and sunny. According to weather reports, a massive snowstorm predicted for Kentucky, Tennessee, and northern Alabama was likely to break over Birmingham and turn into ice for the metropolitan area. Montgomery, 80 miles to the south, was only expecting rain. The last time this had happened, thousands of motorists had been stranded on the roads overnight. Guy remembered the Interstates had looked like something from a zombie-apocalypse movie, with thousands of cars motionless in the ice. The only difference being that the people stranded inside these cars had been alive—evidenced by the occasional dash to the side of the road to answer nature's call.

All off-duty police had been called in to work the storm. The mayor had rescinded leave for firefighters and municipal emergency personnel as well. Word had come down through each department: Everyone was on duty till the ice melted. *Which could be well into tomorrow!* griped Guy as he headed to work on what was supposed to have been his first day off in two weeks.

It had been raining when he'd left home, but by the time he reached University Boulevard, the rain had mixed with sleet. As he always seemed to be lately, Guy was occupied with thoughts of Lindsay and her sleaze-ball pimp. Guy looked forward to the day he'd finally be able to charge Ramirez and lock him up for good. Unfortunately, that day didn't appear to be anytime soon, not unless he could figure out what had happened to Lindsay.

Guy blew his nose. Thankfully, his cold hadn't gone to his chest—he wasn't sure there was room; his heart was too full of sympathy for this poor kid. *The priest was right. He was Lindsay's family now, and he would do everything he could to find her killer!* At New Beginnings, Roxanne had told him about the perverts she'd serviced. Not vermin off the street with money in their pockets, but businessmen and executives. "My clients were lawyers, doctors; *hell, even a preacher,*" she'd told him.

It hit him like a ton of bricks!

He pulled over to the curb and sat with the ignition running. *What preacher could possibly afford a $3,000 hooker?!* He turned off the wipers as the sleet began to ping on the windshield. Only one name came to mind.

It couldn't have been him—could it?

Guy flipped open his computer and checked the database for the names of ministers who had been charged with child pornography in the past five years. Father Flenn's name was not on the list. Guy had already checked the priest out online, enough to know that Flenn had come from a wealthy background, served with honors in the Air Force, left the military to represent his family's business interests overseas for several years, then attended an Episcopal seminary in Tennessee to study for the priesthood. Never married, and no children—at least none on record.

Waiting for the sleet to subside, Guy searched through department files for anything having to do with Father Flenn. The priest's name was listed under several community action groups around town, but Flenn had kept his nose clean—with one notable exception. He had been arrested a few years ago as part of a demonstration down in Montgomery. The protest had been against a controversial ruling by the state legislature concerning suspected illegal immigrants. Guy recalled the furor that had swept the state back then and how he'd viewed that ruling as racist, especially considering its backers. The country had seen some of those same people later rise to national status, only to fall into obscurity soon thereafter.

The report said that Father Flenn had been arrested for intervening in a scuffle between two police officers and a Latino teenager. Interestingly, Flenn had refused to make bond. He'd been released only after surveillance footage showed the officers in question were the ones who'd been out of line. Guy managed to locate the footage on the web: *The priest certainly could handle himself!* The video showed Flenn had little difficulty defending the teenager or deflecting the cops' truncheons when the officers turned on him. *Someone willing to face down two cops to help a skinny, Hispanic kid was not likely the kind of person who would have ever harmed Lindsay.*

He had another idea. Guy pulled out his phone and called the church. Maybe Father Flenn knew other preachers involved with ministries to the girls downtown. Perhaps one of them would turn out to be the preacher Roxanne had mentioned. He'd already called Ashleigh Nieves to request the names of Roxanne's Johns. As expected, Roxanne had said she "couldn't recall" anyone's name.

"Saint Ann's, Iriana Racks speaking," came the voice from over the phone.

"Yes, Miss… *Racks*? Is Father Flenn in today?"

"No sir, I'm afraid he's out this morning. May I take a message?"

He'd never met the priest's secretary but couldn't help wonder what a woman named *Racks* looked like. "Would you ask him to call Detective Rainsford please? Tell him it's important." Guy gave her his number and then tossed the phone onto the passenger seat. The phone rang several minutes later as he pulled into his parking spot at the station.

"Detective Rainsford, good morning. This is Scott Flenn. I hear you're looking for me?"

Guy kept the engine running, unwilling to lose the warmth from the car's heater. "Thank you, Father, for calling me back so quickly."

"My secretary was beside herself! It's not often she gets a phone call from a detective telling her something is urgent."

"Sorry about that. I think the word I used was

important. I didn't mean to pull you out of a meeting or anything."

"It's okay. I'm with a sick friend at the moment." Flenn glanced up at Zack Matteson, who gave him the finger. "A very old friend. Delusional. He won't do anything he's told." Zack rolled his eyes. Flenn had been furious about the surprise phone call this morning announcing that Zack was in Birmingham.

Guy managed to suppress a sneeze. "I'm sorry to hear that, Father. I won't keep you."

"Take all the time you want."

Zack shook his head and walked up the aisle toward the cathedral's altar, muttering something under his breath. Flenn had agreed to meet with Zack inside the Church of the Advent after Zack had called and simply said that, "Thomas Cranmer was on his way into town."

Flenn was angry, but still figured he owed Zack for his help with the laptop. "Meet me at the cathedral," Flenn had told him. "I'll be the one with the huge frown!"

He looked at Zack, who was studying the ornate, wooden pulpit. For all his rough edges, Zack knew quality woodwork when he saw it. Zack used to regale Flenn with stories of his childhood and how he had spent hours in his dad's woodshop. Flenn looked across the church at a stained-glass representation of Joseph, another carpenter's father, and couldn't help but wonder at the irony. Guy Rainsford brought Flenn back to the moment with a question. "Father, I'm wondering if you know of any other pastors that have, or have had, a ministry with the working girls downtown?"

Flenn couldn't think of anyone. "None that come to mind. The ladies don't seem to draw a lot of sympathy from very many churchgoers," he said. "Kind of strange when you think about how much time Jesus spent with prostitutes in his day." Flenn watched as Zack ran his hand across the massive pulpit.

"It's just that, well, one girl told me about this preacher." Guy cleared his throat. "Actually, he had been one of her clients."

"How did she know he was a minister?"

Guy hadn't thought of that. *How had Roxanne known?* "I don't know. Maybe he wore a collar like you do."

"Maybe, but then I think she would have called him a priest. We're usually the only ones wearing these funny looking shirts with the collars turned backwards. Plus, I doubt a minister looking for a prostitute would advertise his vocation. In fact, I'd think he'd have gone to great lengths to hide it."

"I suppose you're right," Guy said. "You should have been a detective, Father."

If only you knew, Flenn thought. "So, is there a reason you're focusing on this preacher?"

"Isn't it obvious?" answered Guy. "I mean, if a minister would solicit a prostitute, then he could do just about anything."

Flenn frowned. "Detective, ministers are just people. Flesh and blood like everyone else. I don't know that you ought to single this one man out simply because he was a pastor." Flenn realized he sounded defensive. *Maybe the detective wondered if he might be hiding something? Still, too many people thought like Guy Rainsford. Ministers were supposed to be above the fray… super-human, unscathed by the real world.* Flenn knew that wasn't the case; he also knew that pastors who tried to live up to that expectation had a long way to fall once their pedestals crumbled, which they nearly always did. "I'm sorry I can't be more helpful. I'll call if I come up with anything."

Flenn stuffed the phone back into his pocket and walked over to Zack, who was still examining the pulpit.

"Not a bad piece of work. In fact," Zack said looking around, "this is actually an interesting building."

"You always seem surprised at what you find when you walk into a church," Flenn clipped. "Maybe you should walk into more of them."

"Is that why you always arrange our meetings in churches? Trying to convert me?"

"If only," Flenn whispered.

"What?"

"We meet in churches, doofus, because I have ready access to them and they're generally free from eavesdroppers."

"Oh?" Zack quipped. "What about that woman up there?" An elderly woman wearing a velvet headband was carrying a roll of cloth into the sanctuary. Flenn explained that the sanctuary was what most protestant churches call the inside of the entire church, but in an Episcopal church, the sanctuary was only the area surrounding the altar. "Maybe that's what is wrong with you religious types," Zack offered. "You can't even agree on your terminology."

Flenn ignored the jibe. "That lady is on their altar guild. She's getting ready for the communion service here this evening."

Zack raised an eyebrow. "During an ice storm?"

"What is it the Hollywood folks like to say? 'The show must go on.'"

"Aha!" Zack jibed. "I always knew it was a show."

Flenn poked Zack's chest. "You're not fooling me, Zack. There's got to be a heart in there… somewhere."

Zack shrugged. "If there is, Donna never found it."

"Yes she did, and so did your kids. That's what scares you. By the way, have you called them yet?" Flenn knew he hadn't.

Zack ignored the jibe and pointed to a nearby pew. "Let's talk before Birmingham becomes a giant popsicle." They sat down underneath a stained-glass representation of Jesus feeding the multitude. Zack reached into his pocket and pulled out a handful of jellybeans. He offered one to Flenn, who refused. "So, have you talked with Willy Rye's wife yet?"

Flenn looked at him. "First, tell me the rest of the story… including all those pieces you left out before."

"Okay; just don't say I didn't warn you." Zack glanced around the nave. "Daniel Romero is about to announce his bid for the presidency. He's in league with some pretty nasty folks."

Flenn nodded. "Yeah, you told me. Iran."

Zack shifted slightly. Pews weren't made to be comfortable. "There's more."

"There always is… "

"It's *why* the Iranians are supporting him. Apparently, there has been a huge breach in the upcoming election."

"All the more reason you need to report this to Langley," Flenn said.

Zack simply looked away.

"Okay, so how does Benji Rye fit into all this?"

Zack glanced around the church again. The woman in the velvet headband had finished arranging the altar linens and was leaving through a side door. "Their price is for Romero to look the other way when Iran decides to attack another country a couple of years from now."

Flenn felt a familiar churning in his gut. *Why did it only happen when Zack Matteson was around?* "Iraq?" he asked.

Zack shook his head.

"Not Syria," Flenn mused. "They're allies. No need to attack them. They hate the Saudis, but they wouldn't... would they?" Again, Zack shook his head. Flenn thought for a moment.

"No! You've got to be kidding me?"

"I wish I were."

"That would be suicide!"

"Ordinarily, yes. But think about it; if America doesn't intervene, then Britain won't and the European Union certainly won't—at least not anymore—which leaves Israel without a friend. And if Iran has gotten as good at infiltrating computer systems as they appear to have, then they must be working on hacking Israel's nuclear strike capability."

"There's a big difference, Zack, between a voting booth and a nuclear command center!"

"I sure hope so; but from what I heard, it looks like Amir is pretty sure of himself."

"Colonel Amir?" Flenn pulled out a copy of the *Book of Common Prayer* from the pew rack in front of him. He needed something to hold onto right now.

"Yeah. Remember him?"

Flenn nodded. "I'll never forget. Still, I can't imagine the United States staying out of something like this," he said. "We've been Israel's strongest ally since '48. Are you sure someone's not pulling your chain?"

"This is legit, Flenn. I watched a dozen people get blown into tiny bits to keep this under wraps."

"Yet somehow you escaped?"

"I know what you're saying, but, no, it wasn't staged for my benefit."

"How do you know for certain? Iran is certainly capable of a stunt like that."

Zack shook his head. "Yeah, but to what purpose? There's no scenario where that would even make sense. No, in every plan there's an unknown... " He looked at his friend. "In this case, *I'm* the unknown."

Zack didn't say anything about the man he had seen shadowing him. *No need... not yet*, he thought. Zack had managed yesterday to get a clear picture of the man who'd been following him. He'd sent it to Langley who informed him that it was Farhad Ahmad, one of Col. Amir's men known to be stationed in London. Zack had seen Ahmad's car park across the street from the cathedral as he was going inside. He figured Ahmad wouldn't be so brazen as to follow him into the church.

Flenn fell back in the pew and looked up toward the altar. "And now we could both be in danger if they find out you are talking with me," he said. "Gee thanks, Zack." Flenn rubbed his forehead. A major headache was on the way. He needed caffeine. "Zack, this is huge! You've got to go to Langley right away."

"And say what? I don't have a shred of proof. Everyone in Washington is walking on eggshells these days. They're all afraid to make waves right now. The people I would normally go to aren't there anymore; they all got fired or quit during all that mess. And the jackasses that replaced them are too consumed with bureaucratic doubletalk and protecting their own jobs to know how to handle anything like this."

Zack always had a reason for not calling in the cavalry until the last minute, but his friend might not be exaggerating this time. The last few years had seen Washington go from reasonable order to outright chaos. It still baffled Flenn how the last man he'd have thought would have been electable had won the nomination against a slate of several very talented individuals. True, President Ripley hadn't lasted a complete term, but everyone seemed to still be overly distrustful of one another in D.C. these days. Flenn drew a deep breath and glanced over at his old friend. "Again, what does this have to do with Benjamin Rye?"

"I was just getting to that." Zack popped a jellybean in his mouth. "It looks as if Iran has its fingers in the new voting software being implemented in several states right now."

Flenn nodded. "I read something about that recently. Most of the Southern states haven't expressed an interest in using it."

Zack grinned. "Yeah; I hear some down here are still using the 'hands up if you're for him' method."

Flenn didn't laugh.

"Anyway, that's why Romero brought Benjamin Rye into all this. Rye has a huge influence with the religious right. None of the other right-leaning, mega-church preachers would dare go against the son of Willy Rye."

"Rye and Romero are old college buddies," Zack said, though Flenn already knew that. "They left quite a wake up at Princeton from what I've been able to find out."

"What kind of wake?"

"Mostly young girls… they had some sort of scam to seduce high schoolers. It was kept under wraps, but I talked with one of the former deans who told me that several principals had complained to him about Romero and Rye back then. He had tried to have them expelled but was told to keep quiet. He suspects someone pulled some strings. No one ever brought charges."

"Money talks," Flenn said, disgusted but not surprised.

"Not as loudly as religion."

"Since when have you been interested in religion?"

Zack shook his head. "Are you kidding? Religion has been the driving force behind most of the world's problems." Flenn shot him a look. "Okay, maybe not religion as it was intended to be, but the religion of narcissistic imams and preachers full of hate—the religion of militias, dictators, white supremacists, and terrorists. What I'm interested in right now, though, is *Willy Rye's type* of religion."

Flenn rubbed his temple, trying to chase the headache away. "Other than backing every Republican candidate since Nixon, Rye hasn't been as politically minded as most of those other television evangelists. To my knowledge the Rye Foundation has always been on the up and up. They do some amazing work with the poor here at home and in third world nations."

Zack seemed unimpressed, but then, Flenn thought, *Zack was unimpressed with almost everyone's accomplishments. He always suspected people in the limelight of having somehow cheated to get there.*

"So, how long have you known Benjamin Rye?"

"Too long," Flenn answered. "Like I told you up in Cullman, our families used to hang out in the summer. Dad was a huge contributor; we went out to their cabin on the Cahaba River a lot. Very nice place, except for Benji being there. He was a bully. Mean as a snake to his brother. Tried that with me—once."

"What happened?"

Flenn smiled. "What do you think happened? I beat the snot out of him."

"That usually works," said Zack.

"Benji was all bluster. Still is, as far as I'm concerned."

Zack considered that for a moment. "You believe all the hype about his so-called conversion awhile back?"

Flenn was silent for a moment. "It's not for me to judge the sincerity of someone's faith," he finally said. "I for one know the power of a changed heart."

"But?"

"I don't trust him. My gut says he's as big a fraud as he was when he used to convince his mama that he was sick and couldn't do his chores at the cabin."

"Oh, he's convinced her of a lot more than that, from what my sources tell me," Zack said. "I've talked to a couple of his other roommates from college, before he and Romero moved in together. They couldn't stand Rye. They said he used to brag for hours about all the things he got away with at home."

"Not to defend the jerk, but being the son of a famous preacher, I expect he felt he had to go to extra lengths to prove he fit in. The ultimate case of preacher's kid syndrome."

"What's that?"

"It's where you try to prove to the world that you're not a goody-two-shoes." Flenn's head was splitting in two. He'd go to the cathedral's kitchen after Zack left and see if he could find some coffee. "Most teens are rebellious, but P.K.'s can take it to the next level."

"So, do you or don't you believe all the hype about Rye's conversion?"

Flenn fidgeted. "I've known his mother for years. She's the one who doesn't believe it. She hasn't come right out and said it, but I've worked with her on some charities here in town and she's hinted at her doubts on occasion. I don't think she's nearly as naïve as you say.

She loves both her sons but isn't particularly proud of either of them. She's been trying for the past two years to convince the old man to fix it so that the foundation's board of directors will have most of the power after he's gone; not Benji. The younger brother, Junior, isn't on the board; doesn't want to be."

Flenn set the *Book of Common Prayer* on the pew beside him. "Willy needed so badly to believe in Benji. It was the ultimate Gospel story... you know, where the sinner sees the error of his ways and everything's changed for good."

Zack nodded. "Sort of like when Scrooge wakes up on Christmas morning?"

"Exactly," Flenn said. "Who wouldn't want to believe their child capable of a change like that?" Flenn thought for a moment. "You really believe Benjamin Rye could sway the fundamentalist vote away from the Republicans?"

"Don't you?"

Flenn didn't answer. "What about an attack on Israel? Evangelicals would revolt right away."

Zack looked around the nave again. "From what I overheard, they're working on an anti-Semitic stance that'll build distrust of Jews in general. If history is any indicator, that won't be such a hard sell." Zack paused, then looked at Flenn. "Let me ask you... do you think Benjamin Rye could actually go that far?"

"What? Sell out Israel? Sure, in a heartbeat if there was something in it for him. But, could he convince the average Bible-toting Christian to ignore Israel? No way."

"What if the two of them could build up enough animosity toward the Jews over the next couple of years?"

Flenn cringed. Part of his and Zack's espionage training had been to learn how to plant seeds of doubt and distrust. *What was it every nation did when they were about to go to war? They demonized their enemy, made them seem less than human. It is always easier to justify violence if you can dehumanize an entire race of people. The Jews had been dehumanized so many times throughout history that a clever administration, with Benjamin Rye's help, might just be able to do it again!*

"Yes," Flenn finally admitted. "I suppose Benji Rye is someone who could do just that."

"That's why I need to know where his support will lie. If he's in bed with Romero then we're in for a rocky road ahead, unless someone intervenes."

"And you're that someone?"

Zack didn't answer.

Flenn fumbled with the *Book of Common Prayer* again, but his eyes couldn't focus. This was all too horrible to fathom. *If Daniel Romero indeed had Iran's help, and Benjamin Rye brought the religious right away from the Republicans, then Romero, as a third-party candidate, was a shoe-in to be elected!*

One question remained. *What was in it for Rye?* There was one obvious answer. Romero had promised Rye a place at the table. The thought of Benji Rye sitting in a position of real power sent chills down Flenn's spine. He hardly knew anything about Daniel Romero, but he knew an awful lot about Benji Rye, and the jerk had a long history as a charlatan and a bully. *There had been too many of those in Washington lately,* Flenn thought.

Flenn's eyes cut over toward Zack. "I've already met with Elizabeth."

Zack tensed. "And?"

"Benji will be supporting Romero."

Zack glanced down at the *Book of Common Prayer* on the pew next to Flenn. He sighed. "Looks like we are going to need some rather *uncommon* prayers pretty soon, huh?"

CHAPTER THIRTY-ONE

Roxanne was dashing through the mall for work when the headline in the bookstore window stopped her dead in her tracks:

"WILLY RYE MEETS HIS LORD"

USA Today had a smaller headline than the *Birmingham Post*: "Famous Evangelist Dead at 93."

Roxanne shuddered as she made her way to *Le Chic*, no longer worried about being late. The television in the back room of the dress shop was tuned to a local news station. Reporters were standing outside the giant, mirrored-glass building that was home to the Rye Foundation. Roxanne turned the sound down as she clocked in for the day.

"Hey, I was watching that!" the assistant manager groused. "That man helped put Birmingham on the map, you know."

Roxanne turned the sound back up. "Sorry," she said, even though she wasn't. Throughout the day, staff and customers kept talking about the preacher's death. Everyone in Birmingham seemed to have a Willy Rye story:

"I saw Willy when mama took us down to Legion Field back in '82..."

"He and his wife came into my daddy's diner once..."

"I met his son; not the good looking one, you know, that really fat one..."

Between the television in the backroom and customers' constant anecdotes, Roxanne was glad when her shift finally ended. She clocked out hurriedly, relieved to be away from the constant praise of the Rye family, and went downstairs to the food court to buy a strawberry smoothie, just as she did every day after work. A big man stepped in line ahead of her, also asking for a strawberry smoothie. His accent sounded a lot like her new boyfriend, Juan, who was from Mexico.

Roxanne smiled for the first time since coming into work. *She couldn't really call Juan her boyfriend,* she reminded herself, *not just yet.* They had only met a few weeks ago. He worked in a shop she liked to browse after work. He was a year younger and lived close to the mall. She'd left work early one day and gone over to his house while his parents were away. They had made out, but she hadn't gone too far, and she wouldn't anytime soon. That was just something she wasn't ready for, not after all she had been through. *Who knows,* she thought as she waited in line, *maybe she'd hold off until she was married.* Roxanne couldn't help but smile. *Wouldn't that be awesome!*

As she turned to leave, the big man bumped into her, sending her drink splattering across the floor. "I am *so* sorry," the man apologized. "I'm such a clumsy fool! Please forgive me. I wasn't watching what I was doing." Roxanne bent down to try and wipe up the mess as the girl behind the counter called to someone in the backroom for a mop. "Here, please, take mine," the man offered. "It's strawberry, the same as yours. I haven't touched it yet."

Roxanne thanked him, but declined.

"No, I insist," he said, pushing the cup into her hand. I'll order another one. Please, I feel bad." He turned to the girl at the register. "Actually, just give me a soda instead," he told her. The girl behind the counter poured his drink as a skinny kid with a mop came grudgingly out from the back to clean up the mess. The big man turned back to Roxanne: "I'm really very sorry."

"No harm done," she replied with a smile. Roxanne walked the length of the Galleria sipping the smoothie and thinking about Juan. She knew he was off work today but hopefully she'd see him tomorrow. She stopped to look at the puppies in the pet store. She checked the time; the bus left at 5:30. She was supposed to be back no later than 6 o'clock; that was the rule. She didn't mind. New Beginnings was helping turn her life around, and if that meant having a curfew and obeying a few rules, then that was a small price to pay.

The puppies looked odd. Their noses began to blend

together, and they seemed to be walking funny. Roxanne rubbed her eyes, remembering she hadn't eaten all day. *That must be it*, she told herself. She took another sip of the sugary drink and shook her head, trying to clear her mind. She hadn't noticed the man with the soda following her, nor had she seen him earlier when he had poured powder into his smoothie—the same one he'd given her.

Roxanne was feeling worse. She looked at the cup in her hand—*rotten strawberries*, she thought, and threw it in a trashcan. The walls around her seemed to be moving, swaying back and forth. She decided to go outside for some air and to wait for the bus. The Guatemalan followed her outside. "Roxanne?" The girl turned, but her eyes couldn't focus on anything. She was starting to lose her balance.

"Yeth?"

He reached around her shoulder to steady her. "Are you okay?"

Roxanne couldn't make the man out; everything was too blurry. "I don't feel good."

"Here let me help you. It's not far." He'd decided against trying to slip into New Beginnings. The guards there were even bigger than he was. No, he'd simply followed her around the mall for a few days. *People were such creatures of habit,* he'd mused. Each day Roxanne went to the food court for a strawberry smoothie before going to talk to some pimply Latino kid.

The Guatemalan led Roxanne to his rental car, which he'd parked away from the only security camera in the area. She was almost completely out. As he pushed her into the back seat, he ran his hands down her lissome body and smelled her sweet perfume. "Que lastima," he whispered. *Unfortunately, there just wasn't enough time.*

He drove to a secluded road several miles out before stopping the car and pulling a syringe from the glove box. He uncapped the needle, took her left arm, and inserted it carefully into the vein. He gave her the full syringe, then drove outside of town to find a secluded spot where he could dump the body.

CHAPTER THIRTY-TWO

Benjamin Rye was worried. Not about the future, Danny had that mapped out in minute detail. Nor about his past, the Guatemalan seemed to be handling that with relative ease; although, Rye still hadn't told Danny about his secretary… or her twins. Rye wasn't quite sure if he was done with them yet. It had been easy enough to buy their silence so far. *If that ever changed… well, a second visit from Danny's gorilla would just have to be arranged.*

No, what worried Rye right now was money.

Rye had set the wheels in motion, just as Danny had instructed, but he was going to need cash soon, and lots of it. Even if he was able to pull strings at the Rye Foundation, he still didn't have access to the ministries' coffers. With a meager three million in his personal accounts, he wasn't about to spend his own money in case Danny's scheme backfired.

Danny, on the other hand, came from real money. Rye knew the story of how Danny's great-great grandfather, Vincenzo Romero, had emigrated with his family to Guatemala from Sicily. Vincenzo's parents had brought with them huge dreams. They had purchased a rum distillery—which they'd promptly run into the ground. Penniless, Vincenzo had been forced to leave home as a boy and hire himself out to a railroad gang run by one of the coffee cartels. It was there where Vincenzo Romero had learned to fight. He'd killed a man when he was just 17, a dozen more by the time he was 20. When the fruit companies had battled the coffee cartels for control of the railways, Vincenzo quickly sized up which side would likely prevail and aligned himself with United Fruit. It wasn't long before his talents were noticed. Thanks to Vincenzo's ruthlessness, the hired guns from the coffee interests began to disappear one by one. Vincenzo had been rewarded handsomely for his work, money which he invested with the fruit conglomerate. He was a rich man by the time he was 30 and went into business on his own. By then, Vincenzo had been able to afford to hire others to do the killing for him.

Four generations later, the Romero's business ventures had made them one of the wealthiest families in Central America. Their most lucrative interest these days was AlphaNet, a telecommunications operation. Danny's father and uncle had established the company in Guatemala before his father had moved the family to America. As cell phones and digital technology rose to the fore, AlphaNet became a major player throughout Central America. After Danny's father died of lung cancer, his uncle had offered him his dad's shares if he would help the company establish a beachhead in the United States. According to Danny, it hadn't been easy. The big-three phone companies had fought AlphaNet at every turn.

"Come on, answer the damn phone!" Rye said aloud.

"Hello?"

"Danny? We need to talk!"

"I thought we agreed not to discuss business over the phone," Romero answered, surprised to hear Benji's voice. It wasn't that Romero was paranoid; he just knew, better than most, how easy it was to listen in on a supposedly private conversation.

"Yeah, well things are getting expensive, Danny. There are more flyers to mail, religious organizations to visit, television and internet adds to pay for; it's getting pretty pricy."

"Again," Romero said, "I'm not talking about this with you over the phone. I'm trying to finalize plans to announce, and I'm knee deep in negotiations for my number two. I've got a huge gala to plan for Brad Cochrane in two weeks."

"The senator from Tennessee? I thought you called him a hillbilly?"

"You do your thing, Benji, and let me do mine. I'll send you what I promised."

"I just… "

"Don't call me again!"

"But… "

"Just do your damn job!" Romero hung up and threw the phone across his office. *He and Benji had too much at stake for things to get mucked up now by a stupid lapse in judgment!* He went to the credenza and poured himself a drink. *Benji was nervous, that was all. Everything was set;* Romero reminded himself, *Benji just needed to have faith in the bigger picture. Of course, faith had never been Benji's long suit.*

He downed the drink and poured a second. *They couldn't risk being seen together from this point on—Benji would need to at least appear to be making a fair and balanced decision when the time came.*

The first phase was already underway. Thanks to Benji, the Rye Foundation was calling for a nation-wide year of prayer for the next election. Phase two had been harder to talk Benji into—a televised crusade to begin in Houston in July and end in Washington just before the election, where Benjamin Rye would do what his daddy never had and publicly endorse someone to be the next President of the United States. As far as he was concerned, Romero didn't care if Benji ever did another crusade, but this one was going to be crucial. It would secure the evangelical base which Romero would need to persuade the country in a couple of years not to interfere with Iran's plans toward Israel.

Romero was no fool. He knew better than to double cross Col. Amir, or his handler, Sadar Abbas. *They wouldn't be able to touch him while he was in office, but afterwards... well, there were a lot fewer Secret Service assigned after one left the White House! No, he'd live up to his part of the bargain. What did Israel matter anyway? Just a headache to one administration after another. He'd be doing America a favor. And if not; well, what the hell... he'd still be the president!*

CHAPTER THIRTY-THREE

"So, what can you tell me about Juanita O'Reilly?" Scott Flenn sat across from his bishop and friend, Tom Morrison, as both men sipped single-malt Scotch in front of the vicarage fireplace. Nights like this had become a ritual ever since Flenn had come to Saint Ann's and the bishop had learned they shared a taste for expensive Scotch.

Flenn picked up his glass of sixteen-year-old Lagavulin, finished it, then reached for the bottle on the mahogany coffee table between them. *Two dead girls, one of them missing; an upcoming presidential election about to be hijacked. Israel facing certain catastrophe in the future; and, Zack Matteson was back—Yes, he definitely could use another drink!*

Flenn leaned back into the sofa. He had given Tom his favorite chair, a leather recliner that didn't just sit comfortably; it embraced you as if it were a lover. The bishop had discovered its charms several years, and even more glasses of Scotch, ago. Tonight, however, Bishop Morrison was having to share it with a sleeping cat who'd refused to budge.

"Juanita? She's an angel," the bishop said. "She's super involved with the diocese, you know. She's on diocesan council this year; just rotated off the standing committee." He took a sip of Scotch. "Of course, she would have to be an angel to be married to Mac O'Reilly. I can't stand that man!"

Tom Morrison was one of the select few who knew about Scott Flenn's clandestine past. Flenn had thought his father-in-God should know the backstory of his new priest six years ago when Flenn had first come into the diocese. It had been a lot to handle, but Tom had processed it all quite well. They had become close friends after that. Flenn figured his bishop knew a lot of secrets, which was exactly why he had invited him over tonight. Flenn was on a fishing expedition. As a lure, he had been sure to tempt Tom with his favorite malt.

Flenn stared down at the amber liquid inside his glass. "I have to agree with you on that one, Tom," Flenn said. "Mac O'Reilly is a pompous ass."

The bishop smiled. "Shame on you, Father! Does your congregation know you curse like that?"

"Probably." Flenn smiled. "They don't know that you do, though."

"Let's keep it that way," the bishop said with a smile. "People like to think their clergy are perfect." He shook his head. "God knows why; we sure screw things up enough." Mama Kitty shifted, draping herself now across the bishop's lap. "Not to mention the ones who are nothing more than wolves in sheep's clothing."

Flenn thought of the mysterious preacher, the one Detective Rainsford had asked about; and then of another preacher—one gaining notoriety of late, one

Flenn couldn't stand. "You mean people like Benjamin Rye?"

Bishop Morrison raised an eyebrow. "Funny you should mention him." He reached for the bottle. "Rye came to my office a couple of weeks ago and wanted to leave a bunch of pamphlets for me to hand out to all our parishes—as if! I mean, I'm sorry about his dad's death and all, but I just don't like that guy. He's always seemed smarmy to me." Tom Morrison looked at Flenn and grinned. "Funny thing, you know; I've always thought you two looked a lot alike."

"Please!" Flenn had heard it before; the first time from his own mother, oddly enough. Flenn leaned forward. "What kind of pamphlets?"

"Apparently, the Rye Foundation is already gearing up for next year's election. They usually wait until after the summer conventions before they start promoting the Republican nominee. Not this year. He's asking for a season of prayer *before* the election, and he's calling out *both* parties for their gross negligence of the spiritual state of our country."

"Both parties? That's unusual." Flenn put down his drink. "I don't suppose I can have a copy?"

"Too late. I filed them."

Flenn grinned. "File 13, I assume?"

The bishop nodded. "I mean, usually they just mail this crap out, but Rye actually made an appointment and came to my office with them. Handed them to me personally."

"Well, the Rye Foundation isn't all that far from the diocesan office," Flenn said.

The bishop made a face. "Don't remind me. Things have a different smell over there since Benjamin Rye began taking over." He looked at Flenn. "I guess I shouldn't say that now that his old man is gone. Willy was a good guy. I didn't always agree with his politics or his theology, but he was authentic."

Flenn hoisted his glass in the air. "I'll drink to that." Flenn planned to skip the funeral at the convention center and pay his condolences to Elizabeth later. There would be too many dignitaries at the funeral, including several from the White House—which meant Secret Service. A few of those agents might remember him; besides, he didn't need any more reminders of his past. Zack Matteson's sudden appearance had been more than enough.

"So, back to Juanita O'Reilly. Why do you say she is an angel?"

"Well, she's served on diocesan council, the standing committee, the diocesan capital funds campaign, the… "

"Yeah, all the stuff that really gets your hands dirty helping people," Flenn said, a bit too brusquely. He set his glass down on the coffee table. *Maybe he'd had enough.*

The bishop shot him a warning glance. "Not everyone shares your passion for every social ministry that comes down the pike, Flenn."

"Fair enough."

"Besides," the bishop said, "you come from her kind… rich, powerful. I'm surprised to hear you talk like that."

"The O'Reilly's are new money. My family is old money."

"What's the difference?"

Flenn winked. "Old money can trace every dime back to our pirate ancestors who originally stole it."

The bishop laughed.

"You think I'm kidding? Old money hangs onto it forever. We wear the soles out of our shoes and drive our cars until they fall apart. New money spends, spends, spends and then spends some more."

"Well, you both have mansions." Tom had accompanied Flenn to his father's funeral a few years back. The Flenn's family home was massive.

"That's true," Flenn countered, "but we keep our thermostat turned down in the winter."

Tom Morrison chuckled. "Okay, I get it, but why the sudden interest in Juanita? Didn't ya'll work together on something once?"

Flenn paused as he considered the glass on the table in front of him. "I'm just interested in what happened to their kid, that's all."

The bishop shook his head. "Awful thing; and still no word of her whereabouts." Tom looked at Flenn suspiciously. "Why are you suddenly so interested in her disappearance?"

"Can't it just be a pastoral concern?"

"They're not your parishioners. Beyond just general concern for their heartache, there'd be no reason for you to be asking me about it six months later. So, what's up?"

"You should have worked with me in my old job," Flenn said. The bishop set his glass down and waited for an answer. "Okay, you've got me. I can't tell you how I got drawn into this, but I'm unofficially helping investigate her daughter's disappearance. I have reason to believe the kid may have been trying to get away from her parents, at least from her stepfather."

"I'd like to get away from him myself," Tom said, "but Mac keeps getting himself posted to things in the diocese just to annoy me. He thinks I'm... how did he put it once... a 'bleeding heart liberal.' That was after I suggested the diocese support a free clinic for the working poor up in Decatur. Seems these days if you want to help people you get labeled." Bishop Morrison thought a moment. "Get away from her stepfather, huh? Well, let me ask the obvious question... Was Mac abusing her?"

"Between me and thee?"

"For now."

"Looks that way." Flenn was on thin ice here and had to be careful. He did not want to bring Minerva Wilson into this.

The bishop's eyes narrowed. "Son of a ... ; well, if Mac was abusing her, then I can sure see why the girl would want to run away."

"Me too, but what I'm wondering, Tom, is do you think Juanita is the kind of woman who could have known, but not said anything?"

The bishop frowned. "I've heard that some mothers do that... but, Juanita? I would hope not." He thought for a moment. "On the other hand, Mac holds the keys to just about everything in that house. I knew her years ago before her first husband died. They were members at Holy Trinity where I was the associate. They were nice; a young couple with no money. Juanita's parents both died when she was young and I think an aunt or someone close to the family raised her. I can't recall her first husband's name right now but I remember he died when Shelly was about a year old. Wait a minute... it was Rob... yeah, Rob Hershey. Anyway, Rob died when Shelly was little, and we were all concerned about what would happen to them."

"What did happen to them?"

"She met Mac O'Reilly, that's what happened. I think it was at a diocesan event of some sort. They asked me to marry them. I said no. You know the rules: in the case of a divorce we have to petition the bishop for permission; and the previously married person has to have been divorced for more than a year."

"Mac wasn't?"

"Nowhere near. The ink wasn't even dry on the documents." Bishop Morrison finished his drink. "They ended up having a civil ceremony. Mac wouldn't speak to me for a long time afterwards. When I was nominated for bishop, I heard he was behind the scenes working against me. It was the fourth ballot before I was elected, and at least one of those ballots was directly because of Mac O'Reilly."

"So," Flenn said, "Juanita raised her station in life by marrying him?"

"Financially, yeah. Everything Mac touched seemed to turn to gold. When he and Juanita married, he was owner of a string of temporary staffing companies across the state. He sold them and made a fortune. He went on to dabble in one thing, then another. Every one of his businesses brought in money, lots of it. I've often wondered, aside from that, just what Juanita could have seen in the man. I mean, come on, you know the guy, he's a jerk."

"No, I believe the word I used was *ass!*" Flenn felt something sharp dig into his left leg. He glanced down as a tiny orange ball of fur mistook him for Mount Everest. It wasn't long before she was joined by two more who climbed his leg onto the couch where they began to chase one another around and behind him. "By the way," Flenn asked, "want a kitten?"

"Not a chance! Where'd they come from?"

"From that lazy dust mop asleep in your lap. As to where that icon of motherhood came from originally, who knows. She certainly likes people; must've been somebody's pet once upon a time. When I found her she was hungry and homeless."

"Of course, she was!" said the bishop. "Why did I ask? If I know you, she was also working for the displaced-feline-Honduran-refugee fund!"

Flenn laughed. "Not that cat! Too much effort." The kittens climbed down the arm of the sofa and ran off toward the kitchen. Their mother never opened an eye. "If you won't take one of those little nuisances, maybe you could take that one in your lap? She seems to like you. She certainly isn't of use around here. I'm not even sure she remembers those fluff balls are hers. Maybe you could take her to that free clinic in Decatur? She could do all their cat scans."

The bishop smiled feebly at the old joke. "Thanks, but no thanks."

Flenn eyed his glass again and decided to finish off the contents. "Back to Juanita; you obviously know her well. I need your honest opinion. Do you think she is the kind of person who could have known something was going on between her husband and daughter and simply kept her mouth shut?"

Tom Morrison was silent for a moment. He had known Juanita O'Reilly for years. Flenn was right; if anyone could answer that question it was probably him. He shook his head. "How does anybody *really* know something like that?"

"Come on, Tom. What does your gut say?" The bishop was clearly uncomfortable, but Flenn pressed. "Could Juanita O'Reilly have known something was up and kept quiet in order to maintain her present lifestyle?"

Bishop Morrison's sighed. "Flenn, I… I hate to say it, but I just don't know."

"I realize you don't *know*, Tom, but what is the first answer that popped into your head?"

Bishop Morrison looked down at the floor, and then back up at Flenn. "I'm afraid that's the best answer I can give."

CHAPTER THIRTY-FOUR

Sunny and seventy-seven degrees. *Who would have thought that there had been crippling sleet and ice here only a few nights ago?* Flenn was on his way to All Saint's in Homewood to drop off a book their rector had asked to borrow last week. It was difficult to concentrate on ordinary tasks right now with so much on his mind. These past few days had sucked him into a whirlwind, not unlike the one that had swept Dorothy into the mythical land of Oz. Instead of a lion, scarecrow, and tinman... he had a priest, a detective and a spy.

Minerva, Rainsford, and Matteson—oh my!

He shouldn't make light, he told himself. As if in confirmation, he looked up to see the giant glass walls of the Rye Foundation looming ahead.

Flenn had almost made it to All Saint's when his phone buzzed. It was the bishop. "Good morning, Tom! Hope you weren't hungover yesterday morning," he teased. "I know that I..."

"Flenn, where are you?" Tom's voice was almost a whisper.

"Over by All Saint's. Something wrong?"

"I need you to come to Saint Latimer's right away. I'll meet you here."

"What's going on?"

"I'll tell you when you get here. It's not good. Be prepared." The bishop hung up before Flenn could ask anything more.

Flenn took a deep breath. *It could be anything. The rector, Jason Witherspoon, was getting on in years, he'd already had one stroke this year. Or, maybe something had happened to the building?* There'd been a recent rash of church fires throughout the state. Flenn pushed a button on his steering wheel and said, "Call Minerva Wilson." The Bluetooth system he'd had installed searched through his contacts and called the number for Minerva.

"Hi, this is Mother Minerva," the recording said cheerily. "Please leave a message and I will get back with you."

Damn!

Beep.

"Hi, Minnie this is Flenn. I just got a message from the Bish telling me to meet him at your place. What's going on? Call me if you get this in the next few minutes, otherwise I'll see you when I get there."

Saint Latimer's parking lot was filled with squad cars as Flenn pulled up to the church. One or two still had their lights flashing, the rest were parked with no occupants inside. There was an ambulance as well.

It had been the rector! Poor Jason, Flenn thought.

Two cops stood just outside the main entrance. Flenn hurried past them into the building. Whether it was his priest's collar or the way he carried himself, neither officer challenged him. He walked into the reception area where police, church staff and paramedics were busily rushing past. He didn't see anyone he recognized. People were ignoring him; with a clerical collar he simply blended into the scenery. Flenn walked up the carpeted steps toward the offices and classrooms. The bishop was at the top of the stairs speaking quietly with the rector, Jason Witherspoon.

So much for that theory!

As soon as Tom Morrison caught sight of Flenn he motioned for him to wait. The bishop put his hand on the rector's shoulder and whispered something, then walked over to Flenn. "Let's go someplace where we can talk privately." Tom opened a nearby conference-room door. Several women were inside; one was crying. They stood as Bishop Morrison entered. "I'm sorry ladies, but could we have this room for a moment?" One of the women came over and hugged the bishop, dabbed her eyes, and then left the room. The others followed.

"Flenn, you were close friends with Minerva Wilson, weren't you?"

Minerva? Alarm bells clanged in Flenn's head! "What's happened?" The bishop put his hand on Flenn's shoulder the way he had with the rector. "Damn it, Tom, tell me!"

The bishop inhaled deeply, then said, "Minerva's been shot."

Flenn staggered backwards and reached for a chair to steady himself.

"Shot? What... where is she... who... "

The bishop cut him off. "It happened sometime last night. The sexton said that there was a light on in

Minerva's office when he got ready to go home. He knocked on her door but she told him she had a late counseling session and asked him to leave the front door unlocked."

Flenn felt as if someone had just pounded his gut with a sledge hammer. "Is she… is she alive?"

Tom shook his head. "She's gone, Flenn."

Flenn collapsed into the chair behind him as a lump the size of Texas filled his chest. "Give me a minute." He choked back the tears. *Yes, he had friends die before, several in fact. Many of them murdered or shot in the line of duty. This was different; this was Minnie!*

Bishop Morrison sat down next to him and waited. A moment later Flenn looked up, ready to hear the rest. "One of the secretaries found Minerva in her office this morning. She'd been shot several times. There's blood everywhere."

Flenn raised an eyebrow. "You went in there?"

The bishop nodded. "Someone needed to say last rites."

Flenn had always respected Tom, but never more so than right now. "What happened? Surely this place has video surveillance?"

"The cameras don't turn on until midnight," the bishop explained. "Jason told me that his assistant, Bill Shelaney, has already reviewed the feed… nothing, no sign of anyone."

"What about Minnie's husband, does he know?"

"Wayne got here about a half hour ago. Bill is with him right now… his office."

Flenn stood. "I need to see her."

"Not like this, Flenn."

"I've seen it before, Tom. Remember?"

"The police won't let you in there."

"You don't understand; I know how to investigate a murder scene."

"So do they. I barely convinced them to let *me* in there. One of them is Catholic, so he let me pass. You're just a priest to them, a novice who would get in the way."

Flenn's emotions were getting the better of him. "I'm no novice, Tom!"

"I know that, and you know that, but do you really want to let the rest of the world in on it?" The bishop stepped in front of the door. "I've kept your secret all these years, but you go in there shouting 'CIA' or something and nobody's going to believe you, or worse, they *will* believe you!"

"I've got to do *something*, Tom!"

"So, go in there and comfort Wayne. I'm sure Bill could use the help."

He didn't want to comfort Wayne; he wanted to see Minerva, to see for himself what had happened, to survey the crime scene, to kick somebody's ass!

"That's an order from your bishop."

Flenn's shoulders sank as he nodded in submission. "I want to know everything that you do, Tom… find out anything you can. Take pictures if they let you. I don't know, tell them you need pictures for diocesan records… they might fall for it. I'll go check on Wayne."

The bishop simply sighed and said, "I'm sorry, Flenn."

What else was there to say?

"Not half as sorry as whoever did this is going to be!" Flenn nudged past the bishop and back out onto the carpeted hallway. A policeman was talking to Father Witherspoon. Flenn went around the corner to Bill Shelaney's office. Two paramedics were standing idle, waiting for word to take Minerva's body to the morgue where the medical examiner would eventually release it to whichever funeral home Wayne chose. *Poor Wayne! The man was now faced with raising his kids without the woman he loved more than anything else in the whole world.* Flenn was silent, remembering his own loss in Edinburgh so long ago.

Flenn knew the story of how Minerva and Wayne had met in high school, married while still in college, and worked for years together in the same office. How Wayne had been supportive of Minnie's decision to go to Sewanee and study for the priesthood. How he had stood beside her through two miscarriages. How elated he'd been at the birth of their children a year later. Flenn had been in the Wilson's home many times, and they in his. He had baptized their oldest child. The youngest had been born at Sewanee, and baptized by the same wonderful professor of New Testament that Flenn had studied under. Flenn walked slowly past Minerva's office but the door remained shut. He knew that the forensics team was in there now: taking pictures, swabbing things, dusting other things... looking for fingerprints, gun powder residue, bullet casings… all the things police lab-rats live for.

Since the computer program Zack had given him had already deleted itself, he'd have to get Zack to break into the police records a second time—although Flenn felt he already knew who had killed Minerva. He stopped just outside Bill's Shelaney's door and crossed himself before opening it. Bill was sitting on a leather couch next to Wayne, who sat with his head buried in his hands.

Bill stood. "Flenn! Glad you're here. This is a horrible day," Bill looked at Wayne, "for all of us." At the mention of Flenn's name, Wayne stood, only to fall headlong into Flenn's arms. Bill squeezed Flenn's shoulder then quietly excused himself.

"Wayne, I'm so… so very sorry."

"Why?" Wayne managed to say through his tears. "Why Minnie? Who would want to hurt such a sweet, wonderful person?"

Flenn thought he knew the answer to that, but instead said, "A sick man, Wayne, a very sick man. I'm sure the police will figure it out. What about the kids, do they know?"

"My sister has them at her house." Wayne wiped his eyes with his sleeve. God, Flenn, how am I going to tell them?"

Flenn squeezed Wayne's hand. "I'll help you." *He would do more than that as soon as he found Mac O'Reilly—a lot more!*

"You're a good friend." Wayne reached for the tissue box on the coffee table. "I just can't get my head around it. She called me last night from the office and told me she'd be late. I put the kids to bed and turned in myself. When I got up this morning and she wasn't home, I freaked. I wasn't up five minutes before the phone rang. They found her around seven this morning. I called my sister. She came over and took the kids." Wayne burst into sobs.

Tom Morrison stuck his head into the room and looked over at Flenn. "You okay?" Flenn nodded, although he was anything but. "I'm still here, if you need me," the bishop said.

The door shut softly as Wayne wiped his eyes. "Tom's a good man," Wayne said. He told me if I needed anything to just let him know. He gave me this, but I don't know what to do with it." Wayne picked up an envelope from the coffee table and handed it to Flenn. Inside was a check for a thousand dollars made out from the bishop's discretionary fund. *That was just like Tom,* thought Flenn. *He knew there would be expenses, meals to buy for the kids, babysitters, funeral costs.*

"He said there would be more… Flenn, I don't want money, I just want my Minerva back!"

Whatever part of Flenn's heart was still intact shattered into a million pieces. "Wayne, I know the police will be asking you all this later, but is there anything that Minerva said yesterday that was at all out of the ordinary?"

"She's been upset for a long time. I don't know why. She kept telling me that it was over some kid at the church, but that was all she'd ever say. She has… had…

such a tender heart, it could have been just about anything." Wayne wiped his eyes again. "I kept after her to go and see a doctor—she'd lost a ton of weight. Finally, last week she told me that she had talked with someone and that she was feeling better. I didn't press her. God, how I wish I had now."

Flenn knew the *someone* Minnie had talked with had been him. "What about yesterday? Did she say anything at all?"

"Yeah, maybe." Wayne blew his nose. "She said she'd come to a conclusion about this kid; that she was going to confront the situation head on. I can't believe I actually told her, 'You go, girl'. A look of horror flashed across Wayne's face. "My God, Flenn, do you think a member of Saint Latimer's did this?"

Flenn thought exactly that, but said, "Let's give the police some room to move. I'm sure they will come up with some answers." *That is, if he gave them time!* Bill returned just then with some coffee. Flenn took a cup and excused himself. He and Bill could tag team with Wayne until the police were finished and Minerva's body was on its way downtown, then he'd go with Wayne to his sister's house to tell the kids. Flenn called the office and told Iriana there had been a pastoral emergency and that he wouldn't be coming in today. She tried her best to fish whatever had happened out of him, but he wouldn't tell her. *She'd know soon enough. It would only be a matter of time before the news was all over town.*

Flenn found Tom and let him know that he needed to speak to him—alone. The bishop asked Father Witherspoon for the use of his office. As polite as Tom had been, it wasn't a request. The two men sat down in the spacious and tastefully decorated office. The expensive carpets, the antique furniture, the nineteenth-century lithographs… none of it was making the intended impression right now.

"Tom, I'm pretty sure I know who did this."

"Who?"

"Mac O'Reilly."

"That's impossible. Mac is at Camp McDowell. I just left him. We were there for the annual board retreat."

Flenn shook his head. "That can't be. He must have left last night…"

"No," Tom said, "he was there all night."

Flenn fell, more than sat, on the chair behind him. *Okay, Mac hadn't pulled the trigger, but he could still be behind this.* "Look, I couldn't tell you the other night, Tom, but I suppose I can now. It was driving Minerva crazy. She's the one who told me about Mac abusing his stepdaughter."

"I wondered where you'd gotten that information."

"Shelly told Minnie during a confession that she was… "

The bishop raised both hands. "Stop right there!" His eyes widened. "You mean to tell me that Minerva repeated something said under the seal?"

Flenn interjected, "Yes, but… "

"There are no 'buts!'" The bishop shook his head angrily. "You're trespassing on holy ground, Flenn. I can't listen to any thing said to another priest in confession; and, you sure as hell shouldn't have!"

"Tom, I understand what you are saying, but Minerva's dead and… "

"No!" The bishop's face was turning red. "Don't say another word! I know you're upset. We all are." He took a breath. "This is too horrible to even imagine; we need to give it some time." Tom looked away. "You might not be, but I'm walking on unchartered ground here. I've never known anyone who has been murdered." Tom took a deep breath. "Maybe somehow Mac was involved, or maybe not. Either way, it will be for the police to figure out." He looked straight at Flenn. "In the meantime, I forbid you from telling the police anything that Minerva said about that girl's confession."

Flenn rose to object. "Tom, please, listen to me!"

"I'm sorry, Flenn, but I want to know you will obey me. You will say nothing to the police, or to Wayne for that matter, about anything said in that confession. Are we clear on that?"

Tom had just turned boss; worse, he had pulled the 'father-in-God' card.

"But, Tom…"

"Father! Are we clear?"

Flenn clenched his fists. "You don't understand; if you will just… "

"I said, are we clear?"

"Crystal!" Flenn nearly tore the door off its hinges as he stormed out.

CHAPTER THIRTY-FIVE

Preachers and prostitutes… nothing seemed to add up. Guy Rainsford was frustrated. He sat at his desk and pored over his notes for the third time this morning. Bits and fragments strewn around like pieces from different puzzles all in the same box—a girl viciously beaten and drowned, a pimp who saw himself as doing society a favor, and an abused teenager in a half-way home desperate to put together the pieces of her own life.

The detective rubbed his temples then looked back down at the yellow notepad, noticing something he had overlooked before, something tiny written in the margin––*Denise.*

Who the hell was Denise?

Then he remembered that Roxanne had mentioned her. Denise was another one of the girls working for Valentino. Guy could have the pimp picked up, but he'd simply deny knowing the kid. *He'd deny knowing his own mother,* Guy told himself, *unless there was something in it for him!* Guy wanted nothing more than to see Ramirez behind bars, but Valentino was no fool. He wasn't about to incriminate himself more than he already had outside the morgue last week. *The pimp had taken a huge risk reporting Lindsay missing in the first place. He wasn't going to start introducing the rest of his girls to the Birmingham Police Department as well!*

Guy's former partner, Teri McCaleb, had looked up Ramirez's phone records—*not exactly legal without a subpoena, but what else were former partners—and lovers— for?* Teri had told him that Ramirez had received dozens of calls during May and June, most of them from private numbers who had gone to some length to make their calls untraceable. Guy recognized a few of the names she had been able to trace—a couple of prominent lawyers, a well-known surgeon—but no preacher.

Could one of those men have killed Lindsay? Ramirez swore up and down that she had not had a date the weekend she went missing, that she had called him saying she was sick that Friday, the last Friday in May. After that, he'd claimed he never heard from her again. Guy sighed. *Maybe the pimp was telling the truth. If the slime-ball had known who had murdered Lindsay, why would he have reported the girl missing in the first place?*

Guy felt like throwing something; he was getting nowhere. He picked up the phone and dialed Ashleigh Nieves' number. He needed to ask Roxanne more about this Denise kid.

"I'm sorry, Detective," the director of New Beginnings said. "She's not here. She didn't come back last night. I was scared to death when they told me the police were on the phone; I thought you might be calling with bad news." Guy could hear the anxiety in her voice. "We called her boss at the mall, but she said Roxanne left right after work. She told me there was some boy

Roxanne's interested in, but she didn't know his name. Frankly, I hope that's all this is," Ashleigh said. "I mean, we don't allow that sort of thing, but I can remember what it was like to be a teenager."

Guy wasn't sure that he could.

"Let me know when you hear from her," he said. Guy hung up the phone and reached for his jacket to head for the mall. *Not another one, not on my watch!*

CHAPTER THIRTY-SIX

"You don't know for sure that the councilman did it." Zack leaned back into his chair at the Cullman Chew and Chat and sipped his soda. Scott Flenn sat across from him. Flenn had needed to vent, and so he'd come to Cullman to find Zack. They spoke in hushed tones, although no one else was sitting nearby.

"Who else could it have been?"

"Maybe it's time you share all this with the police," Zack said.

Flenn pushed his empty coffee cup aside. "I can't."

Zack reached for his hamburger. "Again with the 'can't'. Why the hell not?"

"Under orders." Flenn picked at his salad. "Has to do with a confession." *Technically, the bishop had ordered him not to tell the police or Wayne Wilson; he had said nothing about the CIA.*

"Yeah, you always were the obedient one." Zack salted his French fries and dipped one in a mound of ketchup.

"Unlike you, who used to run off chasing after one hunch or another."

"Hey, they usually paid off." Zack said.

"Oh yeah, like the time you thought the first lady was

264

passing information to the Saudi prince; or how about when you were sure Bin Laden was in Iceland, or the time..."

"Okay, okay!" Zack picked up another fry. "I followed my gut and you followed your brain. That's what made us such a good team." He grinned. "Course, my hunches were usually good ones."

"Wasn't it one of your hunches that got us in a firefight with Colonel Amir and his men that time?" Flenn said.

"I seem to recall we took out some pretty notorious drug lords that day," Zack said. He pointed across the table to Flenn's salad. "You need to eat. Starving yourself won't do any good, and it isn't helping your memory either."

"Father, you fellas okay over there?" Irma called from across the bar. "Clyde's just made some peach pie if you want any."

Flenn shook his head. "No, thanks."

"Speak for yourself," Zack said. He called over to the waitress. "Pie sounds fantastic, I'd love a slice!" He looked across the table at his friend. "You really are getting too thin," Zack said. "That salad isn't even enough to fill a rabbit." He called back over to Irma. "Make that two slices, Ma'am!"

Flenn didn't argue. He had run an extra two miles this morning to try and clear his mind.

"You know, what you're doing right now is exactly what you always accused me of doing?"

Flenn raised an eyebrow. "What?"

"Aren't you just following a hunch about this lady priest? Seems to me anyone could have killed her. A crazy off the street, someone angry about advice she'd given, something like that."

Flenn shook his head. "Her husband said she was meeting someone about a kid."

"Still not enough," he said, his mouth full of hamburger. "I mean it might be enough for me, but not the Scott Flenn I used to know."

"Here you go, gentlemen." Irma handed them each a generous slice of the steaming pie. "Give it a minute, it's right out of the oven." She looked at Flenn's empty cup. "I'll be back in a jiff with more coffee."

Flenn looked at the pie. "I suppose you're right," he said. "Mac O'Reilly is still a monster, though."

"Yeah, I get it," Zack said, "but you're letting that cloud your judgment. Just because he's a molester doesn't mean he's also a murderer. I mean, isn't that what you'd tell me if the situation were reversed?"

Flenn thought about that for a moment. "Okay, so what about what you're doing? Aren't you just following another of your hunches?" Irma returned with the coffee pot and a fresh soda for Zack.

"Absolutely not. Romero's in this up to his neck. I've seen the bodies, remember? Plus," Zack figured it was time to warn Flenn. "I've got a tail. One of Amir's men, I'm fairly sure."

Flenn's eyebrows shot up. "What?"

"He's across the street in the little Honda. Skinny, olive-skinned guy. Check it out."

Flenn knew better than to turn and stare outside, so he got up and excused himself to the men's room. He came back a moment later and chanced a quick look across the street. "I see him. How do you know he's not listening in on us?" Flenn asked as he sat back down.

"I don't. But I'm reasonably sure he's just been sent to keep an eye on me. Iran's not going to have any decent equipment available anywhere near Alabama. Their budget is tighter than ours." Zack pulled the dessert in front of him. "I'm guessing someone saw me in Turkey and he's just making sure I'm not a liability. Which is another reason I don't dare go back to Langley right now. I might be dead before I made it off the plane. No, I'm safer right here... at least for now." Zack took a bite of the pie. "Oh my God, this is heaven!"

Flenn sighed. "So, *you* won't go to Langley, and *I* can't go to the police. I guess this was just a wasted trip, huh?"

Zack looked up. "Are you kidding? I might've missed out on this pie!"

"You never change, do you?" said Flenn, finally sampling the dessert.

"Nah. Besides, you've changed enough for the both of us since you quit the agency."

Flenn shook his head and sighed. "It's starting to feel like I never left."

CHAPTER THIRTY-SEVEN

Saint Latimer's Church was packed. More than 500 clergy, parishioners, city officials, friends, and family members had filled the nave on a Thursday afternoon to pay their final respects and offer their support to Wayne Wilson and his children.

Minerva had been admired by everyone who knew her. That she had been murdered, and in her own church, was heartbreaking. A cry of outrage was being raised by several denominational leaders across town as well as a number of city officials, many of whom were here today for the funeral.

Bishop Morrison was the chief celebrant, as was customary at all clergy funerals. Flenn was listed in the bulletin as the homilist; but, as he stood with the clergy and acolytes in the sacristy before the service, he wondered if he'd be able to make it all the way through his own sermon. Flenn detested ministers who cried from the pulpit—*crying preachers always seemed pretentious and manipulative*—but today he was worried that he might be about to join their ranks. Flenn had rarely shed tears in front of anyone since he was a child… except, of course, for that time in Edinburgh.

The line of acolytes, torchbearers, choristers, deacons,

and priests fell into their respective orders for the processional hymn. Wayne had been asked to carry his wife's ashes; he'd declined. Instead, Flenn bore the simple wooden box down the aisle, his heart breaking with every step. The last person in the procession was Tom Morrison, in full bishop's regalia—cope and mitre, and carrying his bishop's staff. Flenn saw several familiar faces, he even recognized Guy Rainsford standing with some other police officers, which would have surprised him more had Saint Latimer's not had a custom of honoring the police department with a special service each year. Thankfully, Flenn had not seen the one person he was dreading would be here today—Mac O'Reilly.

Even now as he placed the urn near the altar, Flenn was trying to figure out who had done this horrible act. *Minerva had told Wayne that she was staying late that night to confront a parishioner about something. It had to have been Mac! Who else could it be? Still, the bishop himself had confirmed that Mac was far away the night of her murder. Had Mac hired a contract killer? Would he take that kind of a chance?*

The assisting clergy took their place in the chancel as Bishop Morrison began the words of the opening anthem: "I am resurrection and I am life, says the Lord. Whoever has faith in me shall have life, even though he die. And everyone who has life, and has committed himself to me in faith, shall not die forever." Afterward came the prayers, scripture readings and a hymn. The Gospel lesson was from John 14, where Jesus tells his disciples: *"In my father's house are many mansions."* Flenn had prepared his sermon on that text, as well as on the lesson from Romans where the apostle Paul wrote: *"I am convinced that neither death, nor life shall be able to separate us from the love of God."*

As he stood in the massive pulpit and surveyed the congregation, Flenn saw Wayne and the children sitting with Minerva's parents. Priests and deacons, dressed in black and white robes, filled the first six pews on the opposite side. The police chief was also here, along with the mayor. Flenn had served with Minerva on the mayor's community-action task force just last year. Several young people were in attendance, both from Saint Latimer's youth group and from around the diocese. Minerva had been a volunteer counselor at Camp McDowell for several years. Students and faculty from the seminary in Sewanee had also come; Flenn recognized some of his own professors amongst them. Fortunately, he didn't see Mac O'Reilly anywhere in the congregation.

Flenn began his sermon.

"You couldn't help but notice Minnie's smile. As small as she was, that smile always seemed enormous. She greeted everyone with it—rich, poor, black, white, Episcopalian, Baptist—everyone."

Damn!

Mac O'Reilly was sitting about 15 pews back on the left. Juanita wasn't with him. Flenn took a breath. Looking directly at the councilman, he continued. "I suspect Minerva might have even had a smile on her face for the one who walked into her office that night and took her life." Flenn paused to see if O'Reilly would react. Nothing.

"It's too bad that her killer couldn't have seen the wonder, the sincerity, the love that was behind that smile. The very love of one who once looked down even upon those who crucified him and cried out, 'Father, forgive them, they know not what they do."

Where had that just come from?

Flenn hadn't meant to say those words; they'd just seemed to fall out of his mouth. He glanced down at his notes, trying to find his place, but couldn't. He looked up at the congregation and began preaching a sermon he'd never intended. It was as if someone else had commandeered his tongue. He went on for several minutes, preaching about grace, forgiveness, and the unconditional love of God. None of it had been what he'd prepared. As he stepped out of the pulpit, he was asking himself what had just happened. *At least he had managed to get through the sermon without crying.*

The service continued with the Nicene Creed and the prayers. Flenn had been asked to take one of the stations during communion. He would distribute the bread while a deacon would administer the chalice. Anticipating a large crowd, three communion stations had been designated—his was toward the back, on the left-hand side, not far from Mac O'Reilly. His stomach churned. *How could he give communion to that man? Mac O'Reilly may or may not be a murderer, but he was still a child molester!*

Flenn placed the wafer in the hands of the first person

in line and said the familiar words, "The body of Christ, the bread of heaven." The woman took the bread and moved on to the deacon to receive the wine. Flenn thought about withholding communion from the councilman, but to do that was not only to excommunicate him, it could spoil everything. He'd have to give an account of his actions to the bishop, and probably to O'Reilly.

Scores of people passed by him. So far, Mac had not been one of them. *Perhaps he would feel too guilty to receive and would just stay in his pew.*

A young teen with closely cropped hair, wearing tighter jeans than a girl her age should, stood in front of him and held her hands out just as the others in front of her had. Flenn could tell she'd been crying. He forgot about Mac O'Reilly for a moment and gently squeezed the girl's hands as he gave her the bread. "The body of Christ, the bread of heaven," he said tenderly. The girl looked lost, out of place. Flenn's heart went out to her. It was only as she made her way toward the deacon for the wine that he saw O'Reilly. The councilman was only a few communicants away.

Flenn tried to compose himself before giving communion to the next person in line. The boy standing in front of him didn't notice the delay; he was more interested in figuring out who the girl in the tight jeans was. Flenn peered down into the shiny paten in his hands and heard himself say, "The body of Christ." *Just what was that body?* he asked himself as he handed the boy the round wafer. Flenn's head began to spin, yet he didn't exactly feel dizzy. He felt something else…

something he hadn't felt in a long time, not since Edinburgh! A strange feeling of warmth came over him.

Was the body of Christ only the bread on the paten he held? said a voice inside his head. *Or was it the community of faithful people with outstretched hands ready to receive God into their lives? Was it not all the world... the disciples that night gathered in the Upper Room with Jesus—Peter, Thomas, James?*

Then it hit him...

Even Judas! Jesus had not excluded his own betrayer from the holy meal.

Flenn looked up. Mac O'Reilly now stood directly in front of him. Surprisingly, the knot in Flenn's stomach was gone. His nerves didn't tense. His eyes didn't glare. Instead, Flenn found himself placing the bread in the man's hands and simply saying yet again, "The body of Christ, the bread of heaven."

And then it was over. The councilman crossed over to the deacon for the wine and was gone.

Flenn had experienced something he'd only known once before—a penetratingly, deep sense of peace. *But why now? Why here?*

The answer came from out of nowhere: *He had to be true to his calling; and, what he was called to be was a priest, a minister to all people, even to the Mac O'Reillys of the world.*

The remainder of the service seemed to fly by. The experience wasn't something Flenn could have explained had anyone asked; just as he could never explain what had happened in Edinburgh so long ago. It was just that right now Flenn was keenly aware that there was something larger to life, something much bigger than just the present moment. He had spent the first decades of his life denying the existence of that something... but it had just brushed by him again, enabling him to do what he'd thought impossible. This was far from over, he knew that, but for now Flenn simply breathed it all in as the congregation filed by at the end of the service to shake his hand.

The sight of Guy Rainsford making his way toward the door brought Flenn back to earth. Flenn looked down; the girl who had been crying during communion stood in front of him, her eyes still swollen and red. He asked if she was a member of Minerva's youth group. She said no, but that she'd heard from a friend that Mother Minerva had been a great lady, and just wanted to pay her respects. The girl looked up at Flenn and asked, "Did you really mean that part in your sermon about God loving not only good people like Mother Minerva, but everyone... no matter what they've done?"

He scratched the back of his head, *Yes, he supposed he did*. He took a breath. "No matter what," he repeated. Hearing his own words spoken back to him was an eerie reminder of what he'd just experienced. He held out his hand. "I'm Father Flenn, but my friends just call me Flenn. What's your name?"

The girl hesitated, then took his hand.

"I'm Denise."

"Good to meet you, Denise." He smiled, then turned to the next person in line as the slight brunette made her way out the door, presumably to her parents' car.

Denise?

Something about that name. Something important. What was it? Then it hit him: *Juanita had told the police that one of Shelly's friend's name had begun with the letter 'D'! Denise had just said that a friend had told her about Minerva.* His gut was screaming: "It's her!"

He turned, but she was gone. Ignoring the rest of the mourners in line, he called to the detective. "Guy! Guy Rainsford!" The detective couldn't help but hear him—everyone did. The priest motioned for him to come quickly, then whispered in his ear. "A girl with short, dark hair, wearing tight black jeans and a white jacket just left. I can't tell you why right now, but you need to follow her. Don't let her see you. I'll explain later. Trust me, this is important. See if you can find out who she is!"

Guy wondered if the priest had lost his mind.

"Please! Just trust me on this. I'll fill you in later, I promise. All I can tell you is that her name is Denise."

Guy's eyes grew twice their normal size.

No, it couldn't be that Denise! Could this be the girl he had been looking for; and, how on earth had the priest known about her?

Guy bolted out the door, determined to find out.

CHAPTER THIRTY-EIGHT

Large, gray clouds were gathering as the wind blew through the churchyard. Guy sneezed as he pulled his overcoat tightly around his chest. Denise was standing on the corner talking to someone on her phone. He walked past her to his car in the parking lot across the street. A few minutes later, a black Chrysler pulled up and the girl crawled into the back seat. Guy followed two car lengths behind. He called in the tag and discovered that the car belonged to an Anton Jackson, an Uber driver. Guy followed the Chrysler to the Galleria in Hoover where he watched the girl get out in front of an upscale hotel attached to the mall. Guy parked and followed her inside. As he entered the massive lobby and navigated around several small palm trees, all decorated with multi-colored Christmas lights, he saw the girl standing with two men near the silver and brass elevators. He recognized the fat one right away.

Valentino Ramirez!

Fortunately, the pimp didn't notice him as he ducked into the bar and watched from a far corner. Ramirez seemed to be giving instructions to the girl, after which he hugged her and shook hands with the man. The man pressed something into the pimp's palm.

Denise got onto the waiting elevator with the man and the doors shut behind them. Ramirez was smiling as he walked through the lobby and out the door.

It was the Denise he'd been looking for, it had to be! How had Father Flenn known?

There was nothing Guy could do except remain in the bar and try and follow the girl afterwards. He ordered a hamburger with fries but didn't have much of an appetite. An hour and a half later, Denise stepped off the elevator and walked outside where she hailed a taxi. She was a tiny thing—short, brown hair, not more than 15 or 16 at the most. Guy followed the cab to a dilapidated, single-story shack in a run-down neighborhood off Seventh Avenue. He wrote down the address and took some quick pictures with his cell phone, then left. People around here knew a cop's car when they saw one.

Gusts of wind blew debris across broken fences and into the street as the rain began to pour. Tornados weren't unheard of in December, so Guy switched on his radio to check. Sure enough, Birmingham was under a severe weather alert. Instead of driving home, Guy kept an eye on the sky as he headed toward the vicarage next to Saint Ann's Episcopal Church. Father Flenn had some explaining to do.

****

Thunder shook the vicarage, sending the kittens scampering underneath the sofa. Flenn was on his first cup of coffee this morning, trying to shake off the effects of an exhausting week.

Yesterday's funeral had taken a toll, but the night before that had been equally demanding. He'd been up half the night with Ashleigh Nieves; she had been hysterical after the police had found the body of one of her residents. The girl had died from an overdose of heroin. It had been nearly 2 a.m. before he'd finally made it to bed, then up early yesterday to finish his homily for the funeral. To top it off, last night Detective Rainsford had come by during the storm, demanding to know how Flenn had known about Denise. *It hadn't gone particularly well.*

He reached over to top off his coffee when there was a knock at his door. Flenn assumed it was the detective again. His promised explanation had simply been that as a priest he was told things in confidence, things he or she couldn't share with others. It was the best he had been able to come up with. Zack had always been better at lying.

He opened the door as lightening flashed in the distance. "Wayne! What on earth are you doing out so early, especially today of all days?"

Wayne Wilson removed his baseball cap and shook as much rain off as he could before stepping inside. "Sorry, Father, I just wanted to give you this." He handed over a clasped envelope that had been sealed with several layers of tape. It was addressed in ink to: "Mother Minerva Wilson," and marked: "Confidential."

"Here," Flenn said as the rain dripped onto the foyer

tile, "give me your jacket; come have some hot coffee." Wayne followed, apologizing about the water.

"Just tears from heaven," Flenn said, hanging the jacket over a kitchen chair. "Lord knows, we've all shed a lot of those lately." Wayne sat at the table while Flenn poured two steaming cups to the brim. He offered milk and sugar, though Flenn never used the stuff himself.

Father Flenn turned the envelope over. It had no return address. Wayne explained he'd found it on his wife's desk at home. It had been opened, presumably by Minerva, and then re-sealed with tape. "Somehow, it just doesn't feel right for me to read it," Wayne said. "I thought maybe you wouldn't mind taking a look? If it's private church business, then you'll know what to do with it."

Flenn sat down to examine the envelope. The postmark was a local one. Inside was a pink flash drive along with a hand-written note.

Dear Mother Minerva,

I've given this to a friend of mine and asked her to mail it to you in case anything happens to me. You've been such a good friend! I'm so sorry to have burdened you with all my problems.

I want to thank you for keeping my secrets. After you watch this video, please post it on the internet for me. I know you won't want to do that after you see it, but I am begging you—Please!!! It's the last favor I will ever ask of anyone. I would have asked my friend Denise to do it, but I think it would be better coming from someone respectable like you.

P.S. I gave Denise your name and telephone number. She is in the same situation as me. You know what I mean. Anyway, she could use a friend like you.

--Shelly

Flenn looked up at Wayne, summoning every ounce of self-control he could not to run and pop the drive into his computer. He simply said, "You're right, Wayne. This is private church business. How about I take care of it?"

Wayne sipped his coffee. "Thanks," he said, then stared into the mug for a long time. "I guess I should be honest. That envelope was just an excuse to come see you." He shook his head. "I just needed to get out this morning. It's hard having to handle my own grief along with the kids' pain too. How do you tell your children that their mom's never coming back?" He wiped his eyes with a paper napkin. "Flenn, I have no idea how we're going to get through this."

"One day at a time," Flenn said. "One day at a time." He reached over and squeezed Wayne's hand. They spoke for nearly an hour. Wayne hadn't been sleeping much and neither had the kids. He asked the priest for the name of a child therapist; Flenn recommended one at Homewood Counseling Associates. He also suggested that Wayne see someone as well.

They talked a bit more before Wayne said he had to relieve his sister and get back to the kids. Anxious to examine the contents of the flash drive, Flenn didn't try to detain him. After Wayne left, Flenn inserted the drive into the USB port on the computer Zack had left with him. Before viewing the contents, Flenn downloaded a copy directly onto the desktop—not something Zack would have recommended without having first checked for malware, but then Zack's occupation dealt in secrecy, Flenn's in sincerity. Plus, Flenn didn't want to wait any longer.

He opened the attachment and a video began to play. Flenn saw what looked like a kid's bedroom. Judging from the dolls, posters, and toys in the background, it was a girl's room. There was movement off to the left and then a teenager sat down in front of the camera. He knew who it was even though he'd never met Shelly O'Reilly. She was a petite blonde with penetrating, yet, sad eyes.

Um, yeah, it's me, Shelly. I'm making this video to set the record straight. If you're seeing this, then something has happened to me before I could get out of this hellhole!

Behind me you probably see a lot of dolls, toys, and crap. They were all bought by my mother's husband, Douglas MacArthur O'Reilly—Birmingham Councilman Douglas MacArthur O'Reilly! He's the one who gave me all this junk because he felt guilty for all the times he molested me. That's right; Mac O'Reilly—the man who adopted me when I was seven years old and made me change my name to his—is a child molester!

It happened hundreds of times before I figured out how to make him stop. At first, I didn't understand. As I got older, I was too scared to do anything about it, until a few months ago when I finally threatened to expose the creep.

Oh, and in case you're wondering… my mother knew! She knew! She caught him more than once. The only thing she ever said to me about it was that it was all my fault! Great parents, huh? Anyway, I want all their snobby friends to know what he did to me; that I went to work for a pimp downtown named Valentino Ramirez and let other scum use me so that one day I could leave home and start over—far away from here!

If you are seeing this video, then I guess that didn't happen. So please, make sure this goes viral. Send a copy to everyone! I want them all to know exactly what Mac and Juanita O'Reilly did to me.

May they both rot in hell!

The video faded to a white screen as Flenn sat in stunned silence. *Two girls… the same age… both blondes… both working for the same pimp. It was beyond coincidence. Lindsay and Shelly O'Reilly were one and the same!*

CHAPTER THIRTY-NINE

Councilman Mac O'Reilly poured himself another bourbon and sat down behind his desk at home. It was 3 o'clock in the morning. He read through the email for the third time but couldn't bear to watch the video again. The councilman had opened the email just before going to bed, after reading the subject line in bold: **You Molested Shelly**! The sender had been anonymous.

Attached to the email was a two-minute video of his stepdaughter telling… everything!

The ingrate! He was glad now that she was dead.

O'Reilly hadn't identified her at the morgue that day, even after seeing the dwarfed toe. *Deformed little tramp! She deserved to die for the way she'd treated him this past year! He had loved her! Hadn't he told he that repeatedly?*

How, or why, she died, he hadn't a clue, nor did he care anymore. Back at the morgue, he'd made a snap decision not to tell Juanita until later; that it would be better if Shelly simply stayed missing. Should it ever be discovered that the girl was indeed his stepdaughter, he would simply claim that her body had been unrecognizable.

She didn't have to end up like that! Didn't she always like the presents he brought home: dolls and toys at first, and then clothes and makeup? He'd never liked the makeup, *it made her look too grown-up, not a little girl anymore. And, what about all those trips to the country? The pony rides? The trips to the coast? Had all that meant nothing to her?*

Above the attachment, someone had written, "This is about to go viral—just wanted you to know."

Mac knew what that meant—*a call from the mayor's office, police cars outside his house, reporters shouting questions.*

He looked back at the note he'd written. "I'm sorry," was all it said.

It was a lie, but Juanita deserved something for not sending him away when she'd discovered what was going on. Juanita had grown accustomed to his money, which had been his plan all along. It was Shelly he'd wanted from the beginning, but the ungrateful brat turned on him last year—threatened to go public if he didn't leave her alone. Said she had made a video just in case he tried to hurt her again.

This was that very video!

How someone had found it, he hadn't a clue. After she went missing, he had torn her room apart searching for it, and anything else that might implicate him. *Someone else must have been keeping the video for her; and now they were about to post it on the internet!*

He downed the last of the bourbon in a single gulp and set the glass down.

It was time.

He reached into the drawer and pulled out his revolver. He didn't let himself think about it—just pushed the barrel into his mouth and fired.

CHAPTER FORTY

Flenn was on his second cup of coffee when the phone rang. It was a blocked number.

"Have you heard?"

Why even have rules if Zack's not going to follow them? he thought.

"What happened to using Thomas Cranmer?" Flenn said.

"I live that cloak and dagger stuff all the time," Zack answered, popping a green jellybean into his mouth. "Do I have to keep doing it with you?"

Flenn set his cup down on the kitchen table. A kitten stuck her whiskers in to investigate, then shook her head and stalked away in disgust. "You've been taking a lot of liberties, Zack. We set that stuff up in the beginning for a reason."

Zack thought he heard a hissing sound in the background. "Yeah, yeah; we can talk about that some other time. I just wanted to know if you've heard the news?"

"About Mac's suicide? I just got off the phone with the bishop. He didn't sound overly upset."

"From what you've told me, it was long overdue."

Flenn straightened in his chair. "Wait a minute. Zack, what did you do?"

"I don't know what you mean."

If one could hear a smirk in someone's tone, Flenn was hearing one now. "Damn it, Zack! Did you send that video to O'Reilly?"

"You can't prove that I did." Zack answered. "In fact, nobody can."

"I only sent that file to you as a backup! That video was for the police… eventually."

"And it still will be," Zack countered, "… eventually."

Zack's threat to O'Reilly that he was about to post the video on YouTube was only that, a threat. Zack knew Flenn needed some help. He'd taken a swipe at the councilman simply to unnerve him.

"What if they find your email on his computer and trace it back to you?"

"Remember the file I sent you?" Flenn did. It had disappeared 24 hours after being opened.

"Not all of them take a full day to go away," Zack said.

Flenn grunted. "So, what now?"

"Nothing's changed," Zack pointed out. "You can still send your detective friend that file as soon as you help me take care of my little problem." He meant Farhad Ahmad. Zack hadn't seen the man lately, but knew Ahmad was somewhere close. Zack couldn't afford to keep this game of cat and mouse going much longer. *It needed to end, and soon.*

Flenn explained, "I haven't figured out when or how to give this to the police."

"Just tell them the truth... Minerva's husband gave it to you."

"And when they ask why I sat on it for a few days?"

"You're a priest," said Zack. "You keep confidential stuff for people all the time."

"That doesn't always work, you know." Flenn glanced down into his cup of coffee, still trying to absorb the news. "Zack, I can't say that I'm happy about what you did, but I can't say that I'm all that torn up about it either. The man was a monster. Flenn's voice softened. "Still, I'll say a prayer for Mac's soul."

"You are unbelievable, my friend," said Zack. "Simply unbelievable."

CHAPTER FORTY-ONE

The girl in the lobby of the Sheraton could have been anybody's kid: slender and cute, with short brown hair and dark eyes. She wore tight-fitting blue jeans with a low-cut black camisole meant to show more cleavage than she actually had. She'd been told to wait by the elevator. Her "date" would pick her up and escort her to his room. Valentino hadn't offered a description but had told her the man was willing to pay more than usual, a lot more. *She'd go home to her uncle with more than $4,000 tonight... which meant someone had paid $8,000 to Ramirez for her!* Valentino had told her that he hadn't met the man, but that he'd received payment through an online service. She was to get her share afterward. That was how things sometimes worked.

Denise tried not to appear anxious. *Men, who paid more usually expected more.* She'd have to pretend to enjoy it, just like her uncle had shown her ever since her mother had dumped her on him. Still, $4,000 would buy a lot of vodka. The more vodka her uncle drank, the more he left her alone—which was always a good thing. As long as she continued to give him all her money, her uncle saw to it that she had a place to live, plenty of food and whatever clothes she needed.

Before her mom had abandoned her, they'd lived for a year in a dilapidated Ford Focus, traveling across the country, hungry and homeless. Her uncle had taken them in, but then one day Denise woke up to find that her mother had left. Her uncle informed her that she'd have to earn her keep. It wasn't long before she found out what that meant. He soon took her to see a "friend of a friend," who'd turned out to be Valentino Ramirez. The pimp had made her undress, looked her up and down, and then said that she'd have to have some work done before he could send her out. Her uncle made her cut her hair, learn how to wear makeup, and even practice walking seductively in clothes that were way too tight. He'd already taught her how to do the other things—the ones she'd be doing for the men Valentino found for her.

A stocky man with a receding hairline and a too-short tie walked up to her from across the busy lobby. "Are you Denise?"

"That's me," the teenager said, turning on the charm the way she had been taught. "Wow! Nobody told me you were going to be so handsome."

The man ignored the comment. "Come with me."

They rode the elevator to the 14th floor and walked down to Room 1411. He held the door open for her. Inside were two double beds, a flat screen TV, a bureau, a chair... and another man! *Now she knew why she was being so well paid, and how she was going to have to earn that money!*

The other man looked familiar. He smiled and told her not to be afraid. *Didn't they all say that? It always meant just the opposite.* The stocky man sneezed, then said, "Denise, I'm Detective Rainsford. That fellow over there I believe you've already met. He is Father Scott Flenn. He's an Episcopal priest, and the one who arranged this meeting through your pimp, Valentino Ramirez."

An older girl might have tried to bolt, but she was too scared. *What would her uncle say? More importantly, what would he do? She'd never been busted before!*

Guy saw the fear in her eyes. "I'm not here to arrest you."

Denise looked at one man and then the other.

"And we're not here to have sex with you either," added Flenn. "We just want to talk to you about a friend of yours."

"Look mister," she stammered. "I haven't done anything wrong… and I don't have any friends."

Flenn sat down on the bed, close enough to grab her should she try to run for the door. "We know you haven't done anything wrong, Denise. That's why Detective Rainsford is not arresting you." The girl searched their faces, trying to make sense of what was happening.

"Father Flenn wants to help you," the cop said, still trying to figure out how the priest had known about Denise. Flenn had called him two nights ago and asked if Denise worked for Valentino Ramirez. When Guy told him she did, Flenn had set up this elaborate plan. "He's already talked to some people and tells me he can get you a whole new life out west in a place that takes in girls like you."

Denise's eyes narrowed. "What do you mean, 'like me'?"

Flenn chimed in, "Girls who need a second chance." He spoke to her in a reassuring tone. "Denise, we know all about Valentino, and we know about your uncle, too. We also know he doesn't have legal custody of you; so, a friend of mine, a judge here in town, has signed some papers letting me have temporary custody." Flenn wasn't telling a complete lie, but it was important that Guy and Denise both believed him about the judge. Zack was even now calling in favors that would supply papers for Flenn to have temporary custody without having to go to court. Zack had used the CIA server to tap into the uncle's computer remotely. He'd found hundreds of disgusting images, which he had forwarded to the FBI. The man would be arrested in the next day or two.

Denise protested. "I don't need nobody… "

"Just hear me out," Flenn said. "The place I'd like to send you is a ranch. They take in girls who've been abused, or put on the street, and they give them a safe place to stay. They also will give you an education; and, if you decide to stay, they'll teach you a skill."

"Got one, thanks." She looked toward the door; Guy shifted to block her path.

"I know it sounds too good to be true," Flenn said, "but this place is for real. I can even show you pictures of it on my phone. Denise, they can give you a brand-new start. Like I said, they'll teach you a skill and help you get a good job."

Denise scowled. "Like working at McDonald's… not interested."

"Like one day working in a hospital, a doctor's office or a university."

She studied Flenn closely. "College?"

"If you work hard."

Denise looked down at the floor, seeming even smaller than she had before. "I… I can't read," she said.

Flenn and Guy exchanged a glance. "You'll be reading in six months, I promise. With their tutors and teachers, you'll be at grade level within a year."

"Who's going to pay for all this?" she asked, clearly not buying it.

Flenn just said, "It's been taken care of."

"Right… sounds like a place where they trap girls and then force them to work for free."

Guy spoke up. "If you agree, I'll take you to court where you can talk with the judge who signed the order yourself." Flenn hoped it wouldn't come to that. *Zack wouldn't look good in judge's robes.*

"I'll fly out there with you," Flenn said. "Along with a female security officer," he added. "You won't have to stay if you don't like it, but I think you'll want to once you see the place."

She was quiet for a moment, suspicious, yet wanting to believe this miracle could be for real. "My uncle… "

"You won't ever have to see him again," Flenn said, looking up at Guy. "We will make sure he leaves you alone."

"So, let me get this straight: You meet me one time

and now you're doing this for me out of the goodness of your heart?"

"Not exactly," said Guy. "We want some information."

"I knew it! What information?"

Flenn looked at her. "We want to know about a girl named Lindsay."

The girl's eyes widened. She hesitated. "Don't know her."

"Look, Denise," Flenn said, trying not to let on to Guy yet that Shelly O'Reilly and Lindsay were the same person—not until he had a chance to find Minerva's killer. "We know you both worked for Valentino. What we don't know is who killed her."

The girl looked away. "I don't know what you're talking about."

"It's possible that the same person who killed Lindsay may have just killed another girl... and is probably going to kill anyone else who might know his identity. That could mean you, Denise."

"We're just trying to protect you," Guy added.

Denise was fighting back tears. "I don't know anything about Lindsay or the preacher or any of this. Please, just let me go home!"

Guy tensed. *Preacher? He knew it! It was the preacher!*

Flenn held up his hand before Guy started to gloat. The priest had asked Guy to trust him, and so far, the man hadn't let him down. Flenn had promised to explain how he'd managed to put it all together, and how he knew about Denise, if Guy would just support him tonight. It was beyond every rule in the book, but Guy had agreed; surprisingly, he was feeling pretty good about it. *After all,* Guy reminded himself, *he didn't get a chance to rescue a kid from monsters very often.*

They sat in pensive silence as the girl looked from one man to the other, her eyes beginning to tear up.

"Denise," Flenn said, "you haven't done anything wrong. You're the victim in all of this. What we are offering you is a new life, a new beginning. You can become whatever you want to be from this point on, but we need to know who murdered Lindsay."

The girl looked lost, afraid, and so very young. She began to shake. "I don't know… I don't know who killed her."

Guy interjected, "Roxanne told me... "

She cut the detective off, "Roxy? Oh, my God! Is that the other girl who was killed?" Rainsford didn't answer. The girl looked as if she were about to faint.

"Roxy told me something about this preacher," Guy said, "Do you know anything about him? Do you know his name?"

The girl turned as pale as the bedspread on the bed beneath her. "Oh, Jesus… oh sweet Jesus!"

"Denise, we can protect you. We really can." Flenn reached out for her trembling hands. You can be out of town starting a whole new life by this time tomorrow. Just tell us what we need to know."

"I can't! He said he'd kill me if I ever told! He was the one who Lindsay went out with that night. It's my fault! Sometimes… sometimes we do favors for each other to earn more money. I set her up with him that night behind Valentino's back."

She pleaded with the priest, wiping away the tears with the back of her hand. "You don't understand; I owed her! Lindsay had done that for me several times. My uncle... he kept demanding more money. The preacher had my number and called me that night. I was already committed, so I set him up with Lindsay. I had no idea he was going to kill her. I swear I didn't... "

Guy and Flenn looked at each other. *Bingo!*

She looked up in terror. "I swear to you, I didn't know!"

Flenn patted her hand. "We believe you. Now, listen to me, Denise: You didn't do anything to hurt Lindsay. None of this is your fault. Just tell us who he is and let us handle it from here."

"Don't you get it? He said he would kill me if I ever told anyone about him, about what we did... "

"Nobody's going to hurt you," Guy said brusquely.

"I... I think I want a lawyer."

Damn it! Guy wanted to punch his fist through the wall but Flenn kept talking. *The priest obviously didn't know the rules, that once someone requested a lawyer, a cop couldn't ask any more questions.*

Flenn knelt beside the trembling girl. "Listen to me, Denise. You don't have to tell us who he is right now." He gently wiped away her tears. "We'd like for you to, but I don't want you to be scared. We're here to protect you from ever being hurt again. That is the most important thing of all. You can still go to the ranch with me tomorrow where you'll be safe. He can't find you there. You'll sleep here tonight and we can leave in the morning. I already have a security officer ready to stay with you here tonight. You and I can be on that plane in the morning to start your new life." He didn't tell her that he'd already wired a $25,000 deposit. If Denise stayed at the ranch, Flenn had agreed to pay all her expenses—even for her to go to a local college later if she chose to pursue it.

The girl wiped her eyes with the back of her hand. "You mean I get to go to this place even if I don't tell you who the preacher is?"

Guy shot Flenn a warning glance. "Father, may I have a word?"

"That's exactly what I mean." Flenn lifted her chin. "Denise, I don't know if you believe in God or not, but I do, and I believe God thinks that you are *very* special. You are worth so much more than those men, or your uncle, will ever know."

Denise stared into his eyes, wanting to believe him.

"You and I can be on that plane tomorrow morning. You can come back here if you want. I will stay there with you until you decide."

She shook her head. "I… I don't know."

Guy didn't like what he was hearing. The girl had asked for an attorney. "Father… please… outside!"

Flenn got up slowly and stepped out into the hallway. "Look, Guy, I know what you're going to say. I know she just asked for a lawyer and that officially you're supposed to either let her go now or arrest her for soliciting, but if you let her go we may never find her again. And, if you arrest her, she sure as hell isn't going to tell us anything!"

Guy looked as if he was about to explode.

"Please," Flenn said, "I know I'm asking you to go out on a limb here, but I need you to believe me when I say that I know what I am doing. I will take her to Colorado as planned; if she tells me who the preacher is, then great, but if not, then we have at least gotten this one child out of harm's way. Later, maybe you can ask her for help when you charge Valentino."

Guy considered what the priest was telling him. *He hadn't arrested her, so technically he might be okay; but, to let a potential witness skip town? How could he do that?* He thought of the trembling child on the other side of the hotel door. *How many other hotel rooms had she been in? Just how much had this kid gone through… how much evil had been done to her?*

Guy turned away from Flenn. *God, what this priest was asking him to do! Forcing him to choose between his career and his humanity.* He wanted to pull out what was left of his hair. The detective began to pace back and forth as Flenn waited in silence for him to decide. Guy thought of his job, his captain, the system. *He was a part of that system! Up until now, he hadn't questioned it all that much. The years had taken their toll, but he had signed on as a cop long ago with a desire to help people. How was arresting this child going to help anyone? How could he turn his back on this girl? These people in Colorado could help her. Maybe the priest would be able to get the preacher's name out of the kid… maybe not. Even if he didn't, how would things be any worse than before?*

Guy wheeled around and shoved past the priest and pushed open the door. "Denise, the Father here is offering you the best deal you will ever have in your life. You need to take him up on it."

Denise was still crying, but Guy knew she was also thinking. Finally, she looked into Father Flenn's green eyes. "I get to come back if I don't like it, right?"

Success!

In unison, both men answered, "Right!"

Guy nodded to Father Flenn to call the security guard who had been waiting downstairs. Just how the priest had made all these arrangements so quickly, Guy hadn't a clue, but right now he didn't care. He'd made his decision and felt good about it. He would be taking a girl away from Valentino Ramirez; and this one, at least, would be getting away with her life.

CHAPTER FORTY-TWO

Denise fell asleep after eating a hamburger and fries from room service. She'd also asked for a beer, but the security guard had simply laughed and ordered her a soda instead.

In the morning, a fresh change of clothes was sent up to the room. Walmart had been the only store open late, and since Flenn didn't know Denise's size; he'd had to guess. Not at all what she would have picked for herself, and a bit baggy, but she didn't complain when Father Flenn arrived to pick them both up. Flenn had been worried that Denise might change her mind and try to run once they got to the airport, so he'd offered the guard an additional five-grand to go with them to Colorado.

Zack had promised Flenn he'd have the papers overnighted to the camp. Real or forged, Flenn didn't know, but Zack would have been thorough either way. Since the girl's mother was out of the picture, and her uncle would soon be in prison, there was little chance anyone would challenge whatever it was Zack had put together.

Sitting in the Birmingham airport between Flenn and the security officer, Denise seemed more relaxed and reflective.

"You okay?" Flenn asked Denise as he sat back and sipped black coffee from a Styrofoam cup.

"Yeah. Only… "

"What?"

The girl seemed excited and nervous at the same time. "I've never been on an airplane before."

"Neither have I," added the guard.

"Oh, great!" Flenn laughed. "Don't you ladies get airsick on me." Denise smiled for the first time since he'd met her. Flenn rubbed the top of her head without thinking, but she didn't pull away. Later, on the plane, she fell asleep with her head on his shoulder.

"She feels safe with you," the guard said, before dropping off to sleep herself. Flenn leaned back, careful not to disturb either of them. Denise had probably never felt safe a day in her life. He wondered what it had taken last night for her to surrender herself to a stranger and trust that he was taking her to a place where she would be treated like a human being. *Had it been hope… or despair? Probably both,* he told himself.

The trio disembarked at Denver International in the early afternoon. They were met by a large, rosy-cheeked, slightly sunburned woman by the name of Sally. She was wearing worn blue jeans and a pink flannel shirt with a blue bandana and was carrying a heavy jacket for Denise. "You Southern girls don't know what cold is," the woman said cheerily. It had been so warm yesterday that Flenn hadn't thought about a coat. It had been hard enough last night worrying about a parishioner catching him buying young women's underwear.

Sally was around 40 with flaming red hair and a demeanor that Denise took to almost immediately. They said goodbye to the security guard and the three of them climbed into a late model Jeep Cherokee. They drove for over an hour before arriving at the Fresh Start Ranch. Denise was curious, lobbing endless questions at Sally, who didn't seem to be at all annoyed by the girl's chatter. Flenn realized that Denise was probably discovering happiness for the first time in her life… if not happiness, then, at least, safety.

They spent the rest of the afternoon touring the massive ranch. Sally, who was also a licensed psychotherapist, explained the rules. For the first month Denise would not be allowed to make phone calls except to Father Flenn. She was to be present for all meals, and on time for all group therapy sessions; *Corrals*, they called them. She would also be assigned a *Trail Boss*, who was a trained therapist. Flenn had already explained Denise's lack of an education over the phone. Sally said that there would be a tutor to help Denise learn to read beginning next week. Lastly, Sally explained that Father Flenn would be visiting every other month to check on Denise's progress. It was something Sally and Flenn had already worked out. It was a lot for the young girl to take in; but, by the end of the day, Denise had stopped asking questions and seemed lost in her own private thoughts.

Denise had been quiet around the other girls they met, but she seemed to like the dormitory and the school, and her eyes had grown the size of horseshoes when she saw the stables—large red-and-white buildings with more than a dozen horses in each. Every girl, Sally explained, was assigned a horse to feed and groom. Denise admitted she'd always dreamed of riding. One of the girls was cleaning a stall and demonstrated how to approach a gelding, even showed her how to stroke his mane. It was at that moment when Flenn knew Denise would agree to stay.

After dinner, Sally introduced the 15-year-old to her two roommates and took her off to her new room. Flenn was allowed to stay overnight in the guest quarters. The next morning, when he came to say goodbye, Denise hugged the priest tightly. Flenn stood in the lobby of the dormitory holding her for the longest time as she buried her face in his chest. "Thank you," she said, tears rolling down her cheeks. "I still don't understand any of this. None of it seems real! Nobody has ever helped me… not ever. I keep waiting to wake up and find that this was all just a dream." She looked up at him. "I won't ever understand why you did this for me, but thank you, thank you *so* much!"

He took her small chin in his strong, gentle hands; a tear forming in his own eye, which he quickly wiped away. "Remember what I said in that sermon when we first met?"

She nodded.

"God loves you, Denise. I believe that with all my heart, and I hope one day you will come to believe it, too. Just promise me that you will never go back to your old way of life. That's all the thanks I will ever need." Denise hugged him again. He held her for a moment, and then let go. As he turned to leave, Denise pulled him back, then tugged on his shirt until his face was next to hers. She kissed him on the cheek.

He smiled, his cheeks turning bright red. She put her hand up to his ear and whispered, "The preacher—his name is Benjamin Rye."

CHAPTER FORTY-THREE

The Guatemalan was hungry but there was a job to finish first. The apartment house had not been difficult to find, even at midnight. He slid on the thin gloves, carefully attached a suppressor to his Luger, and chambered the first round. Pulling the black ski mask over his face, he looked around. The street was empty.

He quietly managed to unlock the back door with a tool he kept for just such occasions, and found his way upstairs to the pimp's apartment. The door was unlocked. For a man his size, the Guatemalan was amazingly quiet. He slipped noiselessly into the living room. A solitary lamp from the bedroom cast shadows into the hallway. He could see two figures moving. He slowly raised his pistol as he stepped through the bedroom door. A man he'd never seen before bolted upright, pulling the covers up to his chest. Valentino Ramirez turned over.

"Who the hell are you?" shouted the first man. The Guatemalan answered by shooting him twice in the chest. Ramirez sprang for his pants and his pistol, but the Guatemalan shot him through the back of his head just as his feet hit the floor.

The pimp had been a liability to his boss. The

Guatemalan didn't know why, nor was it his place to ask. It was simply his job to eliminate such liabilities. *The girl, her mother, and now her former pimp—only two more to go. Soon he could go home.* He walked over, kicked Ramirez in the side, and, just to be sure, shot him a second time.

As he walked out the back door, the Guatemalan looked at his watch wondering if he might find someplace open this late; he was in the mood for a milkshake.

CHAPTER FORTY-FOUR

"Zack, are you sitting down?" Sally had let Flenn use the privacy of her office to make a phone call right after he'd said goodbye to Denise. "The man who killed Shelly O'Reilly… looks like it may have been Benjamin Rye!"

Flenn was still trying to piece it all together in his head. Rye was a total jerk and a scumbag, but he had no idea Benji was capable of anything like this. *A teenaged prostitute? Definitely. But, murder?*

Zack was silent for a moment, then asked. "How sure are you, on a scale from one to 10?"

"Eight," Flenn said, "…and a half."

"Good enough for me."

"According to Denise, Rye had been with Lindsay... Shelly… the night she disappeared. If he did kill her, I think I have an idea where, and I'm pretty sure he had help."

"I'm all ears," Zack said.

"Shelly went missing the last weekend of school," Flenn recited from memory. "That was a Friday night, May 27… May 27, Zack!"

"Okay, I'll bite; what's so special about May 27?"

"Didn't you say that Romero and Rye were together the last weekend of May?" Flenn waited for it to register. When it did, it hit Zack like a thunderbolt.

"Oh, my God!" Zack shouted.

The Ryes have a cabin they used to stay at in the summer. I'd get dragged there as a kid with my folks. From what Elizabeth has told me, nobody goes out there anymore, except for the caretaker."

"Yeah, so… "

"So, it's right on the Cahaba River, which washes in to Shades Creek! That's where Shelly's body was eventually found. It just took a few months for it to surface."

"You're thinking Rye and Romero killed the kid at the cabin and threw her body in the river?"

"That's exactly what I'm thinking!"

Zack took it all in, then said, "Only one problem."

"I know." Flenn sighed. "We can't prove any of it."

CHAPTER FORTY-FIVE

Guy Rainsford pulled up outside the arrivals terminal at Birmingham International Airport. Flenn was waiting by the curb. The detective reached over and unlocked the door, "I got your message. I can't believe Denise said the preacher is the son of Willy Rye!"

Flenn climbed in, throwing his carry-on in the back seat. "I can, Detective. I can. I've known that jerk for years. Our parents were friends once upon a time. Benji was a jerk even as a kid." Flenn had considered not telling Guy, but he figured he owed the man; the detective had put his badge on the line to save Denise. Flenn just had to figure out how to delay him from pursuing Rye, at least until Zack had pieced enough together to take it all to Langley.

Guy pulled out of the airport onto Messer Road. "Do you think Rye killed Lindsay?"

That's exactly what Flenn thought, but he only said, "I don't know." Flenn needed time to figure out one more detail.

"I'll drop you off at the church and go talk with him," Guy said

"You think that's wise?" Flenn had rehearsed his response. "I mean, we don't know for certain that Rye had anything to do with Lindsay's murder. If you tip your hat now, he'll have plenty of time to hide behind every overpaid lawyer in town."

The detective looked deflated. "I've got to do something! I can't just sit here. You heard Denise; she said she gave Lindsay the preacher's number. He may have been the last person to see her alive, which gives me all I need to bring in that imposter."

"I've got an idea," Flenn offered. "My family is connected with a top-notch detective agency up in New England." He laid it on thick: "They're good, really good. I can have them come down and give us some behind-the-scenes help. We really should gather more evidence before we go after Benjamin Rye."

"We?"

"Sorry, I meant *you.*"

Guy considered the offer. *What could a couple of days hurt? He didn't want to have to hand over the case to Wickes and Hollister. Knowing those two, they'd take all the credit. Plus, how was he going to explain to Toone the Loon about Denise?*

Guy looked at the priest. "How soon could you have those guys here?"

"Day after tomorrow." He'd used this lie twice now— first with Juanita, now Guy.

Guy thought for a moment. "I guess I'm already up to my ass in alligators." The detective shook his head, "Oh well, I hear McDonald's is hiring." Guy pulled onto I-59, heading for Saint Ann's. "While I still have a job, I'm going to bring Lindsay's pimp in for questioning."

Flenn didn't have a problem with that.

"It's time I begin to squeeze that low-life. Any chance Denise will testify against Valentino Ramirez?"

Flenn shook his head. "I don't think so, at least not any time soon. I mean, can you blame her? Two of her friends have already been killed." Flenn wanted Denise to have as much time in Colorado as possible before Guy brought her back to Birmingham to testify. *Hopefully, if Zack was successful, she'd never have to come back!*

Guy passed a semi and crossed into the next lane. "So, are you ready to tell me how you knew about Denise?"

Before Flenn could answer, Guy's radio buzzed and a dispatcher called in a 10-92. Guy turned up the receiver and listened for the address. "That's Valentino Ramirez's neighborhood."

"What's a 10-92?"

Guy switched on the car's blue lights.

"Homicide!"

They sped down I-59 and turned south on Highway 31 before taking University Boulevard to Eighth Avenue. Blue lights flashed on both sides of the street; it reminded Flenn of the scene in front of Saint Latimer's last week. Guy bolted out of the car; Flenn followed, working his way through the crowd of plain clothes and uniformed police. Nobody questioned why a priest was at a crime scene. Clergy were sometimes called to help with the families. They walked up a flight of stairs and found several more cops inside the apartment. Guy and Flenn made their way through the living room and into the bedroom. A guy in a suit was taking photographs.

Two men lay motionless, both naked. One was still in bed, shot twice. The other was on the floor lying face up, shot through the head and chest. Flenn recognized a professional hit when he saw one.

As did Guy.

"My God!" Guy pointed to the body on the floor. "That's Valentino Ramirez!"

Flenn looked at the two bodies and then around the room. Clothes were strewn everywhere. Still in its holster, a Ruger 9-millimeter lay atop a pair of silk trousers draped over a chair near the bed.

One of Ramirez' "employees" had discovered the bodies this morning, a uniformed officer told Guy. The woman was downstairs now being questioned. Guy glanced from the bodies to the walls to nowhere in particular. He looked as if he was about to explode. Without so much as uttering a word, Guy turned and bolted out the door, his face as red as the 'Bama football pennant hanging from the neighbor's porch across the street. Guy stormed over to his car, leaned against the fender and stared off into space. Flenn knew what was coming.

Sure enough, Guy slammed both hands against the hood. "Damn it! That son of a … I'm sorry, Father, but I just don't give a damn right now! That scuzzball knew about Rye and never told me! And now he's dead!"

Wow! Flenn thought. *Two murdered men, but what was troubling the cop was that the pimp had not told him about Rye.* "I suspect the man didn't tell you the names of any of his clients," Flenn said.

"That's not the point! Ramirez knew who the preacher was all along! It's how Roxanne knew that her John had been a preacher. Benjamin Rye's face is all over the place! Everybody in Birmingham knows the Ryes!" Guy hit the hood several more times. "Damn it! I should have pressed when she first told me about him. God, I'm such a fool!"

Flenn needed to give Zack time to expose the Iranian connection. "You are not a fool, Detective. If Benjamin Rye was involved with Lindsay's murder, then you'll figure it out. Just give it time." Flenn figured Rye and Romero had killed Shelly, and then one, or both of them had murdered Roxanne—along with her mother. *And now, they, or someone they'd hired, had just killed their pimp! It was simple; Rye and Romero were covering their tracks.*

"Father, if Rye killed Lindsay, then maybe he's responsible for Roxanne, or this, too. I'm sorry, but I can't wait for your private detective friends. I'm going to have to talk to him."

Flenn took a breath. "Guy, I'm not a cop, but that seems to be quite a leap. Rye was a client, but that doesn't make him the murderer. If he is involved, do you really want to tip him off without conclusive evidence? The killer could have been any one of several people."

"I don't give a…; I'm going over there, over to Rye Ministries! Why do you care anyway?"

"I care about Denise, that's why! I just got her settled into a new life. You saw her: She's scared to death. She's not likely to testify about any of this, not yet at least. All we have is her word whispered to me. Come on, you were in that hotel room with me, you saw her. I'd hate to see her lose out on this one chance. Give my guys time. Let's see what they can find out first. You're still lead investigator on Lindsay's case. Don't we owe it to her to be thorough?"

Guy looked away. He was furious... furious that he hadn't been able to protect Roxanne... furious that Valentino had never told him about Rye... furious that someone had gotten to the pimp before he could... and, most of all, furious that the priest was right! He *should* let Flenn's people help. He could end up blowing everything right now by going off half-cocked. *If Rye was connected to Lindsay's death, he needed to be sure the charges stuck!*

Guy was silent for a long time as the color in his face slowly returned to its normal shade of pale. "Okay," he said at last. "One week. But that's all, Father; no more." He sneezed. "Maybe by then, I'll be over this damned cold."

Flenn whispered a prayer of gratitude. He needed to make a phone call. Someone had to tell Zack Matteson that he had seven days to save the world.

CHAPTER FORTY-SIX

"You're late." Sadar Abbas had summoned Col. Amir into his office once a week since taking over as director of the Ministry of Intelligence.

"I apologize, Excellency. There was traffic this morning. It won't happen again."

Abbas leaned back in his chair and stared at his subordinate. *Amir was as stale as a seven-week-old turnip.* What he lacked in personality, his family made up for in sheer boorishness. Amir lived with his pompous wife and her worthless brother. Abbas had the displeasure of having met both during the festival of Nowruz, the Iranian New Year. Together, Amir's wife and brother-in-law didn't have the combined intelligence of one of the pet dogs the Ministry of Culture was currently rounding up and exterminating throughout the country.

"Colonel, I have been giving the matter of the American spy, Zachary Matteson, much thought these past few days. According to our people in Washington, he has made no report to his superiors. His continual proximity to Mr. Rye, however, is beginning to concern me. Too much is as stake for us to continue take a chance on this man. Eliminating him could be troublesome, but not nearly so much if Matteson becomes aware of our operation."

Sadar Abbas' eyebrows narrowed. "Do you follow me, Colonel?"

"Sir?"

Abbas sighed. *Stupid man!*

He looked directly at the colonel and spoke slowly. "I wish for you to order Farhad Ahmad to kill Matteson. Is that clear enough?"

The colonel's facial muscles never changed. It was as if his boss had just asked for a cup of tea. "Yes sir."

Abbas nodded. "Good. I think it best if this were to happen within the next forty-eight hours."

Amir's brow furrowed ever so slightly.

"Do you have a problem with that, Colonel?"

"No sir… only… "

"What?"

"The Libyan delegation is due this afternoon and you ordered me to stay with their ambassador while he is in Tehran."

Sadar Abbas sank back into his chair. "So, I did," he said, peering down at his desk calendar.

"Would you like me to appoint someone else to keep an eye on the ambassador, Excellency?"

Abbas waved his hand. "No… no, stay with the ambassador and his delegation. This is a matter which is important to our president. Trade negotiations are fragile right now." Abbas pulled out a notepad and pen. "Give me Ahmad's number and I will handle it myself." Amir pulled the satellite phone from the inside of his jacket to retrieve the number. "Better yet, just give me your phone," Abbas said. "That way I will know the moment the job is complete." Amir reluctantly handed the phone over, then showed his boss how to locate the number for Ahmad. Their business for the day concluded, Abbas simply waved his hand and said, "Dismissed."

CHAPTER FORTY-SEVEN

For most travelers, Prattville, Alabama, was simply a name on an exit sign on the way to the beach. Several hotels had sprung up on the edge of the town to accommodate those who weren't up for the final three hours to the Florida Panhandle—what was jokingly referred to by locals as the *Redneck Riviera*.

Zack and Flenn sat underneath a plastic Santa hanging from the patio ceiling of Jimmy-John's Rib Shack in Prattville. Zack was busy wolfing down a baked potato, stuffed with cheese, sour cream, butter, scallions, and a generous helping of North Carolina-style barbecued pork. Flenn thought if Zack stayed in Alabama much longer he might end up as obese as most of Jimmy-John's clientele.

Prattville was an hour south of Birmingham, and, according to Flenn, almost always five degrees hotter; so, dining outside today had been an option. With temperatures in the upper 50s, their windbreakers were sufficient against the breeze as it tried to blow the napkins off the table. Thankfully, the other diners had chosen to eat inside, giving the two men plenty of privacy. Flenn had just explained to Zack how he still wasn't over the fact that Lindsay, the call-girl, and Shelly, the debutante, were one and the same. Zack responded between mouthfuls by saying he'd seen it all before: "Rich girl gone bad."

Flenn stared at him. "You just don't get it, do you?"

"Get what?" Zack said, stuffing in another bite.

"You sound like some of my parishioners, thinking everybody gets what they deserve."

Zack took a gulp of overly sweetened tea before putting down the large plastic cup. "Yeah, pretty much."

Flenn looked away. "Shelly didn't *deserve* being abused by her stepfather for seven years, or a mother who looked the other way."

Zack considered that for a moment, then picked up a pickle and waved it at him. "True, but she did turn to prostitution. I think your good book has a lot to say about that."

"Actually, it does," Flenn said. "What it says is that many of the prostitutes are going to make it into heaven long before the so-called righteous people."

"You mean people like Benjamin Rye?"

Flenn stopped eating. He looked out across the gravel parking lot, past rows of old pickup trucks sporting varying degrees of rust. He nodded. "Shelly must have thought it was her only way out. Raise enough money, then go somewhere to chase whatever dreams an abused teenager keeps in the recesses of her imagination." He sighed. "Who knows? It might even have worked out if Romero and Rye hadn't destroyed those same dreams—and her with them." Flenn pushed his salad away. He wasn't hungry anymore.

Zack took an even bigger bite than before. "You

know," he said, his mouth full, this isn't bad barbecue; not nearly as good as Memphis-style, but good."

Flenn just glared at him.

"No seriously, I've been all over, and nobody beats Tennessee barbecue. It's their vinegar sauce; not this tomato-based stuff."

"Nothing gets to you, does it?" Flenn said.

Zack looked up from his plate. "What?"

"Damn it, Zack, a kid died! Actually, two did, and a third probably would have if I hadn't gotten her to Colorado first."

Zack leaned back in his chair. "You and I have seen dead kids all over the world."

Flenn shook his head as he studied his friend. "I've often wondered if I would have become as callous as you if I'd have stayed with the agency instead of getting out when I did."

"Callous?" Zack thought about that for a minute as he gnawed on a piece of gristle. "Yeah, I guess that pretty much describes me."

"Ever think of leaving?"

"All the time."

"So then, it *does* get to you?"

"Nope."

Flenn kicked him under the table. "You're a liar!"

"Yep."

Zack put down his fork. "What do you want me to say? Yes, a couple of kids are dead. One murdered, and probably another from what you told me. It *is* awful, but we've seen scores of dead kids, you and me. You never get used to it, but you go on and do the job." He reached out and caught his napkin before the wind whisked it away. "You say that I'm callous… well, of course I am. And, no matter what you think now, you used to be just as bad. Come on, Flenn, we had to be to do some of the things we did back then, things I *still* do, all for the greater good."

The conversation came to a halt as the waitress came to ask if they wanted dessert. Flenn wasn't interested. Zack ordered a slice of pecan pie, with a double scoop of ice cream.

"I can't let things faze me," Zack said, after she disappeared. "The moment I do, it will destroy me. Who knows, maybe one day it *will* destroy me. But for now, I just do the job and go on to the next thing. Same as we used to do together, once upon a time."

Ten years, Flenn thought. *Forever-ago… yesterday.*

"Zack, the job's destroying your soul. You just don't see it."

"Nah. I'm fine."

"Called your kids?"

"Shut up."

"See what I mean? Destroying you." Maybe Zack would never leave the agency. Flenn was beginning to wonder, *did anyone ever really leave?*

"Yeah, yeah. So, are you still going to help me with the game plan?" The waitress delivered Zack's pie, along with the bill.

Flenn took a sip of his water, and then glanced around the parking lot to make sure no one was listening. "Have you thought about what we'll do if your new friend doesn't have his phone with him?"

"He'll have it. Amir will have seen to that. All I'll need to do is push redial. Ahmad won't be using it to call anyone else, Amir will have ordered him not to. Just make sure you're out of harm's way, and that I have everything under control first. Keep him quiet while I'm on the phone with Amir. I'll do my best with the language thing. Though, as I recall, Colonel Amir speaks pretty good English."

Zack took a bite of the pie. "You'll need a gun. I assume you still have one?"

"Not going to happen, Zack. I made a promise, remember? You aren't going to use yours either, not in my church!"

"I get it," said Zack, pointing to the decoration hanging over them. "Christmas is coming and you don't want Santa to see. No problem."

Flenn ignored him. "What about the pimp? The hit looked professional to me."

Zack nodded. "Probably. I suspect the girl and her mother were, too. Have you thought of anyone else who might be able to connect the pimp with Rye?"

Flenn had been thinking of nothing else ever since he'd left Ramirez's apartment. There might be several names, but after talking with Guy Rainsford, he knew one that was certain to be on that list—Ashleigh Nieves. Roxanne would have likely told her about her time with Benjamin Rye. Even if she hadn't, Rye would have assumed that the girl would have told the woman who'd been trying to help her. He told Zack his thoughts. Zack thought for a moment, then said, "Okay, I've got an idea, but I'll need your help."

Flenn looked away. He was too deep in this to turn back now. As Zack went over the details to the second plan, Flenn had to admit it might work.

If it didn't?

Flenn felt a shiver run down his spine.

Two plans were on the table; both risky. One would stop a murderer, the other would put a halt to the Iranians. Capturing the hit man was one thing, but what about Zack's other plan? Even if it did work, there would still be two loose ends: Romero and Rye. Romero might still decide to run for election without the Iranians—if not now, then in four years. Rye would most certainly agree to become his prophet, turning the gullible into Romero's minions.

Flenn knew, if given the chance, Rye would push the whole *Divine Right of Kings* argument in defense of Romero—selling the unsophisticated the idea that God had ordained him to be president and, therefore, whatever Romero said had to be God's will. With his father's good name, Rye would be able to gather enormous support behind almost anything Romero wanted to do. Flenn stared across the parking lot at the traffic whizzing past. *Romero and Rye were killing people!* He didn't want to be involved in what Zack had just outlined, but what other choice was there?

It had been all too easy falling back onto the path he'd left behind. Flenn just hoped he'd be able to step away in the end—*before losing himself forever into that abyss!*

CHAPTER FORTY-EIGHT

Only one more job to do, then he could get on a plane and go home. The Guatemalan drove by Ashleigh Nieves's home three times before finding the best place to park his rental car so as not to raise suspicion. He had circled the block several times; the only person around was some guy in a Honda staring at his phone.

The Denise kid had disappeared without a trace. Regrettable, but nothing could be done about that; so, last night, he'd killed her uncle instead. *Wherever she was,* he reasoned, *the kid would figure out the score and keep her mouth shut.*

Dressed in torn chamois pants, a long-sleeved flannel shirt, and yard gloves, he looked like one of the gardeners that frequented the neighborhood. The Guatemalan opened the trunk and retrieved a pair of hedge clippers for effect. He planned to enter through the rear of the house and wait for the young woman to come home from work. *He'd have some fun first—make the cops think that was why she'd been killed.* He smiled. *Sometimes his job had perks.*

The kitchen door was a piece of cake; a simple slip of a credit card into the jamb. He pulled off the yard gloves and replaced them with his favorite thin ones—much easier to handle a knife with—or maybe he'd just strangle her instead. He put the garden gloves and sheers out of sight and made a mental note to collect them on his way out. He looked around. The house was nice enough, just messy. Dirty dishes in the sink, papers strewn on the table—it didn't look like she'd spent much time at home lately. Probably didn't have company over much either. *Pity*, he thought. He'd done his research; Ashleigh Nieves was a looker. Divorced, no children and no steady boyfriend, from what he'd gathered from her Facebook page.

He stepped on something squishy and stopped to examine it. Candy? Something black, a jellybean maybe. The Guatemalan made his way through the dining room and into the den—where he nearly jumped out of his skin! A man was sitting in a recliner, grinning, and pointing a pistol straight at his chest.

"What took you so long?"

"Yo no hablo ingles."

"Bullshit!" Zack stood slowly, maintaining his focus and his aim. "Now, take your gun out with your left hand, nice and easy, and throw it on the sofa; then, put your hands behind your head. You and I are going to have a little talk about your boss, Mr. Romero." At the mention of Romero's name, the man's eyes narrowed. Zack knew what that meant.

The Guatemalan dropped to his knees, as his hand darted behind his back.

Fast.

Just not fast enough. The big man was dead before the gun exited his waistband.

Zack walked over to give the body the customary kick. "Now look at what you've made me do! I've got to clean up this lady's house all because you wouldn't play nice. How inconsiderate, and so close to Christmas, too!"

He pulled out his phone and sent a text. "Cranmer here. Lucifer has fallen." Zack brushed the pocket lent off a jellybean and smiled at his own cleverness. He spent the next hour cleaning up while he waited for Flenn to arrive. He wasn't worried about anyone walking in on him. Ashleigh was staying with a relative. Zack had gone to New Beginnings two days ago to convince her to take a leave of absence. He'd told her his name was Sean Williams and that he was with the FBI. He'd also told her that she was in imminent danger, which she was. His story, however, was that the FBI had gotten intel that a serial killer was stalking her. Zack had said the man was wanted in three states, and was the estranged lover of one of the women who had come through New Beginnings. He wasn't at liberty to say which one. It had helped that Flenn had timed his visit to the shelter that same morning and was in Ashleigh's office when Zack arrived. Flenn had convinced her to take the rest of the week off. She had agreed to go to Pensacola to stay with her sister.

Flenn had figured out the same thing the Guatemalan had: that if anyone other than Ramirez knew about Benjamin Rye's relationship with teenaged prostitutes, it would have been Ashleigh. Posing as FBI Special Agent Williams, Zack had assured Ashleigh that, once captured, her stalker would be extradited to Ohio to face charges there; she would likely never even have to testify.

Standing over the Guatemalan's body, Zack mused whether they had extradition papers in hell. *Probably not for this piece of garbage!* he thought.

He went through the hitman's pockets and found a rental car keychain with one key... for a Toyota. It wouldn't be too hard to find, since the big man would have parked nearby. Zack rolled the body in a sheet of plastic he'd brought with him... just in case.

Flenn arrived by taxi, carrying a satchel and a box of trash bags. He took the key from Zack and went to search for the rental. He wasn't gone five minutes before he pulled a white Camry into the garage next to Zack's car, closing the garage door behind him. Zack noticed that Flenn seemed more of his old self tonight: tough, detached, thorough—*this was the Scott Flenn he remembered!*

After stuffing the body in the Camry's trunk, Zack grinned and jokingly suggested they park it in front of the Rye Foundation. Flenn didn't laugh. Not to be deterred, Zack offered a second option—dragging the body up the street and giving it to Farhad Ahmad.

Zack had found the locator chip hidden in his rental's rear bumper a few days before. It was a tracking device all right, but an ancient one. *With so much at stake, the Iranians should have invested in better equipment.* Zack shook his head. *Things weren't much different in the CIA these days. Apparently, bureaucratic knots, critical budget cuts, and governmental incompetence were borderless.*

Zack was surprised the neighbors hadn't reported a

stranger sitting in the car, but Ahmad had parked in front of a house that was for sale, and no one had paid him much attention. He pulled a jellybean out of his pocket and offered it to Flenn, who refused. "You okay?" Zack asked.

"No."

Zack decided it best to leave the matter alone. The plan was to dump the Guatemalan's car in a parking lot outside the city, someplace with no security cameras. Tomorrow, 'Special Agent Williams' would make a call to Ashleigh to tell her the man had been captured, and that she could return home. However, first Flenn would take Zack's car on an indirect route to Saint Ann's. As dark as it was getting outside, Ahmad wouldn't be able to see who was driving and would undoubtedly follow. Zack would give them a few minutes, then take the Guatemalan's Camry directly to the church and wait.

"So," Zack said, picking up a trash bag full of blood-soaked rags, cleanser, yard gloves and pruning shears. "Are you ready to do this?"

"Can you guarantee nobody else will get hurt?"

Zack smiled. "Sure."

Flenn shook his head. "Liar."

CHAPTER FORTY-NINE

Ahmad raised the window and sighed as he adjusted the car's heater. *Hot one day, cold the next! What was Allah thinking when he made Alabama!*

He was getting listless having spent nearly two weeks following a man who never did anything except go to churches and eat in greasy pig-diners. Then, Matteson had relocated to a hotel in some town called Prattville where Ahmad had to again keep watch from the parking lots of several more *accursed hash-houses full of the offensive stench of meat only infidels consumed.* And then, two days ago, Matteson had left Prattville and come here to Birmingham.

Ahmad was tired of this. *Fortunately, it was all about to change.*

He had gotten the order last night from none other than Sadar Abbas himself. The only stipulation was that he was to make it look like an accident. Ahmad was toying with the idea of sneaking into this house after midnight, killing Matteson, and then placing the body at the bottom of the stairs. He was trying to think of what he might use to hit Zack over the head with when a car drove into the garage. Less than an hour later, Matteson's car pulled out of the driveway and headed North.

Ahmad was hungry and tired, but Matteson was on the move, and he had no other option but to follow. *Why couldn't Allah ever make things easy?*

CHAPTER FIFTY

Darkness fell early in December, a reality which Guy Rainsford cursed every year. It was only 5:30, but he could hardly make out the front door of Saint Ann's Church from across the street. The encroaching fog certainly wasn't helping matters. Something had been nagging him all day; a feeling that the priest knew a lot more than he'd been telling him.

It had dawned on him this morning as he was taking his cold medicine—Father Flenn had followed him onto that murder scene without hesitation. They'd witnessed two bloody, naked bodies sprawled across the room, one of them with the back of his head blown off... *and the priest hadn't reacted!* Most people would have been sickened at seeing something like that; instead, Flenn had spent the next half hour convincing Guy not to confront Benjamin Rye, but rather letting some high-priced detective agency up North look around for clues! *Just where were these detectives, and why hadn't the priest introduced him to any of them by now?* Guy felt he was being manipulated; *but, to what end? Why would Father Flenn try to lead him away from Rye? None if it made any sense.*

Okay, Denise was one thing. Guy had checked the

ranch out and it was legit; so, Flenn had been straight with him about all that. Still, he couldn't get rid of the gnawing feeling that there was a lot more to this mess with Benjamin Rye. *Was the priest protecting Rye?* He remembered that Flenn had said his family had once been friends with the Ryes. Guy didn't like feeling odd-man-out in his own investigation. He'd driven to Saint Ann's tonight to find the priest and demand to meet one of these investigators. Failing that, he was going to take things back into his own hands.

There was something else; something weird. For the past hour, Guy had felt an urgency to find Father Flenn. He couldn't have explained it to anyone; he didn't understand it himself, but Guy couldn't shake the nagging feeling that he *had* to be here tonight. It wasn't the usual instinctive urge a cop develops over the years. No, this was more—it felt as if someone was standing over his shoulder, pushing him to be at Saint Ann's Church.

Find Father Flenn!

That thought kept going through his mind. Guy had tried calling several times, but all he got was the priest's voicemail, so here he was.

There were no cars in Flenn's driveway or next door at the church. Guy pulled out and circled the block for the umpteenth time. The lamppost in front of Saint Ann's flickered dimly and then brightened as he came around the corner. This time, Guy decided to park his car across from the Church and wait.

"This is stupid," he said aloud after watching the

lamppost flicker on and off several times. Nobody was around; nothing was moving. Not a single person had driven by for the past 20 minutes. *This is a waste of time!* Guy reached for the key just as he saw the headlights of an approaching car. The car turned the corner, pulling past the church, and parking just ahead of him. *That's strange,* he thought when no one got out of the car.

Another car rounded the corner and pulled into the church's parking lot. The streetlamp flickered on again and Guy watched Father Flenn get out of a white Toyota and hurry into the church. A second later, the church's stained-glass windows lit up from inside. A third car, a Honda, came around the corner and pulled behind the first. For some reason, Guy felt his stomach tighten.

A man got out of the Honda and crept up to the priest's car. *Wait a minute,* Guy thought, *didn't Flenn own a red convertible?*

Glancing from side to side, the man made his way toward the church. He opened the door slowly, then slipped inside. Guy watched as a second man climbed out of the first car and scurry across the street toward the church. Guy tensed. Just before the second man entered the church, Guy saw him pull a pistol from underneath his jacket.

Procedure was clear in these situations. Call for backup!

He didn't.

Instead, Guy drew his Beretta and rushed toward the door. Taking a deep breath, he slipped inside. In front of him were the two men he'd just seen enter the church, but Father Flenn was nowhere in sight. The second man, the one with the gun, was standing in the aisle with his back to Guy. The other, a man with dark hair and an olive complexion, was kneeling next to the organ, hands behind his head.

Guy sprang into action. "Police! Nobody move!"

The man with the gun wheeled around, and in that split-second, the olive-skinned man pulled something from behind his back. There was a quick pop, and the second man fell. Two more rounds hit the wall near Guy.

The detective hurled himself behind a pew and crawled quickly to the opposite end. He peered around the side, ready to return fire when he saw a shadow come from a darkened door near the organ. In the blink of an eye, Father Flenn brought what looked like a brass candlestick down on the assailant's shoulder. The gun went flying underneath a choir pew as the olive-skinned man fell to the floor.

Staying low, Guy made his way down the far aisle and crouched behind the large wooden pulpit. He glanced past it and saw the man spring to his feet and face off with the priest. For his part, Father Flenn simply set the candlestick carefully on the organist's bench beside him.

Was he surrendering? Guy wondered.

The other man saw the opportunity and moved in, but Flenn was quick, dodging each punch with the skill of a Kung Fu master. Guy stepped out from behind the pulpit, raised his pistol and was just about to shout orders again when he heard it:

"*Wait!*"

The command startled him. Was it from the man lying on the floor? No, he hadn't moved. Someone, or *something*, had just told him to stand down!

The olive-skinned man tried a roundhouse kick, which Father Flenn easily deflected, while driving his right palm hard and fast into the side of the man's extended knee. The man howled in agony.

Guy lowered his weapon. *Where had the priest learned to do that?*

The injured man crumpled backwards toward the choir bench, inches away from where the pistol had fallen. Guy raised his, but Flenn had already assessed the danger and snatched the man's trousers and pulled him away. The assailant tried to kick with his other leg, but Flenn dodged the blows. As Guy moved toward the combatants, the man rolled to the right and managed to get back on his feet. He reached into his belt and whipped out a small knife. In one unbelievably swift motion, Father Flenn caught the man's wrist and bent it backwards, causing the knife to fall harmlessly to the floor. Flenn then swept his attacker's injured leg, dropping him into a heap. This time, the man didn't move.

Guy vaulted the chancel steps toward the altar. "Everybody, freeze! That means you too, Father!"

Flenn ignored him and rushed to the man who'd been shot. Guy held his pistol on the assailant but stood so as he could see the priest. Father Flenn was kneeling over the man, searching for an entry wound while checking for a pulse.

"You know," said the fallen man, "if you keep holding my hand like that, you're going to give people the wrong idea."

The assailant eyed the knife on the floor. "Don't even think about it," Guy warned, kicking it away. Guy kept his gun on the man in front of him but kept glancing over at the priest, who was helping the other man back to his feet. "You okay?" he heard Father Flenn ask.

Zack was stunned, but intact. The Kevlar had deflected the bullet; however, the force had knocked the wind out of him and he'd scratched his arm on a loose nail in the pew. Zack felt of his arm and said, "Yeah, I guess I'm going to make it. Good thing you insisted on bringing your old vest with you. I'm surprised you still had it." He looked at his bleeding arm. "You know, you guys really should do something about that nail."

Flenn smiled. "I will, if you will quit bleeding on my carpet!"

"Couldn't you just tell folks it was a miracle? You know, like those statues with tears?"

"Catholics do the weeping statue thing," Flenn said. "I've never heard of a bleeding carpet."

"It could be a new tradition, just for you Episcopalians."

Whatever semblance of restraint Guy might have had was completely worn away at this point. "Father Flenn, what the hell is going on!"

"Hang on a sec, Detective." Flenn said, examining Zack's arm. "Go into the sacristy and wash up," he told

Zack, pointing to the door by the organ. "There is a sink and some paper towels in there." Zack's arm was sore, but he obediently headed off in the direction of the sacristy. Flenn called after him, "Light switch is on the left."

"Wait a minute!" Guy was incredulous as Zack stepped around him. "Someone tell me what in God's name is going on!" Guy had just been shot at, seen a priest perform martial arts that would've put a karate master to shame, and was now standing over a stranger he might have to shoot at any moment. *Enough was enough!*

Zack stopped, but Flenn motioned for him to go on. "Not to worry, Detective, everything's under control."

"Well, it was until the cops showed up!" yelled Zack from the sacristy.

"Oh, that's right," Flenn said to Guy, "you two haven't met." He called to Zack. "As soon as you're done bleeding, come out here and introduce yourself—and try to be nice! Detective Rainsford is a friend of mine."

"I'm always nice," Zack said, stepping out of the sacristy, pressing a towel to his arm. Zack looked down at Ahmad, then at Guy. "Um, I'd like to get that knife off the floor and away from this fellow; that is, if you don't mind."

"It's fine where it is," Guy said. "Let's just leave everything alone for now." Zack did as he was told and sat on the organ bench next to the candlestick. He reached into his jacket pocket, and Guy swung the pistol toward him. Zack very slowly pulled out a package of jellybeans.

Guy slowly exhaled. "Okay, no one moves again until I know exactly what this is all about." He gestured toward the candlestick. "Except for that. Father, put that thing away. I've already seen what it can do."

The priest went over to the organ bench, tousled Zack's hair, and reminded him that he was going to be responsible for cleaning up the mess. Flenn picked up the candlestick and placed it on the opposite side of the altar rail.

"Okay, who's first?" Guy said. The detective kept his weapon pointed toward the man on the floor.

Zack held up his hand and smiled like a schoolboy. "Detective, my name is Sean Williams. I'm with the FBI. The man behind you is Achmed Najaar. He's wanted for killing the Anglican Archbishop of Yemen. Maybe you've seen his face in the news?" Guy looked down at the man while Flenn restrained a grin.

This should be interesting, Flenn thought.

"The archbishop and the good father here were close friends," Zack said. "Thanks to Father Flenn's generous donations over the years, the archbishop has built several schools and churches in his country."

Flenn looked away. *This was going to be a whopper.*

"There is a group of, shall we say, not-so-silent objectors to what the archbishop and the father have been doing. The man on the floor over there is part of a radical group of Saudis who sent him to teach the padre a lesson. We got wind of the plot when the archbishop arrived here last week. It just so happens that I've also known Father Flenn for a long time, and he very courageously agreed to help me by serving as bait."

Ahmad sat in stunned silence, as fascinated by what he was hearing as were Guy and Flenn.

The policeman looked at Flenn. "Father, is this true?"

Flenn shook his head. "I know," he answered, "it is difficult to believe..." *Zack could lie faster than anyone Flenn had ever known, a fact that had saved both their lives on more than one occasion.*

Zack smiled. "If you'll allow me to reach into my pocket again, I'll show you my identification." Guy nodded, and Zack handed him an FBI badge with his picture above the name *Sean Williams.* Zack carried the fake badge so that if anything ever went wrong the FBI would get the blame.

Guy looked at the priest. "Why didn't you tell me about any of this?"

Flenn glanced at Zack. "It all happened so fast."

"Father Flenn couldn't tell anyone," Zack interrupted. "Which is what I'm afraid I'm going to have to ask of you as well, Detective."

"What!"

"Afraid so," Zack continued. "Matter of national security. Trust me, if people knew just how many of these attacks are happening in our country every day. . . well, I'm sure you understand. Please, let the FBI handle this."

That was the last thing Guy was inclined to do.

Zack went on, "Your chief has already been informed. He knew about our plans to apprehend Najaar—we've had this all worked out for days. No offense, but what we weren't expecting was *you*." Zack looked into the man's eyes. "I assume you understand, and that we'll have your complete cooperation in this matter?"

Guy shook his head. "I don't know. Procedure dictates…"

"There's another reason," Flenn piped up. "If word gets out to the media that I was targeted by a terrorist, then no one would ever come to Saint Ann's anymore; in fact, nobody would allow me to serve in a parish anywhere for fear something like this might happen again. I'd lose my ministry forever."

Guy thought about what Father Flenn had just said. *The priest was a good man. Maybe this had been why he'd felt compelled to be here—to help protect Father Flenn. There was also the matter of the voice… no, that must have simply been his imagination. Still,* Guy told himself, *maybe there were larger forces at work here tonight. Perhaps there had been all along.*

"Detective, I'm not sure why you were here tonight," Flenn continued. "But maybe it was providential. It seems that the future of my ministry is in your hands."

The cop scratched his head. He suspected there was more to this, a lot more, but he didn't want to harm Flenn, and he sure as hell didn't want to get chewed out by Toone the Loon for interfering with the FBI.

"Well, while you're thinking, there's something I need to do," Flenn said. He went over to the fallen man, reached into Ahmad's jacket, and pulled out an odd-looking cell phone with a large antenna. Flenn selected the last call and pressed redial. A voice on the other side of the world answered.

"This is Abbas. I assume you have good news?"

Guy found there was no end to the surprises tonight as the priest began speaking a foreign language. Ahmad, of course, understood the priest perfectly, as Flenn was using nearly perfect Farsi.

"Ah, your Excellency; good." Flenn said. "I assumed I might be speaking to my old friend, Colonel Amir, but then why trust such matters to underlings, right?"

"Who is this?" Abbas demanded.

"Who I am is not important; but what I have to say is. There has been a change in plans. I'm afraid your operative will need new instructions. We know all about your plot to attack Israel, and have for some time." Ahmad raised an eyebrow.

There was silence on the other side of the phone.

"We also know about your infiltration of the American voting system."

Again, silence.

Flenn went on, "Your man is unharmed, although he did put up quite a fight." Flenn looked over at the Iranian. *No sense in jeopardizing Ahmad's life.* "We will be releasing him soon." Ahmad silently thanked Allah.

"You, Excellency, will now call this operation to a halt. If you do, I cannot promise there won't be any repercussions, but they will be far less severe than if you do not."

Ahmad wanted desperately to hear what was being said on the other side of that phone.

Flenn looked at Zack and rolled his eyes as he listened to Abbas' continual denials. "Excellency, please stop. We are beyond the days of people crying 'fake news.' Our government will see what you have done as an act of war. I don't believe it is in your best interest for things to escalate. So, if your people stand down immediately, we can avert just such a catastrophe."

Flenn waited for the reply, then nodded at Zack. "Yes, I believe that will be sufficient; but, as we say over here in America, 'saying it and doing it are two different things.' We will expect immediate results, or else the Israeli Mossad will also be informed of this matter. I'm certain we'd both rather keep *them* out of the loop... Yes, I agree... may I assume we are of one mind?" Flenn waited for the answer, then smiled broadly. "Excellent!"

He glanced over at Guy. "Now one last thing: We cannot be held responsible for your would-be candidate in next year's election. America is still a free country, with laws. We might not be the best ones to take care of this, if you understand what I'm saying. Obviously, he and his friend are a... " Flenn searched for the right word... "liability." He paused, listening. "Yes, I'm sure you will know exactly what to do. I suppose you would like to speak now with your agent?"

Flenn handed the phone to Ahmad, whose face grew two shades of pale. Ahmad put the receiver to his ear and Flenn listened as the man agreed to his new orders. The Iranian spy tried to explain to Abbas what had just happened, but he stopped in mid apology. Abbas had just hung up on him.

The Iranian looked up at Flenn and said in English, "Now what?"

Flenn continued in Farsi. "I assume you have new orders?" Ahmad nodded. "Good. My friend here will now pretend to arrest you. I will see to it that this policeman discovers nothing about who you really are and will send him on his way. At that point, you and my friend will return here and we will give you your car and your weapon back. Then, we never want to see you again. Is that understood?"

Ahmad nodded a second time.

Zack's command of Farsi was not as good as Flenn's, but he'd understood the drift of it. After all, it was what they had agreed to do earlier, before Guy Rainsford had shown up.

Flenn looked across at Guy and said, "Would you mind handcuffing the prisoner so that Agent Williams may take him into custody?"

Guy holstered his weapon, though a bit reluctantly, as Flenn retrieved the two pistols and the knife and handed them over to Zack. Flenn looked at 'Special Agent Williams,' and said "I'm guessing you want to take this man to Washington for interrogation?"

"Huh?" said Zack. "Oh, yeah. Come on you! We have a long trip ahead of us."

Guy shook his head. "Father, this is all highly irregular."

Flenn knew he had to offer the man something. *Maybe it was time.*

"I know it's irregular, but I do have something that may help take your mind off all this. My friend here is actually the one who stumbled on it." He looked at Zack.

"What?"

"The truth about Lindsay."

Guy straightened, his eyes darted across to the faux FBI agent. "What about Lind… "

"Agent Williams," Flenn said, "before you leave, won't you tell the detective what you told me—what the FBI has discovered?"

Zack had just invested all his creativity in the last wild story; he didn't figure he had anything left for a second. "Why don't you, Father, since you've been helping the detective with that case."

Guy stared at Flenn. "What about Lindsay?"

"Not only Lindsay," Flenn said, "but also Shelly O'Reilly." Flenn motioned to the choir pew as Zack escorted Ahmad down the aisle and toward the door. "I think you'd better sit down."

CHAPTER FIFTY-ONE

It had taken a bit of convincing, but Guy had finally agreed not to file a report, especially after learning that he might be on the brink of solving Birmingham's biggest mystery of the past year.

They had walked across the church grounds to the vicarage where Flenn had poured them both a generous glass of Scotch. After half an hour, Flenn excused himself to adjust the thermostat and took a quick look through the kitchen window. Ahmad's car was still there. Zack was no doubt waiting for Flenn to get rid of his guest.

"Guy," he said coming back into the living room. "I'm sorry you got involved in all this; it was quite an evening for us all." It was a gentle way of saying that the night needed to come to an end. "Frankly, I'm not sure how well I'll be able to sleep, but I'm going to go give it a try."

Guy Rainsford stood. "Father, frankly I don't know what to do with any of this. These past couple of weeks you've taken me down paths I've never even imagined." Guy didn't mention anything about the voice he'd heard in the church; he doubted he'd ever tell anyone about that. "There's one thing I do know; this city needs you. And if my reporting something, which seems to have been sufficiently handled by the Feds, will deprive us of you, then to hell with the rules!"

"Well then," said Flenn. "It looks like we hold each other's future in one another's hands." He smiled. "I assure you, yours is safe in mine."

Guy looked down at the flash drive the priest had given him. If this was what Father Flenn had promised it was, then Guy had evidence that would show Lindsay and Shelly were the same girl. *He couldn't wait to see the look on Toone the Loon's face!*

A DNA test would likely be ordered on Juanita O'Reilly to confirm the girl's remains were those of her daughter. No one had ordered it before since the city Councilman had denied that the body from the river was Shelly's. *After all, who cares about a teenaged hooker?*

Guy smiled. *He did, that's who!*

Flenn said good night, figuring Guy would spend the next week gloating about having solved the O'Reilly girl's disappearance. *He hadn't told the detective all that much, not really.* Admittedly, with Mac dead, the councilman would be the logical suspect for her murder. Rye's name might not even surface. The Iranians would take things from here. It was unfortunate, but it would, at least, spare Elizabeth the shame. She'd had enough pain lately. Flenn couldn't bear the thought of her having to watch the Rye Foundation crumble around her. Her beloved husband had invested his heart and soul in it far too long for it all to fall apart now.

Flenn poured himself another Scotch. Benji had caused Elizabeth nothing but heartache all these years.

What Flenn had done tonight was likely going to shorten her son's life. Abbas couldn't afford to leave any loose ends. *Still,* Flenn asked himself, *what other options had there been?* A scandal, a long-drawn out trial, Willy Rye's followers likely to revolt... *hadn't the country been through enough lately? Four murders,* he told himself, *two of them just children... one who'd been thrown on the city's trash heap, the other abused nearly all her life. And, what of Denise? She'd be brought back to testify in an environment that too often treated victims of sexual assault as criminals.*

Flenn sipped the whisky and fantasized of going somewhere far away. He wondered what pastoring a congregation in the Virgin Islands might be like; and just how long it would take Zack Matteson to find him in the West Indies. Flenn shook his head. *Zack would always be able to find him!* They'd been friend and guardian to one another more times than he could count. Flenn thought back on the many missions he and Zack had completed together, culminating in that last one... in Edinburgh. *It always comes back to Edinburgh,* he thought as he gently pushed Mama Kitty aside and leaned back in his favorite chair.

Maybe he'd been foolish to agree so long ago to the clandestine meetings with Zack in Cullman. What was this, the second, or the third time Zack had summoned him there? Flenn had promised himself each time would be the last; and each time, he knew it wouldn't be.

The chime from his new security system signaled that someone had come through the kitchen entrance. Flenn knew without looking who it was. He lifted his glass.

"You didn't waste much time; Rainsford just left a minute ago." Flenn made a sweeping motion with his arm. "I'd offer to show you around my home, but as you've already had the tour, I don't guess there is much point. Your visit, by the way, is why I now have a security system."

Zack helped himself to a Scotch. "Haven't met one yet that could stop me." He sat down across from his old friend, realizing just how much he had missed his friend over the years. "Ahmad is gone," Zack said. "I think you know where he's heading."

"Well, that *was* our game plan," Flenn said, "though not quite how we'd imagined." He and Zack had figured out a way to kill two birds with one stone. Since Ahmad had followed Zack to Ashleigh Nieves's house, it had seemed the opportune time.

"I don't suppose our Iranian friend gave you anything you didn't already know?"

Zack leaned against the fireplace mantel. "He wasn't very talkative. I think he's still trying to figure out who *you* are," he said, rubbing his shoulder.

"Do you need to have that looked after?"

"Nah, just a scratch," Zack said, sitting down on the sofa. "I took the liberty of telling Ahmad about what Rye and Romero did to that girl out at Rye's place. Insurance. His dossier says he has three daughters."

Flenn set his glass on the coffee table. "I guess that sealed it then."

"He won't do anything without orders, but Abbas will want them both out of the way." Zack lifted his glass. "What I don't get is *you*."

Flenn shrugged.

"You know perfectly well what I mean. You pretty much signed Rye and Romero's death warrants on the phone tonight with Abbas."

Flenn picked his glass up and stared into the amber liquid for a long time. "It is what you and I had agreed to do."

"It is what we agreed that *I* would do," Zack said, "not you."

"Your Farsi is not as good as mine."

"You know as well as I do that Abbas speaks English."

Flenn shook his head. "Yes, but the detective didn't need to know what was really going on."

Zack poured back the Scotch and made a face. "I still don't see how you drink this stuff. Give me a Jack Daniel's any day."

"That mean you won't have another?"

Zack picked up the bottle. "I guess it'll do." Flenn shook his head. His friend never could appreciate quality.

"So?" Zack with a crooked grin.

Flenn pretended not to understand the question. "So, what?"

"Don't play innocent with me. Just what are you telling yourself about what you did tonight? Didn't you take a vow against violence back in Edinburgh?"

"Not exactly. I vowed never to *kill* again. Which is why I hit Ahmad's shoulder instead of his head."

"I thought it was just because you were a bad aim."

Zack finished his second drink in a single swallow. "What about that conversation on the phone. You know exactly where that is going to lead, right?"

Flenn drew in a breath. "I suppose."

"And?"

Flenn stared at him. "And… I guess I'm treading a fine line regarding that vow. Technically, I'm not the one who will have to deal with Romero and Rye. They sealed their own fate when they signed a pact with the devil. Now that their mission has failed the Iranians can't afford to let them go free. All I did was simply remind Abbas of that." Flenn glanced down at the floor. "But, I can't get around it either. There are no loopholes with God. I will bear some of the responsibility of whatever's going to happen." He looked up. "As do you, now that you've told Ahmad about what they did to Linds… Shelly."

Zack shrugged. "I can live with that. Question is, can you?"

Flenn raised an eyebrow. "What? You want me to get all theological on you?"

Zack leaned back into the sofa. "Go ahead; I suppose you've earned it. Just be quick."

"Alright," said Flenn. "Remember, you asked for it." He looked at his long-time friend, wondering just how to start. "We're all sinners," he finally said. "Or, as the old Baptist storyteller, Will Campbell, used to say, "We're all bastards."

"Speak for yourself," said Zack.

"Campbell was a preacher who worked in the civil

rights movement back in the day. He spent a lot of years fighting the Ku Klux Klan. Then one day, he had a revelation of sorts. He heard a friend tell him, 'We're all bastards, but God loves us anyway.' It changed his life. He started working *with* the Klan members, trying to convert them instead of fighting against them."

"How'd that work out?"

"He won over a few. More important is what happened to *him*. He gave up the illusion that he was somehow better than anybody else, even the Kluxers he'd hated for so long. Flenn reached for the bottle of Scotch. "I suppose I came to a similar conclusion awhile back." Flenn said.

"Edinburgh?"

Flenn nodded. "Rye and Romero, Abbas and Colonel Amir, Mac and Juanita… they all started out as innocent children once. None of them came into this world saying, "Hey, I think I will become a monster. Along the way they made a series of choices that eventually made them who they were.

"Life can be cruel or kind, but it's always up to us," Flenn said. "We choose to become who we are."

"Even Rochelle O'Reilly?" Zack said. "I know she was just a kid, but… "

"Shelly was simply trying to find a way out. She finally sought help from her priest but she did it in a way that tied Minerva's hands." Flenn looked away. "And cost Minerva her life."

Flenn closed his eyes. "I think Shelly, for whatever reason, didn't really want to be rescued by someone else.

Maybe she felt she had to do it herself, on her own terms. Maybe, with all she'd been through, she just couldn't trust anyone else." He turned back to Zack. "But, you see, even that was a choice! Shelly wanted to find her own way. Probably thought, as so many abused kids do, that *she* was at fault for what had happened." Flenn shook his head. "No doubt, her stepfather had told her just that. I'm guessing she chose prostitution because it was easy money. It's awful to say, but sex was something she knew. She probably told herself that she'd soon be out of the house and out of Alabama forever, that she would meet someone who would sweep her off her feet, and the two of them would start a wonderful new life together."

Zack leaned forward. "Okay, so, bring this back to your reminding Abbas that Rye and Romero were loose ends."

Flenn stared at his glass. "I suppose I also had a choice. I could reinforce Abbas' instinct about what he should do next... or I could stay silent. If I stayed silent, then he might not do anything, thinking that the CIA would handle it."

Flenn looked into his friend's eyes. "And," he said, "part of me wondered if that meant you would end up having to take things into your own hands."

"So, you were protecting *my* soul?"

Flenn grinned. "Good God, no! That's too big a job for me. It's just that you've got enough deaths on your conscious without adding another one."

Zack finished his drink. "All of them were like that Guatemalan. They deserved to die."

Flenn raised an eyebrow. "Really, Zack? All of them? Don't forget, I was there for a lot of them. We both have made choices we'll have to account for one day."

Zack brushed off the implication. "And so, you chose to push Romero and Rye closer to the edge?"

"I suppose you could put it that way." Flenn looked across the room and then back at Zack. "You tell me: What kind of damage could they still inflict on the nation if Romero actually did win the election, even without the Iranians help?"

Zack didn't have to think long. "Okay, I get it, but aren't you still breaking your vow?"

"No… yes… maybe… I don't know. That will be for God to decide. I made the best choice I knew how to make. In the end, that's all any of us can do. In the end, I'm just a bastard too."

Zack was quiet for a moment. Finally, he set his glass on the coffee table next to the half-empty bottle of Lagavulin. "Okay, one last question." He watched two kittens scamper across the room. "Do you really believe that God cares about all these bastards: the O'Reillys? Romero? Rye?"

Flenn didn't hesitate. "Yes."

Zack shook his head. "I don't get it."

"I know you don't." Flenn smiled. "But I haven't given up on you, Zack, and neither has God. How about you ask him for some help in figuring it all out?"

"Now, that would be an uncommon event;" Zack said, "*me*, praying?"

"You never know."

Flenn stood up. "Listen, as long as you're here, I could use some help masking a couple of bullet holes and cleaning bloodstains off the carpet next door. I don't think I can explain those to my congregation on Sunday."

"Ah, still working together after all these years. We do make quite a team, don't we?"

Flenn laughed. "Have I told you lately that I hate you?"

Zack grinned. "No, you don't. Now, go find us some towels and lemon juice! Get some wood putty too while you're at it."

CHAPTER FIFTY-TWO

Colonel Amir stood at attention before his boss. "You sent for me, Excellency?"

Sadar Abbas smiled, he even stood to shake Amir's hand across his large desk. "Yes, Colonel. Thank you. I have good news, very good news."

Amir was relieved. Judging from his boss' demeanor, all had gone according to plan and Zackary Matteson was now dead. Everything could proceed as planned. *Perhaps Abbas would offer him a raise in salary, or better, that vacation his wife had him put in for months ago.*

"I am delighted to hear that, Excellency."

"Yes, yes, my friend. By this time tomorrow, you will be in paradise!"

That settled it. It was a vacation, and right away! Amir could hardly restrain his joy. "My wife and I shall pack immediately."

Abbas shook his head. "No need. Your family is already there. I have seen to it only this morning."

"Already there, Excellency? There must be a mistake, I… "

Abbas came around his desk and took him by the shoulder. "No, my friend, no mistake. Your wife and brother-in-law are waiting there for you." Abbas began walking him toward the door, his right arm firmly wrapped around Col. Amir's shoulder. "You have been a faithful officer, Amir, faithful to Allah, and to me. Which is why I know you will be in paradise and not in *Jahannam*." Abbas had used the Arabic instead of the Farsi word for hell.

Amir stopped dead in his tracks. The look of fear and confusion on Amir's face was one Abbas would have rather have seen on the Israeli prime minister in a few years. *Alas, that was no longer to be,* he told himself. *As the Americans say, 'It was time now for Plan B.'*

"Guards!" Two uniformed men stepped through the doorway and grabbed the colonel by each arm.

"No!" Amir pleaded, struggling to break free. "What have I done? Please sir, I beg you... have I not always done everything you have asked of me? Surely I can still be of use!"

Abbas held up his hand, signaling the guards to wait.

"Yes, Colonel, I suppose there is one more thing you can do for me."

"Anything!" The terrified Amir forced a smile. "Name it, and it shall be done!"

Abbas returned to his desk chair and sat down. "You can overlook my lapse in protocol," Abbas said

"Excellency?"

Abbas's eyes narrowed. "There won't be any officers at the gallows when you arrive. I've decided to make this a private matter."

The guards had to drag the colonel screaming from the room.

CHAPTER FIFTY-THREE

Juanita O'Reilly arrived at Saint Ann's at noon. Flenn had called earlier this morning to tell her he had new information about her daughter. It had been Zack who had figured it all out last night as they were cleaning up.

"Juanita." Flenn set his coffee cup on his desk. "Thank you for coming, especially with so much on your mind right now, settling your husband's affairs and such." The words were gracious enough, but the usual priestly empathy was missing from his voice.

"Hello, Scott." Juanita was dressed in black, telling the world that she was in mourning. "You said you had information about my daughter?"

"Yes. I think the police will be most interested."

"The police?" The blood drained from her face.

Flenn stood and picked up some books from his desk. "Turns out the body your husband said wasn't Shelly actually was… but, I suspect you already know that, don't you?"

"What on earth are you talking about?"

"The way I figure it, Mac probably told you on the way home from the morgue that day. He would have noticed her deformed toe. I understand from someone who has read the examiner's report that Mac asked to see her entire body." Flenn waited to see if Juanita would respond. She didn't. "Or, maybe you only figured it out when you saw what was on the flash drive last night."

She raised an eyebrow. "What flash drive?"

"Oh, that's right. You didn't get the drive; you got the video as an email. He told me he was going to send you a copy."

She stiffened. "Who?"

Flenn scooped up more books from a nearby shelf. Would you walk with me down to the choir room? It's the little room at the end of the hall. I had asked my secretary to take these hymnals down there before I sent her home early, but Iriana forgets sometimes."

To Juanita's amazement, the priest walked right past her and down the hall. She followed. "What are you going on about?" she demanded. The two stood face-to-face in a partitioned room—half of the room was used by the choir, the other half for Sunday school with only a rolling screen in the middle.

"Come on Juanita; drop the act. You know exactly what I'm talking about." He set the books down on a card table near the door. "What I haven't figured out is why Mac didn't just go ahead and identify Shelly. Had you two figured out what she was doing on the weekends; that she was selling her body to make enough money to get away from you, or was Mac just mad because she had cut him off?"

Juanita turned as red as the prayer books on the table.

"I suppose it could have been all that attention your family was getting from Shelly's disappearance. Lord knows, Mac loved attention—making those long, self-righteous speeches at diocesan convention and taking credit for things he claimed he was doing for the city every time a reporter was within earshot." Flenn picked up a single prayer book and set it neatly on a nearby bookshelf. "But then Minerva came along… I must admit, I didn't figure it out until a friend helped me with it."

Flenn shook his head. "At first, I thought it had to have been Mac, but he was with Bishop Morrison when Minerva was murdered." He picked up a second book and placed it on the shelf next to the first. "Then I thought it might have been a professional hit; but it wasn't, was it, Juanita? It was too sloppy." He looked at her. "Tell me, was it your idea to kill Minerva, or Mac's?"

Her eyes widened. "You've gone mad!"

Flenn ignored her. "The other thing I can't figure out is how you knew that Shelly had told Minerva about the abuse. I suppose you must've overheard the two of them talking. Minerva told me you'd seen them together."

He picked up the last two prayer books and set them on the shelf. "What I do know is that you couldn't afford the truth to come out… so, you killed Minerva." He turned and watched as Juanita's face went from pale to red to pale again. *Was the woman about to faint?* Flenn stared at her in disgust. "Or, maybe you didn't know Shelly was planning to leave you, but then I doubt you'd have cared all that much if she did. After all, she had stolen your husband from you, right Juanita?"

Juanita's voice became pressured, her chin like stone. "That little whore! I gave her everything… "

"Including your husband. Really, Juanita, how *do* you live with yourself?"

"It's easy for you," she spat. "You've always had money! You have no idea what it's like to be poor! What it means to have nothing, bills piling up, a child to raise. Mac took us in; he took care of us."

Flenn's eyes flared. "Mac took care of *himself*, and at *your* daughter's expense! Worse, *you* let him do it!"

"You can't possibly know what it was like!" she countered.

"Oh, really? Tell me Juanita, what *is* it like to offer your only child to a pervert? What is it like to sell your soul to the devil?"

Juanita cocked her head; her eyes softened. "But… you're not going to tell anyone, are you? That's why you called me here this morning. That's why the police weren't on my doorstep. You're giving me a chance, aren't you? Okay, I get it. You want me to confess and repent." She took a long, deep breath and nodded. "Yes. You're right. That's what I'll do. Let's go into the church! Go get your stole, Father. I will make my confession to you right now! It will be good to get all of this off my chest."

Flenn shook his head. "I'm afraid you've gotten the wrong idea, Juanita. I don't intend to hear your confession; although, I'm sure the police will be glad to take it."

She snapped. Reaching into her purse, she whipped out a tiny pistol. Her hand was shaking—*was it from fear or rage*, Flenn wondered.

Flenn stared at the gun. "A Glock 26, huh? I suspect that's the same one that killed Minerva. Thank you for bringing it, Juanita. Most helpful." He called behind her. "What do you guys think?"

The partition slid back to reveal Detectives Rainsford, Wickes and Hollister. All three had their weapons drawn and pointed at Juanita. Flenn reached over and plucked the tiny pistol out of the woman's trembling hand and gave it to Guy. "Gentlemen, I assume when you do your ballistics test you'll have all you need. Although, the widow O'Reilly here may be ready to give you a full confession to having killed Minerva Wilson."

Juanita's eyes traveled from Flenn, to the police, then back again. "I couldn't let that woman keep saying those things to me," she blabbered—just as Flenn figured the fallen socialite might do. "Minerva knew too much about Mac. Don't you see? It was why Mac didn't identify Shelly at the morgue. Do you realize what our friends would have said? Do you?!"

Flenn didn't answer.

"Minerva called me into her office that night; she wanted to talk to me about Shelly. She knew what Mac had been doing." Juanita's eyes narrowed. "She had the gall to accuse me of being a bad mother! When she confronted me, I had no choice… I mean, I couldn't let this get out. I had to do it!" She looked pleadingly at Flenn. You come from haut monde; can't you understand, Father?"

Flenn's eyes narrowed. "I understand that you just told these three detectives that your daughter is dead, that your husband refused to identify her at the morgue, and that you killed Minerva Wilson because she knew that your husband was sexually abusing your daughter." He glared at her. "Beyond that? No. I don't understand you at all!"

CHAPTER FIFTY-FOUR

"Senator Cochrane, so glad you could come to my little soiree!" Daniel Romero squeezed the older man's shoulder as they shook hands for the photographer hired for the evening. The two men posed in front of the giant oak fireplace in Romero's palatial Houston home.

"Daniel, I'd hardly call this party *little,*" said Tennessee Senator Bradley Cochrane. He stared out of the two-story windows that led into the gardens where most of the guests were gathered. "There must be more than 300 people here tonight!"

"Four, but who's counting, right?" Romero smiled and turned to a nearby waiter. "Bring me a martini. What about you Senator, something to drink?"

"I'll have a bourbon and branch."

"One martini and a bourbon and branch coming up." The olive-skinned waiter turned toward the bar. Romero had hired a catering service for tonight, the best in town.

"Senator, I'm delighted you could come. I was worried; I'd always heard you Tennesseans didn't like us Texans very much."

Cochrane laughed. "We like you just fine—*in Texas!*"

"Come on, now," Romero quipped, "surely you realize that everything is bigger and better in Texas."

"Tennessee isn't as small as you seem to think," the senator said. "Why, it takes a body a good eight hours to drive across the state from Memphis to Bristol."

"Only eight? Why that's how long it takes us to drive across an average ranch down here!" When he wanted to, Romero could charm the pants off almost anyone… always to their regret.

"Okay, okay. You win! I just hope y'all will allow me to show you around Nashville someday."

Romero smiled. "Absolutely! In fact, I hope the two of us will be spending a great deal of time together in the future." Bradley Cochrane nodded. This was, after all, why he'd been invited tonight. Romero's entourage had been meeting in secret with Cochrane's people for the past three months. They'd made it clear that Romero was going to announce his presidential bid shortly and that he wanted the senator on the ticket. His own party had bypassed him numerous times, and at 68, time was not on Cochrane's side. His fellow Republicans were looking for someone younger, someone who wasn't part of the old establishment.

Cochrane was a moderate whose ability to work both sides of the aisle was well known, although it had been of little use in recent years. Even though Cochrane had friends and allies in both parties, centrists were seen in the current political climate as nothing more than fence-straddlers. Extremism had become the new normal. However, the senator knew one thing above all else, and that was that the American public was fickle. Signs were developing that it was growing weary of the extremism it had so recently craved. A third party might do well in November, *if* there was still time to put it all together. On that score, Romero's people had sounded most convincing. Romero had made it clear that he admired the senator's experience along with his ability to bring people together.

Cochrane was a solid leader with an impeccable reputation. Married to the same woman for more than 35 years, with no affairs or even any flirtations—at least none that Romero's detectives had discovered. He was a faithful Presbyterian, a member of the Lion's Club, and most important, Cochrane was on both the Ways and Means Committee and the Committee on Veterans' Affairs. The connection to the first would be of use in the future; the second would look good to the masses. In short, Bradley Cochrane was the perfect candidate to run alongside him in November— but they would have to start soon, very soon. Assuming Cochrane agreed, Romero was planning to announce on New Year's Day.

The waiter returned with their drinks. "So, Brad, are you any closer to making a decision on this little thing our people have been discussing?"

"There you go Danny, using that word again. It's hardly a *little* thing, or a *little* decision either… any more than this is a *little* get-together."

Romero scratched his head, signaling a young blonde and a brunette, both wearing revealing evening gowns. Romero introduced the women to the senator, but only as eye candy. He didn't think Cochrane could be bribed so easily. Still, the old man wasn't blind. Adding some window dressing couldn't hurt.

Romero took the senator by the elbow after a moment and led him away from the women. Standing in front of a large picture window, he said, "Brad, I know this is a big decision, but it would be perfect for you... and, I admit, perfect for me, too. You know Washington; I don't.

"People are tired of politics as usual. Don't get me wrong, they still want an outsider, just not like that last clown. His two years were more than enough to sour the public. They want someone who can come off as presidential." Romero placed his right hand on the older man's shoulder. "I'm that someone." He tightened his grip ever so slightly. "With your experience, work ethic, and all-around good nature, you're exactly who I want as my second in command!"

Even from a hotter-than-hell state, the senator knew a snow job when he heard one. Still, Cochrane was more than tempted. "I do have some concerns, Danny-boy. My party is going to fight like hell if I jump ship."

Romero finished his martini. "You don't have to bill it that way. Simply make sure people see you as standing up for sensible, conservative values. I'm certain I can appeal to the moderate Democrats by tossing them a few bones on education and the environment. Trust me, the votes will come to us in numbers bigger than you can believe!"

The waiter brought over two fresh drinks. "Danny, I'm tempted, I really am, but... "

"No buts, Brad." Romero waved the olive-skinned waiter away. "I can't hold out any longer. I need a Veep. I can trust, and, frankly, we've been putting all our eggs in one basket, namely you." It was a lie, of course. Romero's team had been cozying up to three other candidates, but none with as strong a resume as Bradley Cochrane. Even with Iran's help, Romero wanted to win as many real votes as possible.

"Let's be honest, Brad," he said, finishing the drink. "There won't be another chance for you to get this close to the Oval Office." Romero tried to appear concerned. "*You* deserve this! Don't forget, eight years from now the road will be clear for you to have a go yourself!" Romero offered a polished smile. "If we're as great a team as I know we will be, then you'll easily be the next POTUS after me!" Another lie. Romero planned to sack Cochrane after the first term and replace him with Benjamin Rye.

Romero's mouth was dry but he couldn't find the waiter. *Just as well,* he thought, *he'd probably had enough.* He pinched the bridge of his nose and shook his head. *No, he definitely didn't need another drink.*

"So, Brad, before we head outside to greet everyone, tell me; what's it going to be? I really want you on my team."

Cochrane smiled. "Well, I'll say this much: If you're as willing to support some of the causes your aides said you would, then I think we can probably work out a deal."

Romero nodded approvingly, in spite of a horrendous headache coming on like gangbusters. "That's great," he said, "that's really… " He dropped the empty glass and looked down at his hands. They were pouring sweat. A sledgehammer felt like it was pounding his insides. He clutched his chest, first with one hand, then the other.

"Danny, what's the matter?" he heard Cochrane shout as he fell to the floor, gasping for breath. The pain in his chest mounted in proportion to the terror racing through his mind.

"Someone, call 911!" At his age, Brad Cochrane had seen heart attacks before, but nothing like this. Romero grabbed the Senator's pants legs, trying to stand. Cochrane peeled him off and stepped back in horror as blood began to pour from Romero's nose and mouth. A crowd of frightened house staff and guests gathered in a semi-circle around him. "Help me!" Romero screamed... but no one could. In all the chaos, nobody noticed the olive-skinned waiter slip off his jacket and disappear through a side door.

Outside, Farhad Ahmad checked his watch... he did not want to miss the next flight to Birmingham.

CHAPTER FIFTY-FIVE

Elizabeth Rye appeared, oddly enough, at peace. The news of the death of her son had not traumatized her the way Flenn had expected. *Maybe it would have,* Flenn thought, *had her son been a decent human being. Benji may have managed to keep his father in the dark the last couple of years, but a mother knows.*

Flenn stood in the entryway of the Rye Mansion. He had come to check on her, as had dozens of friends and family. *Elizabeth was a good woman who hadn't deserved to have to deal with such grief. To lose both her husband and her eldest son, louse that he was, would have been a strain too great for most women to bear; yet here she was greeting well-wishers, still the embodiment of old-South elegance and charm.*

He wondered if Elizabeth had heard about Daniel Romero. *How could she not have?* It had been all over the news last week as media outlets reported that the telecom tycoon had died prematurely of a massive heart attack.

Several people were milling about the mansion—all dressed in their "Sunday best," as Willy would have said. This was the second such gathering in the past two weeks. Dignitaries were dropping by the mansion and sending flowers, just as they had right before her husband's funeral. The president had sent her personal condolences but would not be in attendance. The kind note she'd sent had explained that the first-husband would attend in her stead. Despite going through chemotherapy, President Claxton had managed to make it to Willy's funeral, along with several past presidents, members of congress and heads of state. The only president missing had been the one who sat now in a federal penitentiary. The Israeli prime minister had even attended, although unannounced. *That must have played havoc with security!* Flenn mused.

In his priest's collar, Elizabeth had spotted Flenn the moment he walked into the room. She made her way over to him and took his hands in hers. "Thank you for coming, Scott." She offered her cheek, which he kissed lightly.

"Now Elizabeth," he teased, "there you go again. You know everyone calls me Flenn these days."

She smiled. "Just like your father! He would never let people call him David. He was always Flenn, too, you know. Not to me, though. To me, he was always Davy." Her eyes were no longer looking into his; she appeared to be lost somewhere in the past. She returned to the moment a split-second later. "Please, let's go into the next room where we can speak privately."

Elizabeth led Flenn across a hall into a small, handsomely decorated parlor with dozens of framed photographs of Willy standing with movie stars, sports heroes, and political figures from the past half century. "My husband used this as his study. He rarely let anyone other than family see this room. He didn't want them to

know what a celebrity hound he was." She gestured in a
sweeping motion: "It always tickled him that a country
preacher had gained this much attention from all these
famous people." She sat down on a small leather couch
and patted the seat beside her.

Flenn sat next to her. "Elizabeth, you've been through
so much lately. I'm so very sorry for all your pain." He
meant it. Her son had finally reaped what he had long
sown, but Flenn couldn't help but feel a tinge of guilt for
the sake of the man's sainted mother.

"You're very kind, Scott. I miss my husband so much,
but I wouldn't have him come back to me in the state he
was in these past few months. Please," she said after a
moment's reflection. "I need to ask you something."

"Of course, anything."

"Now that it is just the two of us, I want you to tell me
why my son died."

Flenn raised an eyebrow. "I don't think I can answer
that, Elizabeth. You Baptists are the ones who believe God
takes people to heaven at a designated time, not us
Episcopalians."

"*You* are the only one who *can* answer it; and, that is
not what I mean." The look in her eyes was not that of a
grieving mother, but of a woman determined to know the
truth. "I'm not stupid."

Flenn wasn't sure what to say.

"What I want you to tell me is simply this: Was it our
government or someone else who killed Danny and
Benji."

Flenn stammered, "Elizabeth, I don't… "

She cut him off, her eyes focused directly on his. "Yes, you do. I've known for years. Your father told me all about the CIA."

Flenn's jaw dropped.

"You see, your father and I were... well... let's just say we shared more than a lady customarily speaks about."

Both of Flenn's eyebrows shot straight up. *There are still surprises in this world! Hopefully, she didn't mean what it sounded like she meant.*

"Davy told me that you served with military intelligence and then went to work for the CIA. I also know some about what happened in Scotland—at least as much as you told your father. And... I believe it really did happen." She patted him on the knee. "God works in mysterious ways."

There had been few times in his life when Flenn was at a loss for words. This was one of them. *Elizabeth had known all along? His dad hadn't even told his mom in all those years!*

"Now Scott, dear, you of all people are not about to throw a party for a presidential candidate, Democrat or otherwise. Those of us in the ministry know that we must keep up the appearance of neutrality for the sake of our congregations. I knew something was up the moment you started asking me about Danny." Her eyes flared. "I've always loathed that man! If the devil had a nephew, it would have been Daniel Romero." Elizabeth regained her composure. "What I don't know is what he and Benji were up to. I suspect it was no good. My senses tell me that the powers-that-be in this country would not accept Daniel as the next president." She looked at him. "Is that why he and my son are both gone?"

Flenn sat in stunned silence, not knowing how to respond.

"Benji never went to the cabin anymore." She sighed, "at least not alone. And he certainly wouldn't have gone out on that boat at night. Even if he had, he was an excellent swimmer. I don't care what the police say, there's no way that Benji went night-fishing all by himself last Friday at our old cabin."

Benjamin's body had been found on the shore near the dock. A rowboat was floating several yards out. From what Flenn understood, an anonymous tipster with an accent had called the authorities to report a drowning.

Flenn gazed at the tender old soul across from him. *The pain she must have gone through over the years—covering for her son's faults, secretly making restitution, sending him for counseling over and over again. This woman deserved the truth, at least some of it.*

He hesitated a moment, then took her hands in his. "It wasn't our government." She must have already known how venomous her son could be—how cold and calculating. He wasn't going to tell her that her son was a traitor as well. "Some people were hurt because of Benjamin and Daniel." He paused. "A girl died."

"And so, this girl's family killed my son?" There was a look in her eyes of… *what was it? Relief?*

She needed closure. Maybe Flenn should just let her believe that's what happened. *It was certainly kinder than the truth that her son had been set to become the false prophet to a psychopath!*

"Not exactly, but that's close enough. The girl's family has also paid a high price for all of this. Please trust me, it is better left alone."

Elizabeth didn't respond, just simply looked down at the linen handkerchief in her lap. The two of them sat quietly, holding hands as people milled outside the study; no doubt, searching for her. Finally, she spoke. "Scotty, you are a good man." She paused. "Your father was a good man. My husband was a good man, and Junior, even with all his issues, is a good man." She sighed. "Benjamin was not a good man."

Flenn couldn't argue, so he simply squeezed her hand as a tear materialized in the old woman's eyes.

"I endured so much over the years... I tried, Scotty, I really did."

"I know you did, Elizabeth."

"Somehow, in our quest to do the Lord's work, we lost Benjamin. Willy was gone so much, and I... I had to go it alone. I attempted to be both mother and father to the boys. Junior was easy. He's always been so eager to please. Benji felt the world owed him something. He was always so angry..." Her voice trailed off. She looked back at Flenn. "Your father often told me I was too soft on Benji, that I should let him undergo the consequences of his actions." She looked pleadingly into Flenn's eyes, "But, don't you see, *Davy*, I couldn't, I just couldn't... not with Willy always out there in public. How would it look?"

Flenn was silent at hearing her call him by his father's name. He felt as of he was watching the last of the ancient ocean liners taking on water and going under. In a few short years, Willy Rye would be forgotten. Just as tragic, this dear soul would spend the last of her days going over all the "what ifs" of the past.

As if on cue, a knock came at the study door. "Mom, are you in there?"

"I'll be out in a moment, son." Elizabeth dried her eyes and inhaled deeply. "He's a good boy, my Junior. He always has been. Benji, well… I just so wish he could have been more like his father… or his brothers, either one of them." She searched deeply into Flenn's widening eyes for a moment, as if wanting to make certain he'd understood.

For the second time in the past five minutes, Flenn was utterly speechless. Neither said another word. Instead, they both simply sat there in pained silence.

CHAPTER FIFTY-SIX

The chief of intelligence sealed the large envelope and handed it to his secretary with instructions to hand deliver it to the Iranian president in two days' time. The secretary didn't bat an eye. *Why should he?* Abbas told himself. *It is his job to do as he's told, not to ask questions.*

Abbas looked back at his desk and wondered if the deaths of Daniel Romero, Benjamin Rye, and Col. Amir would be enough to satisfy those in his government who had originally devised this plan. *Probably not*—which was exactly why he had sent his family to Zurich earlier this morning, routing their flights so as not to arouse suspicion. Abbas had long speculated he might one day fall out of favor with the ruling party, as his predecessor had before him. Unlike him, however, Abbas had developed a contingency plan early on—and since *he* was the head of intelligence, no one would know of his defection until it was too late.

His own flight, under an alias, had been scheduled out of Damascus, a city he had visited more than once at a moment's notice. If he were spotted, no one would suspect anything, not until he was safely aboard his next flight at least. By the time anyone understood just what he'd done, Abbas would be safely in Zurich, where he would contact the British Embassy. He'd trade as little intelligence as he could in return for asylum. Abbas sighed. Iran would lose the upper hand in cyber warfare... *for now.*

He picked up his briefcase and looked around his office for the last time. Becoming a traitor was not an easy thing. Sadar Abbas loved his country... he just happened to love breathing even more.

CHAPTER FIFTY-SEVEN

Flenn awoke the next day to three kittens pouncing on his chest. They had somehow managed to escape the laundry room—again. He thought for sure he'd closed that door before turning in last night. There had, of course, been a lot on his mind. Five people had been murdered—two young girls, a woman who'd thrown herself and her child onto the garbage heap of life, a pimp who trafficked in teenagers, and his lover as well. Mac O'Reilly was buried, his socialite wife incarcerated. A Guatemalan hitman and a power-hungry psychopath also dead, as was a narcissistic exploiter of the simple-minded—*a man he'd just found out might well have been his half-brother!*

Flenn moved the kittens to the foot of the bed, where they began to jump on one another instead of him. As usual, their mother was nowhere to be seen. He checked the time—5:30 a.m. He might as well get ready for his morning run. First, he needed to go check that door to see how the kittens had escaped.

Downstairs, Mama Kitty was asleep in his favorite chair, the one she'd just about clawed to pieces. The kittens were still upstairs. *Had she been the least bit concerned as they were taking the treacherous journey up the fourteen carpeted steps to his bedroom?* He envied her. *Untroubled with the plight of the world; just sleep, play, eat.*

"Don't mind me," he said as he passed by the sleeping feline. "I'm just the one taking care of you and your progeny." She stretched at the sound of his voice, then rolled over onto her back.

He went to start the coffee and noticed the folded note on the kitchen table. *That's how the kittens had escaped! Zack had no doubt thought it funny, or maybe he had stopped to play with them—not that Zack Matteson would ever admit to playing with kittens.* Flenn sighed. *So much for the new security alarm!*

He turned on the coffee maker, then read the note propped up on the table like a Boy Scout tent:

> ***Thanks for your help! Wish I could stay, but I'm on my way to London to see if the Brits will play nice. I understand they're entertaining your new phone pal from the other night. I'll be sure to pass along your regards! Merry Christmas!***
>
> ***Until next time. Z.***

Flenn tossed the note in the trash, hoping there wouldn't be a next time, but knowing better. Still, it had been Zack who'd figured out that Juanita had been the one who'd killed Minerva. "It was a sloppy kill, done by someone who was angry," Zack had pointed out. "The councilman had an alibi," he said, "So, who is next on the list of potential killers? The mother, of course." Maybe

Flenn would have figured it out on his own, but then his mind didn't work like Zack's any more... *thank God!*

He sipped his coffee in peace, thankful that at least one girl had been saved in all of this: *Denise.* Perhaps millions more in Israel had been spared as well.

Would Iran have really gone through with the attack? he wondered. *If so, would the United States have stayed out of it?* It was hard to imagine. Flenn took a breath. *Thankfully, he didn't have to think about it anymore.*

He finished his first cup and made a note to reserve a flight to Colorado to visit Denise after Christmas. After pouring a refill, he opened the pantry. The sound of the can opener brought Mama Kitty running into the kitchen. He poured the food into several bowls, one for her and the others for her progeny, who were just learning what solid food was all about. He passed them on his way up the stairs. Yellow balls of fur, falling pell-mell over each other on their way down to the kitchen. He wondered if their mother would notice their arrival.

An hour later, after his morning run, Flenn showered and prepared for the day. He fastened his clerical collar and retrieved his jacket. He planned to stop by the office briefly before he went on to the cemetery. He looked in the mirror and took stock of himself. *Yes, he and Benjamin Rye were both tall and about the same size. Both had brown, wavy hair and green eyes.* Other than that, he didn't see a resemblance.

Maybe he'd simply heard wrong. Maybe Elizabeth had said 'brother,' and not 'brothers.' The thought of Elizabeth and his father together... Flenn shook his head. *Just the remnants of an old woman's fading dream,* he told himself. *A dream of being whisked away from the constant scrutiny of a skeptical world waiting for some member of her family to falter or fail.*

Still, he wondered, *could his dad really have been Benji's father; and, if so, had Willy known?*

Willy Rye had been everything he appeared to be. An honest Baptist preacher who had loved his Lord and the public's esteem in equal proportion. Elizabeth had been an exemplary wife and mother. If there had been more to it once upon a time, then that was between Elizabeth and his dad. Flenn wouldn't let himself forage through yesterday's debris. Today had its own challenges, and the future was looking even more tenuous with Zack Matteson always discovering some new treachery lurking in the shadows. Yet as he stared at his reflection, Flenn couldn't escape wondering if Benji was his half-brother. *If so, was there some of Benji's darkness lurking somewhere deep within him?*

Probably not. At least that's what he told himself as he stood in front of the mirror, and again later at the office when he read the headline on the *Birmingham Post's* website:

First Husband arrives to say Farewell to Benjamin Rye

And the subhead:

Investigation Rules Death an Accidental Drowning

Maybe it was a fantasy that Elizabeth had kept hidden for years… a fantasy she'd clung to in order to escape a harsh world where one slip of impropriety could cost her family everything. There was no way to ever know for certain what had really happened way back then, or whether what was said yesterday was simply the illusion of an old woman who wondered what life would have been like out of the limelight.

At the office, Flenn went through his morning mail, caught up with some correspondence, and then, checking the time, grabbed his coat and headed for the cemetery. He took the long way today, purposefully driving down Fourth Avenue. He slowed as the wind blew garbage across the street in front of him. He wondered if Valentino Ramirez had known that Lindsay and Shelly were the same girl. *Had the pimp eventually figured out that Denise had gone behind his back to set up Shelly with Benjamin Rye? Did he know that Rye had been capable of murder?*

Questions which were unanswerable.

What did it matter now, anyway?

Apart from a stray dog rummaging through a trash can, there weren't any signs of life on the street this morning. Just as well, Flenn thought. Fourth Avenue had been a place of misery and sorrow for far too long. The new councilman appointed to replace Mac O'Reilly was already making overtures that a neighborhood with such a sordid past should be razed and rebuilt into high-rise apartments.

Maybe it should, Flenn thought.

He pulled into the cemetery a few minutes before nine. It was nearly deserted. Not like the one across town would be later this morning—where a crowd would gather to bury Benjamin Rye. Flenn scooped up his *Book of Common Prayer* from the passenger seat and climbed out of his Saab. He hadn't dared put the top down this morning, way too windy.

The rustle of dry leaves was the only sound as he walked up the narrow path toward an oak tree in the distance. Ahead, in the dewy grass, stood a solitary figure.

"Good morning, Detective."

Guy Rainsford nodded. "Father."

The two stood in silence before a newly dug grave, staring at a plain cardboard card on a plastic stake in the ground. The card simply read: "O'Reilly, Rochelle, Age 15." Eventually, a stone would replace the marker—a stone which Shelly's mother would never see. Juanita was currently under suicide watch at Brookwood Hospital. Whether or not she ever left psychiatric care, she would undoubtedly be locked up for the rest of her life.

Flenn was silent for a long time. "An angel," the bishop had mistakenly called her. *Maybe she had been at one time... before selling her soul to Mac O'Reilly.* Flenn wondered if fallen angels were ever given back their wings.

"There's no Anglican Archbishop in Yemen."

"What?"

Guy blew his nose. "Much less one that was murdered. I checked."

Flenn watched as a dried magnolia leaf blew across the grave, recalling the lie Zack had told the detective that night. He took a breath. "No, there's not; but, the truth is… well… complicated."

Guy shoved his handkerchief into his jacket pocket. "It usually is."

Flenn knew the man deserved to know the truth, just as Elizabeth had. *But just how much of that truth was enough?*

"His name isn't Sean Williams, but he is a federal agent."

Guy shifted his weight and looked out beyond the grove of trees to the Birmingham skyline. "Homeland Security?"

"Sort of. He and I knew each other way back—when I was overseas."

The detective wondered, and not for the first time in the past few days, if a priest would lie to him. "Go on," he said.

"The man at Saint Ann's was trying to kill him, not me. My friend knew too much about an upcoming attack. He'd asked me to help catch him."

"And you did it for what? God and country?"

"Let's just say I owed him one. He had agreed to help me help *you*."

Guy raised an eyebrow. "Help *me*? Help me do what?"

Flenn motioned to the newly turned earth.

"Oh."

The priest and detective stood quietly as the wind tossed more dead leaves across the grave. Flenn went on, "He agreed to help me with Denise, with the O'Reillys—

with everything. He's the one I sent Shelly's flash drive to once Minerva's husband gave it to me. He forwarded it to O'Reilly. I suspect that was why Mac committed suicide."

Guy stood still, peering down at the grave. "I take it there's more?"

"Yes."

"Do I want..." he corrected himself, " ...do I *need* to hear it?"

"No."

Guy gazed off in the distance. *The case was likely never going to be solved to his complete satisfaction. At least Lindsay had finally been identified. Hollister and Wickes would take it from here. Shelly O'Reilly, after all, was their case.* He looked down the hill toward a grove of leafless pecan trees. *It wasn't his problem anymore; and there were other mysteries to be solved. Valentino Ramirez's murder, for one.* Plus, Toone the Loon had just assigned him another case equally perplexing. A man's body had been found in a trunk of a Toyota Camry abandoned in a parking lot on the outskirts of town. He was a huge man, with no identification. Shot at point-blank range.

Guy would have his hands full in the days ahead, but he still couldn't put Roxanne out of his head. It all felt connected somehow, though he doubted anyone would ever be able to piece it all together. As he looked back at the grave, he wondered if maybe the main thing was that Lindsay was finally at peace. *Maybe one day he would be, too.*

"Okay," Guy finally said. "I wasn't at Saint Ann's that night."

Flenn simply said, "Thank you."

They both gazed down at the grave, each lost in their own separate thoughts. "She deserved better," Guy said, breaking the silence.

Flenn nodded ever so slightly. "All children do."

Guy buttoned his coat as a chill breeze swept through the cemetery, blowing leaves beyond the grave and down the hill. There had been no funeral for Lindsay… Shelly. Her stepfather's suicide and her mother's arrest were still capturing headlines. Someone had released Shelly's video online, which had gone viral, just as she had wanted. But there had been no service, no memorial, no good-byes—nothing, other than the press hounding the psychiatrists who were attending her mother.

"With parents like that, she never had a chance," Guy said.

Flenn shook his head. "I'd like to think there's always a chance, Detective; always a possibility for good to prevail over evil."

Guy wiped his right eye—whether from his cold, or something else, he didn't know. "Why does God allow such things?" he asked.

Flenn reached over and put his hand on the man's shoulder. "He's probably asking the same question about us."

Guy shook his head. "Everyone always says that. Seems to me that just lets God off the hook."

Flenn drew in a breath of cold air. He looked over his shoulder at the desolate cemetery and then back at the grave at his feet. "I think it's about choices."

"Huh?"

"Something I was talking about with a friend recently," he explained. "God gives us the freedom to make choices. Thing is, we make a lot of the wrong ones."

Guy looked down at the freshly turned dirt. "I don't know, Father. I can't imagine she would have chosen to end up like this."

Flenn looked at him. "The important thing now is the choice *you* made."

Guy raised an eyebrow. "What are you talking about? What choice?"

Father Flenn smiled. "The choice not to abandon her."

No more was said between them. A dove flew by, as Father Flenn opened his *Book of Common Prayer* and began to do what they had come here to do. He read aloud from the burial office:

In the midst of life, we are in death; from whom can we seek help? From you alone, O Lord… Into your hands, we commend your child, Shelly. Acknowledge, we humbly beseech you, a sheep of your own fold, a lamb of your own flock, and a sinner of your own redeeming. Receive her into the arms of your mercy…

At last, the wind was still.

Don't miss Father Flenn's Next Adventure...

Rites of Revenge

Join the Father Flenn Mailing List:
www.fatherflenn.com

Acknowledgments

I'm pretty good at expressing my gratitude... just lousy at remembering everyone I need to thank. Of course, I want to acknowledge my wonderful wife, Diane, and my "kids:" Heather, Sean, Dominic, Jonathan and Amy. My family: mom and dad, for all the love over the years; my brother, Wayne, and sister-in-law, Emily, who were the first to push me toward publishing the *Father Flenn Adventures*; and my Godmother, Sue Sunde, for encouraging me to read as a child. Thank you to my parish family, St. Mark's, who have put up with their quirky priest for nearly 15 years. I owe a huge debt of gratitude to my editor, Margaret Shaw, and cover designer, Peter O'Connor. Thanks also to Jim Brown for the formatting. Thank you Larry and Richard Vinson, Winston Schepps, Michele Burdell and Paul Whaley for all your kind words. Lastly, thank you to my bishop, friend, and fellow author, Kee Sloan—who writes so much better than I do.

56885049R00236

Made in the USA
Columbia, SC
02 May 2019